Impulsive

If you've already read this prequel go to page #99 for the end of Unbound and begin reading IMPULSIVE

A Bound4 Series Novella
Editing by Barren Acres Editing
Cover Design by Just Write Creations

Unbound

Fidgeting in my seat, I try to shake off this restless feeling. I'm no stranger to long international flights, but something about this trip to Canada has me on edge. Spending time with Ethan O'Connell, the VP of International Sales, can be stressful at the best of times, but I highly doubt I'm feeling anxious about my boss's difficult disposition. On the contrary, these days he seems content; he seems happy.

If I had to guess why I'm feeling a little off, it would be the odd dreams that have been haunting my sleep since I found out I'd be flying into Toronto. They're the kind of dreams that linger in your mind, long after you wake. Places and people that seem so familiar to me, yet when I wake, I can't seem to identify them. And then there's her… my mind becomes preoccupied with the memory of her smile. Her image is so clearly burned in my mind, it's as if she were sitting beside me, with those beautiful hazel eyes. I will never forget the way they sparkle an intense green with dramatic flecks of gold and brown. My chest becomes tight, and if it weren't for the sudden turbulence that startles me into taking a breath, I think I would have forgotten to breathe altogether.

I force myself to think of something else. Work. Yeah, that's it; focus on work. I didn't even question why John McCabe, Ethan's right-hand man, asked me to take an earlier flight because when Ethan O'Connell has a need, everyone jumps. That's how it's always been. For me, Carter Brant, it's how it will always be. Ethan can be challenging; difficult if I'm being completely honest.

There's always been an unspoken understanding between us; a brotherly type of connection we formed back in school. It was Ethan who paid for my education when I lost the funding for my scholarship. He skyrocketed up the corporate ladder, and two years later, when the opportunity arose, he hired me to run the Australian office of Aurora Technologies. In short, I'd sooner sever a limb than disappoint him.

All my success and everything I value, I owe to Ethan O'Connell: my boat, my luxury home, my Ferrari F12 Berlinetta, and my big fat bank account. You'd think I'd be happy with all that, but lately, I want more. The playboy lifestyle isn't as fulfilling as it used to be. I long to find a woman I can call my own. One I can start a family with, like the woman in my dreams. That's the kind of love I want to find.

Feeling like I'm being watched, I glance over the headrest of the adjoining seat. The flight attendant looks away, ashamed she's been caught. She's been staring at me since I boarded the plane. After a brief moment, she turns and locks on to my gaze. Unable to hide her reaction to me, her face turns a telltale shade of pink. A mischievous grin slowly curls the edges of my lips. I know where this is going. I'm a longtime member of the mile-high club with an incredible passport of frequent-flyer miles under my belt. There's always a beautiful woman willing to make the long, tiresome flight a little more enjoyable.

A little distraction might just be what I need to settle this anxiety. I push aside my earlier apprehension about my playboy lifestyle. Right now, it's a strong impulse, and I can't fight it. Taking an appreciative look at the blushing flight attendant's long legs, I nod suggestively toward the rear of the plane. My cock twitches when she bites her lip and hesitates. The shy ones are always the ones who surprise me the most behind locked doors. I know how to coax them out of their comfort zones, eliciting responses they themselves didn't know they were capable of. She makes her way down the narrow aisle of the first-class compartment, slowing as she passes my seat she whispers, "Follow me."

Standing under the spray of warm water, I grumble about the barely adequate water pressure in hotel showers. Squirting a dollop of shower gel into my hand, I try to scrub up enough lather to wash my body. I worked up a sweat on that flight, and for some reason, I feel like I need a good cleansing. She was a nice enough girl, and as I suspected, kinky as fuck. The quiet ones always are.

I smile as I lean back and rinse the shampoo out of my hair. My amusement fades as I begin to think about what I've just done. I've done it many times before, but this time I felt a strange regret as we landed, and she slipped me her number while thanking me for flying Air Canada. I tucked it in my pocket, with no intention of calling her. I never call them, but this is the first time I've ever felt guilty about it.

As I step out of the shower, my phone rings. Again. Ethan must be in a ripe mood if John keeps calling to check on my ETA. I already know where we're meeting for dinner, and I have no desire to listen to him rant about O'Connell, so I ignore it, as I did the last four times he called.

The owner smiles as I walk toward the restaurant entrance. Ethan and I have spent many nights here earning his friendship. "Good evening, Mr. Carter. It's so nice to see you again. Ethan is waiting."

I smile and politely overlook his thick European accent. "Good evening, George. It's just, Carter," I remind him.

As I pass, he leans in discreetly. "He has a beautiful woman on his arm tonight."

I reach for the brass handle on the heavy wooden door. "Doesn't he always?"

"Oh no, she's not like the other girls." He gives his head a little shake. "You'll see."

I chuckle as I enter. Ethan is always attracted to the same kind of girls. Those he can easily control; bleach blonde, starry-eyed kittens that will do anything to please him. In my younger years, I admired him for that. Now I find it kind of pathetic.

Through the dimly lit bar, I spot McCabe and make my way toward him. I can hear Ethan's voice as I join them from behind. "Carter is the sales manager at our office in Australia. He'll be here for a few weeks, while we work out a new business plan."

I catch a glimpse of her silhouette, and when the light briefly illuminates her face, it stops me in my tracks. Not the trashy blonde who's rubbing herself against Ethan like a dog in heat; that's not an uncommon sight. It's the brunette that makes me feel as if I've just walked into an invisible brick wall. She's undoubtedly the woman George was referring to.

John catches me standing in the shadows and motions me in. I can tell from the look on his face, he's relieved reinforcements have arrived. Keeping O'Connell out of trouble is a two-man job, most of the time.

A jolt of energy awakens every nerve in my body when I step up behind her. Thoughts race through my mind at lightning speed. I've only ever felt like this when I dream of... *her*. My stomach nervously twists and turns, as I struggle to understand how it could be possible. It's her... it has to be. I recognize the way she breathes; the way she smells. My heart pounds with a strange cadence as I lean in and speak gently in her ear as if we're old friends. "My ears are burnin' so they must be talkin' bout me."

Being this close to her, an intuitive calmness settles my nerves, even though her body tenses at the sound of my voice. Her sudden intake of breath presses against my chest, reminding me that we've actually not met yet. "Carter Brant." I step to her side and extend my hand.

"Olivia James." Her cheeks flush as she reaches for my hand, and it elicits a response from my body that's neither appropriate nor wanted, at this particular moment.

I prolong the release of her hand until I feel the heat of Ethan's glare. I sense her anxiety as he abandons his companion at the bar and heads toward us.

"Carter." Ethan nods and holds out his hand for a brief shake before pulling me into a quick man hug. "Good to see you. How was your flight?"

"Brutal, as usual," I complain. "Thank God for my long-standing membership to the mile-high club," I joke.

He looks past me, curiously. "I thought you were traveling alone?"

"I am." I raise a brow and smirk. "There's never a shortage of eager women on those long flights."

Remembering she's still standing at my side, I become embarrassed. For some reason, I don't want her to think I'm a womanizer. I mean, I guess I could be considered one, but I don't want her to have that impression of me. She seems to be off in a world all of her own at the moment, so I'm hoping the comment went unnoticed.

The sound of Ethan's voice pulls her back to reality. "Olivia?"

"Yes, sorry, what did you say?"

Ethan flashes her an annoyed look, and it really irks me.

"We'll head into the dining room for dinner now," he directs.

Ethan doesn't introduce me to the blonde that flanks in from the side, taking his arm. John has been texting me every ten minutes since my feet hit the ground, so I know who she is and why I'm here. Olivia walks behind everyone, looking disappointed, and I don't like it. I place my hand gently on her back, guiding her to the dining room. It just seems like the natural thing to do. When we reach the table, Ethan's client, Stacey, situates herself beside him to ensure that she captures all his attention.

"I guess you're stuck with me," Olivia says, apologetically, looking at the two empty chairs on the far side of the table.

I smile and settle in beside her, "I wouldn't consider that unpleasant."

Shannon, John's girlfriend, looks over at us, with regret in her eyes. Ethan shoots daggers at me from across the table. I know exactly what his problem is, but I don't care.

Minutes seem like hours while I fake an interest in the small talk going on around me. I'm much more interested in knowing more about Olivia. Although, I feel like I already know everything about her. How do you bring that up in casual conversation with a complete stranger? She stares at me several times, looking as if there's something she wants to say. "Have we met before?" she finally asks me.

I want to answer 'Yes, every night in my dreams,' but it's likely a bad idea. "I don't believe so." Have you ever been to Australia?"

"No," she laughs, "but you seem very familiar to me."

I'm intrigued that she feels it too. "Were you born here?" I ask, ignoring the business conversation on the other side of the table.

"Yes, born and raised. I'm a small-town girl."

"Nothing wrong with that," I add.

"Were you born in Australia?"

"Yes."

She cocks her head to the side. "Sorry, I guess I'm just naïve, but I thought you'd have more of an accent."

I chuckle. "I've heard that before. It comes out more when I'm at home with my mates or talking to my mum. I spent most of my younger years in boarding schools in the U.S. Then I did my business degree at one of the best universities in London. That's where Ethan and I met."

"He mentioned that." She smiles, and I see the curiosity light up her expression. "You and two other friends, right?"

"That's right. Have you met Landon Scott? He's the sales manager for Aurora Tech's division in South Africa."

"Ethan has mentioned him."

Her eyes darken, and I know that look. She has an agenda.

"What can you tell me about Reese Wilson?" she asks coyly.

I knew it. I glance up to ensure Ethan isn't listening to the conversation. I'm not even going to attempt to change the subject. "I lost touch with Reese. I heard he just accepted a job offer and he's moving back to Ireland. Ethan hasn't seen nor heard from him in quite some time. He doesn't plan to, in the future."

She nods, acknowledging that my loyalty to Ethan is something that's not going to falter, but at least she tried. For a long drawn out moment, the golden flecks in her hazel eyes mesmerize me. I envision the lush rolling hills of Ireland, babbling brooks, and the warmth of the summer sun.

I'm annoyed when Ethan ruins my daydream by pulling me into a conversation about business. I'd rather chat with the two extremely intelligent women on this side of the table. I don't know how John McCabe landed such a young, hot lawyer, but good on the old guy.

I have to hand it to him, when entertaining clients of the opposite sex, Ethan has a magnetism about him. I don't know if he's aware of his dalliance, or if it's a well-thought-out plan of attack. He can be the world's biggest asshole, but when he turns on the charm with that bloody Irish accent, women practically toss their panties at him. It's quite something to watch. He'd never jeopardize a business deal at any cost, but what he's doing to Olivia right now is wrong, and I'm having a hard time watching it go down.

I ignore his steely glare from across the table whenever he feels I'm being a little too attentive to her. When the waiter arrives at the table with drinks for Ethan and his business companion, Olivia's expression turns to concern, prompting me to lean over and whisper in her ear, "You look like you need a drink yourself, is everything okay?"

"Yes," she whispers back. "Order me anything with vodka in it." Fumbling with the zipper on her purse, she drops it on the floor, spilling everything out. It amuses me when she curses like a sailor. She disappears under the table for quite some time, making me curious about what's going on down there. Ethan clenches his jaw and begins to look extremely uncomfortable. I lift the edge of the tablecloth and bend down to see what's causing her delay. I close my eyes, wishing I could unsee what I've just witnessed. Olivia watches in horror as Stacey's hand glides upward along Ethan's thigh and doesn't stop.

The look of utter heartbreak on her face fuels an angry urge in me to give O'Connell the ass-kicking he deserves. But I can't. I gather up the few remaining items on the floor and pass them to her. She gives me a forced smile.

I offer her my hand as she gets to her feet. She acknowledges my sympathetic look before glancing at the opposite side of the table. Ethan looks at her with a flash of regret then turns away, unable to look her in the eye. His business conversation with Stacey continues calmly, as if nothing is wrong, but he holds his water glass tightly in both hands, looking like he could crush it under the force. I've got to hand it to him. It's an impressive show of restraint.

"Carter, please excuse me for a moment, I need to freshen up." Sensing her anxiety, I move the chair out of her way, tempted to follow. I have a very strong urge to take care of her right now. Stacey rambles on about the clubs her friends want to check out later on, and how much fun it's going to be. I narrow my eyes and shake my head. Has everyone gone completely mad? I'd really like to tell her to 'shut the hell up.' It's tempting.

Olivia continues walking. "Carter," she calls over her shoulder. "Whatever you order me, make it a double."

I grin. "My kind of girl."

Ethan watches her leave the room with a very stoic expression and then glances over at me. I return his stare, not feeling intimidated at all. I shake my head in disapproval as I return to my seat.

"Is there something you wanna say to me, Brant?" he growls angrily.

I pause a brief moment, giving it consideration; there are quite a few things I'd like to say to him. Thinking the better of it, I decline. "Not at the moment, no."

Shannon frowns when John breathes out a sigh of relief. "This is getting out of hand," she whispers to him. "Take Ethan outside and have a talk with him. He needs to put an end to this. I'll go make sure Olivia's okay. And *you...*" She puts her hand on my shoulder as she passes, "*You...* need to do something about *that*," she states firmly, as she nods in Stacey's direction.

They head in different directions, and I suddenly find myself alone with the woman I overheard Shannon refer to as *the devil* during one of John's calls.

"I love your accent," Stacey says, giving me a demure smile.

"Thank you." I busy myself with my phone, typing everything I can think of into the search engine to get some insight or answers about the feelings I'm having for Olivia: déjà vu, past life regression, dream traveling, alternate universes.

"I heard you drive a Ferrari. Would you take me for a ride?"

I glance up briefly. "If you're ever in Australia. That's where it is."

"What color is it?"

"What?" I ask annoyed.

"The Ferrari. What color is it?"

"It's red."

"Trophy Wife Red like my nails? Or Candy Apple Red like my lips?"

I look up, amazed she's flirting with me. I know John was hoping I'd charm her away from O'Connell, but I just can't bring myself to do it. He made his bed, and now he can lie in it. "Rosso Scuderia is the brand color."

I'm relieved to see Olivia return from the toilet. I start to get to my feet, but she waves me off. Ethan joins us simultaneously and takes his place on the other side of the table. Here we go again.

"Do you have a kangaroo?" Stacey suddenly blurts out, making an awkward silence even more uncomfortable.

"Excuse me?"

"You're from Australia, right?"

"Yes, but there are laws against keeping them as pets in the city."

"Have you ever boxed a kangaroo?" she continues with a very serious expression.

I thank the Lord Ethan takes over the conversation. Olivia tries to keep a straight face, but she has to turn her head to mask her amusement. I lean in to whisper in her ear and rest my arm on the back of her chair. Her long curls brush against my skin, and I resist the urge to brush my fingers through them. "Thank Christ, you're back. After only ten minutes of brilliant conversation, I can safely say, she must have slept her way to the top."

Unable to control herself, Olivia snorts, and it makes me chuckle. Recognizing it as a silent warning when Ethan glares at me, I straighten in my seat. It's not easy being so close when I crave the touch of her skin against mine.

When dinner is finally over, we move around the pub, mingling between the bar and the billiards room. The silence is broken by a shrill scream, as Stacey runs like she's on fire toward the front of the restaurant. I'm disappointed to find out she hasn't burst into flames, but rather, my favorite refuge has become a resort for stiletto-wearing women with perfect hair. Now I know I'm getting old. Once upon a time, I would accept this as a challenge, but now I cringe at the schoolgirl giggling.

Olivia watches them in horror from the bar. "Dear God help us, the rest of the Barbie girls are here. Bartender… two tequila shots and hurry!"

Amused, I take one of the shot glasses out of her hand. After clinking them together, we toss them back in unison.

"Whew!" Olivia's eyes slightly water from the burn in her throat. "Hey, Carter, let me ask you a question. Would you let any of those Barbies join your mile-high club?"

I had seriously hoped she hadn't heard that comment. "Hell, no!"

"Not even Stacey?"

I scrunch up my face and lie. "Even I have standards." Leaning in, I whisper in her ear, "That whole story isn't true. I don't want you to think poorly of me. But don't tell the blokes, they worship me for it." I flash her a charming smile.

Olivia laughs and looks around the room. "Hey? Where's O'Connell? I haven't seen him for awhile."

I slide the empty shot glasses across the bar and indicate to the bartender that I want two more. "I think he's playing darts with John."

I pass her another shot, and laugh at the face she makes when she swallows.

"Bleh! I don't think I can do any more of those." She shudders.

"One more," I wave at the bartender. "And a glass of red wine," I add, as Shannon makes her way over to join us. The door flies open, and a rowdy bunch of blokes fills the room. Olivia introduces them as friends and explains that they were invited to help entertain Stacey and her friends.

Having heard the ruckus, Ethan makes his way to the bar and buys them a round of drinks. Stacey flashes me a seductive grin as she anchors herself to his side. I'll admit, after several tequilas, I'm starting to think she's a very intriguing woman. Or she's completely fucked in the head. I'm not sure yet.

Olivia tenses and takes several deep breaths, trying to calm herself. I pass her another shot. "I can't remember if bitch-slapping was on the list of things that would be frowned on," she mumbles under her breath.

I laugh once and glance up as Ethan approaches. "The boys are going to play a game of pool, and the girls are going to watch," he says to Olivia.

I try to hide my amusement when she dramatically rolls her eyes. It's clear she's had just about enough of Ethan O'Connell and way too much tequila. "Awww. The girls are going to watch? How cute is that?" she says sarcastically. "I suppose the poor things are too delicate to play." She's laser-focused on Ethan, and her stare remains sassy and unwavering. For some reason, it starts to make my cock hard. "It's such a shame," she continues, "because I'm sure everyone in the bar would love the view. Nothing like a little after dinner camel toe."

I burst out laughing. Shannon chokes on her wine, and quickly holds a cocktail napkin over her mouth. With a boldness already fueled by tequila, Olivia picks up another shot glass and tosses its contents deep into the back of her throat, letting it wash down effortlessly. Slamming the glass down hard on the bar, she gives him a smile that unmistakably means fuck off! I think I love this girl. I lean against the bar and cross my legs at the ankle. I can't wait to see what comes next.

Ethan stares at her, his jaw clenched, and his lips pressed in a hard line. Turning to his right, he establishes eye contact with Shannon. "Please take Olivia down to the pool tables, so Carter and I can have a talk."

Olivia raises her eyebrows and laughs. "You can't be serious? You're dismissing me?"

This is getting good. I've never seen a woman take a stand against O'Connell.

Shannon nods and takes Olivia by the arm, trying to steady her as she sways. "Come on, Sweetie. The boys need to talk. We can wait for them down there." Olivia protests but Shannon is clearly stronger than she looks.

Starting to feel the effects of that last shot of tequila myself, I sit on the barstool and wait for them to get out of earshot. "What's up, Boss?" I ask, pretending that I don't know what's about to go down.

"Keep your hands off my girl, Carter," Ethan says harshly.

Well, that was blunt and to the point. Classic O'Connell. I furrow my brow, unable to resist taking a shot at him. "Don't chuck a spaz, Ethan. I haven't had my hands on your girl. She was firmly attached to your dick all through dinner." My boldness makes me smirk. "Find it hard to believe you didn't notice, mate,"

"I'm talking about Olivia." Ethan's jaw tenses and the vein in his temple starts to pulse.

"Olivia?" I scratch my head, pretending to be confused. "Hmm."

"What?" he asks annoyed.

"It's not like you to be so greedy."

"I'm not fooling around with Stacey," he insists.

"Could have fooled me. I have to say, mate, I'm a little shocked." I'm tired of his bullshit.

"At what exactly?" Ethan crosses his arms in front of him, widening his stance.

"Making someone, who's obviously in love with you, watch another girl manhandle your junk at the dinner table. That's a little cruel, don't you think? I don't want to judge you, mate, but it was a dick move. *Literally.*" I'm quite certain I'm going to regret voicing my opinion, but there's no holding back now. "I've only just met Olivia, but I already know she's the kind of woman that deserves a lot more respect than that."

Ethan considers my statement and rakes his hands through his hair in frustration. He establishes eye contact with her across the room and takes on a tortured expression. I know that look, and it causes me concern. "Oh shit. You're serious about Olivia?"

Ethan nods. "Yes, I think I'm in love with her."

If there was any chance of exploring the feelings I have for her, it's fucked now.

"I know…" he corrects himself, "I know I'm in love with her."

I don't understand the jealousy that stirs inside me over a woman who was a complete stranger only a few hours ago, but it feels very real.

"Then, what's going on with Stacey? Don't tell me *nothing*. I have eyes."

He signals the bartender for another scotch. "She's just a client, who's made it very clear about how I'm going to get her approval on our proposal." Lifting himself to sit on the stool beside me, he takes a long pause and then frowns. "My ex, Jessica, is pregnant," he confesses. "She says it's mine."

My eyes open wide. I don't know how one man can get himself involved in so much drama. "Fuck, that's rough. I'm sorry." I know Ethan, and this is going to tear him apart. "I always hated that bitch!" I confess.

"For fuck's sake! Apparently, John did as well," he says angrily. "Why didn't anybody say anything to me at the time?"

I shrug. "Would you have listened?"

Ethan answers into his glass after another mouthful flows smoothly over his tongue. "Probably not, she has magnificent tits."

I nod my acknowledgment and clink his glass as I glance across the room at Olivia. "What are you going to do now?"

"Paternity test, first and foremost."

"Good plan. Does Olivia know?"

"She knows about the pregnancy, but she doesn't know about the other stuff."

I open my mouth and speak my mind for the wrong reason. A selfish one. "You need to tell Olivia everything."

"I want to," Ethan says, swirling what's left of his scotch in the bottom of his glass. "But her last boyfriend was abusive, Carter. I'm afraid if I tell her what I'm being accused of, she'll leave me."

I should bite my tongue, but he just bitched me out for not speaking up about Jessica. "Ah, but you know you can't keep it a secret for long. Better you come clean now and find out if your relationship is strong enough to withstand it. Yeah?" It crosses my mind that I'd have the opportunity to figure out what the connection is between Olivia and me if she leaves him. "Jess is going to fight you tooth and nail. She's just that kind of woman. Eventually, Olivia is going to find out. It should come from you before that happens." I curse my own loyalty. If I told her myself, things would move along quicker.

Ethan nods. "You're right, but not just yet. I'll find the right time after the grand opening." He stops and scrubs his hands over his face. "If she's even talking to me still."

"Only you can fix it, O'Connell. Get your shit sorted." I really like my chances right now. "What's the plan for the evening?"

He watches the crowd of guests at the pool tables. "It looks like they're getting along well. I'm hoping I can send everyone off to the club so I can take Olivia home and try to set things right."

The thought of that makes my blood curdle. "All right then, mate." I slide off the stool. "Let's make that happen."

Ethan gets to his feet, but I can tell there's one more thing on his mind. He reaches over and grasps my arm.

"I'm not joking, Carter. If you so much as get close enough to breathe on her, I'll kill you."

Some things never change, but I'll play it cool until I figure out what's going on with me. "Okay, Boss. I've got it."

"And Carter… don't buy her any more shots. She's pretty feisty when she's sober, but from what I've just seen, if she keeps drinking tequila, she'll have my balls by the end of the night."

I laugh out loud, "Yeah, I think you're right about that. But you have to admit, she's fucking brilliant!"

Ethan grins, "That's why I love her." He indiscreetly adjusts his crotch. "But, I'm rather fond of my balls, as well."

I feel compelled to give my old friend some serious advice… for the right reasons this time. "Ethan, fuck the business, mate. It's not worth it if you lose her."

He raises an eyebrow. "Who are you and what have you done with the real Carter Brant?"

I shrug. "I know, right? I guess old age is starting to mellow me out. Lately, I find myself wanting that kind of love. I think about settling down. I want to come home at the end of the day to a woman I cherish and love. Someone to make babies with and share the rest of my life. I'm getting tired of the jet-setting playboy routine."

Ethan nods his head in understanding. "Thank God, it isn't just me. That's how I felt the moment I saw Olivia."

Me too, and I have no idea what to do about it right now. "No, it's not just you, mate. Amazing what the love of a beautiful woman does to a man."

"No kidding. Olivia has brought me to my knees several times, and I don't think she even realizes how much I love her."

I glance across the room and catch her staring. I wish that look of ardor were for me. "You need to change that before she gets away."

Ethan nods in agreement "I'm going to start right now."

I watch as he makes his way across the room like a man on a mission, completely ignoring Stacey when she tries to intercept him. Grabbing Olivia's hand, he pulls her into a private room, out of sight. I experience a strong feeling of regret over what I've just done. My heart tells me she and I have a destiny together, and yet I just launched O'Connell back into her arms. I shake my head feeling conflicted.

From across the room, I watch as the girls decide to try their hand at billiards. This should be amusing since I noticed when I was under the table that Stacey's not wearing any panties under that very short designer dress. I move to a stool with a better vantage point so I can enjoy the view. I am a man after all. Stacey doesn't disappoint, leaning as far as she can across the table. She glances at me over her shoulder and smiles; fully aware I'm watching. I tip my beer to my lips and watch the show attentively.

A door swings open and Olivia emerges. Ethan takes her by the hand and guides her across the room. I can see from here that her face is flushed pink. The thought of what they might have been doing in there makes my jaw clench. Planting himself on one of the tall stools beside me, Ethan widens his knees and pulls Olivia between them. I know the long sensual kiss he places on her lips is a message to Stacey, but it makes my gut feel like it's tied in knots.

She lays her head to rest on his chest and smiles at me. In this light, her eyes are dark and rich looking, like the most decadent chocolate. I'm drawn back to a time where I remember looking into them and feeling loved. Now I feel even more confused.

Ethan catches a glimpse of Stacey at the billiard table and cocks his head to the side for a quick, *discreet* look. He glances at me through his peripheral vision and offers me a fist bump, behind Olivia's back. She looks at me suspiciously, so I nod and wink. I sit and listen to their banter, pretending that I'm genuinely happy for my friend. I wish I were.

I'm shocked when I hear Olivia tell Ethan, "I take it back… you're not a huge jackass."

Ethan raises his brows in surprise. "Oh? I don't remember you calling me that."

Olivia grins. "Oh, I did, and several other less ladylike things, actually."

"You're definitely my kind of girl," I chuckle. Ethan stops smiling and glares at me.

I shrug. "Just saying, Boss. So don't fuck it up," I warn.

"Uh Oh," Olivia says, as Stacey makes her way toward them.

"The girls want to go over to EUPHORIA and do some dancing," she says to Ethan as if Olivia isn't even there.

Olivia begins to move closer to me, but Ethan grabs her hips, locking her in between his knees.

"Sure, if that's what you want to do. It's only a few doors down. I'll have John call over and get you on the VIP list." Ethan waves John over. "Carter, before you go home, make arrangements to have the tab charged to your room, and then submit it with your expenses."

"Sure thing, mate."

Stacey stares at Ethan with an unimpressed expression. "You're not coming?"

"No, it's been a long day, and I think I'm going to get on my way."

She crosses her arms angrily. "You can kiss my endorsement goodbye if you don't go."

Ethan anxiously scrubs his hand over his stubble. Sensing the tension, Olivia shrugs, trying to put him at ease. "It's okay with me if we go."

Ethan gives her an apologetic look as Stacey storms back across the room to her friends, her heels clicking heavily on the floor as she goes. Ethan meets John halfway across the room to discuss plans. Shannon wanders over to Olivia and me. "What's going on?"

"Barbie wants to go dancing, and she's insisting that Ethan goes, too."

"Wow! She doesn't discourage easily, does she?"

"Apparently not, so I hope you have comfortable dancing shoes on." She looks down at Shannon's feet.

"Oh, I don't think John, and I will go."

"You have to go," Olivia says panicked. "Ethan won't go unless I do. And I'm not setting foot in that place unless you go with me to make sure I don't scratch out their eyes."

I laugh, raising my beer bottle in a salute. "Well, you ladies have fun."

Olivia sneers at him, "Not so fast, Crocodile Dundee. You're going, too. Ethan is going to need you there."

She narrows her eyes at me, giving me a stern warning. I've seen that look before, and it seems it's transcended through time without losing any of its effectiveness. "Fine," I say, giving in reluctantly. "I'll go." I know I don't want to be on the wrong side of Olivia's threats.

"Go where?" Ethan asks as he returns.

"To Euphoria with us," Olivia answers for me.

"Awesome, I'd feel better if you were there. Nice of you to offer."

Shannon lets out a small, well-mannered laugh, while Olivia tries to look innocent. Ethan looks at me, confused. "Oh, I didn't offer," I explain. "I'm going because your girlfriend told me I have to. And quite frankly, mate, I'm afraid of what she'll do to me if I refuse."

Olivia bats her eyelashes at him. Ethan grins and shakes his head. "Wise decision, my friend."

The room erupts into a barrage of giggles. Ethan glances over at them. "John has already gone over to make the arrangements. We'll walk over with the girls."

Stacey firmly grasps Ethan's arm and starts to walk. Ethan looks over his shoulder at Olivia.

"It's okay," she says, putting him at ease.

The lights in the city are bright against the black veil of night.

Standing between the lovely lawyer and the sassy information technology consultant, I present my arms to them. "Ladies. Shall we?"

The girls smile at each other and accept my offer. With one on each arm, I escort them through the city's famous entertainment district. Ethan peeks over his shoulder several times on the short walk, checking on me. I can't believe how ridiculous he is.

John is waiting outside the nightclub, located in one of Toronto's most prestigious hotels. Shannon glows when she sees him. I still don't know what she sees in the old guy.

The minute Stacey leaves Ethan's side, Olivia steps up and claims his hand. The line of patrons waiting to get in extends down the street and around the corner. "Ethan, I don't think they're going to let us in."

Ethan kisses her on the forehead, "Trust me, they'll let us in."

Looking doubtful, Olivia follows him to the door. While he deals with security, she glances over at me and shrugs. An amused grin crosses my lips. "You didn't know that he's part owner?"

Her eyes open wide. "Of the nightclub?" she says, in shock.

Ethan smirks. "No, Baby. I own the hotel."

Arrogant bastard. We bypass the lineup and head to the second floor VIP lounge. Ethan and Olivia head out to the balcony while John stands outside the door, ensuring they get some privacy. I lean against the bar watching the flurry of activity in the room. It brings back memories of our good ole university days. That seems to be so long ago. I usually have no desire to return to those days, but right now, I have a strong impulse to get out on that crowded dance floor. Maybe it's the booze inflating my ego, but I keep catching the girls staring at me, and I could use a little distraction.

Stacey makes her way over to me, smiling. "Hi there, handsome."

"Hello." I give her a longer, more appreciative look. She's a few dingoes short of a pack, but beautiful nonetheless. In this light, she bears a close resemblance to the *other* woman that walks through my dreams. I'm pretty sure it's just the booze because I don't get that feeling when I'm near her, like I do with Olivia. The whole thing just keeps getting more bizarre.

She moves in closer and touches my arm while she talks. "I hope we're not going to spend all night up here."

"What did you have in mind?" I ask curiously.

She leans in and whispers into my ear.

I nod. "Right." I'm not quite sure what I was expecting her to say, or why I'm feeling discontented. I walk away to have a few words with John.

"Why?" he asks me in frustration. "Any other time you'd be all over a challenge like that. The woman is bad news, and I need her away from Ethan."

"He got himself into this mess, he can get himself out."

"I understand now. You've lost it."

"Lost what?"

"Your charm. Your pizzazz. Your sex appeal."

Shots fired! I raise my brow. "Uh, no. She's clearly only interested in O'Connell."

He shakes his head and frowns, then lets me pass. I clear my throat as I enter so they know I'm there. "Sorry to interrupt," I say, as I join them on the balcony. "But I've been sent to inform you, Stacey wants to dance, now." I point at Ethan and smile, unapologetically, "With you."

There's barely room to move on the dance floor, but he does his best to keep Olivia close. She rolls her eyes at Stacey, who continually tries to capture Ethan's attention. I have to give her high regards for her patience. I wouldn't have tolerated that bullshit for long.

A very popular song plays, and everyone explodes onto the dance floor with their best moves. I join them, inspired by the number of hot young women that begin gravitating toward me. Everyone except for Stacey. She's still firmly attached to Ethan on the other side of the dance floor. For some reason, I catch Olivia looking at my feet, and I look down to make sure my shoelaces are tied. She looks embarrassed when I look at her again. I wonder what's going through her mind.

I'm enjoying all the beautiful women dancing around me. I've never set eyes on them before this song, and one of them is now grinding her ass against me. Take that McCabe. I have definitely NOT lost my sex appeal.

"Carter!" Olivia screams in my ear. "Stacey is watching you."

I look over, find her staring, and shrug.

"She's checking you out. Please… please… please… go over and dance with her, and so I can spend some time with Ethan."

The music changes to a slow love song. Olivia tries to get to Ethan in time, but she's too late. Stacey is already pressed against his chest, with her arms locked firmly around him, swaying.

"Fuck," Olivia whispers from the middle of the floor.

It kills me to watch her go through this. I place my hand on her back and escort her off the dance floor. I haven't gotten all the details from John about the Bramtech Corporation, but it must be one hell of a business deal for Ethan to jeopardize his relationship with Olivia. When we reach the other side of the room, I'm flocked by a group of girls who seem to be infatuated with my blue eyes and accent. Screw you, again, McCabe. Tempting as it is, I turn down several invitations to dance. I don't want to leave Olivia standing here alone, but the *grinder* won't take no for an answer. She engages me in a little dirty dancing, right there against the wall. I must admit, I'm not completely hating it; she has a great ass. The booze, the music, and the smoking hot body grinding against me distract me longer than it should. I glance over her shoulder in time to see Olivia heading across the dance floor as if she's just been shot out of a cannon.

It's tempting to let her go and see what unfolds. Instead, loyalty gets the better of me, so I abandon my partner and take off after her, knocking people over in my attempt to reach her in time. I catch her, midway across the dance floor. "Whoa!" I band my arms around her waist from behind, to stop her. "Where are you going?"

"I'm going to peel that SKANK off *my man*!" she says through clenched teeth.

It isn't funny, but I laugh. "Oh no, you're not. Well, at least not while you look like you want to stab someone." I turn her around and escort her back to the other side. Ethan gives me a look of gratitude from across the room. I nod my acknowledgment. She's literally trembling with anger. As an alpha male, it triggers that instinctive need I have to protect her. She becomes my first priority. "Olivia, listen to me. I know it's hard to watch, but I know Ethan. He's an asshole, but he's not a liar. He told me tonight that he loves you."

For the first time since I marched her back over here, she focuses on me. Her expression morphs from anger to sheer terror. Clearly, that wasn't the right thing to say. "I just mean; there must be a good reason he's letting this happen."

Her eyes dart between him and me. "I'm not important enough," she says, looking deflated.

"Don't say that. You're very important to him. For some reason, that woman has latched onto him like a tick on a kangaroo." The darkness doesn't hide the tears in her eyes. "If there weren't a business deal at stake, this wouldn't be happening. I know that's no excuse, but at least it's an explanation." I glance at the dance floor, watching as Ethan consistently moves her hands off his ass. I growl, struggling to accept what I know I have to do. I have to put a stop to this. "Listen, you just stay here. Okay? I'll look after it." Needing liquid encouragement, I tip my bottle to my mouth and drain it.

"Carter? What are you going to do?" she asks, worried.

I like that she's concerned. I pinch her chin and smile. "You look absolutely miserable, and I can't take it anymore. I'm going to do what I should have a few hours ago. I'm going to suck it up and take one for the team."

Olivia lets out a heavy sigh of relief, "Thank you, Carter. You're a good friend."

"Yes, I am. And you're going to owe me one. A huge one, I might add."

"Anything, I promise."

If only. I take a long look at her, remembering the way she looks at me in my dreams. I nod. "All right, let's get on with it. It's your turn to order me a drink. I'm going to need it."

I dodge my admirers and make my way onto the dance floor. Tapping Ethan on the shoulder, I ask to cut in. Stacey glances over at Olivia with hatred in her eyes. Ethan makes a quick exit, leaving me standing there with an extremely pissed off blonde. I've always loved a good challenge. "Don't look so disappointed, beautiful."

She reluctantly takes my outstretched hand, and I reel her in. It takes everything I have to smile and create the illusion that I'm interested in her. Her body remains stiff in my arms, making it difficult to dance.

"Come on, now," I coax. "I don't bite." I lower my mouth to her ear. "That's a lie. I do." I feel her body respond and it pleases me. I know her type. The kind of woman who puts on a strong and dominant facade, but responds to a man who can control her in the bedroom. That's the reason for her attraction to Ethan. The submissive in her is drawn to his alpha personality. She hasn't seen anything yet. As the music vibrates around us, I pull her close and lead her. She responds as I knew she would. I feel her warm breath against my chest as she nuzzles in under my chin and takes refuge there. It's the safest place a submissive could be. My hands firmly anchor her against my body, slowly but surely, staking my claim.

I lower my cheek to hers and breathe in her perfume. It's seductive, yet sophisticated. I'm a sucker for the provocative fragrances women wear. Her hands explore my chest as if there's not a single other person in the room. Instinctively, I tangle my hand in her hair and give it a slow firm tug, discreetly forcing her to look up at me. I watch her chest expand with her quick intake of breath, and it makes me hard. "How wet are you right now?" I already know the answer. Her hips push forward against me as she twitches. The dim lights hide the victorious grin that begins to curl on my lips. I hold her gaze until a silent understanding passes between us.

Suddenly I become the guy I was back in college. The *guy* I've been trying to leave behind. It's an impulse that comes over me, and I can't stop it. "You and I are going to go over to that dark corner under the stairs, and I'm going to fuck you. Do you understand?" I loosen my grip on her and wait for her to comply.

Without a word, she turns, and I steer her across the floor. The moment the darkness conceals us from view, she unzips my trousers and slips my cock out. You'd think I'd be concerned about someone catching us, but I'm not. I press my lips to hers in a hungry kiss and pin her to the wall. I know she's ready for me and there's not a thing beneath this dress to stop me. Discreetly I lift her and slide inside. In a forgotten corner of a crowded bar, I give the girl the pounding of her life. She won't be thinking about O'Connell in the morning. I'll make sure of it.

When I open my eyes the next morning, she's still sleeping at the furthest side of the bed. I'm grateful for the personal space since I'm not the cuddling kind. After a long shower, I escort her to the corner coffee shop. The least I can do is buy the girl breakfast before sending her on her way. Businessmen glance at me over the tops of their newspapers and smirk. I've always bought breakfast for the girls after a casual hookup, and it's never bothered me before. For some reason, today, I feel like I'm doing the walk of shame.

A pair of stunning blue eyes stares at me from behind a computer screen, looking disgusted. When our eyes meet, I get a nervous feeling. A strange energy zips through my veins like a drug.

I slow my pace as I walk past her, feeling as if I should speak to her, but I have no words.

A snide smile, which I don't understand, flashes across Stacey's lips as we pass. As I glance back at her one more time, I see a sadness in her eyes as she closes her laptop and leaves. I don't know why, but I feel like I've disappointed her. I give my head a shake, trying to pull myself back to reality. I'm really beginning to think I need to see a psychiatrist because I'm clearly losing my mind.

Stacey busies herself with her phone the entire time she drinks her coffee. I can't get those sad blue eyes out of my mind. I stare out the window, wondering where she went after she left. Stacey and I barely speak but a few words to each other, before I put her in a cab and say goodbye. There's no exchange of numbers or offers to keep in touch. We both know what last night was. The sex was fucking amazing, and obviously, something we both desired and needed, but that will be the end of it.

Something Ethan said the other night struck a nerve with me. It's been gnawing at me since, so I head into the office. It takes forever to get past the bimbo at the front desk. Why does O'Connell surround himself with this type of clingy women? She detains me, trying to prolong our conversation unnecessarily. I practically have to prostitute myself to get through the door. Now I feel like I need another shower. I walk down the long hallway, hoping to avoid O'Connell and walk straight into John's office. "Hey."

He looks up surprised. "Hey. I didn't expect to see you here so early."

"I'm surprised I'm here at all," I scoff.

"So why are you?"

"Information. About Olivia's ex."

John sits back in his chair. "What do you want to know?"

"Ethan said he was abusive."

"Yes. It appears that way."

"I need the details."

"Carter, if you want information maybe it's better you talk to Ethan."

"I don't want to talk to Ethan. I know you. You've already checked him out, and you're keeping tabs on him." I begin moving papers around on his desk. "You probably have a file here somewhere."

He crosses his arms unimpressed. "And what are you going to do with this information, if I share it with you?"

"Nothing, mate. I just want to help keep her safe. For Ethan."

I can't quite tell by the look he's giving me if he believes me, but he opens the bottom drawer of his desk and takes out a file folder.

"The guy is a real piece of shit," he says, as he hands it to me. "The police report bothers me. I can't put my finger on it, but something doesn't seem right."

I take it out of his hand. "I'll go through it and see if I feel the same."

"Bring it back to me when you're done."

I stuff it in my briefcase. "Will do. And if anybody asks… you haven't seen me."

"Got it."

I spend the next day going over the police reports and checking out details. John is right. Something doesn't add up. I read through some of the witnesses' character statements, and I feel like I'd like to kill the guy for the way that he treated Olivia. I break into a cold sweat as I read through the medical report. My stomach actually begins to feel nauseous. When Scott calls about a delivery that's going to be made at the restaurant and says he needs someone there to sign for it, I volunteer to go. I need the fresh air. It's a coincidence that I run into Olivia at the coffee shop down the street. Okay, so I drove past her work several times until she left for lunch and followed her there. I need to see her.

"Carter!" she says, surprised to see me. "What are you doing here?"

"Running an errand for Scott."

"Do you have time to have lunch with me?"

I smile, pleased that she's asked. "I'll make time for you."

She blushes and looks away as she tucks her hair behind her ear. She's so beautiful. I stand there, like a moron, staring.

"Are you going to get something to eat?"

"No, I'm good." I hold up my coffee.

"Sit," she says looking at the time. "I only get a half an hour for lunch."

I pull the chair out and sit. A sullen look washes over her.

"What's wrong? You can talk to me," I assure her.

"I haven't been sleeping well," she admits, as she picks at her sandwich.

I hold up my hand. "I was wrong. If this has anything to do with the weird kinky sex you're having with O'Connell, I don't want to hear about it."

She wrinkles her nose. "Really? No! Nothing like that." Looking disgusted, she pushes her plate to the side. "I've been having nightmares."

"I can understand why. Dating O'Connell must be terrifying."

She tries to hold off a grin but she can't. "Not about him."

"Your ex?"

Her shoulders fall. "How much do you know?"

I fold my hands on top of the table and come clean. "I know everything."

She looks away and purses her lips.

"Hey." I reach across the table and place my hand over hers. When she turns and looks into my eyes, the muscles in my chest tighten. "John is all over it. I know he's as old as dirt. I think he might have even sat beside Moses in first grade." I pause, enjoying her sudden amusement. "But nobody is better when it comes to security. He'll make sure you're safe."

She nods. "Sometimes I just get this eerie feeling… like I'm sensing the onset of impending doom."

"Well… that's a little dramatic. I push her plate back in front of her. You need to eat."

"I've had no appetite since he called."

As soon as she says it, I sense her anxiety.

"Who called?"

She ignores me. But I'm not going to let it go. "Olivia? Has your ex been in touch with you?" She shakes her head, but I don't believe her. I hold out my hand. "Give me your phone."

"Why?" she asks suspiciously, as she passes it to me. "You won't find his number in there."

"I'm not checking your call history." I quickly punch in my phone number and wait until my phone starts to vibrate. "There. Now you have my number, and I have yours. If you need me, you call me. I promise you, I'll look after you. Whatever it takes."

She gets that look like there's something she wants to say to me. There's a long awkward pause. "Carter, do you ever get the feeling like your living the same life over again?"

Before I can answer, my phone vibrates. The delivery guy is waiting at the restaurant. I look up at her with regret. "I need to go."

"Me too. Lunch is over."

I watch as the waitress clears her barely touched sandwich from the table. "Are you good?"

"Yes."

"A bird eats more than you."

She shrugs and picks up her purse. Ethan better address this issue, or I'll tend to it myself. I'll send him a message later.

I walk her to her car and lock her in. I peruse the parking lot to make sure there's nobody lurking, but I still get an uneasy feeling as she pulls out onto the road. I'd follow her back to work myself, but if I miss this delivery, Scott will throttle me.

I spend the rest of the day working on my business plans until I can't see straight any longer.

I lay awake, staring at the city lights through my bedroom window. I wish I weren't so worried about her, but I'm not convinced she's safe. At three in the morning, my phone rings.

"I shouldn't have called this late," she says quietly.

I laugh once. "I wasn't sleeping."

"I kind of had a feeling."

"So why are *you* awake?" I ask, wondering if she's having the same dreams.

"Nightmares."

I sit up and turn on the bedside lamp. "Where's O'Connell?"

"He stayed in Toronto tonight. He's busy."

"Do you want me to come over?" I have no idea how I'd explain that to Ethan, but I'll figure it out later.

"No. I'm okay."

"It's no problem. I can be there in less than an hour." I move to the side of the bed.

"I don't want you to come all this way. I just thought… maybe you could…"

She pauses so I ask. "Maybe I could, what?"

"Would you mind just talking to me for a little while?"

I feel like I want to get in the car and go anyway, but I know it would only make things more complicated for both of us. It's better if I just stay put. "Of course, anything for you."

I don't feel much like going into the office for the next few days. It's probably a better idea for me to lay low right now, anyway. I've had a few really late nights. I yawn as I sit at the desk in my hotel, doing research on historical Ireland. I've read countless articles and the only thing I'm taking away, is Ireland is thought to be, by many, a very magical place.

I take a break and try to finish up business, but I can barely concentrate on putting my business plan into action. It was a miracle I managed to make the presentation deadline at all. Sales targets, profit margins, and EBITDA stats are all a blurry mound of numbers, continually interrupted by thoughts of the lush green grass of the rolling hills in Ireland, and a life I long to return to. A notion that's disturbingly odd, since I was born and raised in Australia. Most people dream of the love of their life. I dream about the love of my life… times two: Olivia and the alluring blonde. As if it's not enough that I feel like I'm stuck in some kind of weird time warp, I constantly deal with the unyielding push and pull I feel between them.

I dial Olivia's number.

"Hi, Carter."

I pause, thrown off by her use of my name. I don't know what I expected her to call me. "How are you?"

"I'm okay."

"That's not what I heard. Rumor has it that you passed out at dinner last night."

She curses like a foul-mouthed frat boy and brings me up to date. I don't like what I hear about what's gone down in the past few days. "So you told him you loved him and he doesn't remember," I summarize.

"Pretty much."

"I see. And now you're going to torture him, but he has no idea why."

"Right again."

Past and present suddenly blend together, and I become disoriented. "Like the time he ruined your surprise birthday plans by working late at the stable." The moment I say it, I realize what I've done. In the awkward moment of silence that follows, I keep my mouth shut. If I try to explain myself, it'll definitely make it even weirder than it is. I need to get her off the phone before she asks any questions. "I have to go. Promise me you'll take care of yourself and don't be too hard on him."

"Carter," she begins. I pretend I don't hear her and hang up the phone. Now I'm feeling anxious, and I'm wishing I'd taken Ethan up on his earlier offer to go a few rounds at the gym. Maybe kicking his ass would help settle the turmoil inside me. Instead, I'll just stay in my hotel room, do some push-ups and try to burn off some of this energy. I'm just finishing up my last repetition when there's a loud pounding on the hotel door. I knew that sooner or later, he'd figure out I'm avoiding him.

"Open the door, you dick, I know you're in there," Ethan says, as he bangs again, impatiently.

I wipe the sweat from my brow with a towel and take a leisurely walk to the door. He can bloody well wait. When he hears the click of the deadbolt, he pushes the door open and shoulders past me, knocking me to the side.

"Are you alone?" He looks around the room and turns, waiting for an explanation.

"Yes." I have half a mind to call security and have him thrown out, but I doubt that's possible since he owns the hotel.

"What took you so long to answer the door?"

"What are you doing here?" I ask, not hiding my aggravation.

"I came to see what the fuck is wrong with you."

I think about it a minute. "Nothing is wrong." Nothing I'm eager to share with him, that's for sure.

"Really?" He raises his brow. "It's not like you to pass on an opportunity to take a few swings at me." He sits in the chair at the desk by the window and crosses his feet at the ankle. "I'm not leaving until you tell me what's going on."

I glance at John's folder on the desk and hope to hell he doesn't notice it. I might as well give in since it's not in his nature to let anything go, and I really would like to get him out of here. "Let me get my shoes on," I sigh. "We can go down to the pub for a beer."

I'm two beers in, and I still can't bring myself to tell Ethan I've met Olivia in my dreams. Even I've wondered if I'm losing my mind. I consider all the possible outcomes of the conversation where I tell him I think I'm in love with her, and every one of them ends in Ethan blowing an Irish gasket.

I do my best to avoid any questions that would lead to further interrogation, and he's frustrated with my behavior. I can tell. A woman, sitting at a corner table on the other side of the bar captures my attention. I can't seem to take my eyes off her. The shadows mask her identity, but I've seen her somewhere before. Hmmm. That seems to be the new *thing* with me.

While Ethan continues to give me an ear-bashing, the bartender turns the lights up, and I look past him to see what she's doing. Even from across the bar, her raspberry lips look soft and delicious. They're nothing in comparison to the intense blue of her eyes. I've seen those eyes before. It isn't until I see her flash a disapproving look at a drunken admirer that I recognize her as the woman from the coffee shop. That same feeling sizzles through my body like a spark plug trying to fire.

Growing impatient with my lack of interest, Ethan turns completely in his seat to see what has me so captivated. He whistles, "Fuck, man, is that what's got you so twisted?"

"What? No!" I deny.

"Lying bastard." Ethan mutters as he tips his beer glass against his lips. "Have you talked to her?"

I realize she'd be a good diversion for his questions. "What's the point? I'm going home in a week."

"Did you just ask me what the point is? The point is you're still here for a week." His brow furrows. "What the fuck is wrong with you? I seriously think you need to get laid. Apparently going a few weeks without a woman messes up your head."

My jaw clenches. Apparently, he doesn't know about Stacey. I pause, recalling a recent dream... or memory... or whatever the fuck they are. I quickly shake it out of my head. Once upon a time, a good fuck would take the edge off, but not at the moment. Sexual desires seem to be the root of my current affliction.

"Are you going to sulk for the rest of the week? Or are you going to talk to her?" Ethan persists.

"That depends. Are you going to be an annoying dick for the rest of the week?"

Ethan laughs out loud. "Okay, not another word, I swear."

"Thanks, mate, I appreciate it." I get to my feet and look around, spotting the toilet at the back of the bar. "I'll be right back."

I'm only halfway across the room when Ethan takes advantage of the opportunity, walking straight over to the corner table.

"Hi!" I hear her say in a friendly manner.

"Hello." Ethan holds out his hand. "Ethan O'Connell."

"Katherine Ryan," she says, as she reciprocates his firm grip.

"Ah, Ryan is a good old Irish name. Are you from Ireland?" he asks with a glimmer in his eyes.

I shake my head as I disappear down the hallway. Some things never change. The few moments I'm away from them is enough time to wind myself closer to the possibility I might chuck a mental, and it won't be pretty.

When I return, she watches me pass on the way to the bar.

"Australia? No kidding?" I hear her say to Ethan. She lets out a small sweet laugh, and for a brief moment, my heart stalls.

Ethan hands her a pen, and she turns over what looks like his business card and writes something on it. He grins when she hands it to him.

I glare at them from across the room. She senses my stare and looks over. There's something in her eyes that's beyond sensual; it's erotic. Somehow, I know she's hiding some very dark, naughty desires.

Ethan has never been able to resist a beautiful woman, but this is too much. What a dickhead. I can't watch anymore. I turn in my seat and watch the bubbles in my beer float to the top of the glass instead. He certainly doesn't deserve Olivia. My leg jiggles anxiously on the rung of the barstool. I'll kill him if he does anything to break her heart. Repeatedly tapping the drink coaster on the edge of the bar, I'm trying really hard not to lose my mind. "Fuck the friendship!" I slam the coaster down hard and get to my feet. When I turn, I nearly bump into him.

"Whoa! Relax, buddy. It looks like that vein in your forehead is about to explode."

"What the fuck, Ethan?"

"Now, don't jump to conclusions, Brant. I did it for you." Ethan hands me the business card. "In case you change your mind."

I glance down at her name and struggle to think of why it seems familiar to me. "Kate Ryan."

"She was asking questions about you," Ethan continues. "She said she's here on an extended work project, and maybe you could keep each other company next week."

I look across the room as she gets to her feet. She's truly a beautiful woman, with soft, feminine curves to her body. I'm guessing she's close to five foot eleven in those heels, ideal kissing height for me. I become fixated on her. She bears a striking resemblance to a woman in a dream I had some time ago. I'm vaguely aware Ethan is still talking.

"She said she's seen you here every night this week and was hoping you would have said hello."

I mumble excuses as I settle up the bar tab and slide her card into my wallet. I decide I should say hello to her, and keep Ethan off my back for a while, but when I turn, she's gone. I think I might feel disappointed.

Walking back to the hotel, O'Connell doesn't shut his yap for a minute. I'm tired of listening to him. "Do you ever get tired of hearing your own voice?" I ask.

"Not usually."

"Apparently. I don't even know why you need to be in a relationship with a woman. You talk to yourself and answer your own questions," I jest.

"I usually have the best suggestions. Besides, Olivia has an objection to being in a relationship."

Now that sparks my curiosity. "Oh?"

"Yeah," he answers, looking displeased. "She says she doesn't want to be in a monogamous relationship."

"You mean she wants to see other people?" Is the man absolutely nuts? A beautiful, intelligent, amazing woman like Olivia James, and he's not staking his claim? I'd claim her for my own in a minute and make sure there'd be no misunderstanding who she belonged to.

Olivia is one of those girls you come across once in a lifetime: the kind you marry, have babies with and grow old together. You'd have to be a complete idiot to let one of those girls slip through your fingers.

Ethan shakes his head in frustration. "She's still a little freaked out, Carter. She's just learning how to trust again. I only made it worse the other night."

"Are you kidding me, mate? You agreed to a noncommitted relationship? YOU? Didn't you insist that the girls you brought back to the flat gave you their total submission and agreed to complete exclusivity to you? Except for those girls you and Reese…" I stop, deciding it's wise to refrain from finishing my sentence. Ethan looks absolutely pissed off.

"Things have changed since university. And for the record, I am in complete control of my relationship," Ethan assures me.

I laugh. "You're fucked, mate. I've met Olivia."

He gives me an annoyed look. "She's not the kind of girl to be dominated in all areas of her life, Carter. I don't think I would love her so much if she were. Trust me when I tell you she submits in the bedroom. It's the one area she does allow me complete control."

"Obviously that's the place you still need it."

"She can call it a noncommitted relationship if she wants," he argues. "It's completely irrelevant since I have no intention of seeing any other girls."

I shake my head. How can such a brilliant man be so daft? "Have you considered the agreement also gives her permission to see other guys, and there's nothing you can do about it if she does?"

"Oh, there's plenty I can do about it," he says confidently.

"If she were my girl, I'd already have a ring on that finger. Are you willing to share her, mate?"

His face turns red as his anger starts to boil to the surface. "Fuck, no!"

"That's what I thought. Think about it, Ethan. Once again, you've left the door wide open for assholes like Reese to get a foot in."

That comment obviously cuts straight into his heart. "Fuck you, Brant!"

I stop in my tracks and turn to face him. "Sorry. But you needed to hear it. I told you the other night, she loves you. Get your shit sorted out, treat her right, and don't fuck it up because there will always be some prick waiting for a chance with a girl like Olivia."

I hate these ridiculous social gatherings. The only thing worse than the mutilated melodies the town orchestra calls music is the irritating sound of Seán's voice. I've moved away from him twice, but he hasn't gotten the hint. I settle in a spot against the wall, across from the door so I can watch for my brother. The daft redhead follows me and continues with his nonsense. I'm about to tell him to stifle his shit when I glance over his shoulder and see her.

I swallow hard, and my voice abandons me. Even from across the room, Elizabeth O'Connor's smile is capable of stopping my heart. I've always thought my brother's girl is a beautiful woman, but tonight she's absolutely taken my breath away. Seán stops mid-sentence and turns to see what's captured my attention.

"Now, there's a girl I'll be dancing with tonight," Seán says, with a repulsive smile.

I can't take my eyes off her. I follow her every move as she makes her way around the room. I give my head a small shake, trying to rid myself of unwanted thoughts. "I can't see Owen letting you get anywhere near her," I scoff.

Seán looks around the room. "He isn't even here."

"He'll be here," I assure him. "Father made him stay back to do chores." I offered to help, but father said no. I know better than to cross him.

"The old man sure is a lot tougher on Owen."

"I don't get it." I shrug, feeling guilty. "Owen goes out of his way to please father; much more than I do. It just never seems to be enough for him."

"My pa says, Owen's real father is the man that used to work on the horse farm.

I clench my jaws. It's not the first time I've heard that rumor. I work hard at not letting it get to me. Seán's distracted me too long, making me lose track of her. I ignore his comment and desperately search for her in the crowd. When I find her, she's engaged in a very passionate kiss. Angst washes over me. I'm not quite sure when my brother arrived, but I'm glad Elizabeth is no longer unescorted. Watching over her in his absence would be a painful task, this evening.

She wipes her lipstick from his lips, and I wish they were mine. Owen takes her hand and gently pulls her on to the dance floor. She hesitates at first, taking small slow steps. Watching her amuses me. I'm sure letting go of control and allowing Owen to partner her is probably driving her over the edge right now.

Her dress sways sensually around her as he guides her across the room. Seán whistles, reminding me he's still there. "You know," he begins, glancing over at me. "If she were my girl, she wouldn't be walking around, unescorted. She'd be home looking after all the kids we'd have."

I quickly correct him, feeling annoyed. "Well, she's not you're girl, Seán."

"She could be," he justifies, watching Owen glide her across the dance floor. "Think of the beautiful children we'd have. How happy I'd make her," Seán brags.

I feel the tension start to tighten in my muscles. I can't hold my tongue any longer. "Well, that's hilarious, Seán. Since the girl kicked your arse the first day of school."

"She just needs a firm hand, that's all," he says defensively. "To be honest with you, Jamison... I don't think your brother has what it takes to control her. In fact, when he leaves for his fancy medical school, I think I'll take it upon myself to court Elizabeth O'Connor. I'll teach her what her body is for, and how to properly serve a man."

"Shut the fuck up!" The nerve in my temple begins to pulse.

"Look at those luscious lips," Seán says, with a vile smirk. "Every time she showed me disrespect, I'd teach her a lesson. She'd soon learn her place and what her insolent mouth should be used for."

Fire flashes through my veins, "Don't you ever talk about her like that again," I warn through gritted teeth.

"Trust me," Seán says, indiscreetly adjusting himself. "Eventually, she'd learn to enjoy sucking my ..."

Blind rage takes over, and my fist flies through the air, landing on Seán's jaw with a powerful force. Screaming women scurry out of the way. He picks himself up off the floor and throws himself at me. Tackling me with his full body weight, he knocks me backward several feet. Strong hands grab his shoulders from behind and pull him off me.

"I can look after myself," I yell at my brother, as he drags the redheaded asshole away in a chokehold.

"I can see that," he says sarcastically. Seán struggles and breaks away, taking another swing at me. I duck and quickly step to the side. Big burly farmhands step in to break it up, and before I know it, Owen and I are being escorted out of the building by the scruff of the neck. I stumble as I receive a firm push out the door and into the night.

Owen reaches out to steady me, and I push him away. "I said I don't need your help."

He holds his hands in the air in defeat. "Okay." He pulls a hankie out of his pocket and hands it to me. "Here, your nose is bleeding."

I don't really care if it's bleeding or not, all I can think about right now is that she's in there alone with that asshole. I try to shoulder past the largest man I've ever seen, who's guarding the door, but I'm not getting past him. I begin to protest loudly when the door swings open and Elizabeth joins us outside. She looks at me sympathetically and reaches out to touch my arm. Time stands still when our eyes connect, and energy passes between us. I'm convinced she must have feelings for me; I can sense it.

"Go back inside," Owen instructs her. "It's cold out here. There's no reason for you to leave. Stay, and have a good time."

"I'm not staying here alone," she insists.

"I'm sorry, Liz," I say, feeling horrible I've ruined her evening.

She shrugs and gives me a smile that makes my insides churn upside down. "That's okay. I'm not a very good dancer anyway."

"Is there any point in me arguing with you about staying?" Owen asks curiously.

"None at all," she says, assuredly.

"What got into you anyway?" He swats me in the back of the head. "Since when do you let that arsehole, O'Reilly, get to you?"

Thunder rolls in the distance. I look between them, feeling ashamed. Looking up at the cloud-covered moon, I quickly change the topic. "We better get her home before it rains."

The clouds hide the moonlight, making it a long, dark walk. I know from the feel of the air, we aren't going to make it home. The wind picks up as the rain begins to fall in torrential streams. Only a few moments exist between the lightning strikes that brighten the sky. Elizabeth jumps and grabs for Owen's hand. He tries to screen her from the rain, but within seconds, we're all soaked to the bone. She shivers uncontrollably. I curse, angry with myself for not keeping her safe and warm. Over the echoing crack of thunder, I try to get my brother's attention. "We need to get her out of the rain," I yell over the gusting wind. "We're close to the old cabin by the river. I think we should head there for shelter."

Looking around at their surroundings, Owen agrees. Heading off the pathway, we make our way through the heavily wooded area toward the river. The trees provide some protection from the driving force of the rain. Before long, the abandoned wooden shack Owen and I found during a fishing trip comes into view.

My muscles are tired and cramped up from the cold. It takes every ounce of energy I have left to push open the door, so I can get Liz out of the storm. Not much has changed since the last time I was in this rundown cabin, but at least we're dry here. "I'll get a fire started." I walk toward the hearth, bumping into my brother in the dark. "You get her out of those wet clothes and try to get her warmed up."

Owen chuckles, as Elizabeth stands erect, her arms crossed angrily in front of her, "Excuse me, Liam Jamison? I'm perfectly capable of looking after myself. I don't need your brother's help."

Bloody woman is always arguing with me. She's going to catch pneumonia and die if she doesn't get out of those wet clothes. Even with all the money Father has to buy medicine, it might not save her. Why can't she just do what she's told? How hard is that? I establish eye contact with Owen, and he knows my unexpressed thoughts.

"Don't worry, Brother," Owen says, as he lights what's left of the wax candle stubs. "I'll look after it."

Elizabeth gives him an unimpressed eyebrow.

Placing his hand firmly on her back, he ushers her toward a small room and holds back the blanket that's nailed to the doorway.

They seem to be gone forever. I keep myself busy with the fire and try to ignore the giggling and whispers from the other room. I park my ass on a very uncomfortable wooden chair next to the hearth and try to take the chill off. When they return, Elizabeth is holding up a pair of pants that are three times too large for her. I'd make a comment, but it wouldn't go well for me. She doesn't always get my sense of humor. It's earned me a few hard wallops in the arm over the past year.

Owen strips off his wet shirt, laying it out to dry in front of the blazing fire. Elizabeth stares at his broad shoulders and muscular chest. I struggle with jealous feelings when he sits beside her and pulls her into his arms. That should be me. I'm not entirely sure when it was that I fell in love with her, but it doesn't matter. Her heart belongs to my brother.

The fire crackles and roars; when she finally drifts off to sleep in his arms, he carries her to the only bedroom and then returns to the lumpy sofa beside me. At least he's that much of a gentleman. Exhaustion takes over, and as the room quickly warms from the fire, my eyes become heavy, and I'm soon sound asleep. I'm awoken by a strange thumping noise, and I lift my head to see the silhouette of my brother hopping into the room with only one leg in his pants. I can't believe he's going in there. Anxiety prickles through my body and I can't stand it any longer. I'm going to haul his ass out of the room, and then tell her how I feel about her.

I stand outside the door with my hand on the blanket, prepared to pull it to the side and pronounce my love. Instead, I wait, listening to the conversation between them and looking for the right time to interrupt. How do I deny my brother his true love? Then a thought gets stuck in my head. What if I've been imagining the chemistry between us and she doesn't have feelings for me? What then? My brother still gets the girl, and I would live a lonely life of misery and endless awkward Christmas dinners. That's if they ever spoke to me again.

"Owen, I want to," I hear her whisper.

He's my brother. Despite the rumors that suggest otherwise. I love him, and I'd do anything for him. I let my hands drop to my side and take several deep breaths before heading to the couch where he was sleeping. I settle into the dips in the cushions and try to get comfortable. I might as well; he won't be returning to this couch tonight.

All day long I've been haunted by the dream I had this morning. I leave work on time, for a change, to meet John and Shannon for dinner. O'Connell has something going on tonight, and he's not very forthcoming with his plans. I could use a break from him about now anyway. I get an eerie feeling when I enter the underground parking garage at the hotel. I give up on finding a spot near the entrance, so I park in the first spot I find and reach down for my phone. The hair on the back of my neck stands on end when I look up to find an elderly woman standing at the hood of the rental car.

"It's a difficult decision," she says watching me.

I reluctantly get out and quickly lock the door. "What is?" I study her long silver hair and frail body. I'm sure we've never met, but there's something familiar about her.

"You have to let him have her. In this life, she's not your destiny."

We stare at each other for a very long time, remaining silent. As if my life couldn't get any stranger, I nod, acknowledging her message. Now I know I'm out of my mind.

A loud honking distracts me, and I turn to see what's going on. It appears this woman may have some answers to the million questions that have been rolling through my mind. "Why am I having these dreams?" I turn and find myself alone. Baffled, I scratch my head. Great, now I'm hallucinating too?

I'm starting to feel anxious… edgy. The hotel elevator is taking way too long. Slowly, the doors begin to open, and I impatiently push them apart to get inside. On the other side, a woman stands in the doorway, waiting to exit. Her sapphire blue eyes stop me in my tracks. Strange how our paths keep crossing.

"Excuse me," Kate says annoyed.

I shake my head, snapping myself out of it. "Sorry." Feeling like an asshole, I step to the side and press my hand against the heavy elevator door to keep it from closing. She murmurs something about the rudeness of foreigners as she exits and her shoulder brushes against my chest. Normally that kind of comment would bother me, and I'd have a sarcastic comeback, but I breathe in her perfume, and it calms me. I have a very acute sense of smell, and I'm intrigued. All the way to the penthouse, her perfume accompanies me. It's like vanilla cupcakes with a very subtle hint of jasmine… and if I'm not mistaken, kiwi.

It's odd not being harassed by O'Connell every twenty minutes. I wonder what he's up to. The only other time there was complete radio silence between us was the night of all the allegations by his psycho ex-girlfriend.

The new marquee catches my eye as I pull in. Why in God's name he called it Ireland's, I'll never know. It's kind of cheesy, and O'Connell usually has superlative taste and judgment.

Speaking of Ireland… I check for any updates on the arrival of our chums coming for the grand opening. Ethan has asked them to play a few sets of authentic Irish tunes to celebrate his newest restaurant. They're a rather crass bunch, so I keep my interactions with them to a minimum whenever possible, but they're going to be here for the entire week, so I know I can't avoid them.

John and Shannon keep me waiting at the restaurant, giving me time to catch up on all the news back home. Australia, I mean. Not Ireland. Though Ireland is clearly the home in my dreams with her.

"Sorry we're late," John announces, as he pulls out a chair for Shannon to sit.

"About bloody time. What was the holdup?" I look up from my phone and know exactly why they're late. Her face flushes pink, and she can't look me in the eye. John tries to hide a satisfied grin.

I try my hardest not to talk about him, but the conversation always comes back around to O'Connell. John has no idea what he's up to tonight either, and since Scott was the only person he included in the secret plans, we decide we're going to ignore his SOS requests for backup. I laugh at his last plea for help and shut off my phone. "Scott's hidden O'Connell's keys."

"That can't be good," John adds, scrolling through his list of missed calls.

"It's good for us. We don't have to deal with him for a change."

John raises his brow. "Remember last time I wasn't around when he was drinking?"

"Scott can babysit him this time."

John gives Shannon a worried look. "He's right," she assures him. "Scott can deal with him for a change. You deserve a night off."

A few too many drinks later, by Shannon's calculations, she demands my keys. I hate bossy women. I prefer my women much more on the submissive side. After too much discussion, in my opinion, John decides we'll head over to O'Connell's restaurant for a nightcap or two. This has very little to do with having a few more drinks. It's all about McCabe wanting to make sure O'Connell has stayed in line. The poor old guy probably won't sleep unless he checks in on him. Can't say that I blame him, I guess. The last time he left him unsupervised, he made the biggest 'career ending' mistake of his life. I never liked Jessica, but I didn't think Ethan loved her enough to do the things he's being accused of. He could have any woman he wanted with that arrogant Irish accent and swagger. The Ethan O'Connell I know would have walked away and moved on. I don't understand how he has absolutely no recollection of the evening. I've seen the bloke completely hammered and still remember the name of every girl he shagged in university.

Sitting in the back seat of John's car, my knees press uncomfortably into the back of Shannon's seat. I should have taken an Uber.

I begin to curse when John's phone rings, for what I estimate to be at least the tenth time. "The fucker just doesn't know when to stop." I'm in the middle of an angry rant when John shouts my name, trying to get my attention. Shocked, I stop and wait for him to speak.

"It's Olivia."

"You better answer it," Shannon says concerned. "If she's calling, then something's wrong."

She's right, something is wrong. I can sense it. "Hurry up and answer it before she hangs up," I say, as I release my seat belt and move to the edge of the seat.

He glances over his shoulder at me. "Do you mind?" I slide back in my seat as he connects the hands-free call. "McCabe."

"Hi, John," she says in a soft tone.

"Hi, Olivia. It's getting late, is everything okay?"

"I'm sorry, John. You're trying to spend time with Shannon tonight. I'll be fine."

"Don't let her hang up," I shout from the back of the car.

John glances at me in the rearview mirror and furrows his brow.

"Wait!" he says to Olivia, sternly. "Don't hang up. You're not interrupting anything. Tell me what's going on."

"O'Connell and I had a fight, and I walked out…"

I knew it!

"And well, I kept walking, and now I don't know where I am," she sighs heavily.

"Well, that explains why Ethan has called eighteen times in the last half an hour," John says calmly.

"I'm starting to freak out a little. I keep hearing things, and I think someone is following me. Do you think it's Ethan?"

"There's no way Scott gave him back his keys," I add from the back seat.

A look of concern washes over John. "Can you tell me anything about where you are? A street name would be helpful."

"I don't see any signs and it's really dark, I was just so upset I kept walking…"

I can't stand it; I'm going to lose my shit if we don't get to her, right now!

"I have no idea how I even got here," she rambles nervously.

John, as always, remains calm and in control. "Okay, listen to me. I'm going to drive in that direction. Don't walk any farther. Just stay put. If you see anything, a street sign, the name of a business… call me right back. Don't worry, we'll be there shortly."

I fidget nervously. "For fuck's sake, McCabe. Can you drive any slower? Put the hammer down, man. This is not the time to have a senior moment!"

I take out my phone and dial her number.

"Olivia, it's Carter."

"Carter!"

"Are you okay?" I'm no John McCabe, but I try to keep my cool. I read all John's research on her piece of shit ex-boyfriend, so I know what kind of danger she could be in.

"Carter, I keep hearing footsteps, like I'm being followed. I think someone is hiding in the shadows," she says quietly into the phone.

"Listen, I'm with John and Shannon."

"I know. It was kind of hard not to hear you a few minutes ago." She lets out a small laugh.

"I want you to do something for me. Walk in the direction where you started from. Just keep walking, okay? I'm going to stay on the phone with you until we find you." I'm concerned. Beyond concerned. I know the kind of lowlife scum that skulks around in dark alleys. "The minute you see a street sign or something, you let me know."

"Okay. But John said to stay put."

"We've rethought that plan."

"You rethought that plan," Shannon corrects.

I wave her off and keep talking. "Talk to me while you're walking. Tell me what happened."

She lets out a deep breath. "Stupid stuff, really. Ethan was mad because I wouldn't agree to a committed relationship, so he asked one of his coworkers out on a date."

"He did what?" I feel my face turn red, and I know there's little I can do to hide the anger in my voice. "You're messing with me, right? Tell me it wasn't that nasty tramp from reception," I demand, agitated.

"I wish I was joking. It was Hannah."

I feel the tension wind tightly throughout my body. I'm not even sure I can relax my jaw enough to speak. "I see. Have you passed any street signs yet?"

"No, but I see headlights coming toward me."

"Hang on." I hold my phone away from my ear and search for her in the approaching darkness. I bump John as I reach for the switch on the dashboard.

"What the hell are you doing?" he asks me, annoyed.

"Flash the lights. She thinks she see's us."

"I can see you, Carter! I'm just up ahead, on the right."

John screeches to a halt and then jumps out of the car, while I pry my legs out from behind Shannon's seat.

Before I can even get out of the car, John surveys the area for assailants and is on his way to check the alleyways. Old habits never die for some men. He might be ancient, but the old military boy still has some skills left in him.

I rush toward Olivia, giving her the once-over. My heart is pounding in my chest right now. "Are you okay? Are you hurt or anything?"

"I'm fine, Carter."

I cock my head to the side, giving her a look of disbelief.

"My feet hurt." She looks away from me, trying to deflect. I know how frightened she really is. Every emotion this girl has runs through my veins as if they were my own. Unconvinced, I raise my brow and wait.

She sighs. "I'm okay, Carter. Really. I'm just a little freaked out."

I pull her closer and wrap my arms around her body, holding her against my chest. I don't know what possesses me, but I press my lips to the top of her head. "Thank Christ we found you so quickly. We were on our way to the restaurant to have a few drinks when you called." She holds on to me for a long while; her breath warms my chest. I like it. I've dreamt about it. I've longed to feel her body against mine… again… for real.

I begin to think about the things the silver-haired woman said. In this life, she's not mine. There's no denying that Olivia and I had an instant connection the moment we met. I know she feels it too. I can see it in her eyes. There's something there; more than friendship. A past love. I won't act on it, out of respect for Ethan, because that's the kind of man I was raised to be: strong, true, and loyal, right down to my core. But if Ethan fucks things up, well that's a completely different story.

Olivia trembles in my arms. "Come on then." I take off my jacket and wrap it around her shoulders. "Let's get you in the car and take you home."

She responds to my authoritative tone, and it flips a switch inside my brain. My body starts to tense and respond. I slide beside her in the back seat and pull her close, hoping that she doesn't notice the bulging in my trousers. Or maybe I hope she does.

Shannon turns in the front seat and frowns. "Are you okay, Sweetie?" she asks Olivia.

"I just want to go home."

"Of course, we'll take you." She glances over at John, who nods in agreement. "You know what?" Turning back to Olivia, Shannon gives her a sympathetic smile. "Why don't I stay with you tonight? The boys are booked solid tomorrow, and I'll be bored to death. You promised to go dress shopping with me."

"That's a really good idea," John says. "You two can eat ice cream, spend money, and talk about what arseholes we are. I'm sure you'll feel much better after that."

"Hey," I object. "Speak for yourself, mate."

Shannon takes Olivia's silence as acceptance, "It's settled then. I'll stay with you."

There's an unbearable tension in the car when John's phone rings. He decides not to answer the call through the hands-free speaker system. Instead, he picks it up and holds it to his ear. We all know who it is. "Ethan." He holds the phone several inches away from his ear, wincing at the loud screaming. "Ethan, stop screaming and listen to me. ETHAN!"

Now I'm tensing up for completely different reasons. "Let me talk to him," I demand from the back seat. When John ignores me, I undo my seat belt and sit forward so I can hear better.

"Olivia is safe. I have her here with me. Shannon is going to stay with her overnight," he continues.

"I'm going to meet you there." I hear Ethan slur.

"Not a chance, Boss!" McCabe insists. "Scott isn't going to give you back your keys, Ethan, so leave him alone. Carter and I are going to pick you up in about ten minutes. Lay off the scotch."

In the dull glow of the passing streetlights, I can see the tears begin to stream down Olivia's cheeks. She's struggling to maintain her composure. The sight of it is like a sharp knife to my chest. Despite Shannon's assurance that she's got things under control, I walk them to the door. I pause on the landing, outside the open window, long enough to hear her break down into a hard sob.

The sound of it energizes me like a lightning strike. On the way to the restaurant, angry energy surges through my bloodstream, looking for an outlet. John's car hasn't even come to a complete stop when I open the door and jump out.

"Carter!" he yells, knowing me all too well. "Don't do it!" I hear him curse, but I don't give a fuck. I push myself through the crowded bar until I find O'Connell.

I call out his name, and he slowly turns toward me. Before he has a chance to say a word, I swing, hitting him in the jaw with such a powerful right cross that he stumbles back. He looks at me completely stunned and lifts his hand to wipe a small trickle of blood from his lip.

Stepping forward, I poke my finger angrily into his chest. "I told you to take care of her!" I yell. "Treat her right, is what I said!"

"Carter," he begins.

"Don't interrupt me, O'Connell. Is taking the office whore on a date your idea of treating her right?"

"I made a mistake," he says regretfully, rubbing his jaw.

"Olivia loves you! You should be on your fucking knees worshipping her every chance you get!"

I can't contain the rage inside me. It's boiling to the point where I'm going to completely lose my shit. Every muscle in my body is taut and ready. McCabe's hand grips my shoulder from behind, firmly holding me in place. It's going to take military experience to stop me from giving Ethan the ass-kicking he deserves. I shake my head. "You don't deserve her, O'Connell!"

Scott stands guard at Ethan's side, with his arm firmly pressed across his chest, holding him back and encouraging him not to react.

"Okay, Carter, that's enough," John's authoritative voice commands. "Go wait out in the car."

"Fuck that." I'm still furious and tempted to get another good shot in. John gives me a knowing look and nods his head toward the door. It's so infuriating. I hesitate before I turn on my heel, shaking my bruised hand.

"I deserved that," I hear Ethan say as I walk away.

"Bloody right, you did," I answer, agitated. "And you'll get another one if you ever do anything that fucking stupid again." I'm flanked on all sides by restaurant security, making sure I find my way out. One of them places his hand on my back and guides me to the door. I clench my jaw and flash him an unimpressed look. He quickly holds his hands up in the air, acknowledging my aggravation. Believe me, it's best he doesn't press his luck right now.

I toss and turn the entire evening. When I finally drift off into a deep, uninterrupted sleep, I dream. This isn't like the other dreams I've had. I feel at peace. I feel loved.

Under the shade of a large willow tree, I seek shelter from the hot midsummer sun. I lay my head comfortably in the lap of a woman with ocean blue eyes. Her skin is as white and delicate as her name. She smells like vanilla and citrus. It's a very soothing scent. I reach up and stroke my fingertips through the curls of her golden blonde hair. She smiles, presses a kiss to the end of her finger, and then traces my lips.

I want this dream to last, but I wake too soon and feel disappointed at the loss of that feeling. I want to spend more time with this woman. As I go about my morning routine, the memory of her fades, and my mind once again becomes consumed with last night's events.

When Griff messages me to tell me they're on the ground in Toronto and looking for me to meet them for a few drinks, I decline. I give him the *Cliff Notes* version of Ethan's current relationship disaster and come up with an excuse for not joining them.

The more I think about it, the more worked up I get. I pace the floor of my hotel room, feeling extremely agitated. I toss a pair of jeans onto the pile of dirty clothes, and something catches my eye. A small scrap of paper; intentionally tucked under the corner of the lamp to keep it in place. I place my finger on it and slide it into view.

Now that's interesting. I scratch my head. I had no idea she left me her number, and I'll admit at the moment, it's awfully tempting. Thinking twice about it, I crumple it into a ball and toss it into the rubbish.

I look at my watch at least a dozen times, but it doesn't help the time pass any faster. Halfway through my third bowl of cereal, I head to the living area to see what's on the telly. The minute I lie down on the couch, my eyes close; I dream about Ireland and the woman with the daunting blue eyes. The next thing I know, I find myself in the bedroom retrieving the crumpled paper from the trash.

It only takes me a few minutes to walk the four blocks to Stacey's apartment. I knock on the door, grateful she's not the kind of girl who wants to be wined, dined, or romanced. I know exactly what she wants, and I intend to give it to her. The door hasn't even completely closed yet, and she's tugging at my belt, trying to get it undone. I appreciate her enthusiasm. Lifting her effortlessly, I carry her down the hall with no idea where I'm going.

"Bedroom?" I growl.

"Next door on the right."

I push it open with my shoulder and toss her onto the bed.

She wastes no time, stripping her dress off over her head. I smile. I've always been a fan of red lace. At the moment, I'd be a fan of seeing it on the floor. I grab the edges to pull them down, and she stops my hands.

"Use your teeth."

I nip at her skin, making her squeal. This game is taking too long. My cock is hard, and I want inside her. I toss her panties to the floor and crawl over top of her. The bright screen of my cell phone illuminates the floor, as it rings in the pocket of my discarded trousers.

I look down at the floor, tempted to answer it. Stacey runs her fingers through my hair and pulls my mouth to hers. The warmth of her lips and the playful exploration of her tongue distracts me. Until it rings again. I pause. Something tells me that I need to answer it.

"Are you kidding me?" Stacey complains as I get to my feet.

I grab for it quickly. "Hello?"

"Mr. Carter. It's me, George."

There's only one reason George calls. "Is everything okay?"

"No. Everything is not okay."

"Why does that not surprise me?"

Stacey wiggles herself to the side of the bed and guides my cock into her mouth. I almost drop my phone. The girl apparently has no gag reflex at all. "What has he done this time, George?"

"It's Miss Olivia."

Hearing her name catches me by surprise, and I immediately take a step back, pulling myself out of Stacey's mouth.

"What about her?" I ask concerned.

"She came in here a few hours ago. Upset. I'm worried, Mr. Carter. We only served her a couple of drinks, but she is very drunk. She's not herself. The men here, they are not so nice. They will take advantage of a beautiful girl."

I already have one leg back into my pants.

"We tried to call Mr. O'Connell, but he's not answering."

"You're leaving?" Stacey says angrily.

"Sorry, I have to. It's an emergency." I pull my shirt back over my head and put the phone back to my ear.

"Don't let her leave, George. Stand your security guard between her and anybody that tries to get close to her. I'm on my way.

I lean over to give Stacey a quick apology kiss, but she turns her head.

"You're an asshole."

"I know," I admit, as I buckle my belt. "I have to make sure she gets home safe, then I'll come back to look after you. I promise."

I practically sprint the several blocks to the bar. It's quicker than waiting for an Uber. I try to call O'Connell, Parker, and McCabe on the way, but I finally give up. George is waiting outside the door, watching for me.

"Mr. Carter, it's good you have come."

It takes me a few seconds to catch my breath. You'd think my cardio would be better. "Where is she?"

"We're trying to keep her in the bar where we can keep a watchful eye, but Miss Olivia, she's a very stubborn woman."

"Oh, I know it." I make my way to the back of the bar.

"CARTER!" she squeals. Security catches her as she slides off the barstool and her legs turn to jelly.

"Whoa." I hold her until she gets her feet under her. "I've got her," I assure the security staff. They look to George for his approval before reluctantly leaving her in my charge.

"Here, let me help you." I grip her hips and lift her onto the barstool. "Are you okay?"

"I can't feel my nose." She lifts her hand and heavily taps on her face, apparently looking for her nose. As cute as it is, it isn't funny at all.

"Why are you here? I thought you and O'Connell were working things out?"

"Me too." Her eyes begin to tear up. "I called to talk to him."

"He's out with his buddies from Ireland. They arrived tonight," I remind her.

"I know, but I just wanted to hear his voice." She lifts a glass to her mouth and takes a large swig. "So I called," she continues, "and a drunk girl answered the phone."

I raise a brow, surprised.

"She said he just took some girl upstairs to bed."

I'm stunned. "Olivia, don't jump to conclusions, there must be a logical explanation."

"I don't even care. I came down here and spent the night with my friends." She wiggles her fingers, giving a drunken wave to a guy watching from across the room.

"I'm pretty sure none of these guys are your friends."

"Oh, they are. That nice man there has been buying me drinks." She lifts the glass to her mouth.

I grimace. "Jesus, what are you drinking, it smells like turpentine." I acknowledge the douchecanoe watching her from a dark corner of the bar. Immediately, I reach up and stop her hand. "I'm positive *that* guy is not your friend. Let's get you home."

"I'm not ready to go home," she argues. "I'm not going to waste my drink. That would be rude."

I take it out of her hand and down the rest of it. "There." I slam the empty glass on the bar. "Now it's gone, and we're leaving," I say firmly.

I guide her to the door and out into the brisk night air. We've only walked about a block when I start to feel strange. What the fuck is going on?

"Carter. I don't feel so great."

"Me neither." Suddenly I feel like I'm walking through an amusement park funhouse. Shapes become distorted, and my balance is off-kilter. We're almost at the hotel lobby when Olivia collapses. I don't know how I do it, but I pull myself together enough to lift her into my arms.

A woman rushes to open the door and holds it open. "Is she okay?" she asks concerned.

"I think someone slipped something into her drink."

"Do you want me to call an ambulance?"

Everything is foggy, but I recognize her voice. "No. Thank you…" I pause, trying to remember her name.

"Kate," she offers.

"I'm sorry. I'm horrible at names, but I'd never forget a beautiful woman like you."

"How can I help?" she asks, following us to the elevator.

"I just want to get her upstairs so I can make sure she's safe and let her sleep it off." The elevator door closes, and I lean back against the wall to steady myself.

When I step off onto the penthouse floor, I start to feel woozy. My grip feels like it's slipping, so I adjust her weight by tossing her over my shoulder and take her to the bedroom. "Just what the fuck was in that drink?" I wonder out loud.

She begins to giggle. I get her onto the bed, just in time, as she declares the room is starting to spin.

My phone rings and I look down to see Stacey's number. I look at my watch, then over at Olivia. Now that she's safe, I don't see why I couldn't go back and finish what I started.

Something wakes me from a sound sleep. I'm not startled awake but rather coaxed by a gentle force. I can hear her soft whimpering, and I lie a moment, waiting to see if she soothes herself back to sleep. The sound of a softly sung lullaby blends into the silence of the night. Getting to my feet, I quietly join her in the nursery. She turns and places her finger to her lips to silence me.

There is truly nothing more beautiful than the glow of a new mother when she holds her babe. "Is she okay?" I whisper concerned.

After laying the sleeping child down, she smiles at me and takes me by the hand, leading me into the hallway. Gently she pulls the door closed, pauses and listens.

"She's fine," she assures me, as she guides me down the hallway. "Let's go back to bed."

I climb in beside her and wrap my arms around her. "Your feet are cold."

She laughs quietly. "Go to sleep."

Some nights, it's just not that easy. I caress my hands across her skin, trying to soothe myself. "I've always loved you, you know." There's but a split-second pause in her response, but it's enough to cause me grief. She turns in my arms and strokes her fingertips across my cheek. "I know."

She presses her lips against mine for a soft kiss. I return her sweet gift with a growing passion, becoming hungry for more. I want her. I need her. Her nipples become hard and rub against the bare skin of my chest. Sliding my hand under her nightie, I follow the curves of her body to her breast. I squeeze it firmly, making her moan. That quiet expression of her arousal makes me lengthen and grow harder.

I firmly push her shoulder, forcing her on her back. In seconds, I've discarded her panties and lower myself over her body. She welcomes me, adjusting her position for the width of my hips. Supporting my weight on strong forearms, I hover over her, staring into her beautiful hazel eyes. She groans with the first thrust, and the sound of it is almost always my undoing. I've waited for her my whole lifetime, and I don't ever want it to end. I pray every day that I measure up. I have some pretty big shoes to fill.

I wake with a hard cock. I lift my head to look at the tent I'm pitching with the blanket and place my palm on my forehead. It feels like someone took an ax to my head. A feminine hand rests on my chest. She's soft, warm, and comforting. Funny, but I don't remember Stacey being the cuddling type. She sighs and runs her hand across my chest and downward. I love a girl who makes my cock a priority in the morning. My body responds as I breathe in her faded subtle perfume until the very last note of the sweet flowery scent hits me, and I have a shocking realization. This isn't Stacey.

My eyes pop open, and my body stiffens. Jesus, even my eyelashes hurt. A quick look around the room confirms I'm at home. Very small flashes of last night come back to memory: the bar, the booze, Olivia. I gently pry myself from underneath her and get to my feet. I survey the room, the disheveled furniture, and discarded clothing hanging from the most peculiar places. She rolls to her side and tosses the blanket to the floor. It's then that I discover she's wearing nothing but my boxers. "What the fuck have I done?"

My fingertips brush across her skin as I respectfully cover her up. Vague memories start to come back to me. My heart pounds heavily in my chest, and it reverbs like a jackhammer, in my head. I tidy the room and give her some privacy.

I make breakfast with a laser focus, trying to keep the noise down. I don't even hear her enter the room. "Good morning."

Startled, I jump and burn my hand. I curse. She grabs my wrist and guides me across the room to the sink. Holding the burn under cold water, she looks up at me with those beautiful eyes full of sparkling gold flecks. "Better?"

I nod. "Yes, thank you." I didn't think it could get any worse, but I was wrong. Looking at her, standing in front of me wearing my boxers and T-shirt isn't helping. "Olivia…" I pause and exhale deeply. "Do you have any recollection of last night?"

"Very little," she admits, looking ashamed.

"Me neither."

"Do you think anything happened?" I pause, my eyes traveling her body and staring longer than I should. "Between us." I tear my gaze away and look down the hall toward the bedroom. "In there?" I scratch at the day-old growth of stubble on my chin. This is a bloody awkward conversation.

She shakes her head no, struggling to find words. "I… I don't remember, Carter."

"Me neither." My guts twist and turn nervously.

"I don't think either one of us would do anything that would hurt Ethan," she reasons.

I would. I'd go straight to hell, but if I could steal her away and keep her for myself, I'd consider it. "You're right," I lie. "So obviously nothing happened." It's a huge relief and an even bigger disappointment.

"Nothing," she repeats unconvincingly. "So there's no reason to say anything to Ethan about last night. Right?"

"Right." My chest tightens, thinking about my dream. For a brief moment, I consider grabbing her and kissing her to see just what the fuck is going on here. She can tell me *nothing,* but I feel it. There's something here, or there used to be. I'm so fucking confused.

She can't even look at me right now. "I'm going to grab a cab home and get some sleep." She picks up a piece of toast and takes a few bites. "I have a surprise planned for Ethan today."

"I'll take you."

"No!" she says quickly.

Great, now we're back to awkward.

I put her in a cab and head back upstairs to grab some sleep myself. I wish I could dig deep into my memories and sort out the reality from the dreams.

I wake up from my nap, still feeling hungover. I begin to scroll through the barrage of missed messages and calls on my phone. It's clear that I can't avoid the boys any longer, but I have no idea how I'm going to face O'Connell.

I arrive at the hotel restaurant, just as they finish eating. I'm a little shocked to find Ethan isn't with them. As always, it doesn't matter if he's there or not. O'Connell is always the topic of conversation. It feels like my head is in a pair of Vice-Grips, and it gets worse as I sit and listen to the evening's events. When they get to the part of the story where Ethan escorts a very drunk, young girl to her room, I feel my face start to heat up. I look over at Scott and John, hoping they'll deny what I'm hearing. These boys have always had a way of embellishing stories. In fact, most of the time they're full of bullshit. The look on Scott's face says it all.

"How many pints have you had already?" I ask Griff.

"A few. Who's counting?"

"Nobody, mate. I just don't know how you can do it this early in the day."

"North America has made you boys soft," he laughs and gets to his feet. "Time for a smoke."

"Stay out front and don't disappear," John warns. "We've got a car coming to pick you up soon."

"Where's O'Connell?" Trevor asks.

"On his way down."

There's a loud screeching as the chairs are dragged across the hardwood floor. It makes me feel like wooden spikes are being driven into my brain.

"I'll get the bill," John advises.

"I'll supervise outside," Scott jokes.

I chug another glass of water, hoping that rehydrating will help with this pounding pain in my skull. I continue to scroll through my messages. There's one last message from Stacey. I close my eyes, feeling regret. The first few lines contain curse words I've never heard before. I don't blame her.

"Carter?"

John stands at the door, waiting. "Are you coming outside?"

"I'll be there in a minute. I need to make a call."

He nods. "Don't be too long, I have no idea what kind of mood the boss is in."

I flash him an unimpressed look. I can't say I'm surprised when Stacey doesn't answer. She's likely blocked my number by now. Things like this never used to bother me, but I feel like a prick.

I can see O'Connell has joined the boys out front. I might as well get this over with. The sun is blinding, but I squint enough to know that Ethan is watching me, his arms crossed, with an antagonized look on his ugly Irish mug. When my eyes finally adjust to the light, I see her approaching in the background. I stop abruptly, completely stunned. "Holy shit," I say out loud.

O'Connell looks at me, confused. Then turns to look over his shoulder at what has me mesmerized.

"Well I'll be fucked," he says shocked.

I slowly make my way to join them. I'd be full of shit if I said their reunion hasn't gutted me. When the two of them slip away, as if the rest of us don't even exist, Trevor turns to Scott, "Who the hell is that?"

Scott grins, "THAT… is his girlfriend."

Griff's head snaps to the side in shock. "His girlfriend? What the hell does a girl like that see in O'Connell?"

"I've been asking myself the same question," I say out loud. John gives me a disapproving look.

Griff suddenly becomes fixated on her, staring at her, and it bothers me.

"Well, it's no bloody wonder he wouldn't do the blonde last night." Brian starts to laugh.

A villainous grin curls at the corners of Griff's lips. It's positively wicked. Malevolent.

"Hey," Brian continues, "maybe, if we're lucky, the wind will pick up, and we can get a peek at what keeps O'Connell coming back for more."

"Shut the hell up, Brian," I warn.

"Did you see those gorgeous tits?" Trevor asks, looking at his friends. They all nod their acknowledgment, and I begin to experience a very strong moment of déjàvu.

"I was too busy looking at her ass," Nigel says, "I'd love some of that action."

I'm disgusted with their vulgarity. Every Australian muscle in my six foot two body vibrates with anger. Not that I'm surprised about it from this bunch, but they're talking about Olivia, and that, I won't tolerate. "How about, I knock out the teeth of the next asshole that opens his mouth and says something crude about her?" I add to the conversation in an angry tone.

Silence washes over them. I scan the group, establishing eye contact and confirming I'll keep my word. "Are we good?"

Nigel holds up his hands in a surrendering gesture. "I'm good, Brant. Not another word."

The car takes us over to Ethan's restaurant. There's plenty to do to get prepared for the grand opening. He normally puts a lot of money and effort into these things, but for this one, he's really gone all out. It's annoying as fuck that he won't tell anyone what he has planned.

I'm busy lugging boxes of alcohol and sound equipment when my phone rings. This can't be good.

"Hello, Anna."

"Carter," she says formally.

"Is everything all right?"

"Not really, Carter. My husband is a cranky old fart, and Kaylie can't stop crying."

"They miss him."

"Yes," she sighs. "But they're a stubborn lot."

I step out of the room, so I don't have to listen to the protesting about me avoiding all the hard work.

"What can I do for you, Anna? I doubt you called because you need someone to complain to."

"No, Carter. I need your help."

"With what?"

"Madison."

I'm intrigued.

"She's been keeping company with that singer. Ethan's friend."

"Nate?" I ask surprised.

"Yes."

"I'm not sure there's anything I can do about that."

"She's planning to come to Toronto to see him when he plays at Ethan's restaurant opening."

"Ah." The picture's becoming clearer. "And you want me to keep an eye on her?"

"Yes. Ethan doesn't know anything about it."

"That's a good thing. He'd likely blow a gasket."

There's a small pause. "How is he doing, Carter?"

"He's doing fine. He misses his family." I hang up and make my way back inside.

Hmmm. So Nate Ross is flying in to play at the grand opening. That's okay, O'Connell. I have a few secrets of my own now.

"Hey! Look who's back, now that all the work is done," Griff shouts.

"Sorry, mate." I hold up my phone. "Family emergency."

"Right," he says, sounding doubtful.

I shrug. I don't feel the need to convince him. I really don't care what he thinks.

I mindlessly lug beer cases and stack chairs. I need to figure out what this thing is with Olivia. These dreams must mean something, right?

The next day, I pick up Maddie from the airport. I don't let on I know about Nate. She's pretty quiet most of the way until we pull up front of the hotel.

"Carter."

I look at her in the rearview mirror.

"What kind of mood is my brother in these days?"

"Better than expected, I suppose. Why do you ask?"

"If he was to receive some news that normally would upset him, do you think he'd handle it well?"

I open her car door and help her out. "You're brother is trying to be happy, Madison. There's so much going on in his world right now. If this news can wait until after the grand opening, it might be better received."

She frowns at me, and it makes me feel like I just kicked her puppy. I've never really understood the inner workings of this family. I can't imagine how hard it would be to have such an overprotective, controlling brother.

"Madison. You're an adult now. At some point, you're going to have to start making your own decisions. He'll get over it… " I pause when she raises her brow. "Yeah, you're right," I continue. "We're talking about Ethan. He's going to lose his shit and make everybody else miserable."

She sighs. "That's what I'm afraid of. Wait… You know about Nate?"

I shake my head, but I'm not convincing.

"How do you…" Her shoulders fall, and she purses her lips. "Mother!"

There's no point in denying it.

"The woman is bloody terrifying," she continues. "She knows everything. I wonder sometimes where she hides her crystal ball."

I scratch my head. "Okay, but you being here is big enough of a surprise for Ethan. Don't you think? Let's just put your other news aside for tonight."

"Okay," she says, sounding a little more optimistic.

"And maybe tomorrow," I add, as I hand her luggage to the bellhop.

All the way to the grand opening, I think about Olivia. As much as I want to believe her, I feel like something happened between us the other night. I arrive and do a quick security check around the outside of the building. I'm sure McCabe has already done it, but I don't think I'll relax unless I check things out for myself. I need to keep her safe. I'm on my way in to join them when O'Connell texts me, asking my whereabouts. I wasn't prepared for what I see when I pull open the door.

My loud, angry words echo in the room, "What are you wearing?" I take a few steps into the room and stop, shocked. "For fuck's sake! What were you thinking? Do you have any idea the thoughts that are going to go through every man's mind tonight, when they see you in that dress?"

"Carter?" Ethan says, lifting his eyebrows in question.

I can't let it go. Who knows what kind of scum is following her, and what might have happened if George hadn't called me the other night. "Tell her, Ethan. Tell her she's not wearing that dress tonight. Haul her ass home, right now, and make her change into something else." My jaw sets in a rigid line.

Olivia's tenses and looks at me with regret. "Carter," she says softly, as I approach her.

"Christ almighty! Could there be any less material in the front?" I stare at her breasts, and I remember how warm they felt when I closed my lips around the nipples that are hiding, not too far below the neckline of that dress. "Ethan?" I persist, "Are you going to tell me this is okay with you?" Razor-sharp fury dangerously hangs on my words.

Taking another long look at her, Ethan clenches his jaw as he looks back at me. The tension in the air is so thick it creates a heavy feeling that makes everyone struggle to breathe. Shannon and Olivia glance at each with silent acknowledgment.

"I think she looks beautiful, Carter," Ethan finally says. "If this is the dress she wants to wear, then I'm not going to make her change." Smiling at her, he gently rubs his hands up and down her arms, making her feel at ease. "What's wrong with you?" he asks, turning toward me.

I feel my face turn red and I turn sharply to face him, my eyes lit with anger. It's all I can do to stop myself. I'm about to lose it. Erupting like a volcano, I overturn a chair or two and stomp out of the room. Things crash to the ground as I go.

Close on my heels is the Irish military watchdog. "Leave me alone, McCabe," I warn.

"Not going to happen, Brant. Do you want to tell me what that was all about?"

I pace angrily, like a caged animal. "I take it that nobody told Ethan about someone following her?"

John takes a sigh of relief, "Yes. I did. And you know I'm keeping tabs on the ex. He's thousands of miles away, in a different province. It wasn't him."

I growl. "That's no reassurance at all." I stop talking when Ethan walks through the bar, heading toward his office. Olivia stares at me as she follows behind. I lock my gaze to hers, and I know when she looks away, she's experiencing unwanted feelings.

John gauges the dark intensity in my eyes. "Since when do you have this much concern for someone Ethan is dating?"

I clench my jaw. "That was not the only time she was being followed."

"What do you mean?"

I run my fingers through my hair, hesitantly. "Okay, listen. She made me promise not to tell Ethan. So you keep your piehole shut."

"Would you just tell me? I'm supposed to be keeping an eye on her tonight," he says annoyed.

"The other night, someone ruffied her drink at the bar."

"What?" he asks concerned.

"George called me when he couldn't get a hold of Ethan. When I got there, she was completely out of it. The waitress said there was a creepy stranger, lurking in the shadows, watching her all night."

John raises a brow. "And you thought it was a good idea to withhold this information from Ethan?"

I sigh, feeling conflicted. "Yeah, well… maybe not the best idea, but now she's here, in that dress… and Griff and the boys."

John holds his hand in the air. "Say no more. I was there. Well, this is going to be fun. We'll have to keep a close eye on her and not let O'Connell know why."

"There's something else," I admit, feeling the need to come clean. "I drank what was left in her glass before I knew it was doped. Then I took her back to my place, so I'd know she was safe."

John begins to look worried.

"We passed out…in the same bed…n…"

His eyes open wide and he rigorously shakes his head. "No, no, no… I don't want to know."

"Neither of us remembers what happened. Maybe nothing," I continue anyway.

John curses. "I understand why you kept it from him."

"Olivia insists that neither of us would do something like that," I justify.

"Well, it doesn't matter at this point. We just need to make sure she's safe. Madison is on her way. Apparently, we need to keep an eye on her too."

"Lord. Anna got to you too?"

John nods.

"I should give up sales and go into security," I growl.

I spend the evening on high alert. There's a very suspicious man hovering near the door that leads into the alley.

"McCabe, are you there?" I ask into the microphone on the headset.

"Yes."

"Where's Madison?"

"She's with Ethan in his office. What's going on?"

Olivia crosses the room and gives me a small, reassuring smile. I nod.

"There's a creeper at the back door. I don't like the looks of him," I answer once she passes.

John comes into view on the other side of the room. "Got it. I'll check it out. You keep an eye on Olivia."

"Believe me, I'm not going to let her out of my sight." She stands at Ethan's office door but doesn't go in. Griff crosses the floor and places his hand on her shoulder. I can't hear what he's saying, but I don't like it. I move to be closer to them.

"One dance," I hear him demand.

Olivia looks at Ethan's office door and then turns to look for me. I'm already on my way through the crowd to be at a better vantage point. Griff firmly takes hold of her wrist and pulls her out onto the floor. Adrenaline starts to pump through my body as if it senses a need for alertness. There's something really gross and *dirty* about the way that he touches her. I search for John in the crowd. I have a feeling I'm going to need backup. I push my way past people on the dance floor to get to them. Griff leans in, running his tongue across her neck and into her ear.

"Oh, hell no." I'm not waiting for reinforcements. I grab the slimeball by the scruff of the neck.

"Carter? What the fuck?" he screams angrily.

"I'm saving you, Griffin," I say as I pull him away.

"From what?" he protests.

"From O'Connell. Do you have any idea what he'd do to you if he caught you with your tongue in his girl's ear?"

"He'd fucking kill you!" I hear Ethan say furiously, as he approaches from the side. Too late. I let go and take a step back into safety. I know what's coming Griff's way. Ethan's fist connects with his jaw, knocking him to the ground.

"Nice shot," I say in admiration. Stepping aside, I make room for Nigel and Trevor to peel Griff's ass off the floor. I'm sure it's something they do on a regular basis.

Ethan shakes his hand out, opening and closing his fingers, and grimacing as he turns to Olivia, who's staring at him with an open mouth. "Are you okay?" he asks her.

I feel a weird kind of energy like my body has just become a lit sparkler. I look up to find Kate's sapphire blue eyes watching me from the railing. I can't take my eyes off her. I'm tormented by the strange emotional tug-of-war I experience between them. Despite feeling like I'm somehow bound to Olivia, an inexplicable force draws me to Kate.

Right now, I'm jacked up on adrenaline and not sure where I belong, so I make myself fade into the background. I feel like I'm not needed here to protect Olivia any longer. Staying only gets me more confused. A strange rustling noise in the bushes by my parked car heightens my senses. I cautiously approach, ready to react. I'm about to reach in, grab him by the throat, and beat him to a bloody pulp when the frail, gray-haired woman lifts a branch and reveals herself.

"What the?" I lower my clenched fist to my side. "Why are you hiding in there?"

A small green bird flutters its wings and hovers over her shoulder, as she steps out into the dimly lit parking lot.

"You're leaving," she states.

I nod.

"It's not yet time for you to return to Australia."

I laugh once, "I think you're wrong. There's no reason for me to stay."

"Your journey here is not complete. The one you've been looking for is here."

I watch as Ethan escorts Olivia to his car. "I found her, and she's made up her mind." The little green bird squawks as it takes flight, causing me to duck.

"Their journey is a complicated one. They'll still need you to watch over her, boy. But their journey is together. The Universe has another planned for you."

"Oh?" I glance around me to ensure nobody is witnessing me engage in this odd conversation.

"Her eyes are like sapphires and her hair like spun gold."

Now I'm feeling amused. "When will I meet this magical woman?"

She grins, and her appearance seems more youthful as her eyes sparkle in the moonlight. She walks toward me. "You know you've already met her, but you've overlooked her. You're blinded by your memories. You have to let them go. Open your heart and make yourself available for love."

I feel the muscles in my shoulders tighten. "What a crock of shit." I reach for the handle of the car door.

"Liam," she says with an Irish brogue.

The hair stands up on the back of my neck. She reaches out and places her hand on top of mine. I can't move; she's a frail elderly woman, who weighs no more than a small child, and yet, I'm magically pinned in place with her touch.

"She will love you with intense passion and a fierce loyalty. But first, you have to give yourself to her completely. Unconditionally. You let her down in another life."

My chest starts to feel heavy. "She sounds a little *too needy* for me," I joke, trying to divert the tension from an uncomfortable topic.

"It's what you've been looking for. *She's* the one you need."

I grit my teeth, trying to hold back an emotional response.

"Not Olivia. Not this time," she whispers before I can speak. She lifts her hand, and I feel a cool breeze dance around me, lifting away the heaviness and releasing me.

I pull open the car door and pause. "I'm going back to Australia, tomorrow." I wait for her objection, but I'm met with silence. I glance around the parking lot and then settle my gaze toward the holly bushes in front of me. She's gone.

I wake up in the middle of the night in a cold sweat. My dreams haunt me. They're a fucked-up mess of past memories and new adventures. My head is spinning right now. I look at the time and do what every single man faced with conflict does. I call my mother. My anxiety lessens when I hear her voice.

"Hi, Mum."

"Hello, Carter," she says sounding concerned. "Isn't it the middle of the night there?"

"Very early morning," I correct.

"What's wrong, Son?"

"Nothing," I say unconvincingly.

"Mmhmm."

"Really, Mum. I'm okay."

"Who is she?"

"Who?"

"The girl that you're thinking about. The one who's keeping you awake."

I scratch my head. "Yeah, well… it's complicated."

"Don't quote a Facebook status to me, Carter. You've called because you want my advice."

"There's a girl."

"Shocker."

"Come on, Mum. Don't judge."

"Sorry, I'm listening."

"There's something about this girl. Something I can't explain. It's like we've never met before, and yet, we're connected somehow."

"Sounds magical."

"It felt like I loved her."

"Past tense?"

"Yes, we can't be together."

"Why not?"

"She's in love with another man."

"So? If you love her…"

"Ethan," I interrupt.

"Fuckin'ell."

"Right. But here's the problem."

"That's not the problem?" she jokes.

"There's another girl."

"Lord." There's a moment of silence. "Carter, I'm not a young woman, can you get to the part where you need my advice?"

"Sorry, sorry. I was all set to come home. Put everything behind me. Move on."

"But?"

"The crazy lady said the one I'm looking for is here, in Toronto."

"Uhhh. I'm not even going to ask."

"I think she means Kate. The other girl, not Ethan's girl," I explain. "Kate is brilliant and beautiful."

"You sound smitten to me. What's the problem?"

I sigh. "I don't understand why, Mum, but my heart seems connected to Olivia. I'm so confused by it all. I don't know what to do."

"Good Lord, Son. I don't know who's more confused, you or me."

"Definitely me."

"Carter, come home. Take some time off. Spend some time with your friends and family, and learn how to relax and enjoy life. You're going to end up with ulcers or in an early grave, just like your father. For what?"

I roll my eyes. You can always count on your mother for giving you the advice you don't really want to hear. "I've thought about Kate a lot tonight. I think there could be something there if she'll give me a chance."

"Sounds like you know what you're going to do."

I look at my packed suitcase across the room. "I guess I'm staying."

"Brilliant. So… if she's *the one,* does that mean you're whoring bachelor days are over?"

My mouth opens in shock. "MUM!"

"I've often wondered how many grandchildren I have that I don't know about."

"None I'm being held accountable for," I assure her.

"That doesn't make me feel any better."

"I'm joking, Mum."

"Well, my job here is done," she sighs. "Let me know when you're on your way home, Carter. I do miss you."

I throw my suitcase back on the bed and begin to unpack. "Miss you too."

It's not *business, as usual,* these days. Ethan and Olivia have gone to Ireland to settle his business and meet with his family. Thanks to my lack of sleep, I'm cranky, and I hate the new guy brought in by corporate. He's an arrogant French bastard. I get ready for the last-minute call he scheduled, making sure I have all the data and sales stats I need to cover my ass. Since O'Connell fucked up,

Scott, Landon, and I are all under the watchful eye of the board of directors. I don't like it. Ethan has been suspiciously quiet through the call, so far. Landon is midway through his presentation when I realize he isn't even on the call. Asshole. He's the reason everything we do is being scrutinized, he could at least join the call and have our backs. I don't care that he's back home, swooning over the love of his life. Fucker. I shoot him an angry message.

Ethan replies with a series of question marks. I quickly check the list of invited attendees and find his name is suspiciously missing. I should have known there was something shady going on here. What the hell are they up to? I begin to go over my sales reports, containing the prior year's data, when I hear Ethan's voice in the background. Seems he found his way into the boardroom of Aurora Tech's Dublin office. I wait out a very awkward exchange between him and CEO, Charles Hammond.

Scott Parker sticks his head around the corner.

"Hey, we're going to the pub downtown for a little *post-conference* unwinding. You in?"

I mute the line and think about it a moment. I can't think of any reason not to go. Maybe a few drinks will help put to rest my insomnia. I nod. When I finally got to sleep last night, I dreamed of Kate. They're happy dreams, different from the ones I have of Olivia, but still loving, wonderful, pleasant memories.

"Okay, I'll meet you there after the call."

I'm not going to lie; I'm hoping I run into Kate tonight. However, the last time I was in this pub I was with Olivia, and I can't help but think of that night as the rusty hinges squeal when I open the heavy wooden door. "Good evening, Mr. Carter."

"Good evening, George. It's just Carter. I was wondering. Did you ever find out who laced Olivia's drink that night?"

"There was a man the waitress saw lurking in the shadows; watching her. She said that he gave her a bad feeling. He hasn't been back. If he comes, we'll call the police, immediately."

"Thank you. Keep me posted if you get any information."

I find a dark, quiet spot at the back of the bar. Sometimes I like solitude. Unlike O'Connell, I don't need to be the center of attention at all times.

It's hard to keep Olivia out of my thoughts, especially after what happened the last time we were here. I sit and watch the people around me, not as entertained as I usually would be. I order a Jack and Coke, thinking something stronger than beer will help me loosen up.

It seems like I've only taken a few swigs, but already I'm staring past the ice at the bottom of the empty glass, feeling disappointed.

"Another?" the bartender asks, already sliding one toward me.

I nod. "Thanks, mate."

I don't often turn to alcohol as some kind of magic elixir, but I have to admit the music is much more appeasing now. I turn to the crowded room, and that's when I see her, just barely, hiding in the dark shadows in the corner of the room.

Unaware anyone is watching, she sways her hips seductively to the music. I wonder why she's not on the dance floor. Perhaps she's too shy; I like the shy ones. I don't mind the private viewing. She feels my gaze and looks over to see me leaning against the bar, drink in hand, watching her intensely. Our eyes lock, and she hesitates where she stands. I expect her to stop, but instead, she gives me a show. It's even hotter knowing that she knows I'm watching and every move, every sway, every swirl is meant just for me.

I order two more drinks and walk toward her. "Hello, Kate."

"Hey there." She looks around me for something. "I'm not used to seeing you without a woman attached to you somewhere."

"Ouch." For a shy girl, she sure is feisty. "It looked like you were working up a thirst." I hand her a drink.

"I'm not sure I should accept this." She holds it up to the light and looks through the glass. "Rumor has it there's a nasty man spiking women's drinks around here."

"It's not me," I assure her.

"Says the guy I saw carrying an unconscious girl to his room."

"You got me there. You should be careful."

"How is Mr. O'Connell's girlfriend?"

I cock my head to the side. "You've done your homework."

"I was curious."

I raise a brow. "Curious or jealous?"

She laughs once. "Don't flatter yourself, you're not that charming."

"Clearly you're mistaken. Have you heard my accent?"

She has the most beautiful smile. Her friends return to the table and give me the once-over look. I think that's my cue to exit. "I just wanted to say hello. I'll leave you to spend time with your friends."

She raises the glass in the air. "Thanks again, for the drink."

Scott finds me, still sitting at the bar, watching her.

"What's her name?" he asks, as he climbs the stool beside me.

"Kate."

"How did you meet Kate?"

"It's kind of odd, really. It doesn't matter where I am, she seems to be there."

"I see." He slides another drink in front of me. "So she's the reason you stayed?"

I nod.

"I didn't think it had anything to do with the Australian business plan. So what are we talking here? Puppy Love? True Love? Have you even…"

"Hooked up?" I answer for him. "No."

"Why not?"

"I think about it A LOT, but I'm going back to Australia eventually." I put down my beer down and turn in my seat. "She's not the kind of girl you leave behind. I can tell."

"You can tell? How can you tell?" Scott asks curiously, as he glances over at her.

"I just can." I pause trying to think of a way to explain it to him. "Okay, listen… remember how you felt about Rachel the first time you saw her? The way you said she had gotten under your skin, just by the way she looked at you. You said it was as if she saw right through you and past all your bullshit. You told me, you would never forget it."

"And I never have," he confirms.

I glance over my shoulder and catch her looking. A coy grin spreads across her raspberry lips.

"You're afraid that if you spend time with her, you won't be able to hold back," Scott acknowledges.

"Nope." I laugh once and tip my beer to my lips. "I'm afraid once I've had a taste of her, it will kill me to leave her behind."

The girls on the other side of the room get louder. Clearly, they're feeling a little tipsy. They've moved to the dartboard, and I watch amused for a long time. It's a wonder any of them can even hit the board.

"This is painful to watch."

"It certainly is," Scott agrees. "Take a chance, man. I have no idea what this infatuation is you have with Olivia, but it's a nonstarter. That girl there," he nods in Kate's direction, "she could be the love you're looking for. And she's not dating the boss, so it's probably a better choice."

I feel a fleeting moment of anger at his statement, but I wash it away with the last half of my drink.

It's the last throw of the game, and Kate tries to figure out how many points she needs to win. She sways, trying to stay balanced, and I can no longer resist. I hand my beer to Scott and cross the room.

"Go get her, buddy," he chuckles.

Her friends giggle, and she shushes them while she tries to focus.

Stepping up behind her, I place my hand on her shoulder then slide it down her arm. She tenses, tightening her grip on the dart. I try to guide her from behind, but she becomes stiff and nervous. "Relax your arm," I whisper in her ear.

I grip her hip with my free hand and guide her back against my chest, trying to steady her. Her breath hitches and I feel her clench her legs together. She looks up, embarrassed I felt her body's reaction to me. I grin, slightly embarrassed myself, as my semi-hard cock presses firmly into her backside.

"Ready?" I ask.

Slightly turning her head, she brushes her cheek against mine and swallows hard. "Yes," she whispers.

"Me too," I growl softly, pressing my hips against her backside.

"Are you talking about darts or something else?" she giggles, slightly inebriated.

"I'm open to suggestions." I lift her hand, preparing to make the throw. I can't seem to bend her elbow. "You do know how to relax, don't you?" I tease.

"Are you kidding me?" she asks. "It's all I can do to remember to breathe at the moment."

"Try," I encourage, feeling amused.

She takes a deep breath and relaxes her arm. I direct her movement and release the dart, hitting the target she needs.

"You win," I say softly in her ear. I turn and walk away, trailing my fingers across her backside as I go. I don't look back. I can't. If I do, I know how this will end.

My phone rings as I return to the bar. "Hello, John."

"Carter. Do you have any idea what the fuck is going on?"

"None." I hold up a hand to stop Scott from interrupting and start walking until I find a spot in private. I haven't told Ethan I'm still in Toronto, and I don't feel like getting the third degree. Once a day is enough for me.

"I'm worried."

"So am I, mate."

"Between the bullshit going on at Aurora and Olivia terminating the pregnancy, I'm afraid he's going to completely lose his shit soon."

I feel like I've just taken a hard punch to the gut. All the air seems to have left my chest.

"Carter?"

I shake my head in shock. "Um, sorry. What did you just say?"

"I said Hammond's nephew is a…"

"NO!" I interrupt. "About Olivia being pregnant."

"Ethan hasn't called you?"

I pace, considering that our evening together wasn't as uneventful as we both wanted to believe. "No. Tell me."

John sighs, "Olivia was pregnant."

"Was?"

"She kept it from him. He found out she went to a clinic for a termination, then took off to spend some time with her sister. I can't believe he didn't tell you."

"I can't believe *she* didn't tell me," I say under my breath.

"What?"

"How far along was she?" I ask, beginning to feel the tension tightly coiling in every muscle.

"I don't know. Why does it matter?" John asks, confused.

"It just does," I snap. I tilt my head back and take a breath. "Never mind. Where is she now?"

"I just told you. She's at her sister's in Cape Breton. Are you okay, Brant?"

"Yeah, I'm fine." I hang up and dial her number repeatedly while I walk, but she doesn't answer. I'm so consumed with my thoughts that I'm not even sure how I end up home. In a complete fog, I step into the elevator and turn to face the door. I make no effort to stop them from closing as I watch Kate approach.

"Asshole." I hear her yell as it begins to ascend. Finding it difficult to breathe, I run my fingers through my hair and lean back against the wall. I think I'm about to lose my mind.

I head straight to the fridge and open a beer. And then another. Before long, there's a long trail of empties lined up across the coffee table. Cursing, I throw the remote across the room, aggravated there's nothing worth watching on TV. The last thing I remember is dialing Olivia's number again.

It's a long slow process to peel my eyelids open in the morning. The high-pitched shrill of the phone makes my head hurt.

"What?" I groan when I finally find the strength to lift it to my ear.

"It's me."

"Scott?" I try to sit up when I hear sirens. "What's wrong?"

"Someone broke into Olivia's house and trashed it."

"Kids?" I stagger over to the sink for a glass of water.

"No. I'm sure it wasn't. There were photos and messages left behind."

"Jesus." I'm wide-awake now.

"I'm here, dealing with the cops."

The sunshine blazes through the living room window as I pass on my way to the shower. I squint as I stop to lower the blind. "Do you need me there?"

"No. There's nothing you can do right now. They won't let anyone in. They're treating it as a crime scene. So, what happened to you last night? You disappeared."

I scrub my hand over my face, trying to think of an explanation. "I got tired of McCabe's whining, so I went home."

"Did she catch up to you?"

"Who?" I turn the water on in the shower and let it warm up. Even the pounding sound of the water on the glass tile makes my head hurt.

"Kate. She watched you leave, then grabbed her stuff and went after you."

I remember the look on her beautiful face as the heavy metal doors closed shut. "Fuck. I need to track her down and apologize."

"What did you do?"

"I saw her in the lobby, but I didn't hold the elevator door for her."

"There really is something wrong with your head these days, Brant. The girl is into you."

"I get it!" I growl. "I'll make it up to her if she'll ever talk to me again."

"I have to go. They need me here. Get your act together, would ya?"

I stand under the spray of water for what seems like a very long time, hoping the heat will help the stiffness in my neck. Serves me right for sleeping on the couch all night.

I round up all the beer bottles and an empty bottle of tequila. No wonder my head hurts. I abandon the bowl of cereal I've been trying to eat for the past hour. I just can't stomach food right now.

After a brief, unplanned nap, I rummage through a bunch of papers in my briefcase, certain I've kept the card Ethan gave me with Kate's number on it. I sit holding it for a long time, trying to convince myself she'll answer if I call. I take the coward's way out in the way of text message.

Carter: Sorry, I'm an asshole.
Kate: I highly doubt you're sorry about it at all. It seems to come naturally for you.

I deserved that, but at least she's talking to me.

Carter: Let me make it up to you. Can I buy you dinner tonight?
Kate: Why should I go out with you?
Carter: Because I'm irresistible and deserve another chance?
Kate: Fine. But I'm ordering lobster and the most expensive bottle of wine on the menu.
Carter: That sounds fair.

I find myself feeling excited as I get ready. I might even say I'm a little nervous. But it's the good kind of nervous. I haven't felt this way about anyone in a very long time. I wander through the flower shop on the corner, looking for the perfect ones. I'm drawn to the table of daisies, but somehow I just know that they're not the right flowers for Kate. I settle on a beautiful arrangement of pastel green carnations and pale pink roses. I hope I've chosen well. I'm just leaving the shop when my phone rings.

"Hello!" I say cheerfully.

"Well, you're in a good mood now," Scott says surprised.

"I am. I'm on my way to meet Kate for dinner."

"That's great."

I detect a strange hesitation in his voice. "What's going on?"

"Nothing I can't handle. I'll talk to you later."

"Wait! What aren't you telling me?"

"John just called me. Olivia is on a plane on her way here. She found out about the break-in at the house, somehow. I'm betting my loving wife."

My excitement turns to anxiety.

"O'Connell is going to take the company jet," he continues. "But he won't be here until tomorrow. I have to pick her up at the airport in an hour."

"Okay, keep me posted." I let out an angry rant that lasts a few city blocks. I'm sure everyone walking past me thinks I have Tourette's. I take my phone out of my pocket and dial him back. "I'll pick her up and make sure she gets there safely."

"You have plans, Carter. I'll do it."

"No. I just checked the flight details, and it's landing early. You won't get here on time from Dufferin County. I'm ten minutes away. I'll go."

"What about Kate?"

"I'll postpone for an hour. She'll either wait or swear at me again."

I thought I was finally starting to work the girl out from under my skin. Moving on. Standing here, waiting, thinking about what I now know has me twisted in knots. Olivia walks out the gate doors into the main concourse of the airport and meets my unimpressed expression. She pauses, surprised to see me, and forces herself to give me a polite smile.

"What are you doing here?" she asks curiously, as I take the heavy carry-on bag from her shoulder.

"You know why I'm here." I fail at hiding my annoyance. "Did you think he was going to let you go to the house by yourself?"

"I mean, why are you here in Canada?"

I walk toward the parking garage with growing discontent. "I'm here for personal reasons," I say, without turning to look at her. My heavy gait and large steps make it difficult for her to keep up.

"Carter, slow down. I'm tired," she begs.

I reach the car ahead of her and open the trunk to stow her bag. When she finally catches up, she stands at the door watching me. I slam down the trunk and glance over at her, looking her in the eyes for the first time since she got off the plane.

She frowns. "You're angry with me."

I nod my head, breaking eye contact. "Yes, I'm angry. Get in the car," I growl, feeling frustrated.

Olivia sits quietly for most of the ride. My anger doesn't soften at all on the forty-five-minute drive from the airport. She tries a few times to lighten things up with polite conversation, but I thwart her attempts with one-word answers or complete avoidance.

"Carter," she begins, needing to put it to rest.

Determined to focus on the road, I glance sideways for only a brief moment, acknowledging her.

"It's my home, Carter." She continues, "I need to make sure everything is okay there."

"Scott is looking after everything; there was absolutely no reason for you to come."

"All my personal belongings are there, things that belonged to my mother. Surely you understand I need to see for myself."

I bite my tongue. There's no point in voicing my opinion.

Olivia pauses, and then a thought occurs to her. "Oh, Carter, I'm sorry. You're here for personal reasons, and O'Connell has screwed up your plans by assigning you babysitting duties."

According to the crazy lady, I still need to protect her. How do I bring that up? "Let me make it perfectly clear… there's nothing more important to me than keeping you safe."

"So why are you so angry with me?"

"Why? WHY?" I ask agitated. I feel my whole body stiffen. "Do you have any idea just how fucking selfish it was for you to make that decision on your own?"

Regret washes over her. "You're not talking about the house, are you?" She frowns and turns to look out the window, trying to avoid my censure.

"No, I'm not talking about the fucking house."

"It was my decision to make, Carter. Telling people would only have made the decision harder, more painful."

I grip the steering wheel so tightly my fingers turn white. "You're wrong, Olivia. That was a decision for the two parties involved, you and the father."

"O'Connell made it very clear. He doesn't want kids."

I hit the brakes hard, causing us to come to an abrupt stop in front of her townhouse.

"Oh? Let me ask you this." I can't hold back anymore, I need to know. "Are you absolutely sure it was *his* baby?"

Tears well up in her eyes as she locks onto my stare. "Olivia?" I prompt, "I'm going to ask you again, and I want the truth. Are you sure the baby was O'Connell's?"

There's a glimmer of something in her eyes I can't put a name to. Is it sorrow? Guilt? Regret? She answers me, with inarguable confidence, "Yes, Carter. I'm absolutely sure."

"You're that confident nothing happened between you and me that night?"

She fidgets and grimaces from discomfort. It concerns me. "Are you okay?"

She sighs. "Yes, Carter." Tears form in her eyes as she turns to me with a tormented look. "I didn't do it."

I take a deep breath in and digest what she's just confessed. I'm certain this is something Ethan doesn't know. "You didn't terminate the pregnancy?"

She shakes her head. "I couldn't bring myself to do it."

A loud crash and the sound of shattering glass startles her, making her turn in the direction of the noise. Without hesitation, she jumps out of the car and runs toward the house.

"Olivia! Wait!" I holler. Cursing, I take off after her, catching up to her at the front porch. She stands perfectly still, her chest heaving as she tries to catch her breath. Yellow caution tape bars the entrance.

"Just slow down, until I know it's safe," I instruct.

She looks at me defiantly. Raising her trembling hand, she grabs hold of the tape, tugging it firmly and breaking it.

Bloody, stubborn woman. I grab her arm, stopping her in her tracks. "I said, slow down. If you insist on going in there, you're gonna let me go in first and make sure it's safe." I take a few steps toward the door, nudging her behind me as I make my way inside.

Inside, a crew of tradesmen tries to remove the remnants of the smashed windows. Scott looks up from a conversation with one of them.

"Carter." He nods. "I thought you were picking up Olivia from the airport?"

Olivia steps out from behind me and flashes Scott an awkward smile.

He raises a troubled brow. "Ah, well, I'm glad you can smile. You've upset a lot of people."

"I'm sorry, Scott."

"Oh, just wait until Rachel gets her hands on you."

"What is it with you people?" Olivia asks frustrated. "Do none of you understand the concept of privacy?"

Scott signs some papers handed to him by a tradesman. "Oh, you gave up your rights to privacy the moment you fell in love with O'Connell."

Olivia grumbles. "Carter, can you get my bag out of the car?"

"Not a chance."

Scott chuckles. "You're going to stay with Rachel and me."

Olivia looks over at me, distraught. "I want to stay here, Carter. Can't you just stay here with me?"

"NO!" Scott and I answer in unison.

"You'll stay with us until O'Connell gets here," Scott advises.

She frowns in my direction, thinking that I'll give in. "Wait…" she says, suddenly agitated. "Ethan's coming?"

"Of course he is," Scott chuckles. "The minute he found out you were on your way here, he and John booked the company jet. They'll be here in the morning."

Her brow creases. "Oh, just great."

"What exactly did you think was going to happen?" Scott asks curiously.

"Gah! Why is everything always so messed up?"

Is she serious? I glance down at my phone for the time. "She's all yours now," I say to Scott. "I have to go."

She gives me a conflicted look. "Will you be here when Ethan arrives?"

"Not if I can help it." I tuck my phone back in my pocket. "You're on your own. I'll put your bag in Scott's car." I turn, giving her one last look until the long silence between us becomes awkward. "Don't give Scott a hard time and do what you're told." She looks away like a defiant child. "Look at me," I demand. "Please cooperate with the police and answer all their questions."

"Geesh, who died and made you O'Connell?"

I didn't think she could aggravate me any more than she has today, but I was wrong. I establish eye contact, sending a silent message I'm hoping she won't ignore.

"I will," she sighs.

"Don't be going anywhere without one of us."

"Yes, Sir." She salutes me, trying to lighten the mood.

I flash her an unimpressed look. "If you were my girl, I'd have you over my knee, so fast."

Scott laughs once. "Me too." She gasps and her shocked expression makes him grin. "I've got this," he assures me. "Go, get her."

I nod and close the door behind me. I thought I was over Olivia, but I'm not. I head back to the city at a ridiculously unsafe speed. I miss my Ferrari and the wide-open, unrestricted roadways at home. Finding out she's still pregnant felt like a sharp knife to the gut that was twisted slowly as it was withdrawn. It makes my decision easier.

I stuff my clothes in my suitcase without regard to neatness or order. They'll be wrinkled balls of designer fabric by the time I get home, and I really don't care. I'll buy new ones.

As I throw the luggage into the back seat of the car, I pause, looking at the recently purchased flowers. On the way to the airport, I regret leaving them at the front desk with a note. Kate deserves better. It's bad enough my mother thinks I'm a manwhore. I can't imagine how disappointed she'd be with me for bailing on Kate this way. I just can't see her right now. I need to sort out my head, and my heart. My mother was right; I need to take a break. I'm going home.

I push open the door of my Noosa beachfront apartment and drop my stuff on the floor. It's nice to be back home on the beautiful Sunshine Coast. The flight was a killer. Between my conscience and the turbulence, I don't think I got a single moment of rest. When I did close my eyes, I dreamt of myself sitting on the warm golden sand of Sunshine Beach, making sand castles. It's hard to explain the feelings I experienced in this dream, when the adventurous toddler, with curly blond hair and sparkling blue eyes, looked up at me and smiled. I thought about it during the long flight. Olivia may be absolutely positive nothing happened between us that night, but I know every time I look at the boy, I'm going to wonder if he's mine.

The time change has me so messed up, I'm not sure if I'm coming or going. It looks like the sun's coming up, so I guess my day is about to begin. My stomach growls as I wander into the kitchen. I'm not very optimistic I'll find anything to eat. Taped to the fridge is a handwritten note from my mum. Looks like she's stopped in and stocked me up. I wonder who told her I was on my way home. I shrug as I take out the labeled dishes, it doesn't matter much; I'm starving. I sit on the balcony and enjoy the peaceful view as I wolf down the best home-cooked meal I've had in over a month.

The sound of the water is soothing. When my phone rings, it startles me. I suppose I dozed off for a few seconds. I grab it quickly before she hangs up.

"Hello."

"Hi."

I'm relieved to hear from her, even if there's an awkward tone in her voice.

"How are you, Kate?"

"I'm okay. Did you get home safe?"

"Yes, I got in a few hours ago."

"How is your mother?" she asks concerned.

My mother? It takes me a minute. "Oh, yes, my mum. The doctor said she's going to make a full recovery." I close my eyes, ashamed of myself.

"That's good news."

"I'm sorry I had to leave without saying goodbye."

"I understand. It's your mother. You should be there."

"Yes, but I was looking forward to our dinner." There's a long uncomfortable pause that gives me the feeling that I've let her down, again.

"I should go. I just wanted to make sure she was okay and that you made it home safe. Take care of yourself."

The sadness in her voice makes me feel like a first-class asshole. "It sounds like you're saying goodbye. Can't we keep in touch?"

She doesn't respond.

"I see," I say disappointed. "I don't blame you. I don't deserve another chance."

"It's not that. It's just… have you ever felt like you finally found the right one… but at the wrong time?"

That's an understatement. "Yeah, I know exactly what you mean."

"Goodbye, Carter."

"See you around, Kate. Maybe I can take you out for that dinner next time I'm in town."

"Maybe."

I turn off the ringer on my phone, before placing it face down beside me. I don't feel like talking to anybody right now. The glass door behind me slides open, and I know my wish for peace and quiet has fallen on deaf ears. I glance over my shoulder and shake my head. "I thought you'd be gone by now."

"You could at least pretend you're going to miss me."

"Why are you still here, Reese?" I ask impatiently.

He hands me a coffee and joins me at the balcony railing. "There were a few things I needed to finish on the project before I go home."

"Which is when?" I persist.

"Tomorrow. I start the new job next week."

"Safe travels."

"I wanted to be able to thank you in person for letting me crash here."

"You're welcome. Now get lost before anybody finds out."

"You mean before Ethan finds out."

"Yes. That's exactly what I mean."

"Come on, dude. Cut me some slack. You know I didn't sleep with his girlfriend."

"You keep saying that, but it's your word against hers. Besides, it doesn't matter what I think. It only matters what Ethan believes."

"He never gave me the benefit of the doubt. He just cut me out of his life."

"I'm thinking that was the better of the two options."

"What was the other option?"

"Kill you."

"She tried to get me to blackmail him! Why doesn't anybody believe that? When I refused, she turned it around on me. I paid her the ten thousand she wanted from him from my own account, but she said it was too late. She was going to take us both down."

I raise my brow. "*You* paid her the ten grand?"

"Yes!"

Now he has my attention. "He thinks one of his parents did. Why didn't you tell me this before?"

"I tried, but you made me swear I wouldn't talk about it while I was here, or you'd feed me to the sharks."

I laugh once. It's true, I did say that.

"I miss my best friends. I can't stand that everyone thinks I'd do something like that. How do I get Ethan to listen to me?"

I shrug. "I dunno, mate. He doesn't listen to anyone but Olivia, right now."

"She's the new girlfriend?"

"It would appear so. He says he's in love with her." The following moment of silence concerns me. "Reese, I'm warning you. When you get back to Ireland, stay away from her."

"Of course." He takes the empty coffee cup out of my hand. "I'll finish packing up the rest of my stuff and get out of your hair."

I turn at the sound of the sliding door closing. "Reese."

He pauses.

"I'll talk to the new lawyer in charge of his case. Maybe she can find some evidence to support your story."

"Thanks. I appreciate it." He disappears inside.

I rake my fingers through my hair and let out a frustrated growl. A pretty little brunette smiles at me as she jogs past on an early morning run. I nod politely and watch her jiggle up the beach with every stride. Damn, I need a *nonfemale* distraction.

I pick up my phone and search the local buy and sell groups, sending inquiries on every ad under the heading of outdoor sport and adventure vehicles. I want something exciting, and I need something fast. The wind makes the trees on the beach bend and sway. That means one thing… an incredible surf. I grab my board and head out.

Being home is exactly what I needed to refocus. I few weeks and a whole lot of miles away from O'Connell's drama has done me well. I pull up in front of my mother's home in Brisbane and rev the engine of my brand new Ferrari 812. It takes a few minutes, but she eventually opens the door and wanders out.

"What on earth have you bought now?"

"A new car."

"I can see that. Do you need another new car?"

"I think so, yes."

"How much money did you spend importing this one?"

"More than you'd think," I admit.

"Carter," she begins.

"Do you want to go for a ride?"

"No, Son. Dinner is almost ready."

I frown, and she finally gives in.

"Not your normal color choice," she notes, as she opens the passenger side door.

I shine a smudge on the paint with my shirtsleeve. "For some reason, I was really drawn to this shade of blue."

She's barely buckled her seatbelt, and I pull away from the curb. She flashes me an unimpressed look.

I try to hold back an amused grin as I take her for a short and extremely quick trip around the block.

"So why has it taken almost two weeks for you to come visit?" she asks, now that I can't avoid her.

"I got caught up on my sleep then did some shopping."

"For cars."

"And a few other things."

"More toys."

I smirk. She knows me so well.

She thrums her fingers on the armrest, waiting for an acceptable excuse, but I've got nothing.

"Sorry, Mum. I guess I just wanted to avoid talking about it."

"You've come home alone, so I assume it didn't work out."

Rounding the corner a little too quickly, she curses and holds onto the handle. Pulling up to the curb at the front of her house, I slide the shifter into park. "The last time I saw her in person, she was calling me an asshole through a closing elevator door." I frown as I open her car door, feeling ashamed of how I left things with Kate.

She accepts my hand and gets to her feet. "Carter. I know better than anyone you can't change the past. What's done is done. What's important is what you're going to do about it now."

"I'm not sure I want to do anything about it. I'm going to spend a week away on my yacht." I ignore her disapproving look. "Are you going to send me out to sea on an empty stomach?"

She grumbles something and rolls her eyes.

I smirk. "What was that?"

"Come in and eat."

I would never tell my friends this, but I enjoy helping her set the table. I always have, even when I was a small child. I imagine she's happy for the company these days. I've been out of the country a lot. She hums, as she brings the cutlery to the table. I watch, not sure how to handle it when she sets a third place at the table. My dad passed away suddenly a few years ago. Mum tells people he worked himself to death. He never took a sick day or a vacation. He always put his career ahead of his family. Mum begs me not to follow in his footsteps.

She looks really happy right now, so I choose to ignore the additional place setting.

"How is Ethan?" she asks when she sits down. "I haven't seen him in a long time."

"The same as always." I unfold the cloth napkin into my lap.

"And this girl you were telling me about? He loves her?"

"Apparently, so."

"Does she love him?"

I'm about to answer, but she gives me *the look*. I swallow what's in my mouth before I continue. "I believe she does."

She dabs the corner of her mouth and places her napkin on the table. "And you?"

This was exactly the conversation I was trying to avoid. I choose my words carefully. "When I first met Olivia, before I knew she was O'Connell's girl, I felt something between us. I'm drawn to her, and I have a strong need to protect her."

"Where does Kate fit in?"

"This is where I get confused. I look at Kate, and I get a nervous kind of feeling in my stomach."

"Butterflies," she states.

I shake my head. "Nope, more aggressive. Like bumblebees. But bigger. Like pterodactyls."

She laughs. "I missed your sense of humor, Carter."

"Is it possible…" I exhale, "Is it possible for someone to have *two* soul mates?"

"I think it's possible to have different kinds of soul mates. Like friends or family connections. If you think these are romantic feelings you're experiencing for both girls, then you know at some point you're going to have to choose."

I nod in agreement.

"Do you remember the year you brought Ethan home during summer break?"

"I do. It was just after our first year of university."

"Mmhmm. You were both young and wild. Determined to take over the world."

"We were going to conquer every beast, and win over all the ladies," I add.

"What beast did you conquer the weekend you spent in Perth?"

"I don't remember that weekend."

She gives me a disbelieving look. "The weekend after you found out you lost your scholarship. You and Ethan drove to Perth, got drunk, and trashed my car."

My chin drops. "I didn't think you knew about that."

"Don't be ridiculous. When are you boys going to figure out you can't hide anything from a mother?"

"Apparently that moment would be now." I get to my feet and help her clear the table.

"You were so worried I was going to be disappointed in you that Ethan took the blame; paid the ticket and had the car fixed before it was time to come home."

I know where she's going with this reminder of loyalty. "Then he called registration and paid my tuition."

She smiles and nods.

"Thanks, Mum."

I love the smell of the ocean air. I roll to my side, physically exhausted. The gentle waves, rock me to sleep. I'm quickly sucked back through time.

Blue eyes sparkle in the sunshine. My heart feels like it's going to explode with joy. She said yes. I was certain no one could ever love me. Lily came into my life and proved me wrong. My entire world changed the day she got lost and asked me for directions. I knew, the moment she smiled at me; she was the one. Now she's agreed to marry me. It's the first time I've felt happiness since learning about the loss of my brother. Telling Elizabeth will be bittersweet, but I think I should tell her first, before anyone else. Hopefully, she'll be able to stop mourning and be happy for me, for at least a little while.

Nobody's heard from Liz in days. I'm about to knock on the door and become concerned when I notice it's ajar. I push it open and call out to her. In the absence of a reply, I walk in and look around. I've never understood the connection between us, but right now, something doesn't feel right. The house is cold, dark... bare. There's no food in the fridge or evidence anyone has been here for quite some time. It's eerie, really.

I'm drawn to a note on the kitchen table. 'So dear I love him that with him, all deaths I could endure. Without him, live no life.' I know this quote. I scour the bookshelf looking for the leather-bound book with gold-embossed lettering that was a treasured gift from my brother. It's not here. I pick up the note and read it again. A mysterious cool breeze sweeps across my skin, making the hair stand on the back of my neck. I know what she's going to do.

I hurry to the ocean, hoping I'm wrong. I pray that when I get there, I'll find her reading and enjoying the sunshine. As I crest the top of the hill, I see her, knee-deep in the water. My heart pounds in my chest as I run as quickly as I can toward the shore. I call her name, but she doesn't respond. The sand slows my pursuit. She disappears beneath the water, and I fight against the pounding waves, trying to get to her. The sky turns gray, making it harder to search for her in the dark water. I hold my breath and go under.

Wrapping my arms around her, I pull her heavy, lifeless body to the surface. My water soaked clothing weighs me down. I struggle to get to shore, praying I'm not too late.

Distraught, I desperately try to revive her. Tears well up in my eyes as I talk to her unresponsive body, encouraging her to come back to me. I refuse to give up on her. My tireless efforts finally pay off, and she begins to cough, spitting up ocean water and gasping for air. Relieved, I wrap my arms around her and rock her gently as I stroke her hair. "I thought I'd lost you."

She becomes stiff in my arms. "You should have let me go." She begins to cry.

"I couldn't. I couldn't lose you too."

Her body curls tighter in my arms. "I can't live without him. I miss him," she confesses with stuttered breath.

"I miss him too. He went because you both wanted to start a family."

"He didn't need to go."

"He went to learn how to help you carry a child."

"He didn't need to go," she repeats. "I'm pregnant."

I'm shocked by the news. "I thought…"

She interrupts me. "There was so much blood, I thought I lost the baby. Like all the others. The doctor confirmed a few days ago, I'm three months pregnant."

She breaks down, and I try to comfort her.

"I don't know how I'm going to do this," she says sniffling. "Your parents can't even look at me. They blame me for his death. It is my fault. If it weren't for me, he would never have been on that ship."

"Stop it. It's not your fault."

Her crying turns into a gut-wrenching hard sob. It's killing me. "Elizabeth, it's going to be okay."

"I can't. I can't do it. I can't raise this child without him. On my own," she stutters, trying to catch her breath.

I hold her tight, making an immediate decision. I know what I have to do. "You won't have to do it alone. I'll take care of you."

"Liam," she begins to protest. "That's not fair to Lily."

"Lily is strong. She'll understand and move on."
"I can't let you do that. You love her."
"I love you. And I'll love this child as if it's my own. I'll take care of you both. For my brother."

My eyes burst open. Understanding hits me like a bolt of lightning. I roll over to grab my ringing phone, but there's an object in between the nightstand and me. I pull back the covers and expose a pair of feet. "What the?" A head pops up as she reaches out and feels her way across the bed, searching for the table. I watch amused.

Successfully, she gets hold of it and tosses it in my direction. "Thanks."

"Welcome," she says in a sleepy voice.

"Ethan."

"What the fuck took so long?" he growls.

"I'm fine thanks, how are you?" I say sarcastically.

"I need you here."

"Where is *here*, these days?"

"Ireland."

I turn to get out of the other side of the bed, so as not to disturb my guest, and find myself facing an interesting situation. Curiously, I peek under the cover. I grin at the sight of a second pair of feet. I opt to crawl out the bottom of the bed.

"Are you there, Brant?"

"Yes," I grunt, as I struggle to untangle myself from the blankets and get both feet firmly on the ground. "What's going on?"

"I'm going to propose."

"Sorry, mate. You're not my type. You're too fucking bossy."

"You're not funny. I'm going to ask Olivia to marry me at the charity fundraiser."

"In front of all those people? Is that a good idea?" I'm sure it's not, but he won't listen to me.

"It's at Slane Castle, and it just feels like the perfect place."

"Let me guess, it came to you in a dream."

"Yeah, how'd you know?"

"Doesn't matter." I laugh once. "Don't you think you should wait?"

"No. I can't stand the thought of her carrying my child out of wedlock."

"Well, that's awfully noble of you."

"Thank you," he continues without catching on to my sarcasm. "I'm doing it that night, and I want all our friends and family to be there for it."

"What if she says no?"

"Don't be fucking ridiculous."

I laugh. "Silly me. Why would she turn down a man with all your charm?"

"Exactly," he agrees.

For such an intelligent man, I'm amazed he has no clue I'm being facetious.

"Scott was telling me you were seeing a girl in Toronto. Invite her to come."

I hold my breath for a moment. "No, it's okay. I'll come alone."

"I'll pay, you cheap bastard."

"That's not the issue. I sort of left without saying a proper goodbye."

"Well, that's a shame. You're going to need reinforcements."

"For what?"

"I'm assigning you babysitting duties, so Olivia can spend some time with her sister."

"Brilliant," I say sarcastically. I glance over at the two blondes, who are now both awake and watching me from the bed. I consider asking them. That would raise a few eyebrows.

"When is this?" I ask, yawning. One of my friends motions for me to come back to bed.

"In two days. Are you coming or what?" he says impatiently.

I climb into the middle and toss the tangled blankets on the floor. "Yes, I'll be there."

Another flight - another airport. Maybe I should just become a pilot. Ethan sent a car to pick me up and take me to the castle. I wasn't sure how I'd feel about being here once my feet hit the ground. Truth is, I'm feeling good. For the first time in many months, I don't feel anxious. That last dream brought me the clarity I needed. I finally have all the answers to the cryptic ramblings of that strange silver-haired woman. Well, all but that whole baby daddy thing, but it's best I just put that out of my mind forever. It doesn't matter now.

I hate these charity events. If they're so concerned about starving children around the world, why don't they just send them all the money instead of hosting such a grand ball? I hope they accept e-Transfers as a form of contribution because I don't think I even own a checkbook.

I head straight to the bar and run right into Reese. "What the fuck are you doing here?" I ask, shocked.

"The company I work for is also a huge contributor to this charity."

I shake my head, frantically. "No. Nope. You can't be here."

He smirks and lifts his glass to his lips. "Yes, I can."

"Reese. You know Ethan will be here. He's got this big night planned out, and he's going to propose."

"Really? Well, I can't wait to meet the woman my best friend is in love with."

"Jesus, Reese. If he see's you here, he'll probably blow a gasket."

"I'm not leaving. Don't worry, I'll stay out of his way. He won't even know I'm around. Did you talk to his lawyer about me, like you promised?"

"Yes, but if you cause any problems tonight, I'll make sure she finds a way to frame *you* for everything."

"Some things never change, Carter. Everybody is still tippy-toeing around O'Connell."

"Don't ruin this night for them, Reese," I warn.

"I promise, I won't interfere."

I wish I believed him, but I don't. I send a quick message to John, so he knows Reese is in the building.

"Carter!" Megan screams as she throws her arms around me. "Thank you, for doing this. I'm so nervous that I haven't talked to my sister for days, in case I let the cat out of the bag."

She introduces the children by name, but I'm never going to remember them. Maybe she should have given them all nametags or nicknames. I can't believe I didn't try to get out of babysitting duty. I should have designated it to Scott. He's been talking nonstop for the past year about wanting to have children.

It's been over an hour since we've all been hiding out in the main ballroom, waiting for O'Connell to put his plan into action. I don't like that I've lost sight of Reese while I'm in here. What's taking so long? The children are getting a little wound up. I'll take them for a walk and try to keep them occupied. I open the door at the back of the room and find Maddie and Nate sucking face in the hallway.

"Good Lord, get a room, so your brother doesn't see that. Is everyone out to push him over the edge tonight?"

Nate smirks as Maddie pulls away and quickly fixes her dress. "Hi, Carter," she says, as her face flushes. "Can you believe Ethan is going to do this tonight?"

"Nothing he does surprises me." I reach out and grab hold of a wobbly toddler, as he runs past me, chasing his siblings.

"Good catch," Nate says

"I'm worried this is a bad idea," Madison continues. You know how much Olivia hates to be the center of attention. Is the shock good for her and the baby?"

"I agree with you, but he's made up his mind."

"And to make her…" She pauses.

"Make her what?"

"Dance. He's going to invite her onto the dance floor."

I raise my brow.

"It's supposed to be a surprise," she says ashamed.

"Don't worry, I won't say a word."

I look down at the small lad tugging on my pant leg. "Uncle Carter, I have to pee."

Nate laughs. "Let's leave the man-nanny to do his job, Maddie. Katelyn just messaged she's going to get them. You better be in the room when Ethan brings her in."

Before I can respond, I look down to catch Trent heading toward the entrance to the toilets with his pants down around his ankles and his Johnson in his hand. "Whoa, buddy."

"Have fun with that." Nate takes Maddie's hand and leads her back toward the ballroom.

I pick up the small boy and rush him inside to finish business. I should send myself a reminder to ask for a raise.

After rounding up all the strays, I herd them back into the ballroom and find a spot out of the way, where I can keep an eye on them.

I'm guessing from all the commotion, the guest of honor has finally joined the party.

"If I can have everyone's attention, please," the emcee requests. "We have a very special request from one of our long-time supporters, Ethan O'Connell, who would like to dedicate this first waltz to someone very special to him."

I watch Ethan hold out his hand. Olivia looks up at him terrified, and I'm suddenly in the middle of an Irish déjà vu. I wonder this time if she'll let him lead.

I watch from the dark corner. One eye on them, one on the kids, who are chasing each other around with balloons. I blink my eyes rapidly, thinking I've seen that mysterious woman in the shadows on the other side of the room. That's when I see George and Mary. She lifts her hand and gives me a small wave. I nod and smile. I remember the day Ethan, and I ended up in that sad little shop in the middle of nowhere. We were on our way home from an all-night party; hungover, starving, and nearly out of fuel. There was something that drew Ethan into that shop, and I followed. That's when we met the enchanting older couple. Mary welcomed us into her home and made us breakfast, while George filled the car with fuel. I enjoyed looking through their antiques and collectibles and hearing the stories that went along with them. It was sad to learn they had no children to help them look after things, and since business had been slow, the bills were piling up. I picked out a few trinkets and made them accept more money than they were worth. When we left, Ethan vowed to take care of them as long as he could. He said they felt like *family* to him, and he didn't know why, but he had a strong need to make sure they didn't have to worry about money anymore. I knew exactly what he meant. I felt it as well.

The music draws my attention back to the middle of the room, where Ethan confidently dances Olivia around the floor. A calm feeling washes over me, assuring me I no longer need to worry. Things look like they're finally falling into place. When Ethan takes a knee and pulls a small ring box out of his pocket, I can tell the poor bastard is struggling to keep control of his emotions. Since he's met this girl, I swear, he's grown a pair of ovaries.

"Marry me."

Olivia looks down at him, while the entire room awaits her answer. Not me, I know what her answer is.

"Yes, I'll marry you. You're my destiny… I couldn't survive without you."

Ugh, these two are so dramatic. But I know this to be true. She will be his in every life. I think I can finally let go. I have my own destiny to follow in this life. There's going to be a lot of twists and turns on the road to my happily ever after, but I know, after the memories I've been shown in the past few weeks; it's time for me to start that journey.

I make sure the children get some food into them, well, mostly sugar. We'll call that *payback*. Marcus has finally given in and fallen asleep in the middle of the floor. I lift him into my arms before he gets trampled.

After finding him somewhere safe to sleep, I lean against the wall, looking down at my phone, hoping to have a message from Kate. I've tried to keep in touch with her, but things aren't the same. I don't know if that ship has sailed forever, but I hope she'll give me another chance to make it right.

I get the feeling someone is watching me, and look up to find Olivia's eyes on me. For the first time since I laid eyes on her, I don't feel like I'm a ticking time bomb as she walks toward me. She stands in front of me, and we look into each other's eyes.

"Congratulations," I finally say, giving her a sincere smile.

"Thank you, Carter."

"I hope that you two finally find happiness."

She frowns. "Carter…"

"No, I really mean that," I interrupt. "You two belong together. Don't ever let anything, or anybody, come between you."

"Thank you, Carter." She wraps her arms around my chest and pulls me close. I return her hug, close my eyes, and kiss the top of her head.

"I was hoping you'd be here tonight. I wanted to give this to you." She reaches into her bra and takes out a tightly folded document.

"What is it?" I take it out of her hands and try to flatten it.

"The results of the paternity test."

I looked up at her shocked as I read it. "The baby is O'Connell's."

"Yes."

"Why did you do this? I thought you were absolutely sure nothing happened between us that night."

"I was, but you weren't."

I nod. She's a good woman, and she deserves the very best. "You're in good hands with O'Connell," I whisper, squeezing her tightly one last time. "But I'll always be around if you need me."

She swallows hard, trying to hold back a deeply rooted emotional response. "I know, Carter."

"Ahem," a masculine voice interrupts. "Carter."

Olivia loosens her grip and then takes a step back.

I extend my hand. "Congratulations, Ethan."

"You're not trying to steal my girl, are you, Brant?" he inquires in jest, as he shakes my hand.

I laugh out loud. "That wouldn't be possible. It's extremely clear she only loves you."

At that very moment, our eyes lock and something mystical passes between Olivia and I. It brings with it an acknowledgment that sets us both free. The energy that has drawn us together, and kept our souls entwined like branches on a grapevine, magically disappears. After lifetimes of commitment, love, and loyalty, I'm finally **Unbound**.

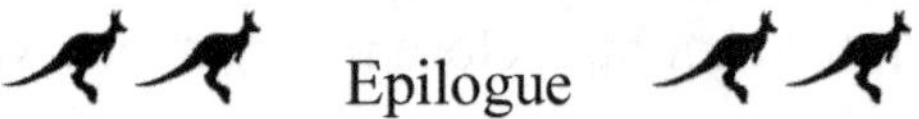 Epilogue

Olivia smiles and tucks herself in under Ethan's protective arm, and he looks down at her in admiration.

"Mmm, I'm a very lucky man. There's someone I want to introduce you to." As he leads her away, he glances back at me and gives me a half-grin. "I'm keeping my eyes on you, Brant," he promises.

"And so you should. I think I've already told you, if you don't worship her the way she deserves, someone else will."

"Stop it, you two. If you ruin my engagement night with your immature, alpha male, pissing contest, I'm not going to be a very happy girl," Olivia says in frustration.

"No worries, Beautiful," I promise. "We're just messing around. I have no intention of ruining this night for you."

I put my hand on Ethan's shoulder and walk with them, giving him a masculine pat on the back. "Just remember what I promised, big guy. If you don't treat her right, I'm going to kick your ass."

Ethan stops walking and gives me a serious look. "Carter. If I don't treat her right, *she's* going to kick my ass."

There's a brief moment of silence before we both throw our heads back in laughter. Olivia stands, with her weight on one hip, arms crossed, and looking unimpressed. "We could start with a double ass-kicking right now if you'd like."

Ethan throws his hands up in the defeat. "No, no, I'm good."

"Me, too," I add, still chuckling.

"Hey… so tell me about this girl you met in Toronto. I hear it might be kind of serious."

"Yes, Carter. For your own safety," Olivia advises. "Tell us about your girl."

"Brilliant subject change," I say, giving Ethan a fist bump. I point down at Olivia's nephew, Marcus, still asleep where I stashed him under one of the tables. "I'll tell you about Kate another time," I promise, as I carefully slide the boy out by his feet. "Tonight, I'm the hired nanny. I'll take the kids back to the hotel, so your sister can stay and celebrate with you."

Olivia watches as I lift the small boy into my arms. "Thank you, Carter. For everything."

I smile and raise two fingers in the air as I walk away. "That's *two* you owe me."

Thank you to my soul mate and my soul friends who have helped me through a couple of difficult years. I am STILL a believer. Love truly does transcend all time, and we can change our destiny.

A Special thank you to Angie, Heather, Tami, Elaine, Crystal B and Crystal O for your help in getting this story ready to share. Shout out to Carol Ann, Andi, Dana and Lee for your patience and support.

In dedication and memory of my Godfather, Brian Johnston. Who always encouraged me to follow my dreams no matter the obstacles. When I needed him, he stepped up. Whatever I needed. Anytime. That's the kind of man he was. He will be missed by many.

Impulsive - Prologue

I'm whisked away to Ireland in that dusty, dark place where dreams and memories blend. So far away, so long ago. I toss, and I turn restlessly. Horses neigh, and suddenly I'm standing right beside them. The girl I vowed to take care of sits beneath a tree in the nearby meadow, reading a book from my family library. I'm anxious for the wedding to take place so I can move her out of the workhouse and the deplorable conditions there. Although my parents argue that she's too young, I will prove to them that I'm responsible enough to start a family and run the family farm when they send my brother off to college. He's not better or brighter than me, although they treat me as if that's the case most of the time.

My sweet Lily has had a rough life, but she has a kind soul and a tender heart despite her tragic childhood. How could I not love her? To me, she's a bright flower, as beautiful as the countryside that surrounds her. The horses frolic, chasing each other around the paddock and bumping into me as I'm trying to get my chores done. It's not to be taken lightly when two tons of free-thinking animal comes at you. Playing or not. I scratch my head. Maybe I should saddle up and take them for a run. Clearly, I'm not the only one who needs to work off some steam. I close the gate and toss my tools into the wooden crate. She gets to her feet and comes to me. I hesitate when she leans in for a kiss. "I'm dirty and sweaty," I warn.

She wipes the sweat from my brow and wipes it on my shirt. "Makes no difference to me, Liam."

Chapter One

Carter

I blink my eyes rapidly, trying to ascertain my whereabouts as I wake. The salty breeze and the roar of the surf disorient me. The surfboard leaning in the corner of the room assures me that I'm home in Australia on the Sunshine Coast.

When I met Kate Ryan, she made me want to end my impulsive behaviour where women are concerned and think about settling down. Once I learned of Olivia's pregnancy, the emotional push and pull I felt between her and Kate was too much. I became confused and feared I couldn't give Kate the relationship she deserves. I'm not proud of how I left. A better man wouldn't have cut and run.

When I arrived back in Australia, I couldn't stop the urge to reacquaint myself with every old flame in my *little black book*. A distraction of epic proportion. I sit up and swing my feet over the side of the bed, and stretch.

"Good morning," says a sleepy, feminine voice from somewhere within the mound of blankets beside me.

I look down at the tousled, freshly-fucked hair on the pillow as she tugs down the sheet and reveals her face.

"Good morning." I pause. Penny? Peggy? Patty? I know it was a 'P'. I worked my way up to that letter a few days ago.

"Do you mind if I grab a quick shower?" she asks, discarding the blanket on the floor and revealing one hell of a smoking hot body.

"Of course not." I'd say make yourself at home, but that's a dangerous thing to suggest to someone with whom you only plan on having casual sex.

"Thank you. I'm a little…." She wrinkles her nose.

"*Sticky?*" I say, amused as I look over at the empty can of whip cream.

She nods her head in agreement. "Can you drop me off at work afterwards?"

I nod as I watch her cross the room completely naked, taking in every beautiful curve of her body. I'd be a complete asshole if I put her in a cab. Besides, I always take them out for breakfast afterwards. It's my *thing*. It somehow eases my conscience a little. Maybe my mother would be less disturbed by my behaviour if she knew I fed the girl a good hearty breakfast before sending her on her way. That's a lot of undue pressure to place on a pancake, but I have hope. Now that she's out of view, I pick up my phone and open the contacts. "Paisley." I feel pathetic for a moment until she calls out from the other room.

"Carter? Are you joining me?"

Oh hell, yes. I didn't spend the extra money on an oversized luxury shower to wash up alone. She grins as I step in under the simulated rainfall and allow her to trace every ridge of muscle on my torso with the soapy washcloth. When she slides her hand further south, I place my hand on hers, forcing her to stop. She looks at me inquisitively.

"It's my turn now," I say, taking the cloth from her.

She turns and leans back against my chest as I wrap my arms around her and caress the soapy washcloth over her body. I take my time around the firm globes, still trying to determine if they're real. If they are, they're impressive. Rubbing against her backside while having a hold on her breasts makes me harden and twitch. I whisper into her ear. "You missed a spot."

She looks at me over her shoulder. "I did? Where?"

She lets out a soft moan as I gently scrub across the small of her back and leave a trail of lather down the crack of her ass. Her muscles tighten and clench as I venture lower. I drop the washcloth to the shower floor and use my hand to separate her legs. She resists me at first, unsure of my intentions. I whisper into her ear. "Don't worry, love. I know my way around." I force her to lean forward and steady herself as I lift her leg and rest her foot on the built-in shower seat. Now I've got her right where I want her. The soothing sound of rainwater is replaced by the sound of my hips thumping against her wet skin, and echoing through the room, as I take her from behind.

Her breathing quickens and becomes shallow, and I purposely slow my movements, sliding almost all the way out before the next thrust. Usually, I'd be concentrating on making her cum, but I'm thinking about pancakes for some odd reason. I become momentarily distracted, and she curses at me, pulling my attention back to the task at hand. I love a sassy girl. A good hard slap on her asscheek leaves a warm, pink mark and the sight of it helps me along. When she purrs and tightens around me, I'm motivated to hit a rhythm that should push her over the edge. As the increasing waves of pleasure grow, I join her. She's a moaning, twitching mess. Job well done if I do say so myself.

As she catches her breath, I turn off the water and reach for a towel. "There's a little coffee shop on the way into work that serves a great breakfast."

She turns to look me in the eyes and takes the towel out of my hand. "You're thinking about your stomach right now?"

"I'm a man. I'm always thinking about my stomach."

She tries to hide her disappointment, but I know that look. It's the look that prompts me to scratch through the entry in my little black book and never look back.

I wasn't wrong. Paisley pouts all through breakfast and picks at her fruit salad while giving me the silent treatment. Ugh. The first night we met, I was honest and upfront with her about my intentions. Nothing has changed. I guess that's women for you. A guy comes back for seconds, and in their twisted little girl brains, they convince themselves there's some basis to begin a committed relationship. My mother would clip me on the backside of my head if she could hear my thoughts right now.

After dropping Paisley off at her work, I head toward my office, engaged in deep thought. I've been with a different girl every night, but that hasn't stopped me from thinking about Kate. My heart beats quickly when I think of those sparkling sapphire blue eyes that I won't soon forget. Going back to Canada would easily sate my addiction to her. Sometimes when the warm breeze glides across the water and gently caresses the waves, I swear I can hear her voice whispering my name. Calling me, luring me back to her.

I find myself staring out my window, completely zoned out when the sound of my name startles me back to reality.

"Carter?"

"Yes, sorry, I'm here."

"You haven't got your video on. Are you sleeping?"

"No, Landon, I'm awake." I switch on my video.

"Sweet Jesus, turn it back off," Ethan begs. "You look like shit."

"Thanks, mate. You're no beauty queen yourself, you ugly bastard."

Ethan laughs, and everyone else on the video call tries to hide their amusement.

Ethan's look becomes serious. "If anyone asks, this is not an Aurora work call. Officially, I'm still suspended."

"Got it," Landon answers for us all.

"For those of you wondering," Ethan begins. "We finally signed the deal with Bramtech. Their connection with the Asian suppliers will save us thousands of dollars and give us a much better margin on the electronic boards for our new electric car partner. Carter, job well done for your part in closing that deal."

Everyone chuckles.

"You're all assholes," I say, annoyed. They laugh harder.

"Well, at least you've got your five minutes of fame," Scott says with a straight face.

"You've even got your own hashtag," Landon adds.

I narrow my eyes. "What the fuck are you talking about?"

"#nightclubguy," Scott says while looking down at his phone.

"Still don't know what you're talking about," I say, growing impatient.

"There's a video circulating of you *closing the deal*," Scott finally says.

"Well, it's arguable, Landon reasons. "The sound is distorted, it's unfocused, and it's dark. It was taken by somebody on the other side of the room."

"Was it me or not?"

John frowns. "Definitely you."

"How long have you all known about this?"

Scott raises a finger in the air. "I just heard about it."

I'm annoyed they all seemed to be amused. "This isn't funny at all. What if my mum sees it?"

They erupt laughing again, and I'm about to lose my shit. "Ethan!"

"Sorry," he says, trying to compose himself. "You're right. I've got your back. John, you're the head of security, work with the team and get this video off the web."

"I think that means that *John* has my back," I grumble.

"Do we know where the video post originated?" John asks.

Scott raises his hand. "One of the guys with us that night said that Stacey's friend posted it on Instagram. And apparently, Stacey knows about it and is quite proud of it. He says she brags about it."

I scrub my hand over my face. "Please tell me I'm not tagged or named in any posts."

Ethan gives me an apologetic look. "Not that we're aware."

"That's the last time, O'Connell. You can pimp out someone else from now on. I have nightmares about that girl. I don't think she's all there."

"I agree," Scott adds. "She seems like she could be the crazy stalker type."

Landon shakes his head in disagreement. "No, you should be okay. She seems like the type who loves to be the centre of attention. I'm sure a fling at the club was enough. As long as you didn't encourage her any."

I purse my lips and rake my fingers through my hair. A silence falls over the group.

"Carter, you left it at the club, right?" Ethan asks.

"Well, no. We went back to my room." Everyone groans. "And I took her for breakfast the next day."

Scott scratches his head. "Okay, so it was only a one-night stand. We shouldn't start worrying for nothing."

I hold my neck and twist it in different directions trying to work out the tension.

John observes my reaction. "Carter?"

"Hmmm?"

"Did you see her after that night?"

I hesitate, causing them to groan again. "Once, maybe twice."

"Have you heard from her at all?" Ethan asks.

"No, not since I came home."

"Good, let's hope she's moved on. If she does contact you, don't engage."

"I'm sure it will just go away on its own," Scott says sympathetically.

I nod my head. "My game plan is AVOID AVOID AVOID. Are we done here? I want to go punch something."

I disconnect the call and lean back in the chair, wondering how I get into these messes. It's been a long time since I've stepped into the boxing ring. I change into my sweats in my private washroom. I think a few hours of sparring will relieve the tension and clear my mind. If nothing else, the drive on this gorgeous afternoon should cheer me up.

I hit the highway and drive quite aggressively until the open road soothes the tension in my soul. My navigation system tells me my next turn is five kilometres, but something tied to the dock catches my eye as I pass the marina. I take the next exit and drive back. A gorgeous red-head greets me as I get out of the Ferrari. She seems overdressed and too stunningly beautiful for someone selling boats.

"Hi!"

"Hello," I say, tipping my designer sunglasses to the top of my head.

"What are you looking for today?"

A distraction. My eyes take a long appreciative look at her long legs and curvy body. "On my way past, I noticed the cabin cruiser for sale."

She leads me to it and then carefully steps aboard. "Let me walk you through."

She gives me a quick tour of the lower deck that houses the bedroom, the eating quarters, and the toilet with a shower. "This is exactly what I'm looking for."

"Great! I assume you have your boaters license?"

I raise my brow and smile. "Yes, I currently own a yacht."

"Oh, are you wanting to downsize? I can get my boss to work you out a trade value tomorrow."

"No, I think I'll keep both. I want something cheaper on fuel when I'm staying locally."

"You're Carter Brant, right? I was at a party on your yacht last summer." She grins and pauses, looking me over from head to toe.

"There's no way that's possible. I don't usually forget beautiful girls."

In the dimly lit cabin, I can tell she's blushing. "There were a lot of pretty girls on that yacht, so you probably didn't notice me."

I put my hand against the wall to steady myself from the rocking of the waves as she loses her footing and falls against my chest. Her hand lands on my cock as she tries to steady herself. It twitches as I think about how good it would feel to have her lips around it. I stare into her eyes. "Well, there aren't any other girls here now. And I've noticed you. What's your name?"

"Julie." She slowly, and I'm sure intentionally, rubs her hand across me, feeling my erection through the fabric of my pants as she attempts to move away from me.

I tighten my grip, preventing her escape and anchoring her against my body. "Are there any other employees here right now?"

She moistens her lips, and it heightens my growing excitement. "No, we closed at noon today. I was locking up when you pulled in."

A boyish grin appears on my lips as I move my hand from her hip to her waist. "Julie, I think I'd like to buy your boat." I venture higher, caressing her with my strong hand and brushing my thumb across her breast. Her intake of breath pleases me.

"I think I'd like to sell you this boat," she says as her body starts to respond to my touch.

I pick her up and move her several feet. "I think before I buy it, I should make sure that the bed is comfortable." I place her down gently on the bed, and without hesitation, she pulls the tie strings on my sweatpants. She stares up into my eyes as she releases my erection from beneath the straining fabric. A wide smile brightens her face when she sees it. "I'd advise you to do so, just to make sure you're making a wise purchase."

She slides down her panties as I climb on top of her.

"You know what's the great part about owning this boat?"

"What's that?" I ask as I part her legs and move between her thighs. Her soft moaning in anticipation of what's to come fuels my want and need.

"As captain, you don't have to ask permission to cum on board."

I grin as my first penetrating thrust makes her gasp. "Right you are."

Chapter Two

Kate

Business meetings make me want to roll on my computer chair out the seventh-floor window. There's nothing like being dragged into the family business kicking and screaming. I, Katherine Ryan, was born into the esteemed Ryan legacy. I couldn't care less for the rich and famous lifestyle, and I'd give it all up and walk out of this boardroom right now if my father would let me.

Sadly, I have a conscience, unlike the rest of my family. They use the old 'don't let your father down' guilt-trip every chance they get, and it works on me most of the time. It's almost as if they thrive on controlling people's lives and using them to benefit their greed. I've wondered on more than one occasion if I was adopted. I don't have that in me.

I want to do something meaningful with my life—something that benefits others and not me. The last time I brought that up at a family dinner, it caused the rest of the talk at the table to come to a complete halt. Everyone stared at me, shocked as if I had gone completely mad. My stepmother was quick to throw out a compliment on a business deal my dad was working on, drawing the attention away from me. For now, I guess I'll soldier on with my family duties and fake interest in the real estate and development industry. I miss my mom every day. She would have understood me.

Chairs screech across the floor as people get to their feet and gather their laptops and coffee cups. Finally! I bolt out the door.

"Miss Ryan," a voice calls from behind. I feel the tension in my shoulders and pick up my pace, moving as fast as possible in my big box store heels. I growl under my breath when a rather stout man ahead of me slows down my escape.

"Katherine!" he calls out again as he pushes past the crowd.

I grimace when I feel his hand brush past my elbow as he reaches for my arm. Damn. I turn to acknowledge him, "Oh, hello, Will."

"I was calling you; didn't you hear me?"

"I'm sorry. I guess my mind was off somewhere." And my body was trying to get someplace else. As far away from you as possible, I think to myself.

He gives me what, I presume to him, is a charming smile. "I thought we could grab lunch."

Good Lord, I've seen horses with better teeth. I smile politely and gently tug my arm out of his grip. "I'm sorry, but I already have plans." I resume walking, hoping he gets the hint.

He frowns and follows. "Of course, you do. A beautiful woman like yourself is likely booked for lunch months in advance."

"You'd be surprised."

"Well, maybe you'll throw this poor guy a bone if you get any cancellations."

That's not likely going to happen, so I'm not giving him any hope at all. "I have to run." I hold up my phone. "Conference call in a few minutes."

He nods. "I'll see you at the morning meeting then."

I glance over my shoulder to make sure he stopped following me. "Yes, of course." Quickly stepping into the elevator, I push the button for the lobby. I have a date with a park bench down on the lakeshore.

I follow the path along the water to a spot that's not quite so busy. The warmth of the sun on my face helps to soothe away some of the morning's anxiety. I'm not the kind of girl who thrives in the boardroom all day. I need air; I need sun; I need freedom. I need to be writhing with pleasure under a particular enticing, muscular Australian. I plop myself down on the wooden bench and peruse through his social media to see what he's been up to. Why can't I get him out of my mind? Ugh. I need to get laid. A jogger passes me and grins as if he could read my mind. I blush like a schoolgirl and reach into my bag for my ham sandwich.

As I dial into my next conference call from my phone, I notice a silver-hair woman observing me from an adjacent bench. I acknowledge her with a smile. A small display of delight momentarily lightens her senescent features.

I nibble on my sandwich while I wait out the boring role call, and my father introduces the new faces on the video conference, a contracting team interested in the new project. I get an overwhelming feeling like I'm being watched, and I glance over at the other bench. The mysterious woman has vanished, and in her place is a small green finch. It cocks its head from one side to the other before taking flight and startling me as it whizzes past my head.

I take a breath, trying to calm my racing heart as I look over my left shoulder and then the right. There's no one around, but I still have an eerie feeling. I try to refocus and do some research on our new partners. I shouldn't be surprised at their repertoire, including several reported lawsuits by past employees and projects I consider poor human-interest choices. I still can't figure out how corporations can put profit ahead of being compassionate toward people.

I break the crust of my sandwich into small pieces and toss it onto the ground for the nearby birds before I start back to the office. All the way, I think about the new real estate project and how much I don't want to do business with these people.

As I breeze into the lobby, the receptionist locks eyes with me.

"What kind of a mood is he in?" I ask quietly.

"He seems to be in a good mood." Dana acknowledges the look of determination on my face and sighs. "You're going to ruin it, aren't you?"

I raise my brow. "Of course not," I assure her.

She rolls her eyes and shakes her head as her attention is demanded by a guest requiring assistance. In the elevator, I practice what I want to say all the way up to the penthouse floor and rush towards his office so that I won't lose my nerve. The door is slightly ajar, so I knock once and peek in. He looks up and smiles.

"Katherine! Come in."

I push the door open and straighten my posture. "Sorry to bother you, Father." I hesitate, and my brow furrows.

"Something on your mind, Kate?" he asks with concern.

I take a deep breath and begin. "Yes, sir. Did you do any research on this new contractor before you agreed to partner with them?"

He sits back in his chair and crosses his arms. "They're a successful firm. Very profitable, I'm assured."

Having his full attention makes me even more nervous, and voicing my opinion just may be crossing the line, but I'm going to do it anyway. "Profitable maybe, but they have questionable ethics."

He cocks his head to the side and narrows his eyes. "Why do you say that?"

"I've been researching them." I ignore his aggravated look and choose my words carefully. "Are these people we want to align our family business with?"

He sighs dramatically. "What are you trying to say?"

I take a few steps closer to him, feeling my nerves start to escalate. "These are people who close down animal shelters and throw seniors out on the street. They underpay their staff and have several outstanding lawsuits against them for breach of contract."

"And?"

My voice goes up an octave. "They aren't stand-up people, Dad. They're shady and untrustworthy. I don't think we should do business with them. I'm afraid they're going to tarnish our reputation and our family name."

He pauses a moment, letting my words sink in. "I've already signed the agreement. What would you have me do? Go back on my word?"

"Yes. ABSOLUTELY, YES."

He frowns. "I'm not going to do that, Katherine. This rejuvenation project in the west end of town is going to happen with or without us. It's a good business investment."

When I think he can't stoop any lower, he goes for the jugular. "Your sister understands. Why can't you?"

A nuclear rush of adrenaline pulses through my veins, and before I can stop myself, I blurt out in anger, "Of course, she does, Dad. I'm pretty sure she's kicked a few puppies in her day to close deals." My brain acknowledges what I've said aloud, so I turn on my heels and get out of there as fast as I can. I hold my breath until I reach the elevator and repeatedly push the button, fearing that any delay will allow him to call me back to his office.

My phone begins to ring as the elevator door opens, and I hurriedly get in. My hand slightly trembles as I turn it to view the caller. Carter. "I can't deal with you right now," I sigh as I slide the ringer to silent.

The elevator door opens, and I look down at the floor as I walk out, hoping to avoid eye contact with the receptionist, but she's on to me. I stop dead at the site of her *sensible* shoes.

I raise my eyes to meet her stern look and crossed arms. "What did you say this time?"

"Errr." I bite my lip and keep walking. "I don't know, something about bad business partners and my sister kicking puppies."

"You didn't?" she says, shocked.

I nod my head then shrug.

"I love you for it, but girl, you better look after your situation before you get fired."

I pause. Getting fired is not a bad idea. "Wait, what situation?"

"All that frustration pent up since that mountain of sexual energy was rubbing on you at the pub."

I lower my brow.

"Girl's night? Playing darts." She throws her hands in the air. "Don't you even try to make it look like you don't know what I'm talking about. Have you heard from him?"

"He bailed on dinner then went back to Australia. His mother is very ill. It sounded like she wasn't going to make it."

"That's horrible. You should call him."

"He called earlier, but I didn't pick up."

"Call him back!"

"Dana, I don't think things are meant to be. I'm attracted to him, but I feel like I'm on high alert every time I'm with him. Something seems *off*."

"A lot of things should be off. Your tendency to overthink things, the wall you've built around yourself."

I flash her an annoyed look.

"Most importantly, your panties. You need to get out of those now and again."

"Are you listening to me? He's in Australia. I'll probably never see him again."

"There's always Will."

I stop dead in my tracks and give her a disapproving look. "I can't even believe you just said that. As soon as I get home, I'm going to unfriend and block you."

She frowns. "Do you want me to call you a cab?"

I resume walking toward the door and wave her off. "No thanks. I need the exercise."

What a day. My mind is pulled into so many different directions I can't put together a single sensible thought. I leave the lakeshore trail and walk up the city block toward the penthouse. Out of the corner of my eye, I see an older woman watching me from the cement steps of a historical building. I turn my head to get a better look and confirm it's the woman from the bench. There's a strange shift in the air as the refreshing wind off the lake seemingly morphs into a warm salty ocean breeze. She gives me a broad smile as I stop to take note of the peculiar event.

The rest of the way home, I think about the ocean. Warm sand and crashing waves recharge my soul. I've never been to Australia, but it's on my mind. Carter is on my mind. A quick shower doesn't help to clear my thoughts. I light my favourite ocean-scented candle and then drop wearily onto the couch, still wrapped in a towel. Lately, when I think about Carter, I think about all the reasons I have to mistrust him. Thanks to Dana, I'm laser-focused on the last night I saw him at the pub. The smell of his cologne, and the firm ridges of muscles pressed against me when he wrapped himself around me from behind, is burned into my mind.

According to Cream Magazine, the Australian dialect ranked in the lower half of the top ten sexiest accents. I would disagree with that ranking. When Carter whispers in my ear with that slow pronunciation and smooth dulcet tone, I'm practically a puddle at his feet. How I manage to resist him is a miraculous feat since I'm sure I'd do anything he demands, given a moment of indiscretion.

I squeeze my legs together, trying to alleviate the ache that's building there. I adjust my position, trying to get comfortable, and the towel spills open, exposing me. I reach for the edge, and my hand skims across my skin. The warmth and gentle pressure feel good. I close my eyes and caress my hand across my thigh and eventually between my legs. I twitch and raise my hips as my hand glides across my clit and rubs with a tenacious force.

An orgasm builds quickly with the long-overdue intimate discovery of my body. As I tease and rub between my legs, my free hand skims across my stomach and upward, squeezing the soft tissue of my breast. As I pinch and squeeze one side and then the other, I close my legs around my fingers, squirming with my impending release. Needing to fulfill my desire, I pull on hardened nipples, making myself moan and unleash waves of pent-up sexual energy so intense I nearly fall off the couch.

As the waves subside and I slowly regain my normal breathing, I grab the towel to cover myself up. My phone rings, and I glance at the display to see Carter's name. There's no chance I could talk to him right now. I shut off the ringer and toss it back on the table. I let out a small laugh at the coincidence. "Sorry, Carter, but you have the worst timing in the world."

Chapter Three

Carter

I consider ignoring the incoming call from Ethan O'Connell. Life has been *enjoyable* lately, and I'm sure from the uneasy feeling I've had all morning, he's about to ruin it.

"Good morning, Ethan."

"Not really."

I note the distress in his tone. "What's going on? Is your father still disowning you? Or is your ex still out for blood?"

"I've left Olivia. I need you to go to Toronto and pack up my stuff at the house. I'm letting the lease go."

That was the last thing I expected to hear. I stand with the phone at my ear, stunned and speechless.

"Did you hear me, Carter? I left her."

"Why in the ever-loving-fuck would you do that? Are you completely mad?" I start to pace.

"I have an excellent reason."

"And what's that?"

"I'm scared."

"Of what? Being tied down to the most wonderful woman in the world for the rest of your life and starting a family?"

"No. Olivia is the only woman for me."

"Then help me understand. She's pregnant with *your* child."

"I know that!" he growls. "Look, Carter. I could lose them both if I stick around. The stress that comes with my family or being in a relationship with me could kill her."

"So, you left her?"

"I didn't know what else to do?"

The man frustrates the hell out of me. I throw my head back and try to ease the tension out of my neck. "You don't leave her, you dumb twat."

"She gave me back her engagement ring. We're finished."

My jaw clenches. "So that's it? You've made up your mind."

"Yes."

I'm aware the long pause is needed to compose himself.

"Carter. I know it's a lot to ask, but I need you to do something else for me. Please don't say no."

I rake my fingers through my hair.

"Just like I said, anxiety is dangerous for them. After I left, the baby went into distress, and Olivia collapsed."

My stomach tightens into knots. "Is she okay?"

"Physically, they're both stable for now. Emotionally, Olivia isn't doing so great. If she doesn't snap out of it, she could lose the baby. I sent Dave to Toronto on the private jet as soon as I heard. He'll oversee their care in Canada."

Concern causes me to pace again. "What can I do?"

"Her sister is with her now, but she has to go home soon to look after her own family. I need you to go to the hospital. Look after Olivia. Make sure she's okay."

I shake my head. "**You** should be doing that," I snarl.

"I can't, Carter. It's the hardest decision I've ever had to make in my life. It's killing me," his voice becomes strained with emotion. "I'm no good for them. If I'm around her, they'll both be at risk. It has to be this way."

It annoys me that he always plays on my unwavering loyalty. This time I'll let him sweat it out a little. "I'm kind of busy right now, Ethan. I'm in the middle of a project."

"I need you to have my back on this one, bro."

I scroll down my contacts list to the next letter on my list. 'R: Ryan, Kate.' I get that nervous, rumbling feeling in my stomach. Strange, her contact sorted itself by the surname instead of the other way around like all the others. Maybe it's a sign. I've been trying hard to keep her out of my thoughts, but perhaps it's the universe's way of giving me a swift kick in the ass.

Ethan continues to rant, and my mind wanders as I stare at her profile picture. I begin to crave her raspberry lips. From the moment I got on that plane to come home to Australia, I have regretted not kissing her. I want to experience her warmth and softness. I need to know how she tastes. I interrupt Ethan's pleading. "Okay, I'll go."

His rant comes to a halt. "What?"

"I said I'll do it. I'll go and check on her."

"Thanks, mate. I don't know what I'd do without you."

"You'd have one of your other groupies do it."

"No, brother. You're the only one I trust to take care of her."

I feel guilty about that. I loved her from the first moment I laid eyes on her, and things have passed between us that Ethan can never know. "What exactly happened between the two of you? Is there anything I need to know?"

"It was ugly, and I'm an asshole. That's all you need to know."

I toss my travel bag onto the bed and double-check for my passport. "Typical O'Connell."

"Carter, she's the only thing I've ever loved. I need her and the baby to be okay."

I pause, acknowledging his sincerity. "Okay, boss," I assure him. "But you need to get your shit sorted out and look after your family yourself."

"Keep her safe until I can."

I'm a few hours into the flight to Toronto's International Airport when the dinner cart starts making its way down the aisle in first class. I eagerly wait for its arrival, not because I think the meal I pre-ordered will be a gourmet experience by any means, but I'm starving. The stewardess places a covered tray in front of the seat beside me and then pushes the cart past us. What just happened? "Did you order dinner?" I ask the man sitting next to me, wondering if he received my meal by mistake.

"Yes, mate. Didn't you?"

"I did." I stretch my neck as far as I can and try to get the stewardess' attention over the top of my seat. "Excuse me." She ignores me while she serves the passengers behind me. I wait until she's done. "Excuse me, miss," I say louder before she moves back another row. I hear a passenger tell her that I'm trying to get her attention. She pauses and then turns to give me a steelie glare. My eyes open wide, and I know that I'm fucked.

"How can I help you?" she asks in a tone that confirms she has no intentions of helping me at all.

Now, this is awkward. "I believe I ordered dinner."

She huffs and walks back to my row. She looks at the printed sheet on the cart and then looks at the seat marker on the overhead. "Can I see your boarding pass, sir?"

I sigh as I search for it. She snatches it out of my hand and studies it carefully. "I'm sorry, I don't have a meal listed here for you."

I know what's going on here. My damn impulses always come back to haunt me.

"I paid for a meal," I assure her.

"I'm afraid you'll have to take it up with the airline's customer service."

"Can I purchase a meal now?"

"Of course, if you have a credit card."

I dig it out of my wallet. "I'll have the beef."

"Sorry, we're all out of the beef."

"Okay, I'll have the chicken."

"We're out of chicken, too."

I take a deep breath. "What do you have?" I keep calm and smile at her, hoping to soften her disposition. I think it might be working. She pauses a moment.

"I can bring you complimentary pretzels."

She's pissed at me. "Okay, if that's all there is, it will have to do. Could I have a couple? I'm starving."

She nods and walks to the front galley. I sit back in my seat and sigh.

"What was that all about?" my curious neighbour asks.

"An international flight, a rather interesting rendezvous in a private section of the plane… and a phone number that I never called afterward."

He ducks, and I grunt as I'm hit with several packages of pretzels tossed at me as she walks past.

"Was it worth it?" he asks, amused.

I give it a moment's thought as I tear open one of the packages and dump the pretzels into my hand. A wide smile spreads across my face. "It was definitely worth it."

I try to get comfortable for the long overnight flight. I don't think there's any point in asking the stewardess for a pillow and blanket. I smile once again as I close my eyes and drift into sleep.

Olivia isn't at the hospital. I can't say I'm surprised that she doesn't answer my call. The woman is as stubborn as O'Connell. I head to the house Ethan is leasing and hope my unannounced arrival doesn't shock her into labour.

As I drive past the small town of Caledon, the hills of Dufferin County remind me of Ireland with green, lush, rolling hills, untouched and undisturbed by growing development needs. It's profound the universe has brought us all together again in a place so much like the home I remember in my dreams. I don't think it's a coincidence at all. Higher powers have been hard at work here.

I pull into the driveway and look at the house with the red door. I'm having an overwhelming and unpleasant déjà-vu. I'm annoyed when I turn the doorknob and find that she's left it unlocked. You'd think she would be more cautious with everything going on. The house is dark and cold. The empty birdcage stands in the corner of the living room. I pick up a familiar leather-bound book off the top of a partially packed box and stare at it for what seems like a very long time. It heightens my anxiety as if touching the soft, worn cover catapults me into the past, to a day I'd rather not relive.

I wander the empty rooms looking for her as my mouth becomes dry with my growing unease. I finally find her in an upstairs bedroom sleeping with a pillow pressed to her chest. I hate to wake her from what seems to be a peaceful sleep, but I need to know that she's okay.

I stand over her and pause for a moment, assessing her vulnerable situation. The sight of her stirs up feelings I thought had long since dissipated. I can't stand this feeling of obsession; the overwhelming need I have to protect her; nurture her; love her. It's a self-destructive path, and I need to find a way to get her out from under my skin.

"Olivia," I whisper so as not to startle her.

She opens her eyes and blinks them rapidly. "Carter?" she says sleepily. "What are you doing here?"

"Do you need to ask? I came to stay with you. You've got a lot of people worried right now."

I climb into bed in the spare room, dead-tired from my long travels and spending the last few hours defending my asshole friend's actions. I never thought, given the opportunity, I would champion his cause and try to convince Olivia not to give up on him. It took some doing to convince her he walked away because he doesn't feel there's any other option. Although I disagree with his decision, I know he's not thinking about himself or his needs, which alone proves how much he loves her.

I try to reach Kate a few more times before my eyes close, and I surrender to exhaustion. Being back in Dufferin County rouses dreams of faraway lands and other lives as if it's a mystical portal with a force too magnetic for me to fight.

I jolt out of a deep sleep and sit upright when she whispers my name from the doorway. "What's wrong?"

"I can't settle. Can I stay in here with you?"

I hesitate for obvious reasons as she moves to the side of the bed and waits. "Please?"

The moonlight shines through the window and illuminates her silhouette giving her an angelic spectral appearance. For the first time being around her doesn't give me those heightened feelings of angst and allegiance.

Feelings that I suddenly realize I've mistaken for love. I hold up the edge of the blanket so she can climb in beside me.

"Do you remember it?" she asks.

I'm acutely aware of the lack of space between us. "Remember what?"

"The farm, the old schoolhouse, the cottage by the river."

The mention of it causes my muscles to become rigid as the feelings of angst return. "I don't know what you're talking about," I deny.

"I don't believe you." She snuggles in against my chest, making me tenser. I try to relax as I wrap my arms around her in what I suppose is a gesture to soothe us both.

"I remember where I know those words from, she continues. "*So dear I love him that with him, all deaths I could endure. Without him, live no life.*"

All this time, I thought I alone had these memories. I place my lips on the top of her head. "It's from *Romeo and Juliet*."

"I was reading it before I walked into the ocean." She recalls.

"You left the book on the rocks, on the shore," I confirm.

"You pulled me out of the water."

"Yes," I admit, quietly, feeling a strange sense of anguish and despair as if I was reliving the moment right now.

"Why? I had nothing left. I couldn't bear to live without him."

"I couldn't bear to live without *you*. I loved you as much as my brother did." I take a deep calming breath. "I suppose I mean as much as *Ethan does*."

At this moment, we acknowledge our past with profound clarity. "How long have you been having the dreams?" she asks quietly.

"For quite some time. When I walked into the restaurant and saw you for the first time, I don't know how to explain it."

"You don't need to. You, me, Ethan, we've all experienced it."

"I thought I was losing my mind."

Olivia lets out a small laugh, understanding a little too well what I mean. "So, what do we do now?"

I think about it for a moment. "We try to save him this time."

She yawns, surrendering to her exhaustion. "Do you think it's possible to change our destiny?"

I remember the things the grey-haired lady said to me, and they suddenly make sense to me now. "I think we have to try. I mean, there's a reason we've been able to recall these memories, right? That's not something normal. I think it's a sign we're supposed to do something different this time."

She guides my arm down to her stomach, and I feel the baby press against my hand. I don't know what to call the emotions I'm experiencing right now. I do know, without a doubt, I want this for myself, but I want it with Kate.

"Carter?"

"Yes?"

"Can you take me to get the car tomorrow? There's something I need to do."

Her breathing slows, and her body softens as she closes her eyes and falls asleep. My mind wanders to thoughts of Kate. I need to see her, and if she doesn't answer her phone, I'll hunt her down and force her to hear me out.

Chapter Four

Kate

I'm avoiding my father since my lack of judgment a few days ago. He and I have had a rocky relationship since my mom passed a few years ago. It's not that I felt I spoke out of turn about my sister. She is the kind of bitch who would destroy others for personal gain. I just shouldn't have mentioned it in front of him. He's not a stupid man, so I'm sure I didn't expose some family secret.

I plan to lay low in the city and forego the Sunday dinners at the family's country home for a few weeks. I'll miss the countryside more than I'll miss my stepmother's overcooked roast and lumpy gravy. Luckily the family business has secured the penthouse of this historic Toronto landmark indefinitely. The intention was for it to be used by out-of-town and international clients, but I've made it my full-time residence since there have been none. I don't mind city life, but I find myself pining for some social distancing and fresh air after spending time here.

I scroll through my emails, occasionally clicking on a few alerts for jobs that might be a good fit. I don't know why I bother because every time someone requests an interview, I decline. I'm not sure if it's because I just haven't found the right career yet or if I'm afraid to tell my father that I'm leaving the family business.

I answer an incoming call.

"Where are you?" Dana asks.

"Working from the penthouse."

"Avoiding your father?"

"That's a definite yes."

"Well, you don't have to. He's not in for a few days. And your sister is leaving for Australia."

"What is she doing there?"

"Some new electronics supplier. What are you doing later?"

"I was going to walk over to the thrift store."

"Why?"

"I need a new purse."

"Buy a new one. There are stores all around you."

"I know, but I hate to spend the money on designer things. I'd rather buy something second-hand and keep it out of the landfill, and the proceeds go to a local charity in need of money. Why did you want to know what I'm doing?"

"I was thinking. I have a cousin. Well, he's a third cousin on my father's side. He's thirty-five."

"NO!"

"He's kind of cute, and he has no debt."

"Are those his best selling points?" I ask.

"Well, I think it's because he lives in his mother's basement."

"I'll pass."

"Kate, I know that you've been hurt in the past."

"Let it go, Dana," I warn.

"Okay, but you should know someone called the switchboard a little while ago looking for you."

"Oh?"

"Someone with an Australian accent."

"What did you tell him?"

"I told him you weren't in the office."

"Good."

"Because you're not in the office."

"Great, thanks."

"Kate."

"Dana."

"If he's calling you, he's thinking about you. Maybe you should suggest you learn more about your sister's side of the business. Tag along with her to Australia. Maybe he's worth getting to know better."

"I don't want to learn her side of the business."

"Why?"

"Because I'd hate it."

"You hate what you're doing now."

She's right. "Just continue to run defence, please."

"Okay, if you insist."

"I do."

I walk the few blocks to the thrift store and wander aimlessly up and down the aisles. I don't even remember why I came in here. Last night I had that dream again. It felt so real. There's a young girl in a faraway land many, many years ago. She stands at an altar in a small stone church with a bouquet of wildflowers wearing a dress that is tattered and worn. She waits for the love of her life. A groom that never shows. I feel her heartache like it's my own.

At times, when I think about Carter, I feel that heartache, as if he's responsible for her pain. Yet something draws me to his ocean blue eyes and chiselled jawline. It's a connection I can't explain. Feeling lost, I leave the store empty-handed.

With Carter still on my mind, I wander into my favourite pub in Toronto's entertainment district and sit at the bar. It's eerily quiet tonight; no sports games, no drunken frat boys playing pool, and not one single shot taken at the dartboard.

I've lost track of how many glasses of wine I've consumed when I begin to reminisce about girl's night and how my body reacted to him. I lower my brow and stare into my glass. "This is an excellent wine," I say to myself. "I can smell his cologne." I shrug and lift the glass to my lips, letting the crimson libation slide effortlessly down my throat.

As I set the empty glass down on the bar, I feel someone behind me. When his warm breath and smooth Australian tone reach my ear, fear turns to arousal.

"Now I know you swallow I'm wondering how long you can hold your breath."

"Carter," I whisper. I'm usually very reserved in my sexual preferences, but Carter makes me have a new appreciation for dirty talkers. As his body presses up against me, I fight hard to refrain from collapsing against his chest and breathing him in.

"Hello, Kate."

I pull myself together. "I didn't know you were going to be back in Toronto."

"You would have if you answered my calls."

He gives me that charming boyish smirk, and my heart flutters. This is not good. "Welcome back." I slide money across the bar to pay my tab and get to my feet.

"Leaving so soon? I just got here."

"That's why I'm leaving." My first step causes me to sway, and he reaches out to steady me.

"Let me call you a cab."

"Not necessary. I'm staying around the corner."

"Well, then let me walk you there."

"I'm fine," I insist as I shoulder past him and out onto the street. The chilly air is sobering, and I'm aware that Carter is following me. It's a short walk, but it gives me time to find the bravery to say all the things I've wanted to say to him since he stood me up for the second time. "I said I don't need you to walk me home."

"I'm not. It appears we're going in the same direction." He holds open the hotel door and grins as I squeeze past him.

Now I'm annoyed. He has a lot of nerve staying here. He knows my family leases the penthouse. "That's something new for you, isn't it?"

He tilts his head slightly and raises a brow curiously. "What?"

"Bringing conscious girls through that door."

His jaw clenches, so I know I've just struck a nerve. I'm glad.

While we wait for the elevator, he studies me silently, taking inventory from head to toe.

Once inside, I lean wearily against the wall opposite where he stands. He says nothing on the ride up. He stares at me silently with an unbelievably powerful presence. Me, I can't keep my big mouth shut. Damn wine. "So, how's your mother?"

He narrows his eyes and then acknowledges my concern. "She's doing much better now."

"Good. I'm glad to hear it." I suddenly feel awkward and fuzzy, and before I can stop myself, I blurt out the question I really want the answer to. "Why are you here?"

"Business," he answers without skipping a beat.

I nod, then look down, trying to conceal my disappointment. "Of course, why else would you come back?"

"You."

My head snaps upright, startled at his answer, and before I can react, he closes the space between us, and I find myself staring at his broad chest. He places one hand on the wall beside me, partially fencing me in. Not that I'd try to escape if I could. It feels like all the oxygen is being sucked out of the space. Or maybe I've just forgotten to breathe. "Me?"

"Mmhmm." He brings his hand to my hip and anchors me to the wall. My body comes alive. "I had to leave before I could do something I wanted to do," he continues.

I force my eyes away from his muscular chest. He licks his dry lips in preparation, and I feel my body pulse with desire and anticipation. "What's that?" I ask breathlessly as I lock onto his ravenous gaze.

A depraved grin curls on his lips as his hand slides up my body and over my throat, cupping my chin and preventing me from turning away. "This."

As he presses his lips against mine, the elevator becomes a time machine, slowing down between floors and making a few short seconds feel like forever. In those moments, a strange feeling of *dominion* wraps around us, tethering us together. It's almost as if the universe has been waiting for our reunion, and it's ensuring we remain aligned. When the elevator door opens, we've only shared an innocent exchange of breath, but it feels much more exhilarating.

With little effort, this man reduces me to a puddle with a single kiss. He extends out his hand as he steps off the elevator and stands before me so purely male, filling the doorway with his masculine lines. I lose sight of all rational thought as I take it and follow him to his door. By the time we get there, I've fought through the haze, and I'm in full-blown panic mode. What am I doing? What am I thinking? I've witnessed this man in questionable moral situations, and I know nothing about him. I build walls to keep out people I know well, and he's a stranger, maybe a serial killer for all I know. When he closes the door behind me, I suddenly have the urge to bolt.

Carter senses my change of heart and lifts my hand to his mouth, kisses it, then gently tugs on it, dragging me closer until my body presses against him. "I'm not going to hurt you," he whispers in his smooth Australian tone. "You can leave whenever you want. I've wanted you so bad since I had to leave. I hope you'll stay. You're in control."

His lips brush against mine in a gentle plea, making me experience intense feelings. Feelings I've been trying to ignore. When he pulls away, his urgent brooding expression summons my submissive soul. Want and desire race through my veins, granting him absolute authority. Clothes are tugged off with fierce need on the way to the bedroom. Carter lifts me with such passion he practically throws me on the bed and falls in on top of me. I grunt, and he repeatedly apologizes as he trails passionate kisses along my neck until he reaches my lips. He parts them with his nibbling and teasing.

His body presses against mine, skin on skin, and I feel every rugged ridge of muscle on his body as he grinds against me, heightening my excitement. Taking my nipple between his teeth, he gives it a hard nip, causing me to gasp and buck beneath him. He expertly guides himself between my thighs, as if he's used that move a thousand times. I don't even care at this point. I need him inside me. With one smooth thrust, he fulfills my desire and then some. Every stroke is masterfully orchestrated to push me over the edge. And it does, way too soon.

Carter lets out a small laugh, and I'm not sure if it's the noise I managed to squeak out at the highest point of passion or how quickly he got me there that he finds amusing. Supporting himself on muscular forearms, he picks up his rhythm and finishes round one. Lowering his body to rest on top of me, he brings his lips to mine. "Don't worry about the swift climax, kitten. I'm very good at what I do and believe me, we're nowhere near done." He nibbles across my throat and down my neck, heading south. "Let's see if I can get you to scream out my name this time. Or at least a full word."

"I make no promises." My body responds as he rubs his rough stubble on the sensitive skin of my thigh and then retraces his steps with his lips. When his hands part me, I wiggle and twitch and squirm beneath the teasing flick of his tongue.

A few hours later, he collapses, exhausted, beside me and tugs me into his arms. When his breathing becomes calm and shallow, he loosens his grip on me. I lay awake feeling conflicted. I have no idea when he's going back to Australia or if I'll ever see him again. Memories of a young girl stranded at the altar haunt me. I'm not a one-night stand kind of girl, and I'm usually not the kind of girl who sleeps with a stranger. Ugh, now I feel awkward and embarrassed.

I channel my sister and find the brass to slip gently out of his arms. On the way out of the bedroom, I gather my clothes and get dressed in the other room before taking the elevator to my penthouse.

I should be exhausted, but I lay awake for a long time. Life was undoubtedly uneventful before Carter Brant came back to town. One thing is for sure: whether I'm feeling happy, sad, angry, or aroused, I'm feeling something for the first time in years. I'm sure these heightened emotions and the inescapable chemistry have something to do with the dreams.

I wish my mom were still alive. I could talk to her about my irrational attraction to him. She'd know what to say. She'd tell me what to do. I've never been around someone who makes my self-control completely unravel when I'm around them. I can't keep him on the right side of the wall, and it's terrifying.

Sleep eludes me, so I get up and get ready for work. A brisk walk in the early morning air helps settle my thoughts. The city wakes early, so I grab a coffee and sit in my favourite spot on the lakeshore. The breeze off the lake is cool and crisp, but it won't stop me from staying to watch the sunrise over the water. Shortly after it crests the horizon, I see a ship in the distance. It appears to be moving very slowly through the water, but by the time I walk down to the lakeside, it approaches, and I watch as it smoothly docks at the Redpath refinery. I'm pleased that I got to experience it on a quiet, peaceful morning before the city traffic drowns out the sound of the wake and the churning of the engines as they reverse to slow down their approach.

Impulsive

Life in Toronto is busy, too busy sometimes. I wonder where this freightliner is coming from and where it's been. I miss the days when my family would fly to different ports around the world and take a cruise ship on an adventure. We used to travel a lot when Mom was alive. She and I would walk the beach looking for shells while Dad finished up a bit of last-minute business. Somehow, she could always tell which seashell came from which beach. She said each one was as unique as the place we found it. That's a skill I didn't inherit.

As I got older and Dad's business got more extensive, family vacations got fewer. I remember he would promise her that we would go next year until no more years were left. I don't recall seeing any of those shells in the home my father shares with his new wife. I don't see *any* memories of my mother there. I'm not angry that he moved on. I'm glad he's found someone, but now and then, I wish that he didn't forget about her. It feels like I've lost both parents.

Carter's number flashes across my phone. I can't. I just can't right now.

Chapter Five

Carter

Well, this is new. I've never woke alone after a night of passion. I walk through the suite, hoping to find her watching the local morning show or making breakfast. I dial her number, and I'm not surprised that she doesn't answer. I shoot her a text and ask her to call. I may have been a little direct in my message, but I'm not happy. There's a tight, uncomfortable feeling in the pit of my stomach when I realize for the first time, I'll be eating pancakes alone.

I get in the shower, but the pulsing heat of the water doesn't clear my thoughts like it usually does. Last night was like nothing I've ever experienced before. And that's saying a lot since I've had some incredible experiences with sexual partners. With Kate, there is something more. A connection. One that arguably began in another life. I'm not saying I believe in all this universal magic and psychic mumbo jumbo, but I must win Kate over to change my destiny if it's true. I'll do anything to make it happen.

"Good morning," I give the girl at the front desk my most alluring smile.

"Good morning, Mr. Brant." She smiles.

"Have you seen Miss Ryan this morning?"

"Yes, sir, she left for the office very early today."

"That's a shame. I was hoping to take her for breakfast."

"Maybe tomorrow, sir." She breathes in my cologne, and a slight blush reddens her cheeks.

I nod, somewhat amused, before turning to leave. "Yes, maybe tomorrow."

She smiles at me. "She will likely be back sometime this evening. I can leave a message here at the desk for her."

"No, that's okay. I'll catch up with her later. Thank you."

I'm halfway to my rental car when I decide to walk the several blocks to the Canadian office. I walk past my car and begin toward the underground ramp that leads to the street when I hear a strange shuffling sound behind me. I look over my shoulder, my eyes straining to see the source in the darkness. If my eyes aren't playing tricks on me, I think I see the silver-hair woman who jumped out of the bushes a while back and scared the fuck out of me. I hesitate, tempted to turn around and confront her. The honking of an approaching car makes me jump, and as it passes, I quickly jog the remaining few steps through the open garage door and onto the street. The sunlight momentarily blinds me, and I wait for my eyes to adjust before walking. A few blocks away, I pause and peer through the large window of the breakfast restaurant where I first saw Kate. I stretch my neck, looking for her around the people who are seated. I walk the rest of the way to the office in a haze.

"Hellooo? Carter?" Scott says as he walks into my temporary office and finds me staring out the window.

"Huh?"

"Where's your mind at?"

I turn to look at him, lost for words.

"Oh, man," Scott says, concerned. "Is Olivia okay?"

"Yes, she's fine. I need to pack up Ethan's stuff over the next few days and get rid of it. She's planning on going to her place, so I'll take her stuff there."

"It's messed up. Her ex-boyfriend has been arrested."

I feel rage pulse through my body. "Ethan should be here with her when she goes to court."

"He's not rational," Scott agrees.

"Oh, I think he's too rational. He knows he'll add to her stress level. That anxiety is toxic to the baby. In his mind, he's doing the right thing."

"Well, there's no arguing he's wrong. I tried."

"We all have," I say, frustrated. "How was Finland?"

"We managed to squeeze in some time to do some site-seeing before we came home."

I nod. "I've gotta say, I'm shocked you went."

"So am I." He pauses, looking uncomfortable. "It wasn't an easy decision."

"One you shouldn't have made without telling Ethan."

"Don't judge me, Brant. Even before he was suspended, Ethan was burning bridges with Hammond's nephew. I need my job."

"Fair enough, but Ethan found out from John that you went, and that was bullshit. We owe him more."

"I don't think he's ever coming back to Aurora."

"You think they'll let him go for a few bumps in the road in his personal life?"

Scott raises a brow.

"Okay, major bumps, but he was still performing and fulfilling his corporate obligations."

He sighs and scratches the back of his neck. "Was he?"

"Fuck, you're right. I don't even believe that."

"I'm not going to lie. Jean-Pierre is a dick."

I nod, feeling agitated. "I know, but he's an intelligent one, and that makes him dangerous."

"I can't stand working for him."

"Me neither, mate. It's not the same working here without Ethan being in charge. I can't imagine working anywhere else right now."

"What are Ethan's plans?"

"I dunno." I shrug. "I thought maybe he'd take over the family business so his father can retire, but John says there's so much tension between the two of them right now it's not likely going to happen." My eyes feel heavy, and I twist my neck, trying to work out a few kinks.

"Are you okay?" Scott asks, looking concerned.

"Yeah, I didn't sleep much last night."

"Everything okay with you and Kate?"

"I don't know. I woke up this morning, and she was gone. She's not returning my calls."

Scott fights off his amusement.

"Hey, I know you think that the shoe is finally on the other foot, but I have never left anyone in the middle of the night," I say defensively.

"That's not why I'm smiling. You're in love."

He walks out the door before I can respond. This doesn't feel like love. Love, I thought, is warm and joyful and uplifting. My heart is heavy and aching.

I can't concentrate on business, so I might as well go back to my hotel.

"Carter."

The sound of his obnoxious French accent is like fingernails on a chalkboard.

"Jean-Pierre."

"How is Australia doing with the new strategic plan? Are we going to hit those new targets?"

"It's going to be tough, but we're progressing."

"Would they progress more successfully if you were in Australia? Why are you here?"

I feel my shoulders stiffen. "I'm here on personal business."

"Personal business for Ethan O'Connell?"

"I'd tell you, but it's *personal.*"

There's a tense pause while he stares me down, trying to intimidate me. "Go home to Australia, Brant. You're needed there. It won't go well if you miss those targets."

"Is that a threat?"

He gives me a cocky half-grin as he turns to leave. "No threat, just a reminder from your boss about contractual obligations."

"*Acting* boss, and I'm pretty sure I didn't sign any contract or agreement that allows for you to change our sales targets midway through the year."

"I guess we'll have to let legal sort that out."

"I guess we will." I shoulder past him, afraid that if I stay another single minute, good ole J.P. will experience the side of my anger that I usually work out in the boxing ring.

"Carter," he calls out as I walk away. "Check your emails. I've asked my secretary to book you a flight, so you'll be home by the end of next week. Whatever personal business you have to tend to, make sure you have it done by then."

So many thoughts are swirling around in my head that I pace in the elevator like a caged animal. When the doors open to the lobby, I hightail it out of there and head for the lakeshore. At home, in Australia, if I had things on my mind, I'd walk along the crystal white sand and throw my board into the surf. Lake Ontario is beautiful, but it doesn't compare to the ocean off the Sunshine Coast. I feel both homesick and lovesick. How the mighty have fallen.

Needing a rest, I sit on a bench not far from the Redpath sugar refinery and try to work out a plan. It's no coincidence I've walked this way; Kate's office is only a few blocks away. Stalking her and forcing myself on her feels like something O'Connell would do, so I need to squash the urge to hunt her down and explain. Instead, I stop at the corner flower shop on my way home and buy a beautiful bouquet of carnations and pink roses, the same as the bouquet I left for her the last time. I'm hoping to deliver this one in person.

I wish I had taken a different way home. Eva sits out front of her shop and watches as I approach. I try to avoid eye contact, but her gaze is magnetic. I glance in her direction, expecting some freaky speech about the universe. Instead, she smiles and nods. It unnerves me more than the mumbo jumbo she tried to feed me the first time our paths crossed.

All this walking and thinking has made me thirsty. I stop at the bar for a drink. I was hoping that Kate might be here, but I make short work of a few shots and pay my bill since she's not. On my way out, I'm sure I hear Stacey's voice, so I *'mission impossible'* myself toward the door.

"Carter Brant!"

I grit my teeth. The sound of her voice grates on me like fingernails on a chalkboard. I slowly turn as she approaches with a rather flashy-looking man at her side.

"Hello, Stacey." I nod at the guy with her, but neither initiates an introduction.

"Why didn't you message me and let me know you were in town?"

"It was a last-minute trip." She can tell I'm lying. The bouquet I'm clutching is a dead giveaway.

"Well, now that you're here, let's have a few drinks."

She reaches for my arm, and the guy beside her clears his throat. "We're on a date."

"Sorry, mate." I pull my arm out of Stacey's grip. "I have somewhere to be. I'll be sure to let you know next time I'm in town."

"Nonsense," she insists. "I'm only here with him because I need a good pounding. Now you're here I don't need him."

I stare at her open-mouthed as a range of different emotions flashes across her date's face. "I still need to be somewhere."

"Disappointing," she says as she takes the arm of her date and turns him back toward the bar. "You were one of the best fuck's I've ever had. Call me after you're finished with whoever the flowers are for."

I shake my head, coming to grips with what she just said and the fact this went down in front of someone she's currently on a date with. He glances over his shoulder as he walks away, strutting as if he's just won the prize. "Good luck to ya, mate," I say as I push open the heavy wooden door to the street.

It's not easy for me to settle the alpha within me and push aside the urges to demand Kate fall in line. I'm confident she would, based on her responses to me last night.

The sweet young girl isn't at the front desk tonight. In her place is a grumpy-looking dude, and I'm pretty sure I could try, but I doubt I can charm him into breaking the rules for me.

"Hi," I strain to see his name tag. "Gary. Have you seen Miss Ryan tonight?"

"No, sir. I haven't."

I hold the bouquet up. "I don't suppose you could give me a pass key to the penthouse so I could deliver these to her in person, could you?"

He looks up from his computer. "No, Mr. Brant. I can't do that."

I frown. "Can you give a guy a break here? I want to surprise her."

"No, sir."

"Okay, Gary. How about I park my ass in the middle of the lobby until she comes down?"

"Don't make me call security, sir."

"Fine." I grab a pen and fold a hotel pamphlet in half. "Can I at least leave them here for her with a note?"

"Yes, of course."

"Thanks, Gary. You're a pal," I say sarcastically.

I wait for the elevator feeling frustrated. As the door opens, my heart begins to beat with a renewed enthusiasm as a familiar fragrance surrounds me. She's been here and quite recently. My eyes grow heavy.

Suddenly I'm standing on the outside of the ornate wooden door of the country church. There is no one inside except the minister and his wife, and of course, Lily. She has lost her family to the famine, and my parents are home, mourning the loss of their eldest son. I decided earlier in the day I would marry the love of my life and take care of her even though I don't have their blessing.

Now that I'm here, I didn't expect to have a change of heart. My father strongly believes it's my duty to support my late brother's bride and raise his soon-to-be-born child. I was gutted to see Liz so broken at the loss that she felt she would have no life without him. This decision weighs heavily on me, but the responsibility falls on me as my father has demanded.

Lily is a brave and strong soul who will survive without a man to provide for her. I take the coward's way out, turning to leave without any explanation. I know she'll be heartbroken for a while, but she'll be fine.

The elevator door opens at the same time as my eyes. I pray that there are no more past-life flashbacks tonight. I'm exhausted, and I need to get some sleep. Thanks to an overbearing asshole of a boss, if I'm going to change my destiny, I only have a few more days to do it.

Chapter Six

Kate

I yawn, trying to keep myself awake. Sneaking out of the hotel at dawn is killing me. I hope by now he's moved on, or at least gone home to Australia. Avoiding him for two days has been more work than I'd like, and it's only a matter of time before we run into each other coming and going.

I stare at the beautiful flowers he left me. The sweet, subtle fragrance accompanied me all the way to work. Who am I kidding? The man is under my skin.

Dana, the receptionist, sticks her head in the doorway of my office. "Kate, your father wants to see you."

"Tell him I'm on a call."

She raises her brow. "Are you asking me to lie to your father for you?"

I pick up my phone and hold it to my ear. "It's not a lie."

She gives me a half-grin. "He's in his office. Your sister just left."

I look out the window at the brilliantly clear and sunny day. "That's odd."

"Katherine, your sister isn't an ancient mythological demon that eats children and brings on bad weather," she insists.

I get to my feet and straighten my skirt. "That's what she wants you to believe." I pick up my phone and round the edge of my desk.

"Try not to upset him today," Dana pleads as she walks with me down the hallway. "He always takes it out on the rest of us when you piss him off."

"I will do my best."

"Your best NOT to upset him, right?"

I pause, making her uncomfortable.

"KATE!"

"YES, of course."

I knock before pushing his office door open and peek in to find him standing at the window staring out onto Lake Ontario.

"There's a file on my desk," he says without turning to look at me.

I flip open the file and quickly skim through some of the documents.

"It's the project I want you to oversee." I glance up to see him watching me in the reflection of the window. I read the second paragraph on page three, and my brow raises. What I read next only adds to my anger.

"They want to tear down the Redpath sugar refinery on the lakeshore?"

He finally turns to look at me directly. "Yes."

"To put up more condos?"

"It's a great business opportunity."

"It's an iconic structure, Dad."

"It's an eyesore."

"Have you ever gone to the shoreline and sat in the chairs they put there and watch the ships come in with the raw materials?"

He furrows his brow. "Why would I want to do that?"

For a moment, I forgot who I was talking with. "I suppose you've never been to the museum either. The entire history of the founder's journey is there."

"No, but you obviously have," he says, growing impatient with me.

"We don't need new condos. We need to continue to honour the Redpath family and how they contribute to our economy. Over forty-eight percent of the sugar in Canada is refined there."

"They'll make it somewhere else going forward. Look, Katherine, I understand why you're upset, but the Redpath company is entertaining offers on the land. Condos will be built there, if not by us, by somebody else."

His indifference infuriates me. "What if I don't want any part of it?"

He walks back to his desk, picks up a few more files, and passes them to me. "Your sister is working on a different project right now. I need you on this."

I bite my tongue and lower my eyes from his as I reach out for the files. My jaws clench tightly as I consider all the things I'd like to say. Instead, I frown as I take possession of them and walk away.

"Katherine."

I stop and turn to meet his censure. "You haven't been to the house for dinner."

"I've been busy."

"I'll expect to see you tomorrow."

I search for an excuse, but before I can speak, he cuts to the chase. "I'm not asking."

I nod, feeling like a small child. "Yes, sir."

Dana catches up with me at the elevator and sneaks in before the door closes.

"Is everything okay? It seemed pretty quiet down there."

"That's because you couldn't hear my silent screams."

"He's forcing you to take on that new project, isn't he?"

I glower.

"I had a feeling you wouldn't like this project, but you'll do a fantastic job on it.

"Seems I don't have a choice."

We step out of the elevator into the bright glass ceiling foyer of the modern waterfront building. "Do you want me to call you an Uber?"

"No, I need to walk and think some things through."

She walks with me. "Is one of those things named Carter Brant? Why didn't you tell me he was back in town?"

My head snaps to the side, and my expression makes her laugh aloud once. "I'm still avoiding his calls."

"I assumed since he's called the switchboard looking for you. Several times."

I lower my head and sigh as I try to rub the tension out of my neck. She stops at the door and turns to face me.

Did you know he works at Aurora Technologies?"

"Yes."

"Did you know your sister is currently partnered with them on a technology project?"

"Yes."

"Katherine, please tell me that you're not giving this guy the brush-off."

"I don't know. Maybe."

"Are you kidding? That Australian accent would make any woman's panties wet. What's wrong with you?"

"I don't know. There's just something that feels a little *off*. I can't put my finger on it."

She raises her brow. "I stalked him on his social media. Please promise me that if you ever get the chance, you'll put more than a finger on it. Use your whole hand…maybe your mouth."

My jaw drops in horror. "Dana!"

"Oh hell," she continues, "Just jump right on top of that thing, and…."

I hold my hands in the air and walk away, escaping into the revolving door and out onto the busy street. I'm drawn in a different direction than I usually walk and find myself not too far away from the Aurora Technologies building. I cross the road quickly and hope that I don't run into Carter. Or worse, my sister.

A few city blocks away, I'm drawn to an old shop hidden away between two modern skyscrapers. "Eva Storm - Psychic. Palm & Tarot Card Readings." The red door and historical architecture lure me in. I push the door open and find myself overwhelmed with the layers of spiritual artifacts and healing gemstones on display.

"You've found me," a frail voice whispers from behind a mystical-looking talisman.

My eyes adjust to the dim light. "Do I know you?" I feel my body tense as she steps out into the open. "I saw you at the lakefront."

She nods and tries to hide a soft smile.

"Oh, but I wasn't trying to find you," I assure her.

"Many are drawn to my shop. It's no coincidence. The universe brings you here. My name is Eva."

She walks toward the back of the shop, and despite my better judgement, I follow. "The universe brought me here?"

She nods and motions for me to sit at a small round table surrounded by candles and a deck of tarot cards in the centre.

"Shuffle and cut the deck."

I hesitate, and she reaches across the table and touches my arm. "Most refuse to believe at first. Soon, everything will become clear."

Curiosity keeps me sitting in the chair. A feral-looking black cat saunters across a countertop knocking things to the ground and adding to the ominous atmosphere as I reach for the deck and do as she asks.

"Cut them into three piles," she instructs, "Then draw cards."

I pull random cards from the deck and slide them in front of her as a heavy feeling washes over me. When I'm done, she deals them into a sequence in front of her. I've never had a reading before, so I'm skeptical, but she wasn't wrong when she said I was drawn here.

"You struggle in relationships with men, yes?"

"I guess so."

"Men often pursue you, but you chose not to have relationships with any of them."

"Correct," I say impatiently, wondering where this is going.

"Why do you think you didn't trust them?"

I feel my pulse quicken. Eva slowly pushes a card toward me. The hero.

"It's because of this guy," she answers in a voice that gives a hint to her age.

"Who is he? My father? My first love?"

She turns over a few extra cards and studies them, leaving me hanging for an uncomfortable amount of time.

"You've only just met him in this life. But in a past life, you knew him very well." She raises her head and locks eyes with me. "You've had dreams."

At that moment, I know exactly who she's talking about. "Everyone dreams," I add, trying to hide my discomfort.

"Not like these. Another time, another place. So real that the emotions stay with you when you wake."

"How do you know that?" I ask, feeling emotionally called out.

"I've heard it before. Many who experience past-life memories seek me out."

"How do I stop them? Exorcism?"

She simpers. "No, child. You face them. Learn from them."

I think about the number of times Carter has already let me down and the disturbing enslavement that Olivia James seems to have on him. I slide the card of the hero across the table toward her. "If this man disappointed me in another life, why is he a 'hero'? And why would I trust him now?"

"He had no choice, in another life. His destiny followed a different path."

"And I'm supposed to believe that won't be true in this life?"

"He wants to change his destiny."

Now I'm skeptical. "If there's such a thing as destiny, how can it be changed? That makes no sense to me."

"All beings have free will. Free will changes our written paths. If you want your future life to be different, then you must make different choices. If you feel love for this man, fight your instincts and trust him."

I startle her when I get to my feet quickly, taking the tablecloth with me. The cards spill to the floor, and I give her an apologetic look as I bend down to pick them up. She crouches beside me, reaching for the ones that strayed from the pile. Her hand brushes mine, and I feel a connection that I can't entirely explain. At that moment, past life memories I thought were dreams flash before my eyes.

"It's time for you to believe that you deserve his love. He's willing to give it to you. He needs you as much as you need him."

As the visions fade, I feel my chest fill with breath as I try to make sense of what's happening to me. I help Eva to her feet and experience an awkward moment as I stumble on my words. "How much do I owe you?"

"Nothing. The road is laid before you. Just take a different path."

I don't even know how I make my way back to the hotel. The several blocks I walked are a complete blur. I get into the elevator and stand there without pushing the button. The door closes, and despite my attempt to press the penthouse floor button, I'm too late, and the elevator goes down to the basement.

I don't need to wait for the doors to open for confirmation. I know who's waiting on the other side. The hair on the back of my neck is standing on end. I look down as the doors begin to open, hoping I'm wrong.

He steps into the elevator and says nothing. The silence is too much, and when I finally find the nerve to look up, he's leaning against the elevator wall staring at me.

"I've missed you. I've looked for you at the lakefront, the corner restaurant, and the bar."

I can't speak. My voice has betrayed me.

"Why are you avoiding me, Kate?"

I look away, unable to answer. When the elevator opens on his floor, I hold my breath waiting for him to leave and end this torture. He turns to go, and I tilt my head back against the elevator wall as he disappears out of sight. I feel a slight jolt, and his wristwatch and school ring come into view as his hand wraps around the edge of the door pushing it back open. Carter steps back in the doorway, stopping it from closing.

"You didn't think I was going to let you go, did you?" He looks at me with a wicked grin so intense I feel like I'm going to pass out.

Before I have a chance to reconsider my actions, I exit and follow him down the hall. What am I doing? I think I've completely lost my mind. He unlocks the door, and my body tenses at the memory of my last visit here.

Once inside, Carter brushes the hair out of my eyes and takes my briefcase out of my hand. "Relax," he says as he guides me into the living area. "I only want to talk. Although it occurred to me that I should put you over my knee and deal with your behaviour."

Chapter Seven

Carter

I pour two glasses of red wine and hand her one. Her hand slightly trembles as she takes it from me, and I'm perplexed by her peculiar behaviour. "Are you afraid of me?"

"No."

"Then you're excited at the thought of a thorough spanking."

"No," she says before taking a few large gulps of her wine. "What did you want to talk about?" she asks as she puts her near-empty glass on the table.

"Let's start with why you left."

Her face turns red.

"Do you think that's acceptable behaviour?"

"No," she agrees.

"Was I just a one-night stand?"

"What?" she bursts into laughter.

"What's so funny?"

"You've bailed on me more than once, and you think that I used YOU for a one-night stand?"

"I've never had a woman sneak out in the middle of the night."

"Is that why you're stalking me? Your delicate ego is hurt?"

I fight hard not to escalate things. Her beauty is enthralling. Her body is intoxicating, but her mind is what keeps me coming back for more. She may have shown me her submissive side, but the bedroom is the only place she's going to let me have control. "You might find this hard to believe, but I *like* you. I want to get to know you, spend time with you. So, be honest with me right now. Why did you leave?"

She finishes her wine in one last mouthful. "I felt…unsure."

"Unsure?"

"Yes."

I sit down across from her and fold my arms. "Please…elaborate."

"I wasn't sure if you wanted me to stay. I thought maybe *I* was the one-night stand."

"Why would you think that?"

"You seem like a player."

My chin drops, and I have a moment of morality that prevents me from denying my past. "I've outgrown that phase of my life."

She scowls. "Tell me the truth about why you're back in Toronto."

"I told you. Business."

"Aurora Technology business?"

When I hesitate, she tilts her head and stares at me as if she can see straight through me.

"Let me explain."

"I knew it!" She gets to her feet and moves to leave.

"Wait! Give me a few more minutes, and I'll tell you everything." I reach for her arm and stall her with a firm grip. "Have you ever had dreams that you can't explain?" I blurt out desperately. Her stiff and rigid stance softens, and I turn her to face me. "I have. I think you have as well."

"Mine are more like nightmares," she says, growing emotional.

"Can we start over? Let me explain who she is and why I'm here."

"I know who she is. Olivia James."

"My Boss's wife." I take Kate's hand and lead her to the other room. "She's pregnant with his child." The nervous energy in her shoulders dissipates, and she closes her eyes briefly.

"So why are *you* here?" she asks in a softer, more accepting tone.

"Well, you're going to think I'm crazy. Lord knows I think I am sometimes. A past life somehow binds together Ethan, Olivia, and me." Her apathetic response to that statement makes me nervous. "I know it sounds crazy; it sounds crazy to me. There's the old silver hair lady who claims she knows stuff, and she keeps jumping out of the bushes and giving me cryptic messages about my future and my destiny," I ramble.

Her eyes open wide while she gives me her full attention. "Why are you telling me this?"

I sit on the coffee table in front of her and take her hands in mine. "Ethan and Olivia are soulmates, destined to find each other in every life."

"So why then are you consumed with their relationship?"

I carefully choose my words. "Nearest I can figure, I made a promise in a past life."

"You're right. It sounds crazy."

I'm losing her, and I panic. "Olivia is in a high-risk pregnancy and nearly lost the baby with all the stress that being in a relationship with Ethan causes. That's why he's left her. On top of it all, she has an abusive ex-boyfriend who just broke into her home, trashed things, and left a threatening note. She's in danger, and since my boss is an asshole, here I am."

"So, you don't have feelings for Olivia?"

I scratch my brow. There's no point in trying to deceive her. She can see right through my bullshit. "It's hard to explain because even I get confused. It's not love in the way Ethan feels love for her. I thought it was at first, but I was wrong."

She lowers her eyes, and I lift her chin with my finger and stare into the sapphire blue. "It was you that I thought of every day after I went home to Australia. Not Olivia. YOU. I'm drawn to you; I feel connected to you."

I pause, expecting her to walk out and never look back. I wouldn't blame her if she did. I squeeze her hands, and she closes her eyes, seemingly trying to come to terms with something. When her lashes flicker open, a renewed spark in her eyes puts my soul at ease.

"Can we order something? I'm starving."

I lift her hand to my lips and place a gentle kiss there. "We can order anything you'd like if it means you'll stay here with me a little longer."

She nods. "I think we still have a lot to learn about each other. I want to know who you are when you're not carrying half-conscious women into elevators."

I shake my head as I begin to grin. "You're never going to let that go, are you?"

She purses her lips. "Not likely."

"Fair enough. I like the idea of getting to know you better."

"I want to know about you in this life," she adds. "I have a lot of questions."

"Let's start right now."

"Like a relationship resumé?"

"Sounds a bit cold, doesn't it?" I rack my brains for something more subtle. "How about we just start by telling each other about our day. The other can ask questions, and we'll go from there."

"Okay, I like that idea."

"Good, I'll start. How was your day, Kate? Did anything exciting happen?"

"Well, I got up at an ungodly hour to avoid a stalker on the way to work."

I love her spunk. "I believe my company has had some business dealings with your family business." I pause and squint, trying to jar my memory. "But I seem to remember you telling me you were here temporarily working on a project. Toronto is home for you, I've come to discover."

"Oh," she says, embarrassed. "Well, that's the standard line to discourage men from thinking there's any chance for a relationship."

Clever, really, but I wonder what else she's not truthful about. "How is it our companies have a technology deal when you do projects with real estate?"

"My father has his fingers in a lot of things. Diversity, in case of disaster within any of the industries," she says. "I'm the senior vice-president of land development."

"You seem less than thrilled with that accomplishment."

She sighs. "I'm having some moral dilemmas with a current project."

"Such as?"

"My father wants me to put together a proposal and work with the town to tear down a historical icon and build condos."

"And what's the dilemma?"

She raises her brow and gives me a look. "I don't want to."

I laugh once. "Oh, okay, well, that is a dilemma."

"What about you? How was your day?"

"Well, my acting boss is a douche canoe. I hate working for him. I suspect he intends to push out those of us who are loyal to Ethan by setting impossible targets."

"What will you do if you're forced to leave there?"

I hadn't thought about it. "I only know how to close sales. I've never thought about doing anything else."

"Have you ever thought about being a full-time stalker?" she asks with a ballsy grin.

"Apparently, Dana can't keep a secret."

"Dana is the president of the Carter Brant Fanclub."

"And you?" I ask, feeling hopeful. "Are you becoming a fan?"

She holds her glass out for a refill. "I haven't decided yet. But the wine is helping to win me over."

I'm amused as she kicks off her shoes and gets comfortable. I follow suit, sitting beside her and stretching out. "Tell me…What's his name?"

"Who?"

"The guy who broke your heart and forced you to build up walls to protect yourself."

"How do you know there was one?"

"There's always a guy."

She tenses, and I study her movements as she tangles and twists her fingers together nervously. "Did he hurt you?" I ask, concerned about her behaviour change.

"No." A long and awkward pause takes place. "Not physically."

"But he broke your heart." I consider that it could be past life me that's the source of her mistrust of men, and I'm just about to abandon the line of questioning when she speaks up.

"His name was Roger. He was my high school sweetheart. I hardly knew what love was back then, but I suppose he was my first love."

I gently stroke my hand on her knee, strangely relieved. "What happened?"

"I don't know."

"How do you not know?"

"Why are you asking these questions?"

"I'm trying to understand the walls you've put up."

The wine is starting to affect her, and she fights the tears, trying to regain her composure. I feel like shit for upsetting her. "You know what, it's not important. Let's talk about something else."

She relaxes against me, feeling unburdened. "Roger and I were best friends. We spent all our time together. One night we were alone in the house, watching a movie, and one thing leads to another and…." She pauses and swallows hard.

"You slept with him that night."

"Yes."

"Your first time?"

"Yes." Talking about it has stirred in her overwhelming feelings of vulnerability. "Afterwards," she continues, "he lay beside me on the bed, and he wouldn't talk to me or touch me. I didn't know what I did wrong. Then he got up and got dressed and asked me to leave." Her voice quivers, and I feel gutted. I move closer, pulling her in and holding her against me.

"I never heard from him again. He stopped taking my calls and started avoiding me at school."

I'm stunned. "You never heard from him again?"

"Nope. I still don't know what I did wrong."

"That's a dick thing to do to someone," I say as I place a gentle kiss on the top of her head.

"He was a seventeen-year-old boy." She says, defending him as she fills her glass for the fourth time.

"I can tell you as a former teenage boy that if that was his reaction after making love to a beautiful girl like yourself, he was gay."

"WHAT?" she asks, opening her eyes wide.

"Yeah, he didn't know it until that minute."

"Oh, do you think?"

I chuckle. "Trust me…I know. I bet if you looked him up today, you'd see I'm right. But even so, you deserved better than that your first time."

"All these years, I thought I'd done something wrong." She lifts her glass, and it's clear that she's feeling the alcohol. "You might want to slow down."

"Pffft, I'm fine."

"I don't think so. I don't want to take any chance that you won't remember everything we talk about in the morning." She giggles as I try to take the glass out of her hand. The liquid sloshes from one side to the other. "Kate," I warn as she tips to the side and doesn't recover. I sigh as the entire glass empties all over her.

"Oops," she says, looking embarrassed. "I better go clean myself up."

"Good idea. I'll clean up out here."

I reach for her as she gets to her feet and sways. "Do you need help?"

She waggles her finger at me and disappears down the hall bumping into walls.

As I clean the wine off the floor, my phone lights up.

Stacey: Are you busy tonight?

The girl has bigger balls than O'Connell. I delete the message and toss my phone on the table as Kate returns wearing nothing but one of my T-shirts. She wriggles beside me, making herself comfortable and leaning against me. "What about you?" she asks, yawning. "Have you ever been in love?"

My body tenses knowing that Conor McGregor's face is the only thing separating me and the most beautiful curves this side of Ireland. Her body goes lax against me, and she's sound asleep before I can answer. Under normal circumstances, if a naked woman sat down beside me, sex would follow. But I haven't slept much in the past two days, and having her here with me creates quietude. I close my eyes.

At four A.M., I gently relocate Kate off my shoulder and reach for my ringing phone.

"Ethan?" I whisper as I move into the hallway. "Do you know what time it is, mate?"

"It's nine A.M."

"Only in your time zone, you thoughtless jackass."

"Sorry, I just wanted you to know that a court date has been set to sentence the scum of the earth, and Olivia insists on attending."

"Listen, she needs you. You need to be here for that."

"I can't."

"Yes, you can. Stop being a prick and show up."

"It's best this way. I can't see her, Carter. It will gut me."

I rake my fingers through my hair and pace. "Fine, I'll be there, but I have my own life to live, so at some point, you're going to have to figure this shit out."

"I just sent you the court details by email. Please take care of her."

The lines goes dead. It's a classic O'Connell move when he doesn't want to hear the truth. I return to the sitting area and clear away the pizza box and empty bottles of wine. Kate looks like an angel still sleeping where I left her, barely clothed. I carefully lift her in my arms and carry her to the bedroom. She opens her eyes and smiles as I lay her down and cover her with the blanket. When I crawl in beside her, she rolls toward me and rests against my chest, safely tucking her head beneath my chin. "Don't leave this time," I whisper. "You're so soft and warm, and I like how you feel in my arms. I want to wake up with you in them." I feel at peace and quickly drift back to sleep.

Chapter Eight

Kate

"What time is it?" I ask sleepily.

Carter lifts his head to look at his phone. "Almost two."

"P.M.?"

He chuckles. "Yes, it was a late night."

I lift the blankets and look beneath them. "When did I put on your T-shirt?"

"Right after you dumped a glass of wine on yourself."

I hold my hand on my throbbing forehead. "How many bottles of wine did we drink?"

"*You* drank a few." He rolls to his side and stares at me as if I'm the Mona Lisa and the Louvre is about to close.

"What are you doing?" I ask, growing self-conscious.

"Feeling thankful that you've given me another chance." He reaches out and caresses his hand along my side, stopping at my hip. "And appreciating every moment of having you here."

In one swift move, he pulls the T-shirt over my head and discards it on the floor. I'm no longer thinking about my hangover.

He brushes his hand across my cheek, and I close my eyes, burning into my memory the endearing nature of his touch.

My arms wrap around him, pulling him closer, anchoring him to my body. Hands grip flesh with a desperate need to get closer. Chests heave with excited breath. Tangled bodies roll across the bed, switching our positions with a heated passion. As my mouth crashes into his, he parts his lips, stoking the fire inside me. Then things take an interesting turn. Rough, impassioned physical contact slows to a doting appreciation of our bodies.

Carter's strong hands gently caress my skin, and his lips follow their path. Every moan, every appreciative sound, encourages him further, and when I part my thighs, giving him access, he makes me purr. I'm sure he feels a grand sense of pride in his skill when he brings me to the edge, and I scream out in pleasure, then go limp. That should keep his ego full for at least the rest of the day.

Startled, I sit straight up, forcing Carter to move out of the way quickly.

"What's wrong?" he asks, concerned as I pull the T-shirt back over my head.

"I'm supposed to attend family dinner tonight. At my father's place, in the country."

"Country?"

I ramble, feeling panicked. "They consider it country since it's more than an hour north of Toronto. I don't want to go, but my presence has been demanded. It's usually on Sunday, but my sister, step-sister actually, is leaving on a business trip to meet with an electronics supplier in China."

Carter leans on his elbow, resting his head in his hand. "Beautiful place. Have you ever been?"

I jump to my feet and dart around the room, gathering my things. "No, I leave the world travel and high-pressure negotiations to her."

"Well, then. We'll have to make a point in seeing the world just for pleasure. Especially Australia. I want to show you around home."

"I'd like that."

"I better get going. I have to shower and see if I can rent a car."

Carter shakes his head, trying to follow. "Wait, where's your car?"

"I took the insurance off it and parked it. I don't need it living in the city."

With all my discarded clothing in my hand, I rush to the door. Carter follows. "I have to go." I lean down and hook my fingers through the ankle straps of my heels before I reach for the door handle. He leans back against the wall, amused. "Kate."

"What?" I ask abruptly.

"If you're heading up to the penthouse, you might want to put pants on."

I look down at my bare legs and curse. I step into my dress and pull it up over his T-shirt. Carter steps up behind me and zips it while placing butterfly kisses across my neck.

"Why are you so worked up about a family dinner?"

"You don't know my family."

He untucks my hair from the back of the dress. "Good point, I'll come with you."

I almost knock him over, pivoting where I stand. "No, no and absolutely, NO!"

"Great, I'll drive. Give me twenty minutes to shower and get dressed."

I can't believe I caved in. I say very little in the car. It didn't take me long to figure out that when Carter makes up his mind to do something, there's little that can deter him. Another thing we have in common.

Carter follows the directions that I entered into the navigation system and glances at me periodically. "You never told me why you're so worked up."

"I try to avoid my family one on one, if possible. Having them all in one room is normally a disaster."

"How so?"

"My dad's current wife came with a few adult children. They fit in well with the family business. My step-sister is ruthless. She is capable of doing anything and everything to close a deal. Let's say her tactics go in the opposite direction of my moral compass. Despite efforts to keep the boardroom separate from the dining room, things always come around to how Kate is the sensitive one and why isn't Kate more aggressively closing deals and contributing to the family business. Sometimes I feel like my dad wishes *she* was his real daughter."

He lays his hand on my knee and gives it a gentle squeeze.

"I feel uncomfortable with putting you through that, Carter. Maybe you could drop me off, and I'll send for a car later."

"Not a chance. I've survived several family meals with the O'Connell family; yours couldn't be worse. Besides, you already told them I was coming." He parks beside my brand new, barely driven Audi, and I notice him admiring it. He grins.

"Wait for me to get your door," he instructs. I'm not usually the 'sit and stay' kind of girl, but I like the way it feels when Carter's attentive. He holds the door with one hand and extends the other to help me to my feet. He pulls me straight into his arms and plants a possessive kiss on my lips. I pull away, feeling like I'm being watched.

Suddenly the light from the house illuminates us as the front door is swung open. "I guess they're waiting for us," Carter chuckles.

I roll my eyes. "They would have seen us arrive on the security cameras."

Carter glances around at the cameras that record our every step to the front door. My father waits for us just inside the entranceway. For a country home, it has an enormous grand foyer. I kiss my father on the cheek.

"Daddy, this is Carter Brant."

Carter shakes his outstretched hand. "Pleased to meet you, sir."

"Call me Joseph. Please come in."

"Let's wait in the study until dinner is ready."

We follow him into the meticulously designed room, where he spends most of his time. Carter peruses the alcohol cart, impressed with my father's collection.

"What can I get you, Carter?" he asks.

"What would you recommend, Joseph?"

He drops a few ice cubes into the bottom of a glass and begins to pour slowly. "This one is my favourite," he says as he passes him the glass. "What kind of work do you do, Carter?"

"Business, marketing, and sales mostly. I run the Australian office for a large technology firm. The head office is here in Toronto."

"Aurora technology, Kate mentioned."

"Yes, sir," Carter answers nervously, wanting to make an impression. It amuses me. He's usually commanding and in control.

My father nods as he tips his glass to his lips and savours the amber liquid as it passes. "I currently have a business agreement with them."

I suddenly get the feeling that we're not alone. Funny how I always know she's nearby. Dread pulses through my veins like I sense something evil afoot.

"Hello, Carter."

Carter's eyes open wide, and he looks like he's about to choke on the expensive whiskey. "Stacey? What are you doing here?" Panic-stricken, he glances in my direction.

"Oh, you didn't know?" A sinister smile curls on her lips. "I'm Kate's sister."

My father and I watch as Carter downs the glass of whiskey in one gulp.

"Step-sister," I add, growing suspicious of the sudden tension in the room. "Do you know each other?"

"You could say that." Stacey walks across the room and takes the empty glass out of his hand. Would you like to tell her how we know each other, Carter?"

I lower a brow as he stumbles on his words while searching for the answer. Curious.

"We met at an Aurora business function," he finally says, locking eyes with Stacey.

I'm an intelligent woman. People underestimate me all the time. Maybe it's because of my hair colour. From my sister's smug smile, I can tell there's something I don't know, and she's going to file it away until she can use it to benefit herself. I'm not surprised that their paths have crossed since she's doing business at his place of employment, but his effort to play it off as *nothing* is a sure indication it was more.

"Dinner is ready, so we can all take a seat in the dining room," My sister announces with an amused smile.

Carter pulls out a chair and waits for me to sit while tentatively watching where Stacey lands. His choice of seating puts him at the furthest possible option. My father's wife flounces into the room carrying a platter and places it in the centre of the table.

"Looks delicious," my father says, reaching in with his fork to stab a slice of roast beef.

She wipes her hands on her apron and walks over to Carter. "You must be Katherine's friend?"

He gets to his feet and smiles. "Yes, I'm Carter. Thank you for having me."

"I'm Lady Tremaine," she simpers as she glances in my direction.

I clench my teeth and glare at my father, but he avoids eye contact.

"Oh, I don't believe that for a minute. You don't look anything like a wicked stepmother to me," Carter says with a tremendous amount of charm.

I think I hear her giggle, and it makes me feel like I've lost my appetite.

"Call me Pat. Please sit down and eat."

And eat, he does. As if it was his last meal. I'm both amused and appalled at how he devours his food. He scrapes his fork across the plate, then looks up, embarrassed we're all watching.

"I haven't had a homecooked meal in a very long time, and this was delicious," he explains.

Pat glows like an enamoured schoolgirl. "I'm glad you enjoyed it."

Stacey drops her napkin on the floor, and fear washes over Carter as he quickly gets to his feet, nearly knocking over his chair.

"Are you okay?" I ask concerned, as my sister emerges from under the table.

"Yes, of course." He picks up our plates. "I just thought that I'd help clear the table so you can give me a tour of the property."

"You don't have to do that," my father adds. "You're a guest. Put your plate down."

Carter does as he's told, focusing his attention on Stacey. Before sitting, he pulls back his chair, putting himself far away from the table edge.

"How long will you be in Toronto," Stacey asks, entertained that he looks like he could throw daggers at her.

"I'm not sure. I'm looking after some personal business for my boss, and when that wraps up, I'll go back to Australia."

"I heard that Ethan and his wife have separated, and she lost the baby. Some people say that it wasn't his baby anyway."

All eyes turn to Carter, and his ears turn red. I'm glad that he's used to dealing with high-pressure situations.

"Well, those are all rumours," he assures everyone.

"Kate," my father says in a serious tone that hints he's about to talk business. "Have you got everything ready for next week?"

"Here we go," I whisper under my breath so only Carter can hear. "Yes," I reassure my father.

"I'm counting on you to get the city on board with our plans, so we don't have any delays getting permits once the deal closes."

I feel my body tense, and Carter reaches over and holds my hand. "I have meetings next week with them."

"Take that young, good-looking lawyer we hired with you."

"There's no need for lawyers yet. I've got the initial meeting covered."

"It wouldn't hurt to have legal there as extra ears."

My anxiety begins to heighten. "It's my first meeting with them. Can I at least introduce myself before I sleep with them and then sneak away in the night with their prized possession?" I snarl. Pat nervously clears the dishes. She drops a fork, and it makes a loud clanging noise as it hits the ground. Carter gives my hand a tight squeeze, stalling my rant. Stacey sits across from me with her elbows on the table, resting her chin in her hands, waiting for me to hang myself.

I take a breath. "I know *how* to negotiate and manage the project. I just don't *want* to." I say sternly, putting an end to the conversation. Carter watches as I get to my feet, sliding my chair back so aggressively it screeches across the floor. I place my hand firmly on Carter's shoulder and stand behind him, daring my family to pursue the conversation with my enraged look. "Carter, I'll show you around the property now."

Without a word, Carter stands and follows me from room to room as I give him the tour that I've heard my stepmother give a million times. This home is her pride and joy, and I know every interesting historical point about its design and architecture. Even a few anecdotal stories that she's heard from neighbours about the original owners of the property.

"Which room is yours?" Carter asks as we wander down the long hardwood hallway.

"I didn't grow up here, but when I stay, I use the guest bedroom on the left. I push open the door to reveal a staged designer bedroom. Carter frowns.

"So, I don't get to see the personality or character of young Kate in this house?"

"I'm afraid not. I grew up in the suburbs of Toronto. My dad sold the family home when he married Pat. Living in the country has always been her dream, and my dad can afford to give that to her."

"Did you get to keep anything from your childhood?" Carter asks as I open the french doors and lead him into the courtyard between the house and the barn.

"There's a box of things my dad has stored for me, but I haven't opened it."

"Why not?"

I shrug, trying not to get emotional. He pulls me into his arms, and I melt into him, letting him hold the broken pieces of me together with his firm embrace. A horse whinnies and Carter laughs once.

"What's amusing?"

"They don't seem like horse people to me."

I grin as I lead him to the barn door and unlatch it. "They aren't. But the stable looked odd empty, so they lease this space to people who are *horse people.*"

Carter brushes his strong hand along the neck of the newest thoroughbred, who moves closer to him, enjoying the attention. "So, she *staged* the barn, like she does the house."

"Exactly. You seem comfortable around them. Are you a horse person?" I ask as I walk the stable, petting and feeding the tenants.

With a single touch, Carter calms the restless fidgeting of a rather spirited stallion. "I've ridden a few in my day, so I guess I'm comfortable with them. I prefer my horses with four wheels."

I raise my brow. "Oh, so you're a car guy."

"You might say that. How about you? What are you passionate about?"

I stumble with my answer. Nobody has ever asked me that before. I know exactly what I don't want to do. But what is it that excites and engages me? "To be honest, I'm not sure."

"Clearly not the family business," Carter laughs.

"Clearly." I rub the nose of the chestnut mare who pushes her head between us. "I have a master's degree in charitable foundations administration. Once upon a time, I wanted to do something that's going to make a difference." We walk to the next stall.

"To?"

"Somebody…anybody. I don't want to just work toward making the rich richer."

"Maybe you need a hobby to offset your corporate world. Participate in a child's charity or animal rescue."

"Preserve historical landmarks," I add ardently.

He cocks his head to one side. "Do I detect a little passion behind that subject?"

"Maybe." I shrug.

With an ardent smile, Carter begins a slow advance toward my lips. As he does, there's a magical moment where time stands still. Even the horses and other barn animals seem to be moving in slow motion. My heart pounds in my chest with anticipation. I have never experienced such a strong connection with someone. It's a desire that has strengthened through time, no matter how hard I try to deny it.

He lifts me in his arms, and the horses get antsy, reacting to the pheromones.

"Point out one spot that's not covered by the cameras," he demands.

A stimulating charge courses through my body, and I quickly point to that covert location.

Chapter Nine

Carter

Somewhere on the edge of consciousness, I float in my dreams, not wanting to put my feet down. Once again, the universe has whisked me away to an ethereal plane where I experience either a past or a parallel life. I'm not sure it matters which one, just that it's a life of joy and happiness. The warmth from her body soothes me as I become fully awake. I'm afraid to open my eyes in fear that it may not be Kate. I strain my senses, searching for the scent of her perfume.

"I'm starving," she says.

The sound of her voice brings a smile to my face. "I think I have an apple I stole from the lobby last week or maybe some lifesavers covered in pocket fluff."

She lifts her head to look at me. "After last night, you best be offering up something a little more substantial."

I open my mouth to speak, and she cuts me off.

"And don't say sausage."

"Damn."

She sits up and pulls the sheet from the bed, and wraps it around her body as she gets to her feet. I'm amused as she crosses the room. "Do you think there's something I haven't already seen? Because, believe me, I've seen it all, and I've committed it to memory."

She rolls her eyes. "I'm cold."

"Come back to bed, and I'll warm you up."

She throws my pants at me. "Food. Now."

"Fine. Breakfast at the diner it is." I pull a T-shirt over my head. "Anything but pancakes."

She stops and gives me a confused look. "What's wrong with pancakes."

"Nothing. I want a fresh start. You know? I'm letting go of old habits."

She raises her brows, then wrinkles her nose. "Like…pancakes?"

I cross the room and gently grip her hips as I press my body against hers. She leans into a warm embrace, and I press my lips to her forehead. "You can order anything you want."

"Oh, I know," she laughs. "I earned it."

My heart beats with joy. As we walk a few blocks to the diner, I reach down and hold her hand, entwining her fingers with mine. She has a certain glow about her this morning, and it's intoxicating.

"What's your schedule today?" she asks me in between bites of her breakfast.

I smile, entertained by her appetite. "I'm going with Olivia to court. I should be back by dinner."

"I'm going to call the city today to see if I can get the Redpath building deemed a historical landmark."

I raise my brow. "Won't that throw a monkey wrench in your father's deal?"

"Mmhmm."

I can't stop smiling. "I'll walk you to work." The sun has never shone brighter, and I wish I didn't have to leave her. This court appearance is the last thing I need to do for O'Connell, and then I'm free to focus one hundred percent of my energy on my relationship with Kate.

I stop at the door and kiss her. "Have a great day. I'll message you later. I should be back by dinner." I glance past her and chuckle at the woman who is not very discreet in her perusal of our goodbyes. Kate looks over her shoulder to see what I'm looking at.

"Dana, I presume?"

"Yes, that's Dana."

"She looks harmless." I wave.

Kate laughs. "She has us all fooled. Be safe today."

"I will. It's babysitting duty, that's all."

"I better get to work."

I kiss her again. "Go get 'em, girl."

"I've got this," she says confidently.

Security at the courthouse is intimidating. Sitting inside the courtroom itself is a whole new kind of awkward.

"She didn't sleep a minute last night," Meghan, Olivia's sister, whispers to me.

Olivia takes one last look around the room.

"He's not coming," I confirm regretfully.

She folds her hands in her lap, looking sorrowful.

Megan frowns and looks over at me. "I wanna kill him," she mouths.

Olivia testifies to the best of her ability, but there are still many blank holes in her memory. After a brief break, they're called back into court for the verdict. For charges that serious, I'm surprised the process is over so quickly.

I leave them out front while I walk the ridiculous distance through the parking lot to get the car. My phone rings, and seeing Kate's name brings the first feeling of happiness I've felt in hours.

"Hello, beautiful."

"How did it go?"

"Not as we had hoped, three years probation and no jail time."

"That's awful."

"Olivia is devastated. She feels like she's never going to be safe."

"I think anyone would feel the same. Obviously, your boss didn't show up."

Tension stiffens my body. "No, and I've got a few words for him when I talk to him. I'm going to take her home."

"Okay. I'm just finishing up at the office, and I'm going to walk home."

I fight the feeling of concern but lose. "I'd rather you didn't. Take a cab."

"Why?"

"Because I've just spent the afternoon at the courthouse and seen firsthand the miscreants that lurk among us. I don't like that I'm not there to protect you. Anything can happen if you're alone."

"Carter, I walk to work every day. The streets are full of people doing the same. I'm hardly alone."

"Just do as I ask. Take a cab."

"Honestly, Carter."

"Kate!" I say in a tone she best not ignore. "I have enough to worry about right now. I need you safe. Do as I ask."

"Okay," she says reluctantly.

"Good girl." There's a moment of silence, and if I had to guess, I'd say she's blushing. I'm attracted to her as a strong independent woman, but I love when she gives in to her submissive side even more.

"Will you be home tonight?"

"I'll be home to you just as soon as I can."

"See you soon."

I pull up to the curb and wait for the girls to get in. It's quite a long drive into the airport during rush hour. Olivia twiddles her fingers restlessly in her lap as I navigate the airport departure terminal.

"I can't stand to leave you alone, especially today," Meg says emotionally.

"I'm not alone. Have you seen the Australian mountain in the driver's seat?"

"Nice try, but I know he's leaving in a couple of days. Why do you always have to pretend to be so strong?" Megan asks sadly.

"I don't think she's pretending," I add.

"Still," Megan objects. "It's okay to be vulnerable sometimes."

"Vulnerable women don't *survive*," Olivia says softly.

I reach over and still her fidgeting hands.

"Well, I'm sorry to have to say this, but there was a time when my sister, the *strong* one, would have been on her way to Ireland to either get her husband back or kick his ass for breaking her heart."

Shock spreads over Olivia's face as she slowly turns to look at her sister. I squeeze her hands tighter as I pull into the loading zone and park.

"That's right," Meg continues, agitated as she gets out of the car. "I said it." Olivia gives her one last hug while I get her luggage out of the trunk. We wait until she crosses the sidewalk and disappears through the doors.

A few steps away from us, a young father tightly hugs his upset daughter. "Daddy will be home before you know it," he says as he places a kiss on her head.

Olivia soothes her hand over her stomach, and I watch in agony as her tears slowly roll down her cheeks. She quickly reaches into her pocket for a tissue and takes a calming breath. "Can we go home now?"

"Of course."

She doesn't say a word in the car. When she turns toward the window and her shoulders soften, I'm sure she's asleep. All the way there, I think about the things I'm going to say to Ethan. By the time I park the car and Olivia opens her eyes, I'm completely charged up.

"I'm going to go lie down," she says as I close the door behind us.

"Can I get you anything?"

"No, I just want this day to end."

"I'm going to call Travis and arrange for security. I'll stay until you fall asleep." I wait until she's upstairs, and I hear the door close before dialing Ethan's number.

"It's about time," Ethan says anxiously.

"Hey, we just got back from taking Meg to the airport. I think you mean to say thank you. You self-centred, selfish dick."

"Sorry, Carter. You're right. Thank you for looking after everyone. I've just been on edge, waiting to find out what happened."

"Well, mate, you wouldn't have to wonder if you got your head out of your ass and flew here to support her. Megan is ready to kill you, and to be honest, the thought has crossed my mind as well."

"We've been through this. I can't. It will put her under too much stress."

"More stress than going it alone? More stress than being heartbroken because the man she vowed for better or worse bailed on her the minute it got worse?"

"It's not like that, and you know it."

If he insists on staying on this path, everything I hoped for with Kate is lost. "Give your head a shake," I yell.

"Carter, calm down. Just tell me what happened."

"Nothing. A slap on the wrist and probation. There wasn't enough evidence to make the other charges stick."

"I was afraid something like that would happen. Call Travis and get her around-the-clock security."

"Already done. You need to get your ass here and make things right with your wife," I yell in frustration.

"I won't. I won't do it. It's not safe."

He hangs up the phone, and I'm left standing in the middle of the room arguing with a dial tone. I sit on the couch and turn on the TV.

I look up to find Olivia standing at the doorway. I lock my gaze with her hazel eyes, clouded with tears. She crosses the room and gently climbs onto my lap, and then lays her head against my chest. "Is he ever coming back to me?"

In the past, this gesture would solicit unwanted reactions, but no longer. Now I'm beginning to feel that strong urge to protect her. "No, Olivia. It doesn't look like it."

I hold her tightly and let her cry until she can't anymore. I'm gutted. My eyes become heavy as a familiar scene unfolds from a past life when certain events turned my life sideways and changed my destiny. This is how it started. With a cry for help, a strong sense of loyalty, and a tug of war with my heart.

Kate. I need to call Kate. My hand searches for my phone as I lose the battle with sleep, and I'm pulled away from reality.

When the sun rises in the morning, Olivia climbs out of my arms. For a moment I'm disoriented.

"What are you doing?" I ask as I finally find my phone and scroll through three missed call notifications from Kate. "Shit."

"Going to work."

I twist my neck to work out the kinks. "Is that a good idea? Are you up to it?"

"I can't sit here playing the victim for the rest of my life. I need to do something."

"Okay, if you're sure. There's someone I need to see before I start getting packed to go home."

"Kate?"

"Yes."

"Do you love her?"

I don't know why that question makes me feel awkward, and I fail to answer.

"Carter. Do you love her?"

"I think I might." Admitting that out loud is liberating.

Olivia smiles. "Then don't fuck it up."

"I'm trying not to."

"Why are you here with me?"

"You are, and always will be, my priority."

"Are you fucking stupid?"

Confusion washes over me. Am I?

"If you love her," Olivia continues, "then she needs to be your priority. There's no way in hell I'm going to be the other woman that fucks it all up. That shit is not acceptable."

"You wouldn't be the only other woman who might fuck it up. Believe me."

"What are you talking about?"

"Do you remember Stacey?"

"Barbie?"

I nod my head. "Yes, Stacey."

"What about her?"

"I found out meeting Kate's family for the first time that she's Kate's step-sister."

Olivia's eyes open wide. "Awkward. Does Kate know about everything that happened that night?"

"I don't think so. Kate knows we're acquainted from a business dealing at Aurora, but I haven't disclosed how."

"There's no gentle way to break that news."

I hold my hands on my head. "I think I've destroyed any chance I had of gaining her trust. Stacey is going to let that cat out of the bag when it has the potential to do the most damage."

"All the more reason to come clean as soon as possible."

"You're probably right."

"Of course I'm right. Get your ass home to your woman. She needs to be your only priority, for fuck's sake. I can look after myself."

I grin. "And that is why we love you."

"Blah, blah, blah. Don't go getting all mushy on me, Brant."

I make my way to the door and turn. "I'm glad to see you're feeling like your old self."

She points at the door. "Get out."

The minute I get into the car, I dial Kate's number, and she answers on the first ring.

"Carter, are you okay?"

"Yes, I'm sorry. Olivia was having a bad night, and I told her I'd stay until she fell asleep. I meant to call you, but I guess I crashed myself."

There's a pause, and it makes me nervous. "Kate?"

"I'm glad you're okay."

"I'm going to drop by your work to see you."

"Oh, I don't know, Carter. I'm kind of busy."

"Lunch, at the bench on the lakeshore. I'll bring sandwiches. I need to see you, and I'm not taking no for an answer."

"I'll meet you there at noon."

I drive straight to the deli near the office and order food. It's not quite an elegant picnic, but it will do.

I arrive early, hoping that the crashing of the waves soothes my nerves. When I see Kate approaching my heart beats with an amorous rhythm, and I get to my feet. I don't know why I feel so jumpy.

She doesn't look happy, and I suppose that's my fault.

I smile and greet her with a quick kiss. "I'm sorry," I say again as I motion for her to sit.

"I suppose I should be used to it."

I deserve that. I pass her a sandwich. "I wish I called you before I fell asleep so I could explain."

"I waited up all night first because I was worried. Then because I was angry."

"I understand. I should have just left her and came home right after I dropped her off. Would you love me if I was the kind of guy to leave a distraught pregnant woman?"

She thinks about it long enough that it makes me smile. I raise my brow. "Forgive me?"

"Hmmm…I'm not sure."

"I hope so because I'm going home. We only have a few days left together."

Her head snaps upward, and she stares in my direction. "To Australia?"

"Yes. That's where home is for me." I study her reaction. "My acting boss wants me back and focusing on the Australian sales market. I'm almost finished doing the things I promised O'Connell I'd help with."

She stares at me, looking like there's something she'd like to say, and then looks away, focusing on the horizon. I'm losing her. She's already building walls and raising the drawbridge. When I leave, she'll put a stop to all communication. I start to lose it. "Kate."

Her hands fidget nervously. "Yes?"

"Come with me."

Her eyes widen. "Oh, I don't know. It's sudden, and you said you're leaving in a few days."

"I don't want to leave without you. Not again."

"Carter. I've got so much going on right now. I can't just pick up and take a vacation."

I take her sandwich out of her hands and wrap it back up. "Not for a vacation. I want you to live there with me."

"Move there? Permanently?"

"Yes."

"We don't know each other that well, and you want me to pick up and leave everything behind and start a new life with you in Australia?"

"Yes."

Her phone rings, and I'm sure she's thankful for the distraction. "Sorry, I need to take this. It's the City calling about the petition for historical status."

I kiss her on the forehead. "I'll see you tonight. Be prepared to be persuaded."

Chapter Ten

Kate

The following day, Dana is busy with a visitor at the front desk when I arrive at the office, so she gives me a quick wave as I pass.

I close my office door to ward off any overzealous hopeful coworkers and spend the morning answering emails, intentionally procrastinating on the correspondence that has to do with the sale of the waterfront property. I look at my phone when I receive a link from Carter. I open it reluctantly and scroll page after page of the most stunning Australian coastline. A few moments later he sends a text.

Carter: I hope you change your mind.
Kate: That's not fair. You're not asking me to go on vacation.
Carter: If I suggested you come for that reason, would you?

Good question. Everything with Carter happens so quickly I don't have time to think, just react.

Kate: I might consider an Australian vacation.

I'm not surprised at all when my phone rings. "Carter, we talked about this until the early hours of the morning. I haven't changed my mind."

"Do I strike you as the kind of guy who gives up easily?"

"Not really, and it's annoying."

Carter laughs. "I wanted to let you know that I have to go back to Dufferin County today. Olivia has a doctor's appointment."

"Is everything okay?" I ask, concerned.

"Yes. She's going to get his approval to fly. She and O'Connell's mother have concocted a plan to set Ethan on the right path."

"Does this plan involve you flying with her to Ireland?"

"No, I'm flying home to Australia tomorrow."

I want to feel relieved about her departure, but I doubt that Carter's involvement with them is over.

"I'll see you in about an hour. I haven't given up hope that you'll go with me."

Again, I have my doubts that he'll be flying home to Australia. It's what's preventing me from saying yes to going with him. The constant disappearing acts and being at Olivia O'Connell's beck and call. I hate that I feel that way. Maybe there's a small amount of jealousy there. It's an ugly feeling, and I'm not too fond of it.

I drop my phone into my purse before swinging it over my shoulder and leaving. I ignore Dana when she calls my name and hope I can make it out to the street before she can catch up to me. A smile blossoms across my face when the warmth of the sunshine hits me.

Kate: let's do something different tonight.
Carter: What did you have in mind?
Kate: I don't know. I just feel like we should go out and celebrate our last night together.
Carter: Don't say it like that.
Kate: You know what I mean. Before you leave.
Carter: Alright. You decide what you want to do.

I knock on the door to Carter's suite. When he opens it, I hand him the stack of things I juggled all the way down in the elevator.

"What's this?"

"Everything you've left in the penthouse."

He raises a brow. "Really? I've left this much up there?"

"Mmhmm. You practically moved in."

I follow him into the other room and frown as he tosses my neatly folded stack of clothes onto the bed.

"No wonder my suitcase seemed so empty."

I suddenly feel sad. I don't want him to go, but he has his own life to live, and I'm not going to ask him to stay.

"Kate?"

"Hmmm?"

"Where are you? You zoned out?"

"Sorry."

"Is everything okay?"

"Yes, of course."

"You look lovely. Did you decide where you want to go?"

"I did."

"Are you going to tell me?"

"I figured we'd just walk there."

Carter opens the door for me. "Well, then let's go."

The smell of his cologne captivates me. I don't think I could get any closer to him if I tried. Believe me, I want to. We walk through the lobby, and I redirect Carter to the side door.

"Where are we going?"

"Nowhere special. I thought we'd stay close so neither of us has to drive. A strange expression forms on Carter's face as he stops in front of the entrance.

"The nightclub? You want to go to the nightclub?"

"Sure, I thought we could dance and have a little fun."

I don't understand why he looks so uncomfortable. There are several people already standing in line, and it's only ten P.M.

The host spots Carter and waves us in. "Oh, special treatment," I say, impressed

"Ethan is part owner of this club. The staff knows me."

They open the gate and welcome us in. "Welcome, Mr. Brant."

"Thank you,"

"We have a new security system, sir."

"Great," Carter says, looking uncomfortable.

"High-quality video from all angles."

Carter clenches his jaw. "Thanks."

"You're welcome, sir. Just thought you should know."

"That was strange," I say as we head into the bar.

Carter scratches at his neck. "Yeah, weird."

We've only just received our drinks when the music slows in pace. Carter takes my glass out of my hand and places it on the table.

"I'm a horrible dancer," I warn.

"I'm not," he assures me.

He leads me to the floor and tugs me in. I do my best not to embarrass myself.

"Relax," he insists.

"I didn't know I wasn't."

I feel his chest rise and fall, and I know he's amused. I do as I'm told and lean in, resting my head under his chin and let him lead. He tightens his grip, forcing our bodies to brush together with every step. "I thought you said you weren't a good dancer?"

"I'm not."

"There's not a thing wrong with the way you move."

I want time to stop right here. This is a moment I want to remember. But the music changes, and we're flanked on all sides by younger, enthusiastic dancers, with lots of rhythm. Carter has moves, but I feel entirely inadequate doing my best sidestep. Carter reaches for my hand and leads me off the floor and back to our table.

He hands me my wine. "What if I told you that I've already bought you a ticket to fly to Australia with me tomorrow."

I take a few huge gulps of alcohol. "I'd say that you're a controlling asshole."

He finishes the rest of his beer and puts it down heavily on the table.

"Are you a controlling asshole?" I ask.

"I don't like the sound of that."

"Me neither."

"What if I told you that I don't want to share you with all these people on my last night in Toronto?"

The smell of his cologne still lingers. "I'd say, pay the bill, and let's go back to the penthouse."

I can't believe Carter leaves for Australia today. It was a long night of him trying to persuade me to go. We talked about every possible scenario of how we might continue in a relationship while on different continents, but I'm certain eventually we'll drift apart. Why prolong it.

He accompanies me to the lobby to say goodbye when I leave for work.

"Are you sure?" he asks one last time.

"I'm sorry. I can't even go with you to the airport today. I have a meeting with the historical committee. One last pitch to rush this status through."

He places sweet kisses on my lips, and I'm crushed. Carter has the potential to fix my broken heart and soul. After years of mistrusting men, I finally believe I'm meant to give my heart to him. He's the one that I want. Tears erupt and fall, and I do nothing to stop them. He wipes them with the pad of his thumb.

"Hey, this isn't forever, it's just for now. We'll find a way to be together. It just might take some time to figure out."

He opens the door to the cab, and I hesitate a moment. There's a sparkle in his brilliant blue eyes as a ghost of a smile crosses his lips. He nods a silent understanding. Stepping back onto the curb, he watches until we're around the corner and out of sight.

I search my favourite thrift store purse for a granola bar, although I don't have much of an appetite. I shuffle through the pockets, moving things. I have no idea why I carry them around. The odd shape of an object in the side pocket makes me curious. I unzip it and pull out my passport. Clearly, the universe is hard at work.

"Driver, can you drop me off down by the lakeshore, please." I'm in no rush to get to a job I hate, even if my father owns the business. Why do I feel like I'm at odds with my life? It's not a bad life. It's a very comfortable life. There isn't much I want for, except Carter.

We get stuck in traffic, and the honking of irate drivers snaps me out of the fog I'm in. "I'll just walk from here, thank you." I pay the fare and get out, hoping the walk will clear my head.

Feeling lost, I walk aimlessly, taking in the architecture of this beautiful city of Toronto until I find myself standing in front of that weathered red door tucked between two magnificent modern high-rises. I swallow hard when the door opens as if she's been expecting me. Her senescence dwindles as her eyes brighten and her mouth begins to curl at the edges into a knowing grin.

"You've decided to go," she says.

I stumble with my thoughts, not knowing which way to shake my head. "I don't know," I finally manage to say. I glance at the signage in the window, then back at Eva. "You're the psychic. What am I going to do?"

She laughs before stepping forward and taking my hands in hers. Energy runs through me as if she's somehow billowed magic through my body and freed me of shadows that weigh me down.

"It doesn't matter how hard the universe pushes you two together. Your free will, my girl, is strong. If I tell you that you will do something, you'll do the exact opposite to exercise your control. So, I'll ask you to do one thing for yourself."

She's not wrong. "What's that?" I ask.

"Stop over-thinking it."

I laugh once. "Have we met?" I say sarcastically.

"Yes," she says convincingly. "In a past life."

I close my eyes for a moment, trying to come to terms with what's she's suggesting. I open them when she squeezes my hands harder.

"Stop worrying about what your family thinks. Stop worrying if he can be trusted. Stop wondering if you can ever feel the love you had for him in that past life. It's real, and you can have it again."

"Eva…" I interrupt. The clarity and peace I was experiencing are now clouded by anxiety.

She smiles and drops my hands. "I know. You can't stop overthinking any more than I can stop meddling." She turns and heads toward the door, leaving me dumbfounded on the street. As she turns the knob and pushes the door open, she pauses and looks over her shoulder. "A simple thought for you today then. You can have what you want. Put everything else aside and ask yourself, do you *want* to go?"

As she disappears inside the building, a protective bubble dissipates, and the busy sidewalk unfolds around me. People slam into me as they rush past on their way to work. I walk with the flow to avoid being knocked over and trampled. I look up at the high-rise building, not sure how I got here, and keep walking until I reach the lakeshore.

I sit on a bench and stare at the rolling water. The roar of the crashing waves on the shoreline is mesmerizing. The water is my power place, but I don't think even it can resolve the conflict I feel inside right now. The loud sound of heavy equipment disrupts my moment of reflection. Curiosity forces me to investigate.

I follow the sound down the pathway, and as I get closer to the Redpath sugar refinery, my heart begins to pound like a hammer in my chest. I pick up the pace, chasing down a guy with a yellow vest and hard hat.

"Excuse me!" I shout to be heard over the noise. "EXCUSE ME!" I scream again as I practically jump in front of him. "What's going on here?" I demand. He stops and pounds a wooden sign into the ground.

"Read the sign, lady," he says abruptly as he walks away.

I quickly read the sign and find myself in shock. "Wait," I say, chasing after him. "There must be some mistake."

"No mistake," he says. "We've got the approval from the town changing the zoning to allow a multiple housing application. We're doing the land survey today."

"No, no, no. There must be some mistake," I say frantically. "I'm in charge of this project. I haven't given the go-ahead on any of this."

He gives me an annoyed look. "I've got signed documents from the company funding this project. For safety reasons, you need to get off the site. If you've got problems, take it up with your boss."

I look around me at the equipment being moved in to start development and demolition. My heart is stuck in my throat. I walk back to the trail feeling dumbfounded. On my way back to the office, my bewilderment morphs into anger. I've purposely delayed this project, so someone has moved things along without my knowledge if development has progressed.

With every step closer to the office, my jaw clenches tighter, and tension overtakes my body. I'm so angry I'm practically shaking when I reach the elevator.

"Kate," Dana says out of breath as she catches up with me at the elevator. "Carter was here and left this for you." I step into the elevator and take it out of her hand. "It's a plane ticket to Australia," she says.

"Controlling asshole," I mumble under my breath as the door closes. We stop on the seventh floor, and to my horror, Will, my lovestruck co-worker, gets into the elevator.

"Hi, Kate."

"Hi," I say, mustering every ounce of energy I have to be cordial.

"Congratulations on closing the Redpath deal. That development is going to make the company a lot of revenue."

"About that…do you happen to know who signed off on the final draft?"

"Well," he says, looking a little embarrassed. "Legally, it was Stacey that signed it, but we all know you did all the work. You should get the credit."

My hands close into tightly formed fists, crumpling the paper I'm holding. "Oh, I don't want any credit for this deal. In fact, I'm embarrassed that my name is associated with it in any way."

When the door opens, I get awkward looks from those who establish eye contact with me as they exit. The others look down or look away. I don't even care anymore. My walk down the hallway is fueled by rage and disgust. When I push open the door to my father's office, I find him and Stacey there.

"Perfect!" I announce.

They turn, startled by my unexpected entry.

"Katherine," my father says in a formal tone as he gets to his feet. Stacey smirks, folding her arms in front of her, preparing for the battle.

"Yes, father? Is there something you'd like to tell me?"

"Yes, sit down."

"Nope." I shake my head. "Nope, I don't think I'm going to sit."

"Let's relax a moment and discuss the Redpath project."

I'm gritting my teeth so tightly I can hear the rapid whooshing of my blood. Why is it that using that R-word has the opposite effect of what's intended? I'm anything but relaxed. "Great, why don't you start with how the project I was working on got pushed through several project phases by someone else."

He twists and turns his neck, working out the tension. Stacey gets to her feet. "I approved the project, Kate."

I feel the excessive rise and fall of my chest as I struggle to keep from losing my shit. "Why?"

"Because you weren't doing it," she adds stoically.

"Who told you to do that? It wasn't your project to interfere with. I was looking after things!" I say through clenched teeth. Stacey glances at my father, who nervously unbuttons his collar and loosens his tie.

"Dad?" I ask, hoping he'll at least lie about it.

"I asked your sister to review the portfolio and act on the tasks you seemed to be struggling with."

I take a prolonged breath, acknowledging his betrayal. I purse my lips and nod my head. "I wasn't struggling. I was trying to look into other solutions."

"Solutions? Solutions for what?"

"To save the historic industrial building," I blurt out.

Stacey laughs out loud, and it fuels my fire.

"Your job was to close this deal and manage the development project. Nothing else."

"You should have talked to me first," I blurt out.

He holds up his hands in an attempt to de-escalate me, but it doesn't work. "Kate, I made a mistake. I should have given this project to Stacey. You weren't on board from the beginning. We'll put you on a different project."

"Well, I'm not available for a different project," I say spitefully.

"Oh, Kate," Stacey says in a condescending tone. "Don't be such a drama queen. I'm sure you've got nothing else going on."

My blood begins to boil.

"Why aren't you available?" Father asks curiously.

"Because…I quit." What have I just done?

"Don't be ridiculous," Stacey says, rolling her eyes. "What would you do without this job."

"Kate." My father advances toward me, and I step back.

"I quit. Let Stacey handle everything from now on."

Stacey shoots daggers at me, and I'm sure it has nothing to do with vacating my position. She's wanted me out of the family business ever since my father married her mother. My father looks heartbroken as I pivot on my heel and storm out, slamming the door behind me.

Dana meets me in the lobby and walks with me to the door. "Before you ask, I quit my job."

"Errr, what?" she asks, shocked.

"I finally did it. I quit my job."

"Tell me you're going to Australia."

I look down at the crumpled papers I'm still clutching in my hand. "Fuck it. I'm going to Australia."

She squeals. "When?"

I squint as I read the boarding time. "Now."

"Right now?"

"In about an hour. I don't have time to pack a bag or anything."

"Do you have your passport with you?"

I unzip the side pocket of my bag and pull it out.

"I'm so excited for you. Why don't you look excited?"

"I think what I'm experiencing right now is panic."

We stop walking, and she throws her arms around me. I feel like I'm going to cry.

"Go, start a new life. One you're going to be happy with," she says emotionally as I flag down a taxi. "Keep in touch."

"I will. After all, I'll need a friend when Stacey gets the family to disown me."

"Meh, I don't think she'll succeed. Your father loves you. He'll understand eventually."

A meeting reminder pops up on my phone.
"Dana, can you do me a huge favour?"

"Sure!"

"It's something that might compromise a company project."

"I'm in. Does Carter have a brother? I'll quit my job and come with you to Australia."

I smile. "I just sent you the contact info for the people with the historical society. Can you call them and let them know I can't do an in-person meeting today and set it up as a conference call? I can talk to them on my way to the airport."

"You're still going to try and convince them?"

"ABSOLUTELY!"

Chapter Eleven

I pace the floor in front of the window that looks out onto the tarmac. I'm not happy I'm going home to Australia alone.

I'm so tense that when my phone rings, I jump, nearly tossing it. "Whatever he wants, John, the answer is no."

"I'll be sure to pass that along, but that's not why I'm calling."

"What then?"

"We've done the best we can on scrubbing that video, but new posts have just started popping up. We're trying to stay ahead of it. Do you have any idea why there's a sudden rebirth in interest?"

"Long story, but I ran into Stacey. It turns out she's Kate's step-sister."

"That probably explains it. A jealous family member is more dangerous than a hateful enemy."

"Great."

"Are you at the airport?"

"Yeah, J.P. Stinkbeau arranged a flight for me. It seems he wants me home in Australia looking after business."

"Never in a million years did I see any of these events unfolding. I thought my career would start gearing down in preparation for retirement."

"I thought Kate and I would be riding off into the sunset and planning a family."

"Is she with you?"

"No, mate. She's staying here."

"So, you're going home without her?"

"What choice do I have?"

John chuckles. "You really have lost it. If it was Olivia, and you were O'Connell would you advise him to leave without her?"

"Of course not."

"You're just going to get on a plane and go home, alone?"

"I don't know what you want me to do, you bastard?"

"You know the answer. I have to go; your boss is calling. He was in a foul mood yesterday when he found out Dave gave Olivia the green light to fly to Ireland."

I hang up the phone and think about what he said. If it were Olivia, would I advise Ethan to get on a plane without her? The answer is no. Fuck it. J.P. can fire me. I'm not leaving her again. The flight begins to board, and I push my way through the crowd heading in the opposite direction. I'm midway through the terminal when my phone rings again with an incoming call from Kate. I stop to answer, but I can't get a good signal. I head toward a door that looks like it leads back out into the concourse when two surly-looking guards stop me. The call drops, and my growing angst makes me consider going the wrong way through airport security.

Another call. "Kate!" I yell, "Can you hear me?"

"Carter…sfawue…sdfasfos…fisisdfj."

I curse, walking near the security exit. A security guard watches me closely. I dial Kate's number and wait.

"Carter!"

"Kate, I keep losing your signal. Can you hear me?"

"Yes, I'm standing right behind you."

Electricity sizzles through my veins. I lower my phone and slowly turn.

She smiles and disconnects the call as I stand in front of her, speechless.

"What are you doing here?" I ask, confused.

"Taking a flight to Australia."

"Don't fuck with me," I warn.

"I'm not. I quit my job, and now I need something to do with my time."

"You're going with me?"

"If we don't miss the flight."

I look at my watch and become anxious. I grab her laptop bag and throw it over my shoulder, then grasp her hand. I don't know how she keeps up with my stride in those heels, but it's impressive. We make it to the runway just as they're preparing to close the door. I quickly stow our bags and look for our seats. I stop in the middle of the aisle in first class, studying the boarding passes.

"What's wrong?" Kate asks, concerned.

"I forgot we're not sitting together. It was the only seat left, and to be honest, I didn't think you'd come."

"Oh. That's okay. Where am I sitting?"

"At the very back of the plane."

She looks down the very long aisle at the people staring at us. I establish eye contact with the guy sitting next to my assigned seat.

"Don't even think of asking," he says.

What a dick.

"You need to take your seats," the stewardess says impatiently.

Kate smiles, trying to calm me. "It's okay."

"No, it's not okay." I grab her hand. "Follow me."

I guide her to the back of the plane, bumping people along the narrow aisles as I go. I stop at Kate's assigned seat and smile at the young woman sitting in the next seat. "Hi. I'm sorry to bother you, but I was wondering if you would switch seats with me so I could sit with my girlfriend."

She looks hesitant, and I promptly show her my boarding pass. "First Class."

"What's the catch?"

"No catch. I want to sit with her."

"Please take your seats," the stewardess says through the speaker system.

The girl grabs her bag and gets to her feet, taking the boarding pass out of my hand as she squeezes out into the aisle.

"Thank you," Kate says as she moves to let her pass. "I'll sit at the window so you can stretch out into the aisle.

I stare at the cramped seats and limited leg room.

"First time sitting in economy?" Kate asks with a smile as she secures her seatbelt.

"Of course not," I lie as I wedge myself into the space with a grunt.

When the plane taxis down the runway with Kate beside me, I feel like I've just steered destiny down the other fork in the road. I hold her hand and try to calm my beating pulse.

"Did you say you quit your job?"

She shrugs and nods. I lift her hand to my mouth and kiss it.

"How many bags did you check-in?"

"Errr. I don't have any bags."

"You didn't pack anything?"

"No time. I quit and came straight to the airport."

I can't stop grinning.

"It's a long story."

"We've got lots of time before we get home."

She lowers a brow. "What's with that smug grin?"

"I suppose it's a good thing I'm a controlling asshole."

"Don't make me get off the plane."

I chuckle. She squeezes my hand tightly as we take off. "Nervous?" I ask.

"Excited," she confirms.

I'm not sorry that I'll never be a member of the mile-high club ever again. Well, unless it's with Kate.

"Hey," I whisper into her ear midway through a very long flight. Her eyes flutter open.

"What's the matter," she asks, sitting up groggily.

"Nothing. I just wondered if you wanted to…." I grin and waggle my eyebrows but meet with a confused look. "You know…" I nod in the direction of the loo.

A knowing look washes over her, and then she laughs. I feel a little hurt. "I'm serious."

"I know. But it's not happening."

I must be losing it. I can't hide my wounded expression. "It will be an experience you'll never forget," I promise.

She raises a brow. "I'm not a horny teenager."

"Neither am I," I say confidently. "I know what I'm doing."

"I wouldn't bother," the stewardess says as she leans over me to pass Kate some pretzels. "He wasn't that impressive." She glares at me before walking away, leaving me pretzel-less once again.

"Fuck me," I grumble.

Kate's face turns a crimson red. "I take it you know her."

"I can't escape her. I'm even on a different airline this time." My ego is wounded, and I feel the need to right her accusation. "And I was brilliant."

Kate raises her hand to stop me. "I don't want to know."

Something in her reaction intrigues me. "Are you jealous?"

"No," she emphatically denies.

She's lying. I reach for her hand and lift it to my mouth. I press a kiss there, lingering to enjoy the sweet fragrance of perfume she dabbed on her wrist. A smile washes away her look of distress. I feel the power of that smile right down to the very core of my soul. "Let's remind each other to look forward. Not back. We learn from our past, and lord knows I can't forget or ignore it, but I'm not going to live in it any longer and ruin my chance of spending the rest of my days with you. The life we're going to build together from this day forward is the only thing that matters."

Her eyes glisten, and she bats her lashes to try and thwart the fall of tears. I brush my thumb across her cheek and then lean in, touching my forehead to hers. The peaceful feeling I get when I'm around her soothes me to sleep.

"Wake up," Kate whispers. "We're getting ready to land."

I return my seat to the upright position as Kate strains to see Australia through the tiny airplane window. She turns her head looking excited. "Wait until you see it from the ground."

"I can't believe I'm here," she says.

"I can't believe it either. I pinched myself a few times during the flight to make sure I wasn't dreaming."

She grins. "You're not dreaming."

"I'm going to do everything possible to make you want to stay," I promise. She looks like she wants to say something, but we're interrupted by the requested regiment to exit the plane.

I keep her close until we finally get out of the crowded international airport and insist that I look after loading her laptop bag into the car. I know that she's a strong independent woman, but I already have an overwhelming need to care for her.

I don't want Kate to think I'm a cheap bastard, so I tip the private transfer driver generously when he drops us at my home. She takes notice and smiles.

"I can hear the ocean," she says excitedly as we walk through the courtyard.

"It's not far away. You can walk there anytime you want. Do you surf? You can use my board."

"Oh, I've never surfed before. But I would like to learn."

"Consider it done. It's not something we have to do today so let us settle in and rest a bit. We can order in dinner if you like." I open the door and welcome her in. I hear her whisper "wow" under her breath as she walks through my professionally decorated place. I drop the bags, eager to show her around. The kitchen and living space don't need any introduction, so I quickly walk through and usher her out onto the balcony. The sunset view never disappoints. We pause there for silent reflection before we enter through the french doors into the sleeping quarters. I can tell she's impressed by the size of my bedroom, and she raises a brow when she sees the shower in the ensuite. It's my pride and joy. I open my mouth, and she immediately raises her hand.

"I don't want to know."

I purse my lips and then grin. "You're right. You don't."

"What's in here?" she asks as we pass a closed door.

"That's another bedroom. I think I may have mentioned that an old friend Reese was staying with me for a while. He moved out weeks ago, but his stuff is still in there. I've told him if it's not gone next week, I'm going to sell it."

"Or you can donate it to a shelter for people who need it."

She's always the humanitarian, looking out for everyone else. "Wait,"

I stop in my tracks. "What?"

She searches the hallway. "Is there another bedroom?"

I furrow my brow. "No, only two." She suddenly looks overwhelmed.

"Where am I going to sleep?"

My heart lurches, and I'm not sure how I'm going to respond. I hadn't considered she would want her own space, at least for the time being. I search for words in my state of panic, and then she bursts out laughing.

"I'm joking, Carter."

I finally resume breathing. "You had me going."

"I know! Let's get unpacked."

I reach for her elbow and stop her. "If you're uncomfortable with staying in my room, I'll pack up Reese's stuff tomorrow or find you a hotel."

"I'm okay sharing your bed."

Hearing that makes me twitch. I've been thinking about making love to her since she arrived at the airport. I was half-hard thinking about it on the plane. "I'm glad." I take her hand and lead her back to the master bedroom. "I'd like to give you a good and proper…*welcome* to Australia."

"Well, I wouldn't want to disappoint you by turning you down."

"Again."

She fights a smile. As I begin to undress her, she slowly falls under my spell. Taking my time, I brush my lips across sensitive skin as I uncover it until she stands in front of me, bare and vulnerable. I sit on the edge of the bed and pull her between my legs. The cool air in the room makes her body feel warm beneath my touch. I suck a nipple into my mouth with a hard pull and give it a teasing lick with my tongue. My hot breath against her wet nipple makes it harden even more.

I get to my feet, and she glides her hands down my hips, peeling my boxers down over my erection. "Get into bed," I demand with an authoritative tone. She complies without haste. I join her, parting her lips and kissing her with driving need. Kate puts her weight on her elbows and raises her upper body, forcing me off and to the side. She throws her leg over me as if she's trying to shift the balance of power.

"What do you think you're doing?"

"It's Australia, right? Everything is backwards here. The toilet water flushes the other way. The girl gets on top."

"You're a smart girl. I know you've figured out that in the bedroom, I'll be in control."

"But."

I stop her with a steely look as I push her onto her back and then force her legs apart with my knee. Grasping her wrists, I pull them over her head and hold her down with gentle, commanding pressure.

"Go ahead and protest. I dare you."

Her breath hitches, and she squeezes her legs together, rubbing herself and twitching against me, silently pleading for me to relieve the ache there. Still fighting for dominance, she circles her hips and forces me in. I don't care. I'm lost in sensation and desire so powerful that I'm almost beyond my ability to focus and stay in control.

I hit a steady rhythm until pressure builds inside us. Unbearably intimate and exciting. We reach our climax together, erupting at the height of passion. As I lay, vibrating inside her, I feel a sense of victory. I am complete. She is finally mine.

Chapter Twelve

Kate

I startle awake feeling disoriented. I jump out of bed and look around the room.

"What are you doing?" Carter asks.

"What time is it?" I ask, feeling panic.

"Kate."

I open my purse and rummage through it with no idea what I'm looking for.

"Come back to bed," Carter insists. "It's eight in the morning. There's no reason to get up so early."

"I need to check my emails and…."

He sits up, revealing his chiselled chest and getting my attention. "Kate, you quit your job. There's nothing you need to check or do today. Besides, Australia is fourteen hours ahead of Toronto, so it's six in the evening there on a Friday. Come back to bed."

I feel silly. "Oh, right." I climb in beside him, and he rolls to his side, pulling the blanket over me.

"Did you sleep well?"

"I did, but I still feel tired."

"It's the jet lag and the time difference. It doesn't matter how often I travel it always kicks my ass when I get home."

"How do you overcome it?"

Carter pulls me against his chest. "Just try to follow the schedule of the time zone we're in, and eventually, your body syncs up."

"You're saying get up now and eat breakfast and then go about a normal day." I pull myself out of his arms and get out of bed. "What do I do in six hours from now when my body says it's time to go to sleep?"

"You'd be surprised how easy it is to stay awake when it's a beautiful sunny day, and you keep yourself busy. We might need to take a few naps in the afternoon the first couple of days."

I put on the only clothes that I have with me. "I like naps."

Carter smirks.

I toss his jeans at him.

"I take it we're not napping now?" he asks as he sits on the side of the bed and pulls them on.

"I boarded a plane with nothing but the clothes on my back. I need to go shopping."

He pulls a T-shirt over his head and tucks his wallet into his pocket. "I'll bring the car around."

I search the enormous bathroom for a washcloth and soak it with warm water to wash my face. I've never been one for wearing a lot of make-up, so it's a good thing I'm comfortable with au naturelle.

I toss my purse over my shoulder, and as I pull the door shut behind me, the strap rips, and everything I brought with me spills all over the ground. I kneel to pick everything up, and Carter joins me to help.

"I love this purse," I say sadly.

"We'll get you a new one today." He hands me the last few things from the ground. "I think we've got it all."

"Thank you." I'm bowled over as I stand and get my first glimpse of his car.

"Kate? Are you okay?"

"Er, yes." He holds the door for me as I get in.

"You look a little thunderstruck," he says when he climbs into the driver's seat.

Carter is a tall man, and crammed into the small sports car he looks like a giant. "It's quite the car."

"You knew I had a Ferrari."

I search my memories. "I guess I forgot."

Carter puffs out his chest like a proud parent. "Do you like it?"

"How much does something like this cost?"

He looks wounded. "Does it matter?"

"Do you know how many children you could send to camp or how many families you could feed with this much money?"

He smiles. "Can't we save the world AND have nice cars?"

I feel embarrassed. "Sorry, it's your money. Of course, you can spend it on whatever you like."

"Going forward, I'll manage the budget accordingly. Something less expensive to drive so we can fill some hungry stomachs too."

I love that he seems to *get me*. Or at least I think he does until he pulls into a high-end shopping complex where most of the store names I only recognize from movies about billionaires and fashion.

"Let's start with getting you a new bag," he says as he navigates the parking garage in front of a costly handbag store. "Unless you'd rather buy one from a different store?"

I wrinkle my nose, trying to gauge if I should say something or just indulge him. There's no point in starting our relationship off under false pretenses. "Is there something *you* need to get here?"

"No. Today we're shopping for you."

This is my opportunity. "Could you pull over for a moment?"

He lowers his brow as he comes to a stop and watches curiously as I search for a thrift shop on the navigation system and hit start.

I'm relieved he seems amused as he pulls out of the parking lot and back onto the street.

"Are you sure this is where you want to shop?" he asks as his navigation directs him to a rather underwhelming parking lot. I wonder if he's ever driven his fancy car through this part of town. My guess would be no since his eyes are darting in every direction, watching who's coming and going. "Yes," I say as I swing open the door.

Carter hesitates. I walk around the hood of the car and open his door. "Trust me, your car will be fine."

He glances at it over his shoulder several times before we reach the door. I smile when we enter through the automatic doors into a bright, clean shop full of random treasures, all priced with stickers that say that all proceeds go to local charities. I'm amused at how uncomfortable Carter looks, but he's a good sport.

I stroll through the aisles picking out a selection of casual summer clothes, and then find myself in the shoe section. Carter stands at the end of the row, looking like he's afraid he'll catch athlete's foot if he joins me. A pair of black patten stilettos adorned with a small white bow, catch my eye. With a broad smile, I hold them up to show Carter.

He scowls from where he stands several feet away. "Pretty but not very practical. Where are you going to wear those?"

I'm aware of the people shopping around me, so I mouth the words. "In the bedroom."

"What?" he shouts.

I sigh and say it a little louder. "In the bedroom."

"In the bathroom?" he says, confused.

The lady standing beside me starts to giggle, and I glance at her with a smile. "Yes, yes, Carter. I'm going to wear these pretty shoes in the bathroom," I say, laughing.

He crosses his arms, annoyed that he's the source of our amusement. "I'm going to look for a purse," he says gruffly as he storms away.

The lady beside me has difficulty containing her laughter, and I admit, so am I. "Well, I guess no pretty bathroom shoes for me then," I say as I put them back on the rack.

She snorts then laughs aloud.

Carter is already perusing the purses hanging in the next aisle. I quickly find the right one. It looks practically brand new. Carter glances at the tag as I turn it over.

"You know you can buy a brand-new purse from any designer store you'd like. I have money."

I walk toward the cash. "So do I. But that's not the point."

Carter concedes and refrains from any further comments when I pick a pair of knock-off designer sunglasses at the cash.

I think I hear him let out a sigh of relief as we leave the store, and he once again has eyes on his precious Ferrari.

I start moving things from the broken purse into the new one and come across a thumb drive that I made for a road trip the girls and I took to Virginia. I hold it up to show him. "Will your car play this?"

"Of course," he says, taking it out of my hand and plugging it into the dash.

"Could we roll down the windows on the way back instead of the air conditioning?"

"You're not worried about your hair? It gets pretty windy along the coast."

I twist it into a pony with an elastic I just found in my bag. "I'm good. I like the fresh air."

As Carter begins to drive through the busy parking lot, the USB loads my playlist, and the first song to play is YMCA by The Village People. My eyes open wide, and I reach over and max out the volume as I slide down in my seat. Everyone walking through the parking lot stops and stares at the Ferrari as Carter navigates the speed bumps with a cautious and slow speed. I place my hand over my mouth to stifle my laughter.

People are still staring after he turns down the volume and skips to the next song. I can't stop laughing. I haven't felt this happy and stress-free in a very long time.

Suddenly the music stops as a call comes through.

"Oh, crikey," he says as it connects through his Bluetooth. "Hi, Mum."

"Hi, Carter. How are you?"

"I'm great."

"You sound a lot less stressed than the last time we talked. When are you coming home?"

I raise my brows, curious about how he's going to answer.

"Well, funny thing."

"You're already home, aren't you," she interrupts.

"Yes, but I only came in last night."

"And did you come home alone?"

"No, Mum. Katherine came with me. She's with me right now."

"That's wonderful," she says excitedly. "So, you're on your way here to introduce her. Right?"

Carter looks uncomfortable and glances at me. I hold my hands in the air in defeat.

"Ah, yes, we're on our way."

"Good answer," she says sternly. "Now stop yapping on the phone and pay attention to the road. I'm sure you're riding around in that death trap."

"I'll drive carefully. Goodbye."

I grin as he hangs up and shakes his head.

"Was your mother that annoying?" he asks.

"More. I think she would have wrapped me in bubble wrap if she could. When I was younger, her habit of being overprotective used to make me so angry. Now, I'd do anything she asked if it meant I could spend more time with her."

Carter reaches for my hand. "I'm sorry, you must miss her."

"I do. Pat tries, but we just have never had that kind of connection."

Carter pulls to a stop in front of a small house in the middle of town. "Are we here already?"

"Don't worry. She's going to love you."

My eyes open wide. "The thought hadn't crossed my mind until you said it. Now I'm worried she won't."

"Sorry." He knocks once and turns the handle as he pushes open the door. "We're here."

"Come in. Carter, I need you to get me down the good serving dish. It's on the top shelf over the refrigerator."

"Got it," he says, kissing her on the cheek on the way past. She dries her hands on her apron and extends her hand. "Come in, come in. I'm Alice. It's nice to meet you finally. You've had my son twisted up in knots for months now."

"Mum," Carter scolds her as he returns to the room.

"The biggest tragedy in life is when a woman has no idea how deeply she affects a man. If she thinks he doesn't care, she might simply walk away without a fight."

I get the feeling she's talking from personal experience. I'm glad to see that she's looking well recovered. "How are you doing?" I ask, concerned.

"I'm fine."

"Just fine? Are you feeling better? What have the doctors said?"

She looks at me, confused. "Doctors?"

"Yes, the specialists? You look great. Are they saying you'll have a full recovery?"

"I have no idea what you're talking about. I haven't been ill."

I glare at Carter. He avoids eye contact with me.

"You sit right here, and I'll be right back. I just made oatmeal raisin cookies. Would you like a cup of tea with them?"

"Yes, please. That would be lovely." When she's out of the room, I turn to Carter and punch him hard in the bicep.

"Ouch!"

"Did you lie to me about your mother being sick?" I snarl.

"No. She was sick."

I narrow my eyes.

"She was." A look of guilt washes over him. "Well, she had a cough."

My mouth opens, and I blink my eyes rapidly, trying to get my head around it. "You made it sound like she was dying of cancer."

"Is that what you thought?" he asks, trying to fake his surprise. "Heavens, no. But in all fairness, it could have been pneumonia. You never know at her age."

"You're unbelievable. What else have you lied about?"

"Nothing. I didn't lie. She wasn't well. I'm her only son, so I had to come home."

I raise my hand. "Stop."

"Here you go," she says as she returns to the room with a tray. "These were William's favourite cookies." She pauses. "You should wrap some up and take them to him when you go see him."

"I have no plans to see him, Mum."

"Don't be ridiculous, Carter. Of course, you're going to take Kate to meet your stepdad."

"Nope, hadn't planned on it. And he's not my stepdad. You were never married. He's probably off galivanting anyway."

"No, Mavis told Beatrice, who told Mary that she saw him in town yesterday."

Carter looks frustrated. "The man abandoned you twenty-five years ago, so why are you still making his favourite cookies?" He walks into the kitchen to get more milk for the tea.

Alice leans in and places her hand on top of mine. "When you truly love someone, you never give up hope."

I smile. After all these years, she still loves the man.

"Or in Carter's case," she continues, "if you truly love him, you have to look past his stupidity."

"Mum!" Carter says again as he enters the room.

"Stop lying to the girl and just apologize for being an asshole."

I put my hand over my mouth to hide my laughter.

"Do it!" she insists.

Carter puffs out a frustrated breath. "Kate. I'm sorry I'm an asshole."

"Was that so hard?" Alice asks him.

"No, Ma'am."

She looks in my direction. "If I know Carter, I suspect you'll be hearing that a lot."

"What was he like as a boy?" I ask curiously.

"Oh, here we go," Carter says as he plops himself down on a chair.

"Carter was the cutest baby I had ever seen. I'll dig out some pictures to show you the next time you visit."

"Perfect!" I say, showing interest.

"He was a sweet and kind child. Always sticking up for the underdog and rescuing stray animals."

"Really? I didn't take you for the compassionate animal lover type."

He rolls his eyes. "Name any ten-year-old who would pass by a wounded or stranded animal and ignore it?"

"Fair point, I guess. What activities did he like to do?"

"Well, when he was younger, the other kids would run around and play games. If I took my eyes off Carter for a moment, I'd find him eating dirt."

I burst out laughing.

He folds his arms in front of him. "That's not funny."

"He used to daydream about traveling the world with his father."

"Again, not my father or my stepfather," Carter adds before heading back into the kitchen for more cookies.

"William wanted desperately for us to go with him, but that wasn't the life suited for a woman with a young child. We stayed home, and I did the best I could on my own. William would write every week begging me to send Carter with him, even if for a short while. I guess back then, he was so much like him I was afraid if he went, I'd lose him too."

How sad. Carter enters the room and looks concerned by my sombre expression. "What's going on?"

"Eventually, he hit his stride," she continues. "He started excelling in school and sports. He grew eighteen inches in one summer when he turned sixteen."

"Wow, what an overachiever."

"You seemed to appreciate that about me last night," he says as he passes me another cookie.

My face turns red. I can't believe he said that in front of his mother.

"I have always been grateful for the scholarship money he received so he could go to university and get the best education possible."

"Ethan." He mouths so only I can see.

I place my empty teacup on the table. "Thank you, Alice, for sharing that with me. I can't wait to hear more stories about Carter growing up."

"Are you leaving so soon?"

"Sorry, mum, you know we've only been back a few hours, and that time change is still messing up our internal clocks. We'll come back to visit soon. I promise."

She walks us to the door and gives me a tight hug. As she releases me, she tucks a few wrapped cookies into my hand. "For William," she whispers.

I smile. "I'll make sure he gets them."

"What are you two up to?" Carter asks suspiciously.

"Not a thing, boy. You mind your business."

"Yes, Ma'am."

Chapter Thirteen

Carter.

"Ethan!" I interrupt. "For the love of God, just take over the family business. That's all your father wants you to do. Everything is happening for a reason. You're home, and Olivia is there."

"That reminds me, I'm going to kick your ass for not telling me my mother was in Canada, and they were coming back to Ireland together."

"I'm more afraid of your mother than I am of you."

"That's probably wise."

"Oh, I know it. Now, John said, you look like shit, and you smell worse. Have you even talked to Olivia yet?"

"No."

"Bloody stubborn asshole! Do you not realize that you're causing her more stress by pushing her away in your attempt to limit her stress? The Doctor said it's not uncommon for babies under duress to come early."

"Carter, I've let things get to a point where I just don't know how to fix it now."

"You pick up the phone and say, Honey, I'm a twat. I want to come home."

"It's not that easy."

"It is JUST THAT EASY!" I yell into the phone. "It's easier than dealing with that douchebag nephew of Hammond's."

"I've heard he's making things tough on you. Do you think it's because you're loyal to me?"

"Scott and I think that's the reason. Look, I didn't call you to argue over this stuff. I wanted to talk to you about Kate."

"Is everything okay?"

"Yes. Remember the night I met Olivia, and we were talking in the bar? We talked about finding the kind of love that you want to come home to at the end of the day. Someone to love and share the rest of your life with. The right woman to settle down and make babies with."

"I remember, Carter. Get to the point."

"I think…I mean, *I know* I want that with Kate."

"Congratulations. Does Kate want that with you?"

"I think so. I mean, she left everything behind and got on a plane to come to Australia with me. That means something, right?"

"I think it does."

"Do you think it's too soon to ask her to marry me?"

"Carter, have you not been following the O'Connell chronicles? My life is like a bad Netflix drama. I'm the wrong person to ask about rushing into relationships."

"Fair point."

"All I can say is that if it feels right, do it. And then be prepared to give her reasons to keep you around."

"If I do it, and by some miracle, she says yes, will you be my best man?"

"You know I'd be honoured."

"Thank you. I'll call you later in the week. Keep this between you and me for now. In case it doesn't go so well. I'm taking her to meet my step-father today."

"Tell William I say hello."

"I will. Now, stop being a dick. Olivia loves you. For better or for worse."

I'm left with a dial tone, and I'm not surprised.

"I'm ready to go," Kate says, entering the room with a handful of things. "Who's on the phone?"

"It was Ethan, but he hung up on me."

"I figured. I could hear you yelling."

"Strangely enough, I still haven't gotten through to him."

"He sounds pretty stubborn."

I laugh aloud. "That's an understatement."

She kneels on the floor and sorts through the pile of things, adding them to different compartments of her new handbag. The sight of her on her knees in front of me awakens something deep within. I'm tempted to pull her to her feet, throw her over my shoulder and give her a proper pounding. One she'll remember for several days.

"Where did you say your dad lives?" she asks as she stands.

"Errr…" I stumble with my thoughts. "Step-dad."

Kate narrows her eyes. "You don't know where he lives?"

"Of course, I know. My mind was elsewhere for a moment. He lives up the coast. Not too far."

"Can I drive?"

I think about it longer than I should, then hand her the keys. "Of course."

She laughs. "I was only joking. I'm not driving your Ferrari."

"Now I feel hurt."

"You'll get over it."

"Explain to me again why I had to call him and arrange dinner for tonight?" I ask as I make the relatively short drive up the coastal highway.

"I'm on a mission for your Mum, and I won't disappoint her."

"I have no idea what that means."

"I was thinking it's curious she kept referring to William as your father and commenting on how much alike you were."

I pull into the marina and park. "The man she married, the man I was told was my father, died when I was very young. William stepped up after that. I know what you're thinking, and I've had that thought myself."

"If they never married, why do you both refer to him as your step-dad from time to time?"

"I was a young boy, and he was my only male role model. He wasn't always the best option, but there were times he filled the fatherly role."

"What are we doing here?" Kate asks, confused.

"This is where William lives."

"At the marina?"

I round the hood of the car and open her door. "On a boat in the marina."

I hold her hand as we walk the narrow dock that floats and shifts with the waves.

"Hello!" a voice calls from the end of the plank.

"Hi."

He greets us midway. "I'm William," he confirms as he extends his hand. "You must be Katherine."

"Yes, it's nice to meet you."

"You must be a very important young lady if he's bringing you here to meet me."

Kate glances at me, unsure how to respond.

I smile. "Yes, she's very important to me, so let's not keep her standing out here on the dock."

"Oh! Of course. Let's go to the boat, shall we."

Kate follows him, and I walk closely behind her ensuring her safety as she steps up and onto the cabin cruiser.

"Welcome to the *Alice Rose*. I've got tonight's catch on the grill. I hope you like fish."

That's an excellent question. "Do you like fish?" I ask curiously. I lean closer and whisper. "It's not my favourite, so I'll be stopping for takeaway on the way home."

"I'm fine with fish," she assures me as she sits on the weathered vinyl bench seat.

"So, you met Carter in Canada?" he asks as he flips the large filet.

"I did."

"Always travelling, this boy. He's never home."

"I hear you like to travel as well," Kate says, making conversation.

"Grass has never grown under his feet," I add.

"It must have been hard travelling when you have a family."

I feel the tension in my neck and shoulders. "It wasn't hard at all. He left us at home."

William fidgets awkwardly with the food on the grill. "Carter's mother didn't have the desire to travel as I did. When I felt the calling, I had to go."

"In other words, you had no desire to settle down," I add with an acidic tone.

Kate raises her brow, somewhat shocked at my honesty. "Isn't that right, Dad?" I persist as he places plates in front of us on the table.

"I know why you're angry, Carter. I also know you understand the call to wander. There's a reason you've stayed single with nothing to tie you down."

"You forced the woman you supposedly loved to raise me as a single mother."

"I didn't abandon you. I kept in touch. I begged your mother to come with me."

"This looks delicious," Kate says, changing the subject.

I try to calm the raging storm bubbling to the emotional surface. The truth is, it wasn't William's duty to look after us. But a good man would have.

"Carter,"

I glance in her direction. "Let it go," she mouths quietly.

I hadn't intended for things to go off the rail so quickly, but here we are. I nod.

"So, where was your most recent trip?" Kate asks curiously.

"I haven't ventured out of the slip for quite some time."

I shovel the charred fish into my mouth at a great rate of speed to rid myself of it from the plate. I have never been one to enjoy seafood and the catch of the day overcooked and burnt on a grill held by two bolts to the back of a boat is even less enjoyable.

"Of all the places in the world you've travelled, why drop anchor here?" Kate asks curiously.

William raises his eyes, and there's an emotion there that I can't put a name to. Kate gives him a knowing smile. I'm not sure what I missed, but they've shared something. "We need to get going. I have to make a stop on the way home."

Kate looks annoyed at me as we help tidy the dishes from the table. "Are you miffed at me?"

"What's so important that we have to rush off?"

"I have to stop and pick up my watch. I dropped it off for repairs, and they close soon."

She gives me a stoic look, and from the corner of my eye, I can see William try to hide a smile.

"Thank you so much," Kate says as we walk toward the dock.

William follows us. "I'm happy to meet you. Hopefully, you'll come back to visit this old man again."

She doesn't wait for my answer or my approval.

"Of course." She tucks something into his hand and leans in close. "These are from Alice."

An expression I can't put a name to washes over his weathered face. I say nothing as I turn to follow her, staying close in case there's a sudden swell of waves that jars the dock.

I reach for her hand, expecting her to pull away since she's not pleased with me. Instead, she accepts my offer and allows me to escort her to the car. Guilt builds inside me even though she hasn't said a word. She gives one last wave goodbye before we disappear into the parking lot. I close my door and pause, mulling over my behaviour. "I was rather harsh, wasn't I?"

Kate gives me a sympathetic smile. "You don't judge me for how my family makes me feel. I was a young adult, but you were only a child. I can't imagine how it felt to watch your only father figure sail away and leave you behind. Little boys need their dads."

"Women need their partners," I add. She looks down, once again breaking our connection and strengthening those walls she's spent years building around herself. That, too, is likely my fault, and I'm determined to do whatever it takes to make it right. I reach over and squeeze her hand. "Hey, I like to travel, but I'm not hitting the road without you. Ever. Whatever fear of abandonment you're holding on to, let it go."

She swallows hard and meets my gaze, locking her eyes to mine. "I'm here to stay," I assure her. "Where's your head at? Is this just a vacation for you? Or is this home now?"

"I think I can call this home."

Excited about her answer, I pull into the jewellers a few moments before it closes. "Come in with me."

I hold the door and usher her in.

The owner meets us as we enter. "Mr. Brant. I didn't think you were going to make it today. I'll get your watch."

"Do you want to look around?" I ask, intentionally steering her toward the showcase of engagement rings. I'd like to get some input on what she likes and doesn't without her getting suspicious.

Silently, she scans the glass display, but she gives me no clues.

"See anything you like?" I ask, growing impatient as I see the owner returning from the back office.

"They're beautiful," she says to appease me.

"Nothing jumps out at you?" I ask curiously.

She glances over at the owner as he approaches. "Not my style," she says quietly.

What does that mean? It bothers me most of the way home. I pull into one of my favourite drive-thru restaurants and order takeaway since I'm starving. I stop at a spot on the beach and watch the moon rise over the ocean.

"It's gorgeous," Kate declares as she eats my fries.

"Can I ask you something?"

"Sure."

"In that entire wall of rings, there wasn't one there that you'd like for yourself?"

She picks up my drink and sucks on the straw before placing it back down. "Not really."

"How is that possible?" I ask, dumbfounded. "Miceli is a world-renowned jewelry designer."

She smiles, and it confuses me even more. "You don't know me very well."

"I know you well enough, but you don't wear a lot of jewelry. I don't know what your style is."

She laughs, and I feel myself becoming frustrated.

"Carter, do I strike you as the kind of girl who cares how many carats a diamond is, or if a ring is made of platinum?"

I pause and think about it, and when I don't answer, she raises her brow. "Do I?"

I scruff the stubble on my chin and concede. "No."

"Money is not important to me. You should know that."

"What is important?" I ask. "If someone wanted to buy you jewelry?" I add.

She smiles. "The story. The history."

I'm a bit baffled. "You think I'm pretentious, don't you?"

"You drive a Ferrari and live in a million-dollar neighbourhood in a luxury townhouse near the beach that you hired an interior designer to furnish," she blurts out without missing a beat.

I'm not sure if I should feel proud or ashamed. "Fair point. Wait to you see my boat," I say, feeling conflicted.

"You have a boat?" she asks, sounding astounded.

"Two."

"How much money do you have?"

I shrug. "If I quit my job today, I'd have enough to keep us comfortable for a very long time." I pause. "We'd never have to worry about money."

"Really?

"Yes, but only if we sold everything and moved in with my mother."

She laughs aloud as we get out of the car and lean against the hood. "Got ya."

"The upside of that is we have a built-in babysitter for when we do some of that travelling."

"Wouldn't we take the kids with us? I mean, you just said how hard it was to watch William leave without you, and I'd want them to see the world and learn about different cultures. Have as many different experiences in life as possible."

I pull her closer, stoked that she's talking about kids and our future. "I like that idea. As long as occasionally we can leave the kids and have a date vacation."

"Date vacation? Not date night?"

"We can do both. But I want us to get married first."

"Married?" she asks nervously. "Nobody gets married anymore, Carter."

"I'm one hundred percent in this relationship, and I'm going to prove to you that I'm committed to you. Nothing will come between us, Kate. Whatever comes our way, we'll face together."

"I like the sound of that, but everything is happening so fast."

"I'm a very possessive man. I want you for myself. I'm not leaving you available for anyone to think they'd have a chance to steal you away. You've always been mine."

"Forever, Carter?" she asks softly.

"Yes, forever." I hush her with my lips until she relaxes in my arms. I'm confident that I've just torn down a significant section of the wall she's been guarding.

"Carter."

"Mmmhmm."

She leans back to stare into my eyes. "I'd like you to make love to me on the beach, under the moon."

"No, you don't. Trust me."

"Why would you say that?"

"Because you never want to experience sand in the crack of your ass, believe me."

Her stare is intense. "I don't care. I just want you to make love to me right now."

I give her a wide smile as I lock the Ferrari and lift her into my arms. "Well then, my lady. As you wish." I walk toward the shoreline and a large group of rocks that will provide us with some privacy. "Just don't say I didn't warn you."

Chapter Fourteen

Kate

Carter gets ready to meet with a few of his sales associates to go over the new targets. I can tell this job is making him miserable. If it weren't for the money, I'm sure he would have told the new boss to kiss his ass long ago. It's crazy how working for Ethan O'Connell made this a desirable career. Now he seems defeated.

"What are you going to do today?" he asks as I walk him to the door.

"Besides, have another shower to wash the sand out of my crack? I'm not sure."

"I warned you. But the crab was a new one. I've never had one pinch my ass before."

I burst out laughing as I recall the loud pitch shrill he let out when a small sand crab felt threatened by our presence and decided to give Carter a warning. "Maybe I'll download a book and head down to the beach."

He smiles and kisses me goodbye. It seems like the most natural thing in the world for me to be here.

"I wish I didn't have to leave you today."

I'm sure he's still reeling from our lovemaking last night. I stayed awake all night thinking about the promises he made. "I'm sure you'd get sick of me if we were together all the time."

"Never."

I laugh. It's a nice dream, but the thought of two people spending eternity together and not getting on each other's nerves occasionally seems like a long shot. I think what my mother and father had was a rare gift. I love that Carter believes that kind of relationship is our destiny as well. I'm cautiously hopeful, but I'm not sure that our discussion last night was intended to be an official proposal. Everything about our relationship so far has been impulsive. Things change. People change. When things slow down and we settle into the pace of two adults raising children, I suspect he may feel the call just as his step-father did.

He stands holding my hands and staring at me with a sincere adoration. For a fleeting moment, I allow myself to feel what truly passes between us; Love.

"Have a wonderful day. Don't forget this isn't Lake Ontario. The salty air will take a lot out of you. Make sure if you go in the water to rinse off before you lay out in the sun."

"Got it."

"The spare key is on the counter. There's a waterproof pack on the table. Take it, put your phone, your money, the key, anything valuable inside it, and take it with you in the water. Don't leave anything on the beach."

"Even my phone?"

He smiles. "Even your phone. Trust me. It's completely waterproof if you close it properly. I've used it dozens of times when I surf."

"You're going to be late."

"I'm the boss. I can't be late for my meeting."

"Fair point."

He abruptly stops as he reaches the door. "You did buy a bathing suit, right?"

I laugh. "Yes." I take one last appreciative look at his rugged chin and ocean blue eyes. "I'll see you tonight." He kisses me one last time, and I watch from the front stoop until he reappears in the Ferrari. He slows down to wave, and I blow him a kiss. I feel giddy like this is still all just a dream.

My phone rings as I gather up my things to go to the beach. I hesitate, not sure if I should answer the call.

"Hello, Dad."

"Katherine, I haven't heard from you in days. Why haven't you been in the office?"

My heart begins to pound. "Because I quit, remember?"

"No, you didn't."

I furrow my brow. "Yes, I definitely did. I was there. You were there too. And your favourite daughter Stacey, the brown noser. She's always there."

"Kate, you were angry. You weren't serious. Nobody took you seriously."

Now my blood starts to boil. "Trust me. I was serious."

"Where are you? Come into the office so we can talk."

"Uhh. I can't do that, Dad. I'm out of the country."

"What do you mean?"

"I mean, I'm not in Canada."

I hear the frustration in his voice. "Where are you, Katherine?"

"In Australia."

There's a long pause where I hear his grumbled curses. "With Carter Brant?"

"Yes."

"When will you be home."

"It's hard to say. Let's go with *I'll be here indefinitely.*"

"You're not being reasonable. You can't just up and leave everything behind that we've been working so hard for."

"That's the problem. Those are your dreams. It's not what I want to do with my life."

"Come home, and we'll talk."

"Okay, I'll let you know when I'm coming home for a visit."

"Any idea when that will be?"

"Soon. I'll have to come to get my things."

"I'm not happy about this, Katherine. Not happy about it one bit. What would your mother think?"

I feel every muscle in my body tighten as I choke back the tears. "Don't, Dad. Don't you dare bring Mom into this. If she were still alive, she would have never let you force me into doing something I didn't want to do. She would have told me to follow my heart. And that's what I'm doing."

He sighs emotionally. "I'm sorry, you're right. It was unfair of me to mention your mother. I don't want to lose you too, Kate."

"You're not going to lose me. I just need to live my own life."

"Come home."

I feel the tension start to subside. "Soon."

"I love you. Be safe."

The words coax a small smile. "I will, Dad. I love you too. I need some time to decompress and figure out what I want to do. I'll call you next week."

Well, that was some way to start the morning. I feel like I've just taken the bipolar express from one station to the next. I'm emotionally exhausted before lunch. I make a sandwich and grab some snacks while my book finishes downloading, then grab the beach bag from the hall. Carter must spend a lot of time at the beach because it's already packed with everything I'll need.

I'm surprised how busy the beach is at this time of day. I always assumed that everyone works from nine to five every day, just because I did.

I find a quiet spot away from everyone else and spear the sun umbrella into the sand, securing it from the ocean breeze. I roll out the beach mat and drop my things. I chase my straw hat down the beach more than once before deciding to use my shoes to weigh it down. The fresh warm air is soothing, and before long, I feel the stress leave my body. I reach for my tablet and get the strangest feeling I'm being watched. A few feet away, a small grey furry face pops up over a pile of rocks and then quickly disappears when he sees me looking. Strange.

I'm a few chapters into my book when something soft rubs against me. I look down to see those sparkling blue eyes and whiskers. "Hey, kitty." I put down my tablet and slowly lower my hand. "Where did you come from?" I look around to see if I could spot anyone looking for him. He backs away as my hand gets closer to him. I stop so I won't spook him. He sits and watches me for the longest time. I go back to reading my book, but I'm aware he's still there. Suddenly a soft fluffy head pops up from under my book, and a tiny meow demands my attention. I move slowly and let him smell my hand before stroking him gently between the ears.

He purrs, and it makes me smile. "You're a wee guy," I say as I check him over to make sure he's okay. "I don't think you should be away from your momma just yet."

He continues to communicate with me, meowing and telling stories. I finally understand what he's trying to say. I reach for my sandwich and pull out some of the ham. He sniffs it and keeps one eye on me at all times before finally deciding to eat it. When he does, he loves it. "Meow." He says again.

"I'm pretty sure this is not good for you. Let's see if we can find your momma."

I pick him up and walk along the strip of sidewalk that separates the buildings from the beach. In the alley of one of the hotels, several employees are taking a break. "Excuse me," I interrupt. "I've found this kitten, and I was wondering if anybody knows who the owner might be?"

One of the younger girls walks over to scratch him between the ears. "He's probably a stray. There are a lot of feral cats around here."

"Is there a rescue or animal control I can call? He looks little," I say, concerned.

"Nah, just put him down over there by the dumpster, and natural selection will look after things."

I blink my eyes, trying not to look shocked at the suggestion. "Thank you. I'll wait to see if someone comes looking for him."

I walk back to my spot on the beach, and the kitten starts to wiggle in my arms. I try to calm him, but he twists and turns, then leaps out of my hands and lands on his feet in the sand. I follow him as he chases a small sand crab down to the shoreline and laugh as the tide comes in quicker than he anticipated and makes him jump back onto dry sand. He is the tiniest little furball I have ever seen except for his ears. They look way too large for his head. The sun behind us casts a shadow that makes him look like Batman. I'm amused. He digs in the sand and uncovers a seashell that I promptly pick up and admire. I carry it with me back to the blanket and sit in the shade. Kitty follows closely behind. I pick up my tablet, then lay back to continue reading. It's hard to concentrate with the tiny purring going on in front of me. I watch him walk in circles trying to find just the right spot as close to me as he possibly can. "Are you comfy?" I ask before holding my tablet in front of me and begin reading.

He pushes his head beneath it and nudges it upward. Damn my tender heart. "Okay, buddy." I abandon my hopes of reading and focus on the tiny furball demanding my attention. I'm mesmerized by how brilliant blue his eyes are.

I open my eyes, feeling like I'm being watched. I look over my shoulder to see Carter wearing a pair of bright orange surf shorts lying beside me.

"Hi! Did you finish early? Why didn't you call me? I would have met you at home."

"I did call, but apparently, you were napping."

I sit up and look for my phone, careful not to disturb the kitten. "What time is it?"

"It's almost four o'clock. Is there something you want to tell me?"

"Huh?"

"Who's your friend?"

Little blue eyes open and follow my every movement. "Oh. I don't know. He just found me. I walked up and down the beach and asked if anyone was missing him, but everyone said he was likely a stray."

Kitten stands up and stretches. "He looks kind of small to be on his own." Carter reaches over and picks him up, holding him so he can see his wee face. "What's wrong with his head?" he asks, grimacing.

"Nothing," I say defensively.

"Look at the size of those ears. Are you part bat, little man?"

I snicker. "I thought the same thing."

"I did a little surfing while you were sleeping. Are you ready to go home?"

"Sure, I'm starving."

"You fed your lunch to the kitten, didn't you?"

I smile mischievously. "Maybe."

Carter grabs his surfboard while I roll up the blanket and gather up my stuff. Kitten watches with curious eyes, jumping playfully at things as I pick them up.

I look at Carter, and he gives me a sympathetic look. "Oh no. I'm not ten years old anymore. My pet rescue days are over."

"He's so little."

"Exactly, it's likely his mother is nearby watching. If this is where you found him, we should leave him here in familiar territory."

I know he's right, so I nod, but I feel torn. Kitten watches as we walk away.

"Don't look back. The minute you look back and establish eye contact, we're done for."

I frown. "Why does this feel wrong?"

It's a short walk back, and I look forward the entire way.

"My dad called me today."

Carter raises a brow. "What did he have to say?"

"They didn't think I was serious about quitting."

"You're kidding?"

"Nope. He was shocked and angry when I told him where I was."

"So, have you left things on bad terms?"

"No, I told him I needed time to figure things out and that I'd be home to collect my things at some point. I'd come by to talk to him then."

Carter looks concerned as he leans his surfboard against the porch railing then unlocks the door. "Did you hear that thud?" he asks.

"What was that? A squirrel or something?"

Carter walks past me to the top of the steps. "Kate."

"What's wrong?" I ask, joining him.

Carter steps to the side and points down. At the bottom, the little grey kitten with giant ears is trying to climb the steps, but they are too tall for his little legs. He stretches as far as he can, digging in his claws and trying to pull himself up before letting go and falling back to the ground. Strangely my eyes fill with tears, and Carter turns into a puddle.

"Oh, for the love of… please don't cry," Carter says as he steps down and picks up the kitten. It looks even smaller in his large, strong hands as he delicately passes him to me. Kitten purrs, and I lock eyes with Carter.

"I don't know what we're going to feed him tonight," he says as he walks past me and pushes the door open.

I follow him in. "He likes ham."

Carter brings in the bags I abandoned at the front door and then turns to see my wide smile as the kitten nuzzles beneath my chin and purrs. "You two are killing me. Have you already named this kitten?"

I stare down at him and grin. "Bruce."

"Bruce?" Carter confirms.

I nod.

"I must be out of my mind. Okay, Batman, you can stay until someone comes looking for you. But don't poop in my hundred-dollar sneakers."

"Like he'd know the difference between those and the cheap ones."

"I don't own any cheap sneakers."

I roll my eyes. "Okay, the cheaper ones."

Carter suddenly looks panicked. "Why don't I find a box and put some sand in it."

"Good idea."

He stops to kiss me on the forehead on the way past. "You do realize this has fast-forwarded our relationship to the point of no return. We're now fur parents."

"That's a very serious commitment," I acknowledge.

"It is. Are you in?"

My heart, for the first time, feels whole. No cracks, no breaks, no longer empty. I don't have this crushing feeling like Carter will abandon me and leave me completely gutted. Life finally feels like it's on the right path. I look down at Bruce and then lock eyes with Carter. "I'm not going anywhere."

Chapter Fifteen

Carter

I wake up this morning from that same dream—me on the beach with a beautiful woman and a small child. The universe is sending me effective messages. Today is the day.

"Kate."

"What's up?" she asks as she gets out of the shower.

"I have to run out for something."

"Now? Can't we stop on the way out?"

"No."

"Do you want me to come with you?"

"No, I'm good. You stay here and make us a picnic lunch and make sure Bruce has enough food and water for the day. I'm not sure what time we'll be back."

She looks at me concerned, and I give her a reassuring smile. "I won't be long, I promise."

I rush to the car because I'm literally a man on a mission. A few days ago, Kate and I wandered into a small shop on the outskirts of town, and she spent hours mulling over the antique jewelry that they've acquired over the years. It's the solution to a serious problem. I waste no time in getting there. The owner smiles when he sees me return.

"I thought I might see you again. Where's the pretty lady?"

"She's at home. I've snuck away to buy her a gift. It needs to be an extraordinary gift. I'm planning on proposing today."

He smiles and pulls a tray of rings out of the display. "She didn't care about the jewels, only the story."

"Yes, you're right. She's interested in the history." I want Kate to feel like this was well-thought-out and not an impulsive purchase.

He searches through the rings one row at a time until he finds the one he's looking for. "This one. I bought it at an estate sale."

He passes it to me, and I stare at it, mesmerized by the simple beauty and design. I can see that the inside band was once engraved, but time has made the message illegible. "It's sterling silver, and the coloured jewels are only costume jewelry quality. The diamond is real."

I scowl. "It's kind of tiny."

"But it's real—only a quarter of a carat. I believe what attracted her to it is the shape. It is no easy task to cut a diamond that small into a heart shape."

I squint. "That's a heart?"

He holds up a magnifying glass so I can see it better. I will admit that if the monetary value was not a consideration for someone, this ring is simple and stunning.

"The story, as told by the seller, is that there was a wealthy man who took on an orphan of Ireland in the late eighteen hundreds."

I perk up. "The Earl Grey Scheme, if I remember my history correctly."

"That's right," he says enthusiastically. "This young girl had a very tragic life. She lost her parents to the famine when she was ten and lived in the horrific environment of the Irish workhouses, where she watched two sisters die. It's said that at the age of fourteen, she had met a young man, and they were to be wed, but on the day of the ceremony, she stood at the altar alone."

I raise a brow. "He stood her up?"

He cocks his head to one side and then the other. "I can only share with you the story I was told. Of course, no one knows why the young lad didn't show."

"That is quite the tragic story. Why would Kate be interested in this ring?" I ask, bewildered.

"Ah, this is not the wedding ring of the young Irish lad. No. After her groom didn't show, the young girl was sent to Australia to help populate the new colony. Lord Brant was the man who obtained her service."

My chin drops, and I blink a few times. "Lord Brant?"

"Yes, and it's said that when she arrived, he fell immediately in love with her."

I listen intently, wholly immersed in the story. "You don't say?"

"Even though she arrived already expecting a child from the other man, Lord Brant took her in and raised the babe as his own. Their wedding was the social event of the year."

"If he was so well off that he could afford a grand wedding, why such a simple, inexpensive ring?"

"There was a news clipping about that. Lord Brant had bought the love of his life the finest gold and diamond ring that money could buy. She made him sell it and use the money to set up a charitable fund to help women, who didn't want to be part of the project, start a new life."

I laugh once, aloud. "Of course, she did."

"This," He holds up the heart-shaped diamond ring, "is the ring she chose in its place."

I feel like a divine force has just hit me in the face with a chair.

"I have the bill of sale and information on the charity as well as newspaper clippings. I even have their marriage certificates."

I feel the excitement building inside me. This is a formidable sign. Well played, universe, well played. "I would like to buy this ring. Would you part with those documents as well?" I ask.

"Of course. It would only be right for them to stay with the ring."

I place my credit card on the counter. "What if I need to get it sized? Are you able to do that?"

He glances at the name on my card and smiles. "There's no need to get it sized, Mr. Brant. She tried that ring on at least four times the day you were here. It fits her ring finger perfectly."

Strange energy fills the room.

"Shall I leave it in its original ring box, or would you like me to put it in a new one and wrap it?

"Do you even have to ask?"

"No." He hands me the worn velvet ring box and a clear protective plastic envelope with all the documents he obtained when he bought the ring at auction.

"She's going to love this. Thank you."

"May your marriage always be full of love."

I look at my watch and panic. "I have to go." I push open the door and rush to the Ferrari. Kate's going to kill me.

My phone rings as I'm pulling up in front of the townhouse. "I'm here, sorry." I jump out and rush to meet her as she comes out the door with a large cooler bag.

"Is this all for just the two of us?" I joke as I try to figure out how I'm getting it in the Ferrari.

As I drive down to the marina, I notice there's a large bag on her lap. "Please tell me you didn't bring Bruce."

She grins. "Oh, I wasn't supposed to?"

"How do you expect the kitten to stay in the boat in this heat?"

"Won't it be cool when we're moving?"

"Yes, if he doesn't bloody blow away. He weighs less than a stick of gum for fuck sakes."

She laughs and opens the bag. "I'm only messing with you. Bruce is at home."

What a relief. The only use for something that small and fluffy on a boat is for bait. Thank the lord I didn't say that out loud. "What have you got in that huge bag then?"

"Everything we need for a romantic evening on the water."

I think I just fell in love with her a little more, and I'm confident this is the perfect night to propose. I want to do it right. As we walk to the dock, Kate stops to read the registered name proudly displayed on the side of the boat. *Lily*. A silent understanding passes between us as Kate reaches for my hand. Her eyes glisten, and I swallow hard, wishing that I could offer her an explanation or an apology for choices made in a past life. I choose to look forward and not back.

No words are spoken as I help her aboard. "What do you think?"

"It's a nice wee boat," she says as she looks around.

My jaw drops. "Nice wee boat? Would you prefer to take the fifty-foot yacht?"

She begins to laugh, and it helps me loosen up. I'm just a little tense today.

"Where are we going?" She loosens the rope, and I steer out into the open water.

"Not far, just a short trip up the coast from Noosa to Rainbow Beach. Maybe we can check out Fraser Island. There's a wildlife sanctuary there I thought you might enjoy. I hear the dingoes come down to the water."

"Well, now I'm glad I didn't bring Bruce."

I don't think I've ever felt so free. Kate ties her hair up to keep it from blowing wildly in the wind as we head to deeper waters and pick up a little speed. It's a relief Kate seems to enjoy being out on the water as much as I do. When we reach the island, I drop the speed and take a leisurely trip around. It's a gorgeous day, and we're able to spot many different species of animals and birds native to Australia. When I find the right spot, I drop the anchor and help Kate unpack the food.

"Look, Carter!" she yells, startling me so that I almost drop my sandwich into the water.

"What?"

"Koala bears!"

I squint. "I don't think the island habitat supports anything like kangaroos or koala bears." She looks disappointed, so I wrap my arms around her as we stand at the back of the boat, watching as the sun starts to get lower on the horizon. "Are you happy?"

"Very. Happier than I ever thought I could be."

I kiss her shoulder. "I have one more thing I want to show you before the sun goes down."

I drive the yacht to the public docks and tie off.

"Where are we going?" she asks as I help her out of the boat.

"Rainbow Beach. Just follow me, and you'll see."

I'm starting to feel nervous now. I've been rehearsing this in my head all day long. She follows me to where I've arranged for two horses for us to ride to the south side of the beach.

She raises her brow. "Are you kidding me?"

I think she's more reluctant than she's letting on as I help her get into the saddle. It never occurred to me that she didn't know how to ride. "I've been assured they're tired old trail horses who know where they're going and don't get excited."

"Have you ever done this before?" she asks as I get up onto my horse.

"A time or two."

"With other women?"

"Do you want the truth?" I ask as I move beside her and help her along.

"Not really."

I grin. "You're the first woman I've ever taken on this ride."

"Good answer. WOW!" she exclaims as we move along the beach, and she gets her first glimpse of the multiple layers of coloured sand that gives Rainbow Beach its name. "That's amazing."

As we make our way back toward the dock, the sun begins to set, and the burnt orange to dark reddish colours of the sand dunes along the horizon are mesmerizing. I return the reigns to the horse handler and help Kate to the ground.

I get that nervous feeling in the pit of my stomach. Too strong for butterflies. I brush the hair from her eyes and take both her hands.

"Kate, when I think about my future, I see only you. I see small children laughing and building sandcastles on the beach."

She gives me a knowing look and finishes my thought. "With curly blond hair and sapphire blue eyes."

"*Your* eyes, Kate. I know it seems like it's happening fast, but I love you. I feel like I've known you all my life. This is our destiny. I feel it deep in my soul." I reach into my pocket and pull out the velvet box. She stares down at it, and I see her eyes well up with tears. I promptly get to one knee and open the box, presenting it to her. "Kate, will you marry me?"

"You bought me Lady Lily's wedding ring?"

A tear streams down her cheek, and I experience a moment of panic. "Yes, but if you don't like it, you can pick any ring you want."

She puts her hand over her mouth, trying to hide her emotion. "It's perfect."

I get to my feet and take it out of the box. I feel a little awkward. I'm not sure what the next move should be. She hasn't actually agreed. I search her eyes for some kind of a clue. She smiles and manages to speak a barely audible, emotional "Yes, I'll marry you." She extends her hand for me to slide the ring on her finger.

She jumps into my arms, and I spin her around until I feel a bit lightheaded. Overwhelming emotions hit me as I lower her, and her body slides along mine until her feet touch the ground. I claim her lips in a possessive kiss, getting intoxicated by our exchange of breath. I need to get her home and make love to her so intimately that our souls will be forever imprinted. It's a barbaric, feral instinct, but Kate brings that out in me.

Firmly holding her hand, we walk along the shore as I lead her back to the boat. The sun is beginning to set as we start making our way back home. I look down at the ring on her finger, and it gives me a significant amount of joy. "Soon, you will be the new Lady Brant."

"Really?" she says, mocking me. "Are you a Lord now?"

"You only need to call me Lord Brant in the bedroom."

She snickers. "Forgive me if I forgo the formality."

I shrug. "It was worth a try. Maybe you could try it just once."

"Not going to happen, my lord." She smirks.

The quiet evening is disturbed by the call of the dingoes as it echoes over the water. Along the shoreline, we can see the shine from their eyes as they pace back and forth. "It's starting to get dark out here," Kate says, concerned.

"Don't worry. We have very bright lights."

She looks very unnerved as she sits beside me. The night air is cool, and we're only a few moments on the water when it starts to rain. I stop the engines and begin to put up the rain covers. Kate follows my instructions and tries to help get it done as quickly as possible. When we're finished, she's drenched to the bone, and I can see every curve of her body and the swell of her breast. My cock twitches and I know I can't wait until I get her home. I pull her into my arms and kiss her passionately, tugging wet clothes from her body with incredible difficulty. She gives me a mischievous grin and runs her hand across my erection before undoing my shorts and forcing them to the ground. I lift her and pin her to the wall. She wraps her legs around me as I thrust inside her. She feels so good, and my emotion is ramped up right now. With her legs still anchored around my waist and her arms around my neck, I lift her and move to the table. It's the perfect height for me to get deeper. She pants as I quickly find the rhythm that's guaranteed to push her over the edge as I grasp her breasts and firmly squeeze them in my palms.

Suddenly and quite inconveniently, I'm blinded by a bright light shining through the cabin window.

Alarmed, Kate lifts her head. "What's that?"

I become still, hoping the light is from a passing vessel. I watch through the porthole as the distinct markings of a rescue boat pulls up alongside us.

"Shit, shit, SHIT!" I ramble as I try to get my shorts up and fastened. Kate gets to her feet in a panic. "What do I do?"

"If you have dry clothes, I suggest you grab them and put them on. In the bedroom." She grabs her bag and bolts to the room and pulls across the bifold door just in time.

"This is the Coastguard. We are preparing to board your ship."

Chapter Sixteen

Kate

Before I met Carter, I wouldn't consider my life to be a story worth telling. In a short time together, we've created an endless number of humorous anecdotes to share with our children. For example, such a beautiful, well-thought-out day for our marriage proposal was followed by an hour-long interrogation by the coast guard. It was hard to keep a straight face while Carter tried to explain why we were drifting offshore in the dark during a rainstorm. Despite his reassurance that he was an accomplished captain and navigator, they insisted on escorting us back to the marina.

I return from the shower to find Carter starfished, face down, and buck naked on the bed. I can't resist climbing in beside him and smacking his bare ass cheeks like a set of bongos.

He lazily lifts his head and stares at me. "What are you doing?"

"Playing the drums," I say, amused.

"I didn't know you had musical talent. Let me roll over, and you can show me how you play the flute."

I snort and throw my hand over my mouth. Carter laughs out loud.

I wiggle up beside him, feeling a little nervous. "I need to talk to you about something."

"It sounds serious. I hope you haven't changed your mind."

"No, but I need to talk some things through with you."

"Like, wedding plans?"

"No. I haven't even thought about that yet."

Carter rolls over and props himself up on his elbow. "What's on your mind?"

I gesture at his nether region. "Can you put that thing away? I can't have a serious conversation with you after your last comment while that's out there."

He grins as he pulls the bedsheet over himself. "Better?"

"Much." I lay down beside him and try to decide where to begin. "When we get married, what am I going to do?"

"You don't have to do anything."

I knew that was going to be his answer. "I can't just sit around all day and do nothing and let you support me."

"Why not?"

I glare at him. I should have known he wouldn't make this easy.

He chuckles. "I guess that's not an option then. What do you want to do? If you want to work, then get a job but pick something you're passionate about. Something you get up every day and want to do."

That sounds too incredibly easy. "Does that job exist?"

"Well, until you find it, you can always volunteer to help for causes you care about."

"I'm not going to lie. I've been thinking about that."

"Start making phone calls and apply for positions."

"I will, but there's something I need to do first."

"What's that?"

"The way I left things with my family feels wrong."

"And you want to make things right with your father?"

"Yes."

"Then you should go home and talk to him."

I feel an enormous weight lift off my shoulders. "Yes, I should."

"Do you want me to go with you? I can move my schedule around. I couldn't care less if I miss a few meetings with Pépé Le Pew."

"I think this is something I need to do on my own."

He nods and tries to hide a look of concern. "When are you thinking of going?"

"On the next available flight."

"That soon? What about Bruce?"

I smile. I could take him with me, but I'm sure you're capable of looking after him while I'm gone."

Speak of the devil. I must have left the door cracked open, and the tiny kitten climbs his way up the side of the mattress and plops himself down on Carter's pillow. "See? You're best friends."

In the cab, on my way to the penthouse, I think about how strange it felt when Carter took me to the airport. He was nervous about me getting on a plane and flying to Toronto. I feel somewhat distraught when we pass the century-old building with the red door tucked between modern-day giants. Except for the 'for lease' sign, the windows are bare, and I wonder if she has passed or just moved on.

I tip the cabby and carry my only bag into the lobby on my own.

"Hi, Miss Ryan, it's great to see you. Welcome back," the girl at the front desk says when she sees me. "Are you back in town for good?"

"No, just temporarily."

"You'll be needing a room then?"

I look at her, a little confused. "Is the family penthouse not available?"

"No, Miss. Someone moved in there a few weeks ago. I could put you in another room. A suite so you'll be comfortable." She begins to tap on the keyboard, searching for an available room.

I feel a little silly. "You know what, don't worry about it. I'll just stay with my dad while I'm here."

"Are you sure? It's no trouble. I can have someone get a suite ready for you quickly."

"No, it's fine. Really."

I swing my bag over my shoulder and walk down to the lake on my way to the office. The Redpath project seems to have stalled. I've only been gone a few weeks, but I figured by now, the land would be levelled and construction underway.

Dana squeals when she sees me enter the lobby. She knocks people over, pulling me into a forceful hug.

"This place is horrible without you," she confesses as she pulls away. "Wait. Where is that gorgeous Australian god? Why are you here alone? You're not coming back, are you? Would you please tell me that you're not coming home? Did you break up? Didn't it work out?"

I try to answer, but she doesn't take a break between questions. "Give me a chance to answer, would you."

She takes a deep breath and pauses. "Sorry. I just miss you. Are you okay?"

I smile and hold up my left hand. "I'm very okay."

"YES!" she shouts. "Your sister is going to shit her pants. I love it!"

"Dana!" I say, shocked.

"Oops." She looks to see who is around us.

"Is my father in?"

"Yes, he is. But I don't think he's expecting you."

"Don't call up," I insist as I walk toward the elevator.

"Err, you know he hates surprises, right?"

"I know."

I ignore the odd looks and whispering as I walk the hallway to my father's office. I push open the door and walk in.

"Kate!" he says, surprised.

"Hi, Dad. You got my message that I was coming home?"

"Yes. It's been crazy since you left. I just finished my sixth meeting today. Is there any possibility of me coaxing you back to work?"

"Not a chance."

"I hate meetings," he grumbles.

"Me too."

"Someone is living in the penthouse."

He nods. "Yes, Stacey moved in there a few weeks ago."

I feel my blood start to boil. Why couldn't it be anybody but her? "What happened to my things?"

"I hired a moving company to pack it up and take it to the house."

"Thank you, I guess. A little heads up would have been nice."

He looks over the top rim of his glasses, and I immediately get his unspoken point.

"Would it be okay if I stayed in the guest bedroom?"

"Of course, Katherine. There's always room for you. I'll call Pat and let her know to get it ready."

"Thanks, Dad."

"I'm done here for the day, so I'll go get the car."

"Okay. I'll go grab whatever is left in my office and meet you out front." I cross the hall and turn on the light. "Fucking scavengers," I mutter as I open empty drawers. "They've even taken my stapler." The only thing left untaken is a seashell pencil holder that I got during a trip to the Bahamas. "Well, at least they left me this." I pick it up and head toward the elevator.

"KATE!" a voice yells from the end of the hall. "Kate!"

I keep walking, pretending that I don't hear him, but he's getting closer.

"Kate! I heard you were here!" he pants when he finally catches up to me.

"Hi, Will. I have to go. Father is waiting for me downstairs."

"Oh, yes, of course, but I was wondering if you'd have dinner with me one night."

"Oh, I'm sorry, Will," I say as I step into the elevator and hold up my hand. "But I'm very engaged." As the door closes, I see him throw his hands up in the air and then cover his face. "I KNEW I SHOULD HAVE ASKED BEFORE SHE LEFT." I hear him growl as I start to descend.

I settle into the spare room and take a shower before dinner. I tried to stay awake for most of the very long flight to sleep at the regular hour in this time zone. I had only just got myself sorted around on the other side, and now I start all over again. My phone rings, and I answer it quickly.

"Good morning, beautiful. I miss you."

I love hearing those words. "Good morning. I miss you too. How's Bruce?"

"He's very needy."

"He's a kitten," I remind him.

"He's pretty high maintenance if you ask me. Always staring at me, looking for attention. Feed me; pet me; nap with me."

I stifle a giggle. "You're napping with him?"

"Let's get this straight. I'm the dominant species."

"Right."

"So technically, he's napping with me."

I snicker. "Glad we got that straight. What's that noise?"

"My boss is calling. For the third time this morning."

"Do you need to go? I can call you before I go to bed."

"Nope. I don't want to talk to him again today. Everything he's doing adds up to him squeezing Ethan out permanently. I think he's just waiting for a way to do it with cause."

"That's awful."

"Let's face it. O'Connell brought this on himself."

"How is Olivia doing?"

"She called me today."

"Oh?" my blood runs cold. How is it that I still feel a wave of jealousy?

"She wants to talk to me about an idea she has."

"Regarding?" I urge him on. For Pete's sake, can he be any more cryptic?

"She wants us all to take on new positions at O'Connell industries and force Ethan to take over for his dad."

"All of you?"

"Yes, Scott, John, Landon. Even Reese."

"Isn't Reese the one his ex-girlfriend cheated with?"

"He was accused of it, but he didn't. He's innocent. She tried to convince him to blackmail O'Connell, and when he refused, she named him anyway. Ethan wouldn't even listen to Reese's side of the story."

"I don't know why you're so loyal to Ethan. He sounds like a dick."

"Well, he is a dick. But if it weren't for him, I wouldn't have received the education I did or the job I have now. He's not that bad of a guy. Just a little misguided. And stubborn. And selfish. Fuck me. I need new friends."

"Mmhmm. You're going to be busy with a new wife soon, so I wouldn't put out any 'bros wanted' ads just yet."

He laughs once. "I love your sense of humour. How are things going with your dad?"

"Well, he didn't throw me out, and he let me stay at the house. I'll talk to him tonight about some of the other things going on. I think everything is going to be okay."

"That's good to hear. When are you coming home?"

"Probably on Monday. I need the weekend to pack up a few things I want to bring home with me. And some stuff I'll need to donate somewhere."

"It makes me happy to hear you call Australia home."

"I guess home to me from now on is wherever we are together."

"I suppose you have to endure another Ryan Sunday family dinner."

"Yes, one last one. Except for the occasional Christmas or Thanksgiving that we come back for."

"You'll have to remind me about Thanksgiving. That's only a North American holiday."

"What are your thoughts about Olivia's plan?"

"I don't know. I mean, working for Ethan or his father wouldn't be much of a change from what I'm doing now. If there were a formal job offer on the table, I'd review it."

"Would it mean we'd have to move to Ireland?"

"She didn't have all the details ironed out, but it sounded like her plan was international expansion, and we'd each run the business in our geographic areas. The same as we do now with Aurora."

"You'd stay in Australia?"

"Right, and Landon would be the business manager for South Africa."

"Well, you're miserable working for Aurora right now. Maybe it wouldn't be a bad thing."

"Let's see how things roll out. I'm not much of a gambler."

I burst out laughing.

"Why is that so funny?"

"You're kidding, right? Everything you do is on impulse. You ask me to come to Australia while you're practically on your way to the airport. Then, you propose shortly after."

"That's different."

"How?"

"I have to go. Bruce is staring at me."

I shake my head and smile as I start my way downstairs. "I'll call you later."

"I love you."

I look through the rooms and find my father alone in the study. "Look after Bruce."

"Hurry home."

I turn off my ringer and stuff my phone in my pocket. "Hi, Dad. Do you have a moment before dinner?"

He pours himself a bourbon and motions for me to sit.

"I wanted to say that I'm sorry for the way I left."

"Me too. I always hoped I could harness you into the family business, but your heart has always been too emotional."

"Is that a bad thing?"

"No, not at all. I shouldn't have forced you to do a job I knew you'd hate. Why did you do it for so many years?"

"Because I love you, dad. I didn't want to disappoint you."

His eyes fill up with tears, and my heart feels heavy. "My girl, you could never disappoint me."

"Since Mom passed, I feel like you die inside every time you look at me."

He stares at me, eyes full of sorrow. "I see your mother every time I look at you. I don't want you to feel that way. I love you. You are precious to me."

"Sometimes, it feels like you're prouder of Stacey than you are of me."

He lifts his drink to his mouth and pauses a moment, thinking carefully about what he wants to say. "I love Pat. She tolerates my bullshit. She will never replace your mother, and Stacey will never replace you. As a business partner, she's exemplary. As a daughter, she falls short."

"Can you love me for the person that I am? The girl who wants to save historical buildings and host fundraisers for soup kitchens." I fidget nervously, twisting and turning my engagement ring.

"Yes. And it cuts deep that you don't think I do. But I guess I have myself to blame for that."

I glance down at my finger. "Carter and I are engaged."

"I noticed your ring. I figured you'd tell me when you were ready."

"I wasn't keeping it a secret. I just wanted to get those other things out of the way first."

"Do you love him?"

"Yes."

"You didn't hesitate to answer. You're that sure?"

"I am. He's the one. It's like we have a connection I can't explain. He gets me."

"As long as you're not marrying him to get away from us."

Is that what I'm doing? I swallow hard, weighing his suggestion, and quickly decide that it's not. "No, I love him."

"Well then, you have my blessings. Will I get an invitation to the wedding?"

"Of course, we haven't set dates or anything. I wanted to make sure everything was squared away between us. You'll walk me down the aisle, won't you?"

He gleams. "I hoped you'd ask."

He escorts me into the dining room, where Stacey and her mother are placing out the food.

"Kate," Pat puts down a bowl of mashed potatoes and then extends her arms for a hug. "It's so nice to have you home."

"Thank you," I notice the daggers Stacey is throwing my way.

"Did you really move to Australia?" she asks.

"Yes, with Carter. We have a lovely luxury townhouse near the beach in the Noosa area."

"How long will you be staying with us?" Pat asks as she passes my dad the basket of freshly baked buns.

"Only a few days. I just came to talk to Dad and gather up my things."

"Well, if you're talking about the stuff at the penthouse, there was nothing there worth taking halfway across the world," Stacey says in a malicious tone.

Pat glances across the table and gives Stacey a disapproving look. I feel my face turn red. "Well, I'd still like to go through it just the same."

"Of course," my dad answers. "Everything is in boxes out in the storage shed."

My eyes open wide. "You mean the stable?"

"Well, you know we store the horses out there too. But your stuff is safe in there. All the things from your childhood bedroom are still packed up out there as well," he adds before cramming a fork full of chicken in his mouth.

"Great." Time for a subject change. "Dad, I know it's none of my business, but I was wondering about the Redpath project."

"There is no Redpath project," Stacey says, staring me down.

"Oh? Why's that?"

"Because someone," my dad says with his eyes on his dinner, "filed a request for historical status. It was granted right after you left."

I feel a great deal of pride, and I have to be careful not to show it.

Stacey continues to stare me down. "We received a cease and desist order."

My dad glances at me and hides a ghost of a smile.

"Kate! Oh my gosh," Stacey says suddenly with such great excitement she startles me. "You're wearing an engagement ring."

"Oh," I look down at the ring that means the world to me. "Yes, Carter and I are getting married."

"Congratulations, Katherine. That's wonderful," Pat says, gauging my father's reaction from the other end of the table.

"Let me get a closer look," Stacey insists. "The diamond is so tiny I can hardly see it from here."

I clench my jaw as she pulls my hand over in front of her. "Well, it's cute. I thought Carter could afford something much more elaborate."

I look across the table at my dad and Pat. They are both avoiding the conversation with their heads down and shovelling food into their mouths. Don't let her get to you, I repeat to myself. "He can. I picked this one from a local antique store. It has some wonderful history and an amazing love story."

"How quaint. I hope you had it disinfected."

"Stacey!" Pat warns.

"Do you think Carter Brant has it in him to settle down with one girl? You?"

"Those days are over. He loves me."

"Of course, he does," she laughs.

It's hard to ignore the growing tension in the room. I narrow my eyes. "If there's something you want to tell me about Carter, now would be a good time to clear the air."

She smirks but declines to elaborate.

"So, what's your plan? How are you going to make a living out there?" Pat asks, trying to break the tension.

"For now, we'll live in Australia. I'm not sure what I'll do there once I get settled, but for now, I'm going to look into charitable foundations that need managing or volunteer work to keep busy until I figure it out."

"How very 'Bondi Housewife' of you," Stacey says with animosity.

I'm startled by the loud clanging noise of father's fork as he drops it to his plate and gets to his feet. "Stacey, it's time for you to shut the hell up. Help your mother clear the table."

Without a word, Pat and Stacey stand and collect the dishes. I mouth the words "Thank you" in my father's direction. He responds with a nod and, if I'm not mistaken, a look of pride.

Chapter Seventeen

Carter

"What do you mean you're not coming home for a few more days? I'm going out of my mind without you."

"Carter, you were the one who told me to start looking for a position that I'd enjoy doing. It's a coincidence that they reached out to me on LinkedIn. But the fact that the head office is here in Toronto so that I could do the interview in person is a sign. I'm sure of it."

"You're right. You can't pass up this opportunity. Stay, as long as you need."

"I knew you'd understand."

"The position is in Australia, right?"

"Yes."

"Okay, I just wanted to make sure you're coming back."

"I'm coming back. Australia is home for me now."

I wish hearing her say it made me feel less unnerved, but my stomach has been twisted in knots all day. Like the universe is trying to warn me of some impending doom.

"Sweetheart, I have to go. My boss is calling. I'll talk to you later."

"Love you, goodbye."

I quickly switch calls. "J.P.! What can I do for you?"

"Brant. You've been avoiding my calls for days."

"That's not true, I've just been busy trying to hit my new sales targets, and you always seem to call when I'm busy with a customer." I'm a salesman. I can sell anything, even a crock of bullshit. "What's so important that you've been chasing me down? I still have fourteen days until the end of the period."

"It seems that one of our important clients is travelling to Australia. She arrives today and is staying at a hotel close to you. It would be fitting for you to entertain her while she is there."

What the fuck? "Thanks anyway, boss, but I don't have time for babysitting duty."

"Carter, I'm not asking. I'm telling. You'll pick her up tonight at dinner time and make sure she has a good time during her stay. I'll have my secretary send you the hotel information. And Carter, if you don't show up, your job will be at risk."

"You can't do that. It's unethical and against our contractual agreement. Legal will back me up on this."

"Very well, contact the legal department and exercise your right to break the contract."

This is precisely what he wants. It takes every ounce of self-control I have not to tell him to shove his job up his ass. "Fine, I'll send one of my younger, single sales associates."

"No, it must be you. It was her specific request that she be joined by the man in charge of sales. That's you."

I curse under my breath, feeling trapped. "Alright, if she's that important to your business, I'll take her to dinner, but nothing else."

"I trust that you will fulfill her entertainment needs for this evening. A critical business deal is at stake. Over three million dollars of business in the first year."

What the fuck? Why do I feel like I'm being pimped out? This feels dirtier than when O'Connell does it. "Dinner. That's where I draw the line." I hang up, angry with myself for even agreeing to that. My phone rings, and I answer it without looking at the display.

"Well? How did it go?"

"Ethan? I forgot to call you back. It went well. Kate and I are engaged."

"Congratulations!"

"You'll be my best man, right?"

"Of course. When?"

"Good question. We haven't planned anything yet. She went home to work things out with her father."

"Well, that's a good thing. The last thing you need as newlyweds is to have family problems looming over your heads."

"I guess you would know."

"All too well."

"John told me that you're not the father of Jessica's baby."

"Yes, someone tampered with the original test results."

"I'm glad you're finally getting some justice. John thinks all charges might be dropped with the new evidence."

"I'm ready to put this mess behind me."

"John also told me that you're having secret meetings with an investment banker that you don't think he knows about."

"Fuck, remind me not to hire any more ex-military security experts."

"What's going on? The truth. Everything. Don't bullshit me."

"I'm thinking about selling my shares in OCI and tendering my resignation at Aurora."

I'm shocked. "I'm close to tendering my resignation at Aurora myself. Hammond's nephew has asked me to pimp myself out tonight to entertain an important client."

"There was a time you didn't mind doing that."

"Yeah, well, those days are over. So why sell your shares at OCI? It's a great opportunity for you to take over for your dad and expand the business."

"I don't know, Carter. I feel like nothing will ever be the same. Maybe I just need a fresh start."

"You had better mean a fresh start with your wife and your new baby."

"It's getting hard to avoid her. She's more stubborn than I am."

"Proof you were made for each other. Have I ever given you bad business advice?"

"No."

"Then listen to me. Turn the family business into the same type of empire you created for Aurora Technologies and stop punishing yourself. Olivia loves you. Let her back in. Everything else is almost behind you now."

"I don't know."

"I have to go. It's almost time for my escort service to begin. Think about it, okay? Don't make any decisions right now. When things settle in a few days, we'll get together like old times and figure it out together."

"Thanks, Carter. I don't know what I'd do without you."

"Well, you would have lost fewer demerit points on your license and never met the Maloney twins."

"They were a lot of fun."

"Pamela and Patricia. It was a night I'll never forget."

"Neither will they," he chuckles.

"It's good to hear you laugh again, old friend. I'll talk to you soon."

The hotel bar where I'm meeting this client is on the south end of the beach, but it's too far to walk. I dab on my favourite cologne and hop into the Ferrari. I leave the car with the valet and head to the bar.

"Do you have reservations?" the girl asks me at the desk.

I scroll through the details sent by my boss's secretary. "I don't think so; I'm not sure. I'm meeting a client here."

"Oh, what's his name? Maybe the reservation is under that."

I scroll back and forth through the data. "I don't seem to have that information." I shake my head, annoyed. "Why would they set up a dinner and not provide the client's name?"

"Because if they did, you wouldn't show up."

Terror runs through my veins. I turn slowly and confirm my worst nightmare. "Stacey, what are you doing here?"

"I'm here on a trip?"

"A business trip?"

"No, more like a trip for pleasure."

"This is not happening," I mumble under my breath.

"Right this way," the waitress says, ushering us into the dimly lit restaurant and a quiet corner.

"Do you have a table somewhere where it's brighter? Like maybe in the kitchen?" I ask. The waitress gives me an odd look.

"He's just joking," Stacey assures her.

"Nope, I'm not. You can't be here. WE can't be here together. Does your sister know you're here?"

She gives me a grin that makes me feel like I've just gone down the rabbit hole. "Kate has no idea I'm here. As far as I know, she's still in Canada waiting on an interview for an international charity position that I set up."

"You were behind that? She'll be crushed."

"The job is real. She still has to get hired on her own. I just pushed the recruiters in her direction."

"Why? I thought you and she didn't see eye to eye?"

"Oh, we don't. But I needed her to stay in Canada a few more days so that you and I can spend some time together."

"Time together? There is no WE. I'm only here because my boss is going to terminate my contract if I don't have dinner with you."

"Ah, yes. J.P. He was even easier to get wound up than O'Connell was. It wouldn't be necessary to get him involved if you had answered my calls the last time I was here on business."

"I won't do anything that will jeopardize my relationship with Kate."

"Dear sister never has to know. You amuse me. I enjoyed our time together. She can go off and save the world, and you and I can play on the side."

Did I hear what I thought I heard? "Are you insane?" I'm marrying, Kate. There will be no playtime with you on the side."

She reaches over and places her hand on my knee, and I feel like I'm going to lose my mind. "We had fun, you and me? Don't you miss it? The excitement. The passion."

"Nope. Not a bit. In fact, the only reason you and I were together in that club that night was so that I could distract you from trying to set your claws into O'Connell."

"I don't believe that for a minute. You're not that good of an actor. You enjoyed yourself. You REALLY enjoyed yourself. And you enjoyed yourself several more times in the following days. What do you think Kate would think if she was to find out?"

"You wouldn't dare."

"Oh, but I would. Clearly, you don't want Kate to know about our past, or you would have told her already."

I raise a brow and get to my feet. "What is it with women and blackmail these days?"

"Sit down. We haven't had dinner yet, and I have an agreement with your boss."

"If you learned anything about me back then, it's that I prefer to be the dominant one in the relationship."

She smirks. "I can switch."

"Jesus. What is wrong with you? I'm in love with your sister. I'm not interested in having an affair with you."

She takes her phone out of her pocket and shows me my boss's number. I begrudgingly sit. "Dinner. That's all."

"We'll see," she says as she opens the menu in front of her.

"You can eat. I've lost my appetite."

She puts the menu down in front of her as the waitress returns. "I'll have the blackened swordfish,"

"I'll have a double whiskey. Keep them coming."

There's something pure evil in her grin. If I were younger and single, I'd be eager to explore the darkness behind it. It's enticing; it's exciting. I shake my head. What am I doing? I shouldn't be here. I've been struggling with coming clean with Kate, and I'm just digging myself in deeper. How would I argue that what happened was before we met when I've just met with Stacey in a hotel while Kate is out of town? I've screwed myself. I lose my job if I leave, and I'm likely to lose Kate either way.

Food and drinks are placed on the table. Stacey isn't discreet about moving closer and closing the space between us. I'm physically exhausted watching her every move and trying to thwart off any physical contact.

"I'm curious," she says between mouthfuls. "What do you see in Kate. She isn't homely looking, I'll give her that, but she's weak."

I take several large gulps of whiskey and wait for the burn to subside before I speak. "She's not weak. She's kind and charitable."

"Weak," she repeats.

"If all the people in the world were exactly like you, who would help those who need it?"

She laughs once. "If all the people in the world were exactly like me, they wouldn't need help."

I search the room, ensuring no one is taking video.

"Don't go anywhere," Stacey orders as she gets to her feet. "I need to go to the restroom. Then I want to go dancing."

Oh, fuck no! I take my phone out of my pocket and call Olivia. "Thank god you picked up."

"What's going on?" she asks, alarmed.

"I need details."

"On?"

"Your job offer. I need to know exactly what I can expect. Salary, expenses, vacation, benefits, bonuses."

"Carter, I'm just trying to put it together. What's going on?"

"I'm about to quit my job."

"What? What happened?"

"I received instructions from Hammond's nephew to entertain an important client on a trip here in Australia. My attendance was non-negotiable."

"He can't do that."

"Oh, but he did. The worst part is the client."

"Who is it?"

"Stacey."

"GET THE FUCK OUT!"

"And she's not taking no for an answer."

"Where's Kate?"

"Still in Canada. She has an interview with an international charity that's looking for an administrator for their Australian branch."

"That's fantastic!"

"It is because she may be the only income we have soon."

"She may not even stay if she finds out."

I get to my feet and peek around the corner to see where Stacey is. "I was trying not to think about that."

"Did you tell her about Toronto?"

"No. I was waiting for the right time." Peeking around things, I cautiously make my way to the lobby.

"You're screwed."

"Can you just send me a job offer?"

"Of course. But Carter, I'm not sure I can match what you're making at Aurora currently. Not to start."

"I know. But I'm about to walk out this door, and when I do, my career will come to a screeching halt." I walk as far as I can away from the door and pace as I wait for the valet to bring my car around.

"I'll have legal put it together right away."

"Thank you." I jump into my car and squeal tires, trying to get out of there. I didn't even tip the poor valet. I'll make it up to him another time. When I get home, I sit in my car in the parking garage for the longest time, thinking about what needs to be done. I take my phone out of my pocket, take a selfie of myself flipping the bird, and attach it to a message that simply says I QUIT.

The moment I hit send, I have regrets—short-lived ones. Changing jobs will be the easy part. Explaining everything to Kate is a whole different level of complicated.

Chapter Eighteen

I swing open the heavy wooden barn door and hold the bottom of my T-shirt over my mouth and nose until the dust settles. I'm annoyed that Pat decided to store everything I own and all my childhood memories, including things that belonged to my mother in the dusty, damp, and musty barn. Heaven forbid she find space for two boxes inside the four thousand square foot home my father bought for her.

I drop the roll of bubble wrap I brought on the floor, then climb a few rungs of the rickety ladder to pull down a couple of old suitcases from the mezzanine.

I unzip them on the floor beside me and then open the flaps of the first box to see if anything inside is ruined. "Lovely," I grumble as I discover my mother's favourite teacup and saucer full of stuffing, straw, and various bits of string. A tiny brown field mouse pokes her head through the fluff and stares me down.

"Sorry little momma," I say as I gently dump the teacup and all the nest material into a small pile of hay in the corner of the room. "I'm pretty sure I'd have trouble getting you through customs."

One by one, I take things out of the box and wrap them. I'll take the most delicate items with sentimental value with me on the plane and check the rest. I'm not sure how gently they treat things marked fragile at the airport. I've watched them from the plane window as they toss stuff on the conveyer belt to load into cargo. I look around at the leaky shed they call a barn. I guess I have nothing to lose. Obviously, things of my mothers aren't of any value to my dad or his new wife.

I'm about halfway through moving things to the suitcases when I begin to feel emotional. I was a young adult when my mother passed away, but that didn't make it any easier to sort through her belongings and purge my childhood memories when my dad sold the family house I grew up in. I check my phone to see what time it is in Australia and dial Carter. "Hey."

"Hey, how did the interview go?" he asks.

"I thought it went well. When I left, she had me convinced I had it in the bag."

"That's great!"

"Not really. They called me late last night to tell me they chose somebody else."

Carter curses under his breath. "There will be other positions," he assures me. "Are you packed and ready to come home?"

"Almost." I choke back emotions.

"Are you okay?"

"Yes. I guess going through everything has made me a little emotional."

"I should have just come with you."

"I love that you wanted to, but I can handle it."

"Sweetheart, you know that being in a relationship means you don't have to do things alone anymore. I've got your back, and I'll always show up for you."

"I know." At least I think I know. I want to believe. So far, everyone I thought I could count on has let me down.

"Hurry home. I miss you."

"I'll be there tomorrow. I better go. I've only got a few hours to repack the stuff I want to bring with me."

"No regrets?"

"No regrets. I miss you too."

I disconnect my call and stare at the last box. I'm not sure why I've kept all these silly sentimental keepsakes. I struggle to find a logical reason in support of taking them with me. I drag the garbage bin across the room and toss old schoolwork and drawings, report cards, and letters.

"Are you sure you want to get rid of those memories?" A voice asks from the doorway.

"Hey, Dad." I look around at the piles I had started sorting. "What am I going to do with this stuff?"

"Keep it to show your children one day."

I pause and give it thought. He walks over and picks up a pile of school papers and flips through them before picking up a box of seashells I had collected from various summer trips.

"You always had some kind of fascination with the ocean," he says as he hands me the box.

I pick them up one at a time and read the date and location I wrote on each one with a marker. "It's always called to me, for some reason."

"Australia must fulfill that calling."

"We're right on the ocean, Dad. I can't wait for you to visit."

"Lots of shells to collect then."

I smile. "It seems I've moved on to collecting other things."

"Oh?"

"On my last beach trip, I brought home a kitten." I flip open my phone and show him a picture. "His name is Bruce."

My dad squints. "What's wrong with his ears? Are you sure it's a kitten? It looks like a wombat."

I open my eyes wide and take a closer look at the picture. "No. He's a kitten." I zoom in. "I'm sure it's a kitten. I think."

My dad laughs, and it fills my heart with so much joy. It seems like we haven't shared laughter since I was a very young girl. I had forgotten how his eyes sparkle when he's happy.

"When do you leave?"

"In a few hours. I'm just going to pack these things up and go straight to the airport."

He nods. "You are always welcome home, Kate. I know this isn't the house that we shared with your mother, and it must feel odd to you, but there will always be room for you here."

"Thanks, Dad."

He turns and walks away. "Just leave the stuff you don't have room for. There's an old trunk in one of the spare bedrooms. I'll move it in there for you until you're ready for it."

I watch as he fades into the darkness. At that moment, I realize that I'm not the only one who fell apart when my mother passed. He, too, has built up some mighty walls over the years. He hasn't been the perfect father. He hasn't been the most understanding father. But I realize now that he's trying to be the best father he can be, and that's enough for me. I no longer feel hurt or betrayed.

I'm anxious to get home and see Carter and Bruce. I walk up and down the curb at the international arrivals terminal, but Carter is nowhere to be found. I take my phone off airplane mode and call him. "Where are you?"

"Right in front of you."

I lower my phone and step off the curb, glancing to the left and right for his car. "Honestly, the Ferrari isn't that hard to spot. Are you sure you're at the right terminal?"

"I'm sure."

"Well, honk your horn then." The large silver Range Rover in front of me makes a loud, obnoxious honking sound, startling me. I jump back and hold my hand on my heart, trying to slow it down. Slowly the heavily tinted passenger side window goes down. Expecting an apology for scaring the bejeezus out of me, I look inside. Carter greets me with a wide smile.

"You have got to be kidding me!"

"Do you like it?" He jumps out without waiting for an answer and starts to load my baggage into the back.

"Look how much room we have now."

I'm trying to wrap my head around it. "I see that."

"Now, when we want to go on a picnic or a trip, you don't have to sit with everything on your lap."

"You bought a brand-new Range Rover?"

He pulls away from the curb and hops on the highway. "Yes. We can't carpool the kids to school in my Ferrari."

There's a long silence in which I ponder the reality of what he just said.

"Kate?" He says, concerned.

I zone back in and realize that we're already home. "I kind of liked the Ferrari," I admit, feeling disappointed.

"You did?"

I nod, feeling like a hypocrite.

Carter chuckles as he unlocks the door. "Well, that's good because I still have it. I bought this as well. You're going to need a way to get around to do your thing as soon as you figure out what your thing is."

"Bondi Housewife," I mumble under my breath as I pick up Bruce and plop down on the couch.

"Pardon?"

"Something Stacey said. Are you going to unload the Rover?"

"I will in a minute. Since you brought her up, there's something I need to tell you."

My blood runs cold. "About Stacey?"

He sits down beside me with an extreme expression of guilt. "I don't want our marriage to begin with skeletons in the closet."

I feel ill. I had a feeling there was something, but now he's about to spill the beans, and I'm not sure I want to know.

"Kate, while you were away, your sister came to Australia."

"She came here? To the townhouse?"

"No, to a hotel, just down the road."

"Is she still there?"

"I don't know."

"Why is she here?"

"Well," he says, looking uncomfortable. "She came here to see me. Because she knew you were in Canada."

"I don't understand. Why would she do that?"

"Last year, before you and I met," he clarifies, "Stacey and I met at a business dinner."

I nod. "It wasn't just a business dinner, was it?"

"No," he says regretfully.

I feel myself starting to get agitated. "Was it just a one-night stand? A fling? How long did it go on?"

Picking up on my tension Carter reaches for my hand. "We got together a few times over a period of several weeks."

I pull my hand out of his, needing some space and time to process it. "Did you have feelings for her?"

"No! It was purely a physical thing."

I place my hand on my forehead and close my eyes.

"It didn't even start as a thing."

"Now, you're not even making any sense," I say, feeling hurt.

"At the time, I was single. You and I hadn't met. Stacey was a client of Ethan's who had requested an evening out. Ethan was supposed to be her entertainment, but he was there with Olivia, and the whole thing was rather awkward, so I." He pauses.

"You what?"

"I took one for the team."

I stare at him, open-mouthed. "You took one for the team?"

"Yes. To get Stacey's attention away from Ethan."

I get to my feet and try to remember to breathe.

"Where are you going?" he asks, concerned.

"I'm going to get my luggage."

He reaches for my arm. "I'll get it."

"No, Carter, I just really need some air right now."

He drops his hand and lets me go. He unlocks the door to the Range Rover from the deck and watches as I pull my life's belongings out of the back. I struggle with one of the suitcases and feel his body next to me, lifting from the other side.

I'm not sure how I'm feeling right now. I'm fighting back the tears, but I don't know if I'm hurt or angry. I let Carter take the heavy luggage to the house and sit on the top porch step.

He gives me a few minutes alone, then joins me. We sit in silence until Carter puts his arm around me and pulls me close. My instinct is to pull away, but I don't.

"Why didn't you tell me?"

"I had no idea that Stacey was your sister until the night I had dinner at your father's house."

"Anytime after that would have been a good time." I point out.

He growls. "You're right. I'm not proud of the way things went. I'm embarrassed we hooked up at all, and I should have come clean right from the beginning, but I was afraid you wouldn't give me a chance. Then time passed, and things were so good between us that it felt too late to say anything."

"So, if there's nothing still going on, why is she here?"

"My boss called me. Said an important client was in town and he wanted me to take her to dinner and show her the town. I was going to send one of my associates, but he insisted that it has to be me, and if I didn't make this client happy, I could kiss my job goodbye."

"And you went?"

Carter looks embarrassed. "I went. And when I got there, I discovered the client was Stacey."

I clench my jaws. "I hate that bitch."

"I told her that I love you, and there won't be any side-action for her."

"How'd she take it?"

"Not well. I'm afraid she's going to keep trying."

"Can you drive me to the hotel?"

"Why?"

"Because I'm going to murder her and feed her body to the dingoes."

He pulls me closer and kisses me on the forehead. "Let's not resort to violence. Besides, I don't even know if she's still there. I left while she was in the restroom and then immediately blocked her number."

"You left while she was in the toilet?" I ask, amused.

Carter nods his head. "Are we okay?"

"I don't like that it happened. But I trust you. And it was before you and I met, so I think I can be an adult about it. Have you been tested for STDs?"

Carter looks at me, horrified.

I shrug. "It's Stacey. I know the kind of lowlifes she sleeps with."

"I'd quite like it if you didn't include me in that category."

"Hey, if the ho fits."

"Okay, that's enough." He presses his lips against mine. "We're looking forward, not back. That's our plan, right?"

I nod.

Chapter Nineteen

I wake in the morning with my arms wrapped around the most beautiful woman in the world and a rather homely-looking kitten on my pillow.

Although she was gone for less than a week, we both missed her here. I'll do everything I can to make sure the times we're without her are limited.

Kate stretches. Her lashes flutter as she wakes.

"Good morning," I say in a gruff voice.

"Good morning."

"How did you sleep?"

She smiles. "You made sure that I slept very well."

"Good." After I came clean about Stacey, I'm thankful that she didn't leave my ass and fly back to Canada. "That was the goal."

Bruce strolls down to the edge of the bed, stretches, and then yawns.

"Do you think he looks like a wombat?"

I lift my head. "A wombat?"

"I showed my dad a picture, and he asked me if I was sure he wasn't a wombat."

I stare at Bruce as I pick up my phone and do a google search. "No, he's not a wombat," I confirm. "He's just ugly."

Kate gasps and puts her hands over his massive pointy ears. "Don't say that," she whispers. "You'll hurt his feelings."

I chuckle as I get out of bed. "He's a cat, Kate."

"Where are you going? You haven't told me what you've decided to do about Olivia's job offer."

"I thought I'd go and make breakfast." How am I going to break the news about this one? I should have dropped all the bombs last night and be done with it. "I'm starving."

"Pancakes?" she jokes.

"I was thinking something a little more substantial."

"Sausage?" Kate gets out of bed and reaches for her suitcase, throwing it up on the bed. "So, have you given it any thought?"

"I have, but I'm curious what you think."

"Well, you hate your job, and it sounds like a good opportunity. Which way are you leaning?"

"I quit my job. Don't unpack; we're leaving for Ireland."

She raises her brow. "When?"

"Today."

"Good lord, I won't have to worry about jet lag. I'll be recovering from whiplash."

She pauses and looks at me, alarmed. "What about Bruce."

"Bruce is going to stay with my mum. Are you okay with that?"

She takes a very noticeable deep breath. "I guess. I mean, what choice do I have?"

"You could take him with us, but I don't think that's a wise decision."

"No, you're right. He'll be fine with your mum. She'll probably enjoy the company."

"Since he's seemingly going to be a permanent member of our family, however, it is a homely one."

"CARTER!"

I laugh. "Sorry, I couldn't resist. I made an appointment with a veterinarian to get his shots and give him the once over. She'll take him while we're away."

"Oh," she picks him up and gives him cuddles. I can hear him purring from the other side of the room. "That's nice of her. I'm quite fond of him, and I'd like to make sure we take proper care of him."

"I assumed that would be the case."

"How long will we be gone?" she asks as she scratches his ears and nuzzles him under her chin.

The maternal way she cares for that kitten stirs something inside me. It strengthens that primal need I feel to protect her. Not because she's weak, but because she's important. "Only a few days. Ireland is a beautiful place, and I want you to see some of it before we come home."

"I'd like that. You're going to love spending some time with Grandma," she says to Bruce as I leave the room chuckling.

It's a long flight, and we spend most of it sleeping or watching a movie. Becoming restless, Kate takes out an envelope of pictures my mother gave her of me when I was a boy. "Who's this?" She passes me the old polaroid photo.

"That's me, obviously. This is my dad. And this guy looks like William." I flip it over to read the handwriting on the back.

"William?"

"It is. That's what it says on the back." I squint. "I didn't know they were friends. This would have been taken just before my father died."

"William was around when your father was alive?"

"Apparently so."

She studies the picture for a long time. "Huh."

She piques my curiosity. "What?"

"Nothing."

"You can't do that. You have to tell me what you're thinking. I can see those gears are turning."

"Look at the picture carefully."

I study it as best I can in the dim light of the airplane cabin.

"Do you see any resemblance between the two men?"

I raise a brow. Now that she's mentioned it, it's uncanny. "Do you think he's a cousin or something?"

Kate gathers up the photos and puts them away as we're advised we're about to land. "I don't know. But if William is related to your father, why wouldn't that be something they would tell you?"

In the cab, on the way to the hotel in Dublin, I think about that picture and wonder if there are family secrets I'm not aware of. Kate stares out the window, and I lean forward to try and get her attention. "Are you okay?"

"Do you think Bruce is alright? He looked sad. Like he thinks we're never coming back."

I furrow a brow. "I was talking about sleep and jet lag and time changes."

"Oh," she says, looking embarrassed.

"How can you tell he looked sad? He always looks that pathetic and melancholy to me."

"Maybe it was just me that felt sad."

I reach over and squeeze her hand. "I'm sure he's fine."

"Were you in love with her?"

I'm stunned. What just happened? "I told you, I had no feelings for your sister."

"I mean Olivia."

My stomach churns a little, and I feel a tightness in my chest. "Is that what you've been thinking about all the way here?"

"It's crossed my mind. Please be honest with me."

"Okay." Honesty is easy. I don't even have to think about it. "I think I will always feel the need to protect her. But love her, no. It's you that I love. Even then, it was you. This time I'm choosing."

She turns her head to look at me for the first time during the ride. In her eyes, I see acceptance. We don't talk about our dreams and our past, but we both know that it has profoundly affected the people we are today. If it weren't for the universe pushing us together, I'm sure we would have gone our separate ways, never to realize our destiny. I can't say I fully believe in past lives or universal power, but one thing is for sure; free will is a powerful thing.

We slow down in front of the hotel, and I blink my eyes, certain that I'm seeing things. Kate sits straight up alert.

"Did you see her too?" Kate asks, alarmed. "Did you see the psychic lady from Toronto? She was right there."

"That's impossible. Why would she be in Ireland? It must be someone who looks like her," I say, trying to calm Kate and convince myself.

"You're right."

"Maybe we're just delirious from lack of sleep. We should probably check in and have a nap."

"I don't think I can sleep right now." Kate watches over her shoulder the entire time the porter unloads our luggage. From the corner of my eye, I see a familiar smile.

"Landon!"

"You're looking alright, Brant. How've you been?"

"I'm fantastic," I say as we embrace each other in a bro hug. "This is Kate."

"Landon from South Africa, right?" Kate confirms as she extends her hand.

He pulls her into a firm hug. "I've heard a lot about you. Do you speak french?"

"No, I'm from a different part of Canada," she says, gasping for air.

"Easy buddy, don't squish my girl," I warn.

Landon releases his hold and laughs. "I'm sorry, I am just so pleased to meet you."

"What time are we supposed to meet with Olivia?"

Landon looks at his watch as he walks with us into the lobby. "In a few hours. Check your itinerary. She just emailed it."

"And Ethan still has no idea?"

"Not as far as I know. He would have called us both out if he did."

"True."

"Go! Eat and have a rest. It was a long flight."

"I'll see you in a few hours. We still need to get checked in."

Kate enjoys the beautifully decorated lobby while I get the keys. "Is there a beach close to the hotel?" she asks the concierge on our way to the elevator.

"About a half an hour away by car, miss. I can arrange a taxi if you like."

"Not right now, but I'll be sure to call if I need to make arrangements."

"Missing the beach?" I ask curiously on our way up in the elevator.

"There's something I want to look for."

"You won't come home with another ugly kitten, will you?"

She gives me the side-eye. "No! I just want to get a shell."

"There are plenty of shells in Australia."

"It's kind of my thing when I travel."

I raise a brow.

"You know, like how some people collect magnets? I collect shells. When I was a kid, my mom and I used a marker to add the location and date of our vacation. I brought a box home with me that was stored at my dad's."

"I get it now." I pull her in close and kiss her. "We'll make sure you get one from Ireland."

After the bellhop leaves the luggage, we drop on the bed, literally exhausted. In just a few moments, Kate is fast asleep. I watch her for some time, counting my blessings.

My alarm goes off and startles me awake. I quickly hit the stop button and lift my head to watch Kate stir, and then roll over and go back to sleep.

I'll leave her resting.

I meet with Olivia in the foyer outside the conference room at the hotel.

"You made it!" she says, relieved.

"We did."

"We?"

"I brought Kate with me."

"That's wonderful. Has she ever been to Ireland before?"

"No, and she can't wait to do some touristy things."

"How long are you staying?"

"Only a few days. But I assume we'll be returning at least quarterly for sales reporting?"

"I haven't even thought that far ahead. I'm nervous."

"Is everybody on board?"

"Everybody. John, Reese, Landon, Scott. Ethan's father."

"I thought I saw your sister in the hotel."

"I found a way to hire her husband, Rick. A lot of friends and family have put their livelihood on the line for us."

I reach for her fidgeting hands. "You'll be fine."

"I hope so. He's beyond a stubborn asshole."

"Yeah, well, that's his gig these days."

"What if you've all quit your jobs and joined us, and he still sells his shares and walks away?"

"He won't."

"But what if…."

I squeeze her hand, stalling her. "He won't."

"How did your conversation with Kate go?"

"I came clean."

"Good. And?"

"She wasn't happy about our history, but we're trying to look forward and not back."

"Well, that's very mature of you both."

"It's the only thing I've got to combat this whole past life nonsense."

"Nonsense?" Olivia laughs.

"I don't want to talk about it anymore. It makes us sound like crazy people."

"Agreed. How did Kate's interview go?"

"Not so good. Stacey had connections with the organization, and when I bailed, she contacted her friend and had them go with someone else."

"What a bitch."

"Kate doesn't know. I just wish I had connections that she could benefit from. Everybody I know is all for profit."

Olivia raises her finger in the air. "I might be able to help you."

"How?"

"My mother-in-law. She sits on the board with several charities. Some of them are global."

I feel excitement wash over me. "Do you think she would meet with Kate?"

"I'm sure she would. I can't make any promises that it will result in a position, but it couldn't hurt."

I grab her, and without thinking, I kiss her on the lips.

She pulls away, startled. "Carter!"

"Thank you, that's all. I'm just thanking you."

She laughs. "Okay, let's get through this briefing, and when things are finalized, I'll see what I can do about making that video disappear for good."

"John's doing his best, but I'd appreciate it if you could give it a go." She smirks. "Anything for you #nightclub guy."

After a few hours of hashing over business plans and having a few beers in the lobby with a few old friends, I'm anxious to get back upstairs to see Kate. I hear the shower when I walk through the sitting area. I pick up a shell with Ireland 2021 written on it in her beautiful handwriting. I begin to discard my clothing to join her, but an unknown number comes up on my phone.

Despite my better judgement, I open the message, and a video automatically plays. A video that reminds me of the very night I'm trying to put behind me. I don't know if Stacey has acquired a different number to contact me or if she's had someone else send it. Either way, she's making it clear that she has no intentions of taking the high road and moving on. I hope Olivia is about to erase this memory for good.

It terrifies me to know that someone filmed what happened that night and although it's dark and fuzzy from a distance, who and what's going on is clear enough. I block the number and delete the video before Kate sees it as she emerges into the bedroom wrapped in a towel.

"How was your day?" She smiles, happy to see me. Or maybe she's making fun of the sight of me standing buck naked except for my argyle business socks. I push my concerns about the video to the back of my mind for now and make my way toward her.

"It was uneventful."

I hold her hips and search her brilliant blue eyes. "Does uneventful mean boring?"

"No, it means peaceful and relaxing."

"And you found what you were looking for?"

"Yes, I did." She brushes her hands along my forearms and upward, then firmly squeezes my biceps.

"Did you miss me?" I ask, caressing her sides and appreciating the curves of her body. "You smell nice." I tug at the knot in the towel and let it fall to the ground.

Chapter Twenty

Kate

Today is the day that Olivia announces the new direction of O'Connell Industries, naming Ethan's most loyal friends in new positions. I can't tell if Carter is nervous or not. I lay on the bed and watch him get ready.

My mind involuntarily wanders. I love it when he wears that three-piece suit. I also love it when he wears those plaid cotton casual shirts and his faded black jeans. Hell, I love it when he wears his sweaty grey tracksuit after he's just come from boxing at the gym. I REALLY love it when he wears absolutely nothing at all. I start to overheat at the thought of his naked body hovering over top of me. Dear God, it isn't the clothes at all. I'm in love with the man, and it doesn't matter at all what he wears. I jump when he waves to get my attention.

"Zoned out again?" A warm mischievous smile spreads over his face as if he could read my thoughts. I smile back at him as I sit up.

"I've got a surprise for you," he says, piquing my interest.

"Oh? What's going on?"

"Olivia's mother-in-law, Anna, has arranged for you to meet with a few human resource people today."

He reads the confusion on my face.

"She's on the board of directors for several global charities and non-profit organizations. She felt you would be a good fit."

I feel a moment of excitement, and then I pause and lower my brow. How would she know I'm a good fit?"

Carter does something on his phone while avoiding eye contact. It's a telltale sign he's done something he knows he shouldn't have. "From your resume."

"That she got how?"

He looks up momentarily. "You left one out, and I copied it."

I bite my tongue. "I see."

"I just sent the itinerary to your email. One today and two tomorrow. I've arranged a car and driver for today. Tomorrow I'll take you."

"Carter!" I'm dumbfounded. "It's not okay for you to go ahead and organize interviews for me."

He holds his hands in the air, stalling my upcoming scolding. "Wait, before you get upset with me, let me explain."

I fold my arms.

"I didn't do it to control you. That's the last thing on my mind. I did it because I want to help you."

"You know there's a very fine line that differentiates between those two intentions, right? Have you ever been in a relationship where you and the other person were equal partners?"

"I'm trying. It's kind of new to me," he reasons.

He is trying. I'll give him that. "The right thing would be for you to talk to me about it. Not just send out my resume and assume I'm interested in positions."

"I'll file that away for future reference. Do you want me to cancel everything?"

"No. I'd like to see what's available, and if nothing else, I should sharpen my interview skills. I was so sure that I had that last one in the bag. I don't know what I did wrong."

A look of guilt washes over him. "I'm sure it wasn't anything you did wrong. I have to leave now. I'm sorry, I have no idea how today is going to go. If all goes well, only a few hours. If It's a shit show, well, there's no way of knowing."

I can feel his anxiety from clear across the room. I walk to him and wrap my arms around him. "Are you worried?"

He relaxes in my arms. "Yes and No. I've signed a contract with O'Connell Industries, so I have a job. How successful the business is, depends on Ethan."

I pull away and try to give him a reassuring look. "I have a feeling that even if Ethan lets you down, Olivia has what it takes to keep things going."

He nods. "You're not wrong. She'll move mountains if she sets her mind on it. I want everything to start rolling the way it's supposed to so we can get home and start planning a wedding."

Every time he brings that up it catches me off-guard. I better start thinking about it since he's made it clear there will be no long engagement for us.

I walk him to the door, and he kisses me on the forehead. "You best go get ready to wow 'em. The car will be here shortly."

With growing excitement, I rush to get dressed and grab my bag on the way out the door. My step-sister's number comes up on my phone as I make my way through the lobby. I don't have time to deal with her right now. I need to focus on this interview. I decline the call and turn off the notifications before tossing it into my purse.

I have no idea why I'm not nervous at all. I research this organization on the way over in the car, and I like what they stand for.

International donations are distributed globally for several humanitarian causes, from clean drinking water in indigenous regions and wildlife preservation to local assistance like feeding the homeless and domestic animal rescue.

"Miss Ryan, come on in."

I smile and get to my feet. I've got this.

When Carter opens the door, I jump into his arms.

He grunts and then wraps his arms around me to keep me from falling. "Does this enthusiasm mean you've had a good day?"

I wrap my legs around him, anchoring myself to his body. "Mmhmm."

He walks into the room and lets the heavy door slam behind him. "And have you secured yourself a career that you feel passionate about?"

"I'm finally going to get to use my master's degree in charitable foundations administration."

"That's fantastic news, baby."

"And the position allows me to work from my home office with only ten percent travelling time and event attendance when warranted."

He lowers me to the ground and takes my hand, leading me to the other room. "I have something to tell you."

"What's wrong?"

"I don't want to spoil your wonderful news, but you'll want to know this."

"Okay, what's going on?"

He scratches his head. "It's Bruce."

"Is he okay?"

Carter sits on the bed and pulls me in front of him. "Sit with me."

I feel a sick feeling in the pit of my stomach. "Carter? What's going on?"

"My mum called. She took Bruce to the veterinarian today for his appointment."

The suspense is killing me. "Stop staling and tell me."

"Kate, Bruce is a very sick little kitty."

"What do you mean, sick?"

"He has feline immunodeficiency virus. FIV."

"I've heard of it, but he's going to be okay, right?"

He squeezes my hand tightly. "I'm sorry, sweetheart. He's not going to live for very long."

I shake my head, sure I misheard him. "No," I say in denial. "That can't be. I've heard of cats that live a very long time with that disease."

"Those are older, stronger cats, Kate. It's an immune deficiency disease. His little body can't fight off all the things that are attacking his system."

I'm not prepared for the wave of emotion that swallows me whole in a single gulp. "No. No, that can't be right. We can fatten him up as soon as we get home. He'll get stronger."

"We can try. We'll make sure he gets good care and that he's not suffering."

Tears well up in my eyes, and he pulls me against his chest and rocks me gently as I try to come to terms with the news.

"I'm sorry. I'm so sorry. I know I just hit you with some sad news, but why don't we go out for dinner and celebrate all the *good* things that happened today."

I sit up and wipe my eyes. "Things went well?"

He nods. "I tried to call you when we were done, but I couldn't get a hold of you."

"Oh, I turned it off during the interview. I forgot to put it back on."

"Just leave it off for now. Let's go get something to eat."

I admit food would be welcome. I'm not sure if my body is five hours ahead of eastern daylight time or nine hours behind Australian eastern standard time.

"Is it supper time or breakfast?" I ask in the elevator on the way down. "I'm confused."

He grins. "I'm craving a big traditional Irish breakfast myself, but I doubt that's on the hotel menu at this time."

"That sounds good. Can we order that tomorrow?"

"Sure. Just don't ask any questions about the stuff you don't recognize."

I raise a brow. "Maybe I'll just have pancakes."

The elevator door opens, and the moment we step into the lobby, we can hear a loud commotion at the bar.

"I guess the boys are still celebrating."

Carter smiles. "It's hard to tell. That's their normal tone."

I glance at the familiar faces in the bar and prepare to join them when Carter gently steers me in the opposite direction.

"Let's opt for something a little quieter."

"But they're your friends," I reason.

Carter raises a brow. "You want to eat dinner and hang out with them tonight?"

I wrinkle my nose. "Not really."

He laughs. "Me neither. We can hide on the other side of the dining room. I'm sure they won't be leaving the bar."

So much has happened today. I welcome the time to sit down and decompress.

Carter studies the menu. "Do you know what you're having?"

"I'm ordering the Irish Stew. It says it's a staff favourite. How about you?"

"Apparently, the locals are crazy for the creamy fish pie."

I put my hand over my mouth and try to contain my laughter, but Carter's look of confusion makes me giggle aloud.

He shakes his head and places his menu on the table.

The waitress returns with a bottle of wine and pours us each a glass. "Would this pair well with the creamy fish pie?" Carter tastes it and gives his approval.

I snort and look away, my shoulders jiggling with laughter. It could be the jet lag or the excitement, maybe both with the heartbreak I feel over my kitten. "I'm sorry," I say when she leaves the table. "I'm having trouble controlling my emotions right now."

"Don't be. I love your smile. If I had known fish pie was…."

"CREAMY fish pie," I correct.

"If I had known *creamy* fish pie was so funny, I would have ordered it sooner."

I'm amused, for no reason at all.

"Tell me, what is your dream wedding?"

I take a sip of wine and make a face.

"Too dry?"

I pucker my lips.

"Sorry. Are you avoiding my question?"

I feel a little awkward. "Can I come clean about something?"

He sits back and gives me his full attention. "Of course,"

"What I told you about my first time."

"It wasn't true?" he asks, shocked.

"No, it was true. And you were right, I stalked him on social media, and he's been out of the closet for a long time."

"Told you."

I pause, trying to think of a way to say it. "Roger is not the reason I build up walls."

"I had a feeling."

"I've always felt that if I gave my heart to someone, they would smash it into a million bits and hand me back a bag of parts. I turned *keeping people at a distance* into an Olympic event and hit the podium every time."

"I think we both know why you feel that way."

"As strange as it seems."

"Thank you for letting me in. It would have crushed me if you chose not to, but I would have understood."

"When I first met you, my intuition screamed RUN. Things just kept pushing us together, and no matter how hard I tried to keep my emotions out of it, I couldn't."

Carter looks into my eyes with unquestionable sincerity. "I will do everything in my power to give you reasons to keep loving me."

"No broken hearts?"

"Not on my watch. We're looking forward. Not back, remember?"

"So, since I never intended being in a serious relationship, I don't have a dream wedding." I shrug.

"I'm going to guess you don't want to be a princess bride and get married in a castle."

I laugh once. "Correct."

"Well, what then? Church? Justice of the peace?"

I start to feel a little overwhelmed. "I don't want something expensive or showy."

"No pretentious wedding? There's a shock. What about attendants?"

"I'm assuming Ethan will be your best man."

"I'm assuming your step-sister won't be your maid of honour."

"Pffft. I wouldn't even invite her to the wedding."

"How would your father feel?"

I shrug. "It's my day, isn't it?"

"Speaking of your sister, have you heard from her lately?"

"She called earlier, but I didn't pick up. Has she been calling you?"

"I'm getting calls from unknown numbers."

"I wouldn't put it past her."

"Long white dress?"

I feel my face slightly warm.

"You're blushing?" He asks, amused as he leans in and whispers. "Is it because you're not a virgin?"

I roll my eyes.

"Oh wait, I know," he says dramatically.

I narrow my eyes suspiciously. "What?"

"A sensible dress that you can wear again to the office, but you can spice it up with bathroom shoes."

I burst out laughing.

Carter stares at me with adoration. "Seriously, I want to give you a special and memorable wedding. Help me out."

I search for something to say. "I don't know. I've seriously never thought about it."

"Never?" he says unconvinced.

The waitress returns with our meals and places them on the table. "Well, maybe when I was a small girl, but I'm not that little girl anymore."

"I don't think that little girl is gone. I think she's hiding in there somewhere, afraid to speak up for what she wants."

I look away for a minute, and he knows that he's struck a nerve. "Would you like to try my fish pie?"

I look at his plate and then lock onto his gaze. "Oh hell no. That looks worse than it sounds."

He laughs as he takes his first mouthful. I wait curiously for his reaction. When he shrugs and takes another bite, I smile. All the good news/bad news is curbing my appetite.

"What about a destination wedding," he asks between mouthfuls.

"How do you have a destination wedding when you live at a destination?"

"We could go to a different destination."

"Why would we spend the money to go somewhere on the ocean with a beach when we live on one of the most beautiful beaches in the world?"

Carter pauses and looks up. "That's it. We'll have a beach wedding."

"I like that idea. We can keep it simple yet elegant."

I can tell his wheels are still turning as we get into the elevator. "We can give all the guests two shells. One with our names and the date for them to take home, and the second we'll get them to sign their name on and leave them for us to keep."

His excitement over the subject makes my heart beat with a welcome ardour.

When we get to the suite, Carter steps into the other room to change. I follow my regular habit of plugging my phone into the charger before bed and remember that it's been off all day. I turn it on and watch as the messages and notifications start loading. Stacey's name comes up, and I figure I better read her message in case something is going on with my father.

Stacey: I think you should know the truth about your fiancé.

Reluctantly I click on the attached video and watch as a heart-wrenching scene unfolds. My blood runs cold, but I'm unable to turn away.

Carter returns, unaware of the event unfolding. "I was thinking for our honeymoon we could go on a safari in the outback. Unless you want to go somewhere else."

Chapter Twenty-One

Carter

The hair on the back of my neck stands on end when I hear the unmistakable distorted music of the video. Kate stands with her phone in her hand, watching intently before raising her head slowly. Her usually brilliant blue eyes are grey and full of sadness. I feel like I've just been stabbed in the chest.

"You're *nightclub guy*?"

I don't know how to respond. "Kate."

She refuses to make eye contact with me. "She used to brag about that night. Her friends still talk about it."

"I'm sorry. I should have told you."

Without another word, she puts her phone on the nightstand and continues to get ready for bed. Not another word. This is bad. Really bad. "I think we should talk about this."

"What's there to say?"

"I'm sure you're angry."

Her eyes finally meet mine, and there is a cold hardened look that I've never seen before. "Don't even begin to think that you know how I feel right now."

I remember my mum's advice. "Kate. I'm sorry I'm an asshole."

She raises her hand and stops me. "I just want to go to bed."

Despite my better judgement, I zip my big mouth and climb in beside her. She turns away from me and pulls the blanket over her body. I want to hold her; I want to assure her she has nothing to worry about, but I know it won't be received well right now. Busy days and time changes pull me quickly into a deep sleep.

Semi-conscious, I reach for her in the middle of the night. My eyes spring open when I discover she's gone. I get out of bed and stumble across the floor in the dark, searching for the light switch. She's gone. No notes, no explanation. Just gone.

My phone rings, and it makes me jump. "Reese?"

"What's going on?"

"What do you mean?"

"I couldn't sleep, so I was sitting down in the lobby chatting up the pretty brunette at the front desk, and I just saw Kate leave with her luggage."

"Can you stop her?"

"No, a car already picked her up. What happened?"

"She saw the video of Stacey and me at the nightclub. If I had to guess, Stacey sent it to her."

"She didn't know about it before now?"

"I told her that Stacey and I saw each other a few times before we met. I didn't go into the details."

"You're a dick. You've spent too much time with O'Connell. You'll be lucky to charm your way out of this one, Brant."

"For the love of God, I didn't even know Kate back then. It's not like I cheated on her," I yell.

"That's not the point. You should have told her everything the minute you found out who she was. You kept it from her."

I scrub my hand over my face. "So, everyone keeps telling me. Listen, if you hear anything, let me know. I'm going to try and call her."

Reese chuckles. "Good luck with that."

Annoyed, I disconnect his call and dial Kate's number, relieved when she answers on the second ring.

"Hey, where are you going?"

"I don't know."

"Come back, let's talk."

She sniffles, and it makes my heart ache. "I need some time alone right now."

"You just leave in the middle of the night without saying goodbye, not even a note."

"I sent you a text."

"I didn't get it. I woke up, and you're gone."

"I'm sorry."

"Don't shut me out. Please, tell me where you're going?"

"I'd rather not say. You'll show up."

"Damn right I will."

"I just need some space right now, Carter."

"Not acceptable," I say in a rough growl.

"Really, Carter? Why don't you tell me why you felt keeping that from me was acceptable! You promised me no broken heart."

My voice catches in the back of my throat. "Are you leaving me?"

There's a long uncomfortable pause. "I just need to get my head around some things."

"Like?"

"Maybe things are just moving too quickly."

"Things?"

"Like the wedding."

I feel like I've just been stabbed in the chest. "Maybe we should call it off then."

"Maybe we should."

I'm clenching my jaw so tightly right now that I'm beginning to see stars. "Fine," I say, feeling defeated. "I'll reach out in a couple of days when I figure things out."

"We should be figuring things out together," I say in desperation, trying to stop her from building walls. "Damn it, Kate. I didn't mean to hurt you."

"Okay, Carter, you tell me how I look forward and not back now that I know?"

"I don't know. Can't you try? Am I important enough to you to try?"

There's another long silence. "I guess not." I disconnect the call and sit on the side of the bed. I might as well change the date of my return flight to Australia. There's no point in me staying here.

Being home in Australia hasn't lessened my heartache any. I knock once on the door to my mother's home before letting myself in. It's been a long restless flight.

Shocked to see me, she stops dead in the hallway. "You look like shit."

"Thanks, Mum." I take Bruce out of her hands. "How is he?"

"He's a sweet wee thing. You wouldn't know he's got such a horrible disease." She looks around me at the door.

"Where's Kate?"

"I don't know."

"What do you mean you don't know?"

Exhaustion and emotion mix, making it impossible for me to hold it in any longer. My eyes well up with tears.

"What's going on?"

I rub Bruce's chin and try to compose myself while he purrs and nuzzles against me.

"Carter? Come in and sit down."

I follow her into the other room and sit down across from her. She reaches over the coffee table and touches my hand. "Talk to me."

"It turns out that a girl I spent time with is Kate's step-sister."

"Was it serious?"

"No. It was just a casual fling."

She moves to sit beside me. "And Kate is upset about that?"

"I told her about it and assured her it was in the past, and I had no feelings for her sister."

"So, what's the problem?"

"Things were okay. But Kate's sister is not a very nice girl."

"Son, I'm not getting any younger. Can you speed this up," she says, growing impatient.

"When I first met Stacey, we had some fun when I was in Toronto."

"By fun, do you mean sex?"

"Yes."

My mother looks at me disappointed.

"In a very public place."

She raises a brow.

"And somebody filmed us."

She places her hand over her heart. "Dear Lord, please tell me that Kate didn't see the video."

"She did. Her sister sent it to her."

I feel a dull thud as my mother cuffs me on the back of the head.

"Mum!"

"What's wrong with you? It's bad enough you couldn't keep your dick in your pants, but you couldn't have at least done it in a private place?"

"You don't understand."

"Oh, I don't? And under what circumstances are you going to try and convince me that boning a girl in a public place where you can be seen AND FILMED is acceptable?"

"You're right, Mum." I rub the back of my head and sit in silence. There's nothing I can say that will redeem me. "My actions were immature and unprofessional."

"Try embarrassing."

"I thought the IT team at work was successful in scrubbing the video from all existence. Ouch!" I rub my head again.

"There shouldn't have been a video in the first place."

"I got it. Stop hitting me. I made a mistake, and it cost me the love of my life. Is that not enough punishment?"

Her disposition softens. "So, is it over?"

"It seems like it. She left in the middle of the night. I talked to her on the phone, and she said she needed some time and that maybe things were happening too fast. I told her that maybe we should cancel the wedding." I frown, and my mother looks at me with sympathetic eyes.

"Is that what you want?"

"No. I love her so much my heart hurts."

"Then what are you doing here?"

"I came to get Bruce."

She looks to the ceiling and mutters something. "No, Carter. I mean, why are you here? Why are you not fighting for Kate?"

"I don't think she wants me to fight for her."

"Nonsense. Don't make the same mistake I made."

I furrow my brow. "What do you mean?"

"Do you think I stopped loving your stepfather?"

"I thought you hated each other."

"Boy, you know nothing."

"Apparently," I admit feeling confused. "Kate said something to me the night she met him. She said she thought he still loved you, and he felt like you wanted him to go."

"I wish we had just talked more."

"I begged Kate to talk. She wanted no part of it. She's spent years perfecting how to build walls around herself. Now I've given her proof that she needs them. She'll never trust anyone again."

"Go after her, son. I suspect she still loves you. Love is worth fighting for."

"Can I ask you a question?"

"Of course,"

"Kate and I found a picture in the envelope you sent. It was a picture of me with Dad AND William."

She looks at me with fear in her eyes.

"I didn't know they knew each other. And Kate mentioned that they looked a lot alike."

She looks at her fidgeting hands.

"Mum, is there something you want to tell me?"

"No."

"Is there something you *need* to tell me?" I reach over and place my hand over hers. "I think it's time you tell me."

"William is your father's brother."

"He's my uncle? That explains the resemblance. Wait!" I say, confused. "Why would you keep that a secret?"

Her eyes fill with tears, and I pause, putting together the pieces. "Oh."

"William is your biological father, Carter. He was the love of my life, but he didn't want to settle down. He had taken off on a grand adventure with no idea when he'd be back when I learned that I was pregnant with you.

His brother, Alan, was a wonderful man. He stepped up, and I eventually learned to love him. He loved you like you were his own. We never thought we'd see William again, so there was no point in telling you. Then Alan passed, and William came home."

I listen, open-mouthed. "Does William know?"

"Yes, I told him, and he tried to make things right. He wanted to spend time with you and get to know you. I was afraid that one day he would leave again, so I encouraged him to go. Deep down, I didn't want him to leave us. I thought I was important to him and that he'd reconsider and stay, but he didn't fight for me. He just sailed away with my heart. I was so hurt that my heartache eventually turned into anger. But even after all these years, I still love him."

"Does he know that?"

"If he didn't know it then, I doubt he knows now."

I look down at the sleeping kitten in my lap. "Can you watch Bruce for a while longer?"

She nods. "Bring her home, son."

I grab my carry-on and rush to get to customs in the Toronto international airport. Three-time zones in three days is a new personal record, and I'm not entirely sure what end is up right now. I know I have to get to Kate. I check the time zone on my phone before stuffing it in my pocket. Finally, I catch a break. It's Sunday, and I'm confident she'll be at her father's country home for dinner.

I jump in a rental car and spare no time getting there. I rehearse in my head all the things I want to say when I see her. I squeal the breaks as I pull upfront of the brightly lit home and jump out. My heart is racing as I take quick steps to the front door and knock.

The door opens slowly, and Kate's dad stands in front of me, looking confused. "Hi, Carter."

"Mr. Ryan. May I come in?"

He reluctantly stands to the side and allows me into the foyer. "Come in. We're just finishing dinner."

I follow him into the dining room and look around the table. Pat gets to her feet. "I can get you a plate if you're hungry." She glances at her husband nervously.

"No, thank you. I ate on the plane." There's an awkward tension in the room.

"What can I do for you, Carter?" he finally asks.

"I came to talk to Kate, sir."

"Kate?"

"Yes, sir."

"She's not here."

I try to still the anger growing inside. "I'm sure she told you to tell me that, but I need to talk to her."

"Who?" Pat asks, returning from the kitchen with dessert.

"Kate."

She looks at me and then back at her husband. "Kate's not here, Carter. Wasn't she with you in Australia?"

I've had enough of these games. "Kate!" I yell, walking past the table and heading towards the stairs. "KATE!"

I hear footsteps descending the wooden stairs. "Kate!" I call again. "Please, I need to talk to you!" Suddenly a figure comes into view on the staircase.

"She's not here," Stacey says as she steps into the bright light of the hall.

Rage rushes through my veins the moment I see her. "Where is she? When was the last time you heard from her?"

"Carter, calm down. You're starting to concern me. Where's my daughter? Has something happened?"

I realize they're telling me the truth, and anger turns to fear. "You mean, she's really not here?"

"No," Pat adds. "We haven't heard from her since she called to tell us she got a job."

"Has she disappeared?" her father asks with growing concern. "Should we call the police?"

"No, No. I'm sure she's fine. She just wanted some time to herself."

"Why? What happened?"

I turn to look at Stacey's smug smile. "She's what happened."

"Stacey?" Pat asks, confused.

"I'm sorry to tell you this, but your daughter is a manipulating, blackmailing, horrible bitch."

Around the table, chins drop. I reach into my pocket for my phone and pull up the video. I might as well get it all out in the open. "Before I met Kate, Stacey and I spent some time together. It's not something I'm very proud of. When we were out one night, someone recorded us at a nightclub.

Since Kate and I fell in love, Stacey has done everything to try and cause problems between us. She even coerced my boss into forcing me to maintain a relationship with her behind Kate's back."

"What?" Everyone stares at Stacey.

"Don't be ridiculous. Why would I do that?"

"You tell me? I don't think it's because you particularly like me. Is it because you only want what you can't have? Or is it because you want Kate to be miserable?"

She smiles.

"And when I refused to play her games or carry on a relationship because I'm in love with Kate, she sent her this." I hand Kate's father my phone, and he and Pat watch a few moments of it together.

"You're '*nightclub guy*'?" Stacey's brother asks.

"Steven," Pat says, appalled.

"I've seen enough," Kate's dad says as he hands back my phone and then locks eyes with Stacey.

"Is this true?" Pat asks. "Did you send this to Kate?"

Stacey shrugs. "Why not? I thought she should know. After all, Carter is going to be my brother-in-law."

"Get out of my house." Kate's dad demands.

Stacey's eyes open wide. "You can't throw me out. My mother lives at this house."

"I'm with him on this, Stacey. Kate has always been a kind and loving person. I don't understand why you would do something so hateful. The only purpose of showing her this video would be to crush her and break her heart. What kind of person have you become if you're capable of such malice?"

"The kind who always gets what she wants," she says, glancing in my direction.

"Not this time," I add

"Get out. You can stay at the penthouse until the end of the month. Don't come back here," Joseph insists.

Stacey stomps towards the steps. "Fine," she says as she disappears out of sight. "I hate this family anyway!"

Kate's father returns his attention to me. "Carter, where's my daughter?"

"If she's not here, I don't know."

"You've got to find her. She'll be crushed."

I pace, trying to think rationally when it hits me. "I know someone she might have told." I dial his number and wait for several rings before he answers sleepily.

"O'Connell."

"I fucked up."

"Brant?"

"She left me, Ethan."

"Kate? What the fuck happened?"

"It's a long story, and I'll fill you in later."

"Do you love her?"

"Yes. You know how much."

"Then you have to go after her and make her understand. Don't make the same mistake I did."

Not another one. I mumble a curse and rake my fingers through my hair. "I don't know where she is right now. She's not in Toronto or Australia. Ask Olivia if she's talked to her. I need to find her. I need to make it right."

Ethan sighs. "Okay, don't lose your shit, Brant. Let me ask Liv."

I hear him call to her, and then he must have put his hand over the speaker because all I hear is muffled voices.

"Exactly what the fuck did you do, Carter? Olivia said that you're an asshole, and there's not a chance in hell she's telling you a thing."

"Stacey sent her the video of her and me."

"I thought we had security get rid of that video."

"Stacey must have had a copy on her phone. When I refused to agree to see her on the sly, she sent it to Kate."

"That bitch is pure evil."

Feeling awkward, I look around the room to see where Stacey's mother is and walk further out of earshot.

"I have to find her. Tell Olivia that she owes me one, and I'm calling in that favour now."

"Hang on." He doesn't mute the phone this time. "I don't know why he didn't just call you himself, but he says you owe him, and he's calling in his favour."

I can hear Olivia cursing in the background and then an amused chuckle from Ethan. "Nice mouth, Love. Hang on a moment, Carter."

I pace in silence while waiting for him to come back on the phone.

"Liv says she's staying at our cottage in the country. Before you ask, I had no idea. Apparently, my wife keeps secrets from me."

"Tell Olivia I said thank you."

"Brant…do I want to know why my wife owes you a favour?" he asks with jealousy on the edge of his tone.

"She never told you?"

"Thanks, Carter, I have to tell him now," she yells in the background.

"Damn right," Ethan replies. "You're going to tell me the minute I hang up the phone. Then we're going to have a little talk about owing favours to my friends."

"Calm down, Ethan. It's not what you think, mate. I'll talk to you later. I've got to book a flight to Ireland."

I can faintly still hear Olivia in the background. "Okay, woman! I said I'll tell him," Ethan says, aggravated. "Carter, you should know that if you fuck this up, you're going to have to deal with my wife, and believe me, man, it's not going to be pretty. You're going to wish I kicked your ass instead."

"Got it! The plan is to bring her on home."

"Go get her."

Chapter Twenty-Two

I walk the room, mingling with wealthy supporters hoping to coax them to part with some of their money. When Anna asked if I wanted to jump right into my position and attend this fundraising event, I didn't bat an eye. I need the distraction, so I stayed awake most of the night, stalking each and every one of our attendees on social media. I couldn't sleep anyways thinking about Carter.

A familiar face appears in the crowd, and I skim through the guest list, certain his name wasn't there.

"Hi, Kate. You look beautiful."

My face turns red. "Hi, Reese. What are you doing here?"

"Anna O'Connell. She makes sure we all get the invitations."

"Ah, she is committed."

He smiles, and it puts me at ease. "Committed to making sure all my hard-earned money gets filtered back into the community. This cause is one very near to my heart."

"Oh? You're a supporter of The Animal Welfare Institute."

He looks around the room at the promotional material. "Of course, isn't everybody?"

I scowl. "Did Carter send you?"

"No. I heard Anna talking at the office today, and I knew you'd be here."

I put my hand on his elbow and steer him away from the crowd. "Who knows?"

"Just me as far as I can tell. Nobody is talking about it. I only know because I was sitting in the lobby when you left."

I was excited about my first fundraiser with this organization, and now that nervous feeling is replaced by angst. "I hope he doesn't show up here and make a scene."

He looks at me sympathetically. "He's not here, Kate. He went back to Australia."

Shock jolts through me. "He went home without me?"

A look of regret washes over him. "You didn't know?"

My hands begin to tremble, and I try to hold off the tears welling up in my eyes.

He pauses, looking uncomfortable. "He thinks you changed your mind. Wait…didn't you leave him?"

"No, I just needed some space to cool down. He can be smothering at times."

"Yeah, I lived with him. I know."

I feel betrayed, and it's an unreasonable response since I was the one who walked away. "I guess he's done with me."

"Kate, I know what you're thinking, and I'm going to stop you right there. That's not Carter's thing."

I laugh once through the emotion starting to bubble to the surface. "That's exactly his thing, Reese. His first impulse is to cut and run."

"Are you telling me that he didn't try to talk to you and work things out? He just let you walk away?"

I replay the evening in my head and feel ashamed.

"Well? Did he?" he persists.

"He wanted to talk, but I wasn't ready. I was going to call him tomorrow after I had a chance to deal with everything that's going on."

"He thinks you don't want him in your life. He's crushed."

I grab a fluted champagne glass from the tray of a passing waiter. I finish it in a few gulps, and then Reese takes the empty glass out of my hands. "That's not how we're going to resolve this. You need to ask yourself what you want."

"I don't know," I say, flustered.

"Figure it out."

Anna flanks me from the side. "Katherine, here you are. I've been looking for you. Hello Reese, are you ready to lighten your bank account?"

He flashes me a sly grin. "Of course, Anna. Why else would I be here?"

I follow as Anna steers Reese to the table where he can make his donation. I glance across all the information on the table for other charities looking for support and stop at a brochure for feline rescue in Peru. The little grey kitten on the front page reminds me of Bruce. My heart hurts knowing that he won't be with us for long. Then I realize I might not ever see him again. I wish Carter were here. He would heal my heart. He's always soothed my sorrow and made me feel safe. My world is currently in turmoil, and it's all of my own doing.

"Are you okay, dear?" Anna O'Connell asks, concerned as she drives me back to the cottage with the red door in the beautiful Irish countryside.

I look up, embarrassed my mind was elsewhere. "Yes, sorry, I've got a lot on my mind."

"Carter?"

The sound of his name makes my heart squeeze tightly in my chest. "Yes, I've messed things up."

She pats her hand sympathetically on my knee. "Nonsense. People in love do stupid things. Sometimes without even knowing it. Relationships are hard, and they take a lot of work."

"Carter left for Australia a few days ago. Without me."

"Well, I'm no relationship expert, Kate, but I suspect that has something to do with you leaving and staying at the cottage by yourself. If I left every time Aiden did something to upset me, we would never be together in a room long enough to have four children."

I feel miserable inside. "I told you I messed things up."

"Being in love means that you're going to be vulnerable sometimes. You'll learn when to give each other space and when to call each other out on the bullshit. But you do it together."

She puts the car in park and turns to look at me. "Now, go inside and make yourself a cup of tea and call the boy. Put him out of his misery."

I nod my head. "Yes, ma'am."

It's a long walk up the cobblestone walkway in an evening gown and three-inch heels. I turn and wave as Anna backs out of the driveway and the tail lights disappear into the night.

I slip out of my borrowed evening gown just inside the door and kick off the heels. After plopping myself down on the couch, I pull the blanket over me and dial Carter's number. I'm not surprised but still gutted that it goes straight to his voicemail. "Hi, it's me. I'm ready to talk. Please call me."

I look around the meticulously decorated cottage as I start to drift off to sleep. Images of the Irish country knickknacks are replaced in my thoughts with the warm sandy ocean décor of the home I share with Carter. *The sounds of the waves on the shore soothe me into a deeper sleep where I find myself walking in the warm sand with a toddler, picking up shells. He insists on carrying the plastic bucket filled to the brim, without any help, back to the spot where Carter is sleeping under the shelter in the shade.*

Mini Carter, still covered in sand, crawls beside him, lays down, and closes his eyes. The sound of the ocean, the breeze, the birds…the snoring, all create a glorious picture of what's supposed to be. I wake several times during the night with my phone still in my hand. When my eyes open at sunrise and refuse to close again, I check voicemails, texts, and emails. Still nothing.

I pack up my things and leave the Irish countryside. There's only one thing to do, and that's go home and say I'm sorry and hope he'll give me another chance. The earliest flight I can get on isn't until the morning, so I check into the hotel for one last night.

The elevator door opens, and I walk straight into Reese. He raises a brow. "I didn't expect to see you here again."

"I've decided to go home."

He grasps my elbow and turns me toward the lobby as he begins to walk. "And home is where now? Toronto?"

I purse my lips and shake my head. "Home is in Australia."

"And Carter?"

"I'm hoping he'll forgive me. I've been calling, but he doesn't answer."

"He will," he assures me as we walk through the front doors toward his waiting car. "When do you leave?"

"Tomorrow morning. I figured I'd stay closer to the airport and maybe take one more walk on the beach before I go."

"You're in luck. I'm running an errand for Olivia, and I'll be going right past there. I'll give you a ride, and you can send for a car when you want to come back."

"That would be great." I reach for the handle, and he chuckles. "Are you driving?"

I roll my eyes. "I forgot."

He walks around the hood of the car and opens the passenger door for me. "Can I ask you a question?" I ask as he turns off the main road and heads out of town.

"Sure."

"I don't understand the loyalty you all have for O'Connell. He seems like a dick."

He laughs aloud. "That's not a question. It's a statement."

"I'm wondering why, after the things he wrongfully accused you of, are you still so loyal to him?"

"Because in a different time, he stood by me, without judgement or questions. He was the one person I could count on."

"You mean in another life?"

He gives me a curious look and tries not to smile. "No, I mean at the beginning of university."

"Oh," I say, feeling embarrassed.

"Ethan had somewhat of a *royal* upbringing compared to Carter and me. It was a miracle that either of us made it to that university at all. We met in a rather boring economics class our first year. He accepted us and befriended us. Myself, I would have folded under the financial pressure midway through the year. I suspect Carter would say the same. Ethan made sure that we only had to worry about our grades and not our finances."

"So, you feel like you owe him?"

"No, not at all. You don't understand. There were no strings attached. No feelings of guilt. We became close, like brothers. The best kind of family, the kind you get to choose. As we learned, growing up with money didn't guarantee happiness. Life growing up as an O'Connell was difficult, and he struggled like the rest of us, just in different ways. If you're asking why we do so much for him, it's because he deserves that kind of friend. Not too many people see that side of him."

I get it now, and I'm glad I asked. It helps me understand Carter's need to serve and protect. Reese pulls off the road at the top of the pathway to the beach. "Be careful out here alone. The beach is full of all sorts of dangers if you're not careful."

I glance at my phone one more time before I get out of the car.

"Don't worry, he'll find you. This time, it's your destiny." He assures me before driving away. So, he did know what I was talking about when I brought up past lives.

The sun is bright, and the warm salty breeze off the ocean calls me to the beach. I watch my footing as I carefully decline the narrow rocky pathway to the sand.

Once I reach the beach, a frail voice speaks from behind a rock. "What did you decide?"

Startled, I hold my hand to my chest. "I knew I saw you in town. What are you doing here?"

"Looking for clams."

"I mean in Ireland."

The grey-haired psychic smiles. "If everyone is here, there's no reason for me to be there."

"Are you following me?"

"I was here first," she reminds me.

"Oh, right. Well, enjoy your day."

"What did you decide?" she asks again.

"My heart is telling me Carter is the one."

"Then let it be so." She smiles.

"It's not that easy. My sister will never let it go. She won't stop until she destroys us."

"Don't give her that power."

"You don't know my family."

"I'm being told your family is helping."

"How's that?"

"Spirit says she's been given a full-time assignment. In Asia. She'll move there soon."

I hope she's got that one right. "Thank you, if you'll excuse me, I have to figure out what I'm going to say when Carter calls." I turn to walk away, and she calls out a name.

"Lily,"

I turn, as if hearing that name was a natural thing.

"There's a small one, with blue eyes and rather large ears. He's very ill."

"Bruce, my kitten."

She nods, and her eyes begin to twinkle in the sun. "He will pass soon. Spirit says not to mourn his death. He has a much more important role to fill."

"Oh. I was hoping he would get better," I say sadly.

"All things come back, sometimes different than they were."

I hear a car screech to a stop at the top of the hill, and I look up, straining to see what all the commotion is. When I draw my attention back to Eva, she's gone. Her footprints in the sand have inexplicably vanished.

It's moments like this when I question my sanity. The ocean is calling, and it draws me to the shore. I slip off my sandals and let the warmth of the sand soothe me. "Where is he? Please bring him back to me," I say aloud. I'm not sure what I believe anymore, but if there's an ocean spirit, I hope he's listening. I suddenly become alert. "What was that?" I strain, listening over the roaring of the incoming tide, and I hear it again. My name. I look both directions along the beach, and when I hear it once more, I know where it's coming from.

I turn to see him coming down the rocky terrain of the hill at full speed and then struggling to run in the sand.

"Carter!" I rush to him, meeting him halfway. The weight of the world has been lifted, and my soul fills with joy.

"I went to Toronto, but you weren't there," he pants through short breaths. "I arrived in Ireland, and you weren't at the cottage." He gasps for air.

"I left you messages."

He holds a finger in the air and then bends over, taking deep breaths. When he stands, he still struggles to breathe. "When we get home, I better get back to the gym. My cardio is shit."

A wide smile blossoms across my face. "I'm sorry. I'm sorry for everything." I throw myself against his chest and wrap my arms around him firmly.

"Okay, easy on the bear hug. I'm barely getting enough air as it is."

I loosen my grip and lean back to look up into his magnificent blue eyes. Eyes I saw mirrored in the innocent face of a small child in my dream this morning.

He kisses my lips and pulls away. "I'm the one that's sorry. I shouldn't have left Ireland. I should have just given you time to process."

"You begged me to stay and talk it through."

He cocks his head to the side and makes a face. "Yeah, that's true, I did. So that one's on you."

"Give me another chance?"

"I wouldn't be here if I wasn't totally head over heels in love with you. I'm not giving up on us."

"Let's get married as soon as we get home."

"Whoa, now who's being impulsive? What about your sister?"

"I don't care. She could never have had a relationship with you because she's not woman enough to keep you."

"Exactly. You've got that right."

He smiles, and it brings happy tears to my eyes. "I promise. No more walls, no worrying about the past, or past lives, or whatever. I want to spend the rest of my life with you. It's where I'm meant to be."

"No more running, Kate. True love is not just love that lasts through all time. Love is when we've both been stripped bare, exposing all our faults and ugliness, and yet here we are together. Still needing and wanting each other."

"And loving each other," I interrupt.

"That's my favourite part. I can't promise you that I won't make mistakes along the way, but I'll do my best."

"I can make you that promise as well."

He holds my hand as we walk in the water along the shoreline. "We've got this, right?"

"I think we do."

"Are you sure you want to get married?"

"Yes."

"On the beach."

"Mmhmmm," I confirm.

"Okay, if you're sure, then let's make that happen."

"I have questions."

"Okay, shoot."

"Did you think I left you and went home to Toronto?"

"I did."

"How did you know I was in Ireland staying at the cottage?"

"Olivia caved."

"And how did you know that I was at the beach today."

"Reese called."

"I see. So, I have no chance of ever hiding from you."

"Nope."

"Note to self. Never plan a surprise party. Nobody can keep a secret."

He picks me up and tries to carry me up the hill. He makes it halfway before he has to put me down. "Fucking cardio." He holds out his hand, and we continue the climb side by side. "Guess what I learned from my mother when I went home."

"That William is your real father."

Carter stops short. "How did you know that?"

I laugh. "I've gotten good at identifying what love looks like."

"That's amazing."

"Plus, Olivia introduced me to John McCabe, and I asked him to look into it. That guy is amazing."

"There's no hiding anything from McCabe."

"Olivia and I had a long talk, and I think I finally understand it all. How everyone is connected, I mean."

"Mind-boggling, isn't it?"

I lean against his chest and tuck my head under his chin. Right where I belong. "I'm very thankful that true love really does transcend all time."

Epilogue

Carter

I don't know how she pulled it off, but my beautiful bride-to-be organized a wedding in three weeks. Friends and family are gathering this evening at our favourite restaurant for what would be our rehearsal dinner if we were, in fact, rehearsing anything.

One of the things I love about Kate is she's always on time. There's never any tension or angst getting anywhere because she's always ready to go. I watch from the doorway as she dabs a small amount of perfume behind her ear. The breeze gently carries it through the room. One of my first memories of Kate was brushing past her, and for the rest of the day, I could smell the subtle aroma of vanilla cupcakes and jasmine.

It draws me in, and I watch in the mirror as I wrap myself around her and nibble at her neck.

"Stop," she giggles.

"Make love to me one last time while we're still single."

"Do you have cold feet?" she asks, watching my reaction in the mirror.

"Not at all. I like the way you smell like a cupcake, and it's making me hungry." I waggle my eyebrows, and she struggles to keep a straight face.

"We have somewhere to be," she says, looking at the time.

"It's our party. You think they'll start without us?" I nibble across her shoulder and along her neck.

"That's not going to work."

I grab her waist and spin her around. "How about this? Is this going to work?" Before she can answer, I claim her lips in a possessive kiss, growing in passion as her lips part and receive me in. Her hands stop pushing against me and grasp my biceps, squeezing them firmly.

"Here or in the bedroom," I ask as I lift her.

"Bedroom."

I carry her down the hall and grab the bottom of her dress, prepared to pull it straight up and discard it on the floor.

"Wait, wait... we don't have time, just lift it."

I'm so worked up I don't even care. "I need you, now." I grab the sides of her underwear, and again she interrupts.

"Wait, wait, wait... don't rip them. Let me take them off."

"Oh, for fucks sakes," I say, feeling frustrated.

"It's okay, see, I've got them off already. Carry on."

I trail open-mouth kisses across her body and stop to pleasure her with my warm roaming tongue. She squirms, trying to position herself, so friction is her best friend. Becoming impatient, she moves. Forcing me out of the way, she climbs on top, straddling me. She lowers her hips and slides over me. So intense, so deep. My hands travel down her body from her breasts to her hips, touching what belongs to me.

Kate lets out a moan. And then another. She calls out my name as she leans back and bucks several times. I pause and watch the theatrics.

"Oh baby, that was so good," she says with excessive panting.

"Mmhmm."

"Quick, let's freshen up and get going."

"You faked it."

"No, I didn't!" she says, offended.

"You looked over at the clock."

"Honestly, it was just that good. So hard and deep."

"Do you think I don't know when you have an orgasm?"

"That was an orgasm."

"Nice try. You owe me one."

When we arrive at the restaurant, we try our best not to draw attention to our arrival. The first person to see us is Ethan O'Connell, and he's making a b-line straight for us.

"I can't believe you faked it," I say to Kate, feeling wounded as we enter the room."

She locks her eyes to mine. "I didn't fake it," she insists in a whisper.

"Brant! Where have you been? It's not like you to be late. I hope you weren't working."

"No, no. It was more like a workout than work. At least for one of us." I glance over at Kate and watch as her face begins with a mild blush of colour and then turns a crimson red.

Noticing her reaction and the freshly-fucked appearance of my hair, Olivia elbows Ethan. He looks at her with knit brows. She raises her eyebrows, looks in my direction, and smiles, trying to send him a silent message.

Ethan looks at the red flush on her face and then scratches his eyebrows. I'm sure Kate is just about to die of embarrassment. I reach down and hold her hand as I give her a reassuring smile. The waiter walks past, and

Ethan grabs two glasses of wine and hands them to us. "You're a few behind. Drink up. We're celebrating."

Olivia holds up her glass. "Cheers, tomorrow you'll marry your best friend."

Ethan makes a face. "Don't be ridiculous, woman. I'm already married."

"I was talking about Kate. And you're cut off."

I take a sip from my glass and put it down on the table before taking Kate's out of her hand. Olivia narrows her eyes suspiciously.

"How is the baby doing?" I ask, trying to draw the focus away from Kate.

"She's doing well."

Ethan's phone rings and he jumps, startling all of us. "Yes, yes, I called. How is the baby? Is she okay? Everything is fine here. Did she take her bottles? How is she sleeping?" We stand, staring at him, and his wife crosses her arms in front.

"I guess it's a new dad thing. You know, first time leaving the baby with a sitter." I explain.

Olivia shakes her head. "He's driving me nuts. He calls the babysitter every half an hour."

When Ethan hangs up, he looks at his wife's disapproving glare. She holds her hand out. "Okay, give me the phone." He looks at her almost as if he has an addiction, and she's trying to claim his stash. "Ethan," she warns, "give me your phone."

He passes it to her reluctantly, and she quickly tucks it into her bra. I laugh at the look she gives him. She rolls her eyes and tries to hide the smile starting to form on her lips. "Honestly. How are you going to behave when she starts dating?"

"Oh hell, NO! Our daughter is never going to date. I'll make sure of that."

Olivia looks at me, crossing her eyes in exasperation. I chuckle, but It's kind of pathetic.

"I'm so sorry to hear about your kitten," Olivia says, changing the subject.

"Thank you," Kate says, frowning. "He passed a few weeks ago. We did everything we could to make him comfortable in the end."

I anchor her to my side and kiss the top of her head, hoping to prevent any of that pent-up emotion from bubbling to the surface.

"I'm so sorry to hear. He was so cute."

"Cute?" I mock. "You know we're talking about Bruce? The little goofy grey kitten whose ears were three times too big for his head."

"I know who we're talking about," she scolds.

"It was very sad. I miss him terribly," Kate says softly.

"It was sad, but we did get some good news at the same time," I announce.

"Carter," Kate says, unsure.

Ethan grabs two more drinks from the waiter. "I heard. You've started a charity to raise research funds to try and discover a cure for that feline disease."

"Yes," Kate says, relieved.

A ghost of a smile washes across Olivia's face. "Nice try, girl, but you're glowing."

I glance over at Ethan's confused look. "What does that have to do with anything? It's fucking warm in here."

Olivia smiles and pulls Kate into a loving embrace.

"Do you know what they're talking about?" He asks.

I nod.

"What in the ever-loving-fuck is wrong with you, O'Connell?" Olivia says. "She's pregnant."

"Pregnant? How did you get that from sweaty skin? Is it true?" he asks me.

I chuckle. "Yes."

"That's fantastic!"

"We hadn't planned on becoming pregnant so soon," Kate says as we walk into the room where we'll be dining. "But Carter slipped one past all the defence. If life has that strong of a will, how do you question it?"

"You don't." Olivia smiles, and Kate glows, and I feel like I'm the luckiest man in the world.

Kate draws my attention to my mum on the other side of the room. William sits beside her, holding her hand. He seems to be listening attentively to every word she says. Her smile is as bright as the sparkle that's returned to her eyes. It seems I may not be the only one to change my destiny in this life.

Coming Summer 2023

Another Secondary Journey in the Bound4Ireland Series.

LOVE OUT OF BOUNDS

When you're the daughter of the wealthiest Irishman in the county, there are certain expectations thrust upon you. My brother, Ethan, climbed the corporate ladder at record speed, maintaining the family standards. My younger sister, McKenna, followed in my brother's footsteps, marrying her soulmate after college, and then working at the family business. Kaylie is the youngest of the O'Connell children. She was an unexpected blessing that came later in my parent's lives and the surviving twin of a difficult pregnancy. She will never have to prove herself to my parents.

Rockstar, Nate Ross was everything my over-protective Irish brother warned me about. He was older, impulsive and a player. He was always on the road with the band and would eventually leave me broken-hearted. I am Madison O'Connell, and in my brother's opinion, his long-time friend Nate isn't good enough for me. Now I lie to my family about falling in love with him.

Impulsive